Cape May Ever After

KIMBERLY BRIGHTON

Published in the United States of America by Cape Island Publishers

CapeIslandPublishers.com

Library of Congress Control Number: 2024908617

Printed book ISBN: 979-8-9879070-6-1

Ebook ISBN: 979-8-9879070-5-4

This is a work of fiction. Names, characters, places, and incidents either are the product of the author's imagination or are used fictitiously. Any resemblance to actual persons, living or dead, business establishments, events, or locales is entirely coincidental.

To my daughter ~

May you always stay true to yourself as you seek your happily ever after, and know we're cheering you on with all our love and support.

Thank you for the light and joy you've brought to both our lives.

We love you to London and back!

June

Marley

MARLEY MAGUIRE SHIELDED HER EYES FROM THE blinding spotlights as she stepped onto the stage of the Channel Six newsroom, wishing the floor would open up and take her out.

"You good?" her fiancé, Sam, asked as he squeezed her elbow.

"I'm gonna pass out."

She tried to steady her wobbling knees as she struggled to breathe. While she was accustomed to being center stage in a courtroom—thrived on it, actually—any other type of public appearance was terrifying. Especially knowing she was about to have millions of eyes upon her, considering the wild popularity of the station's upcoming segment, *PheelGoodPhilly*.

Who could blame her for her reticence? It wasn't that long ago that her ex-boyfriend had called her out as a villain on national TV when he was a contestant on a popular reality TV dating show. Targeted by social media trolls and hounded by media for months, Marley had suffered personal losses as a result. The last thing she needed was to be cast into the spotlight again. For any reason.

"Do we really have to do this?" she pleaded with Sam.

"Come on, Mar," he cajoled. "It'll be fun. Where's your sense of adventure?"

"At home. Under the covers, where I should be."

"Good thing I've got enough for both of us, then."

Glancing around, Marley wrapped an auburn curl around her finger as she chewed her lip.

"Aww, don't be nervous, Mar. I got us." Sam grinned as he clasped a strong hand around hers.

The assistant producer directed them to join the five other couples lined up onstage. All here for the same reason: to compete in the station's first annual Battle of the Betrothed competition.

It wasn't in Marley's plan to wage war against other wedding-bound couples. Nope, this was all Sam's brilliant idea. He'd entered the contest without her knowledge, submitting the lyrics to the song he'd written, "A Cape May Kind of Love." The song was selected from among thousands of other entries as a finalist, advancing them to the second round of the competition, bringing them to the news station that day.

The song was, without a doubt, award-worthy. Sam swept her off her feet whenever he sang it to her, but it belonged between the two of them, not the entirety of southeast Pennsylvania. While she loved the song, she didn't love the fact it had catapulted them to this portion of the contest as one of six couples to compete for the grand prize: a free wedding and a bunch of cash.

"Cold, *hard* cash," Sam had emphasized when he'd revealed to her earlier that morning, not only that he'd entered the contest, but that they'd been selected to go on to the next round. And she'd better hurry and dress nicely as they were about to go on live TV.

She'd barely had time to register what was happening before she found herself in the local newsroom, getting mic'd up beneath the sweltering glare of studio lights, at o-dark-thirty on a Friday morning.

"We got this," Sam whispered as he guided her to the end of the line.

"Okay, listen up," the producer addressed the couples. "First, congratulations on making it to this round. The purpose of today's broadcast is to introduce you to our viewers, who will ultimately decide your fate. With that—" she swept her arm in the direction of a woman who looked like a real-life Barbie doll, perched on a director's chair, "—I'm sure you're all familiar with the host of *PheelGoodPhilly*, Amanda Bacharach."

Marley wasn't. But whatever.

A chorus of greetings arose from the couples. Amanda, who was inspecting her fingernails as if she might find the body of Jimmy Hoffa under one of them, cast them a look of undeniable disinterest. Apathetic AF, as if she'd rather be swimming in shark-infested waters than on set with a bunch of pie-eyed contest hopefuls.

I hear ya, girl.

"I want to give you a rundown of what to expect today," the producer continued. "Amanda will kick off the segment by introducing Battle of the Betrothed and explaining what the contest involves. Then, we'll go down the line so you can introduce yourselves. Tell viewers your first names, where you live, and why you think you should win. After that, we'll invite our audience to tune in every month to see the couples in action and vote for their favorite. Finally, we'll wrap up today's segment with a practice challenge. Questions? Comments?"

Sam raised his hand. "Which member of each couple gets to do the introductions?" he asked, wagging a finger between the two of them.

The producer shot Sam a puzzled glance. Marley followed with one of her own. Really? *That* was the burning question in his mind? How about: why on God's green earth are we doing this?

"I guess it's between the two of you to decide," the producer said, chuckling. "Hopefully that's something you can agree upon."

She sounded polite, but Marley could see the veritable thought bubble over her head, questioning how good a team they could be if they were about to spar over something as trivial as introductions.

The producer moved down the line to adjust another contestant's mic as Sam's fist pumped up and down, signaling the onslaught of a rock-paper-scissors battle.

"What are you doing?" she whispered.

"Seeing which one of us gets to speak. On three."

On two, he thrust out a flattened palm. She absentmindedly followed with rock.

"You lose," he proclaimed smugly as he smothered her fist with his hand.

"Oh my God, Sam," she muttered. They always had a bit of a competitive thing going between them, but this was ridiculous. She couldn't care less who spoke. "Have at it. If I have to open my mouth on live TV, I'm gonna puke."

"I won't let us down, Mar." Then he added, "But do me a fave. If you *do* puke, turn the other way. I gotta be in court in an hour, and my other suits are at the dry cleaners."

The producer counted down from five. With the point of a finger, the host sprang to life.

"Hey, everyone, Amanda here with *PheelGoodPhilly*, the hap-hap-*happy* show brought to you by Channel Six news." She sang out with enthusiasm, as if someone had shot Red Bull directly into her veins. "If you've ever planned a wedding, you know what a drain on your budget it can be." Then, under her breath, she added, "Not that I would know, having never been engaged before. Thank you, Eddie."

Uncomfortable! The couples glanced around in an attempt to figure out who Eddie was and what role he'd played in Amanda's ringless status.

"But I *am* told by friends who've snagged a man that, between the venue, the professionals, and *all* the things, costs can really add up to rob you of the hap-hap-*happi*ness you deserve. That's why Channel Six has partnered with local wedding vendors to make you feel good, Philly, with its latest contest, Battle of the Betrothed. Over the course of the next six months, these six...*lucky* couples will compete to win an all-expenses-paid wedding and $10,000 cash."

"Oh, yeah! Bring it," a man called out.

How crass. Marley frowned down the line to see which uncouth lowbrow was responsible for the outburst, until she realized it had come from the man she was standing beside. Her very own groom.

Amanda's eyelids fluttered in an apparent attempt to keep them from rolling back into her head. Through a forced smile, she explained the rules. Each month, the contestants would compete in a wedding prep challenge. The audience would vote for their favorite couple. Whoever received the lowest number of votes that month would be eliminated until there was only one standing.

The couples' challenge: get the most votes.

Marley's challenge: get eliminated in the first round.

She didn't have time for such folly, spending the next six months—*six months!*— in a competition she wasn't the least bit interested in. She had real work to do. Not only running a law firm but planning their wedding. They'd agreed upon a two-year engagement to ensure their newly opened law firm was well established before shifting their focus to wedding planning. Their date was now a year away, and most everything had yet to be done. Fortunately, they'd booked their venue—Congress Hall, Cape May's prestigious beachfront resort—as soon as they'd settled on a date. That left everything else to be done. It made Marley's head swim just thinking about it.

Now, instead of serious wedding planning, they'd be engaging in mind-numbing nuptial nonsense.

It was important to Marley and Sam that they pay for their wedding themselves. Marley's dad had been laid off a year earlier, and her parents needed to keep their modest savings for her younger brothers' educations. Sam's family, who were practically made of money, had offered to foot the entire bill, but the couple didn't want to relinquish control and have their wedding become the social event of the century, given his dad was a law firm partner and his mom a popular dermatologist. Marley and Sam wanted to keep it simple.

"We should just elope," she'd suggested, only half-joking.

"And rob everyone of the opportunity to witness me marrying the hell outta you?" Sam had asked, incredulous. "No fucking way. We're doing this big, and we're doing it right."

"Big?" Marley hoped his parents' taste for grandeur wasn't rubbing off on him.

"Emotionally big. Our way. Surrounded by our favorite people."

Once their firm turned a profit, they began socking away as much money as they could—not only to pay for the wedding, but also to eventually purchase a shore house. Another reason to keep wedding costs down. They had their sights set on Cape May, where their good friends had a vacation home. Both avid beach lovers, Marley and Sam yearned to escape from their tiny apartment during sweltering city summers to a place where they could wiggle their toes in the sand, drinks in hand. The quaint seaside town on the tip of the Jersey Cape would provide the perfect refuge.

Amanda's voice brought Marley back to the present as she began listing all that the grand prize would entail. "In addition to $10,000 in cash, the winning couple will receive an all-expenses-paid wedding, including a florist package valued at $2,500. A photo/video package valued at $3,500..."

Marley did the math in her head as Amanda rattled off prize values. If they won, their entire savings, combined with the cash prize, could go far as a down payment.

Sam must have seen the lightbulb going off above her. Looking down at her, he smiled. "Cape May shore house, here we come. Cha-*ching*!"

Marley's trepidation began to melt away as she warmed to the idea of Sam's zany plan.

Each couple introduced themselves and gave a cutesy pitch

as to why they should win. One couple recited lines from their winning poem. Another announced they were expecting a child. A third promised to donate the cash to charity. All tough to top, but Marley had unshakable faith in Sam, knowing he'd pull something equally spectacular out of his ass. An eloquent trial attorney who thought fast on his feet (not to mention a hopeless romantic), Sam would surely come up with something that would drop the mic on the others.

Finally, when it was their turn, Sam raked a hand through his sun-kissed surfer hair, aqua eyes twinkling at Marley before he cast a sultry stare at the camera. Marley grinned expectantly, preparing to *in yo' face* the other contestants.

"Hi, I'm Sam," he said, his tone as smooth as melted butter. "And this is my gorgeous bride-to-be, Marley. We live in Society Hill and we're here to win this challenge because..."

He trailed off, then remained silent.

Uh oh.

Sam's eyes locked with the camera lens. His mouth dropped open, and he made a gurgling sound as if he'd been stabbed in the neck. Marley had never seen this look before. Sam was a natural-born ham, but this was his first time on TV before an audience of millions. And it must've just hit him.

"Because why, Sam?" Amanda tittered nervously.

"Uhhh..." His unwavering gaze was accompanied by a swallow so hard, his Adam's apple nearly popped onto the stage. "That's why," he croaked.

The others laughed. Amanda looked amused for the first time since the segment began, and Sam looked like someone had just thrown a pie in his face.

"Well, viewers, you heard it." Amanda recovered like a pro and turned to the camera. "Marley and Sam should win because...that's why."

"That was *so hot*, Sam," Marley teased under her breath. "*Damn*, you have a way with words."

"I froze, Mar," he whispered.

"No shit, Elsa."

"I fucked up."

"Let it go."

Amanda spun to them and spoke from the side of her mouth. "You guys know you're mic'd, right?"

"Oh, shit," Sam blurted out, then clamped his hand over his mouth. "Sorry."

Amanda gave a terse smile. "So those are your six couples, ladies and gentlemen, while I stand here without a ring. Thanks again, Eddie."

Awkward! Every eye in the studio was drawn to the man behind Camera One, who'd just gone into an epic coughing fit. Possibly Eddie-the-Non-Engager himself.

"Switch to Camera Two," the producer hissed.

Amanda gave Camera Two a big, fake smile. "To give you a little preview of what to expect with this competition, we're going to start off with a practice challenge. Everyone ready?"

"Yes!" the couples answered enthusiastically.

"No!" Marley screamed to herself—or so she thought. Apparently not, as all heads in the studio swiveled toward her. It was her natural instinct to object, momentarily forgetting that a shore house was on the line.

"*Heh heh*, just kidding," she muttered, making a street gesture with her hands as if she were signaling fellow gang members. "Keepin' it real, Philly."

Dear God, strike me down now.

Amanda, crossing the stage to a table where six small gift bags were neatly lined up, cast a look of appreciation at Marley as if they were partners in crime, kindred spirits who also saw the contest for the silliness it was. Or, perhaps, hoping to enlist Marley's gang connections to off Eddie.

"Today, we're giving our audience a sample of the types of challenges you'll be engaged in. Since they didn't get to witness your proposals firsthand, we're going to have you re-enact them right here. But there's a twist. In each of these bags are three items that you're going to use during your proposal. Men, come pick out a bag."

The men shuffled to the table, looking nervous. With the exception of Sam. He didn't shuffle, he sauntered. With all that natural swag, boy couldn't help it. After all, he put the *rizz* in charisma. Marley caught the side eye he shot the camera, the one he considered his "sexy look"—head down, brows slightly raised, suggestive half-smile. Seemingly over his crippling stage fright, Sam was already working the audience, trying to win votes.

"He's dreamy," the woman next to her swooned.

"Please. Don't encourage him."

Nonetheless, her comment stoked Marley's pride. She felt her own competitive tendencies clicking into place so strongly they almost made a sound. Suddenly, she was all in.

Work it, Sam. Let's win this thing!

The men claimed their bags as Amanda continued. "Your challenge is to make a three-sentence proposal using the items in your bag. I'll give you a moment to compose your thoughts."

Sam rejoined Marley and opened his bag, giving her a mixed look of concern and humor. She peered in to see a knife, a spoon, and another object she couldn't make out.

"What's the third thing?"

He pulled it out.

"We're screwed. Literally." Bearing a six-inch screw and a lascivious grin, he gave an evil laugh. "Dare me?"

Oh boy.

"Sam. No." She shook her head as if she were admonishing a toddler.

He wouldn't dare. As an attorney and otherwise respectful member of modern society, Sam would know better than to break FCC rules by being brazenly suggestive on live daytime TV.

Or so she hoped.

The other men worked their random objects into clunky proposal lines, but none appeared to have the same gift of gab as Sam. Filled with adrenaline over the thrill of competition and excited by the prospect of winning (with a dash of cautious trepidation thrown in), Marley said a silent prayer Sam would kill it.

He grinned mischievously as he went down on one knee.

"It would be *knife* if you would be my wife," he said as he held up the knife, smiling at her.

Marley laughed out loud at the adorable look on his face, the teasing gleam in his eye.

He pulled out the spoon. "And I'm over the moon whenever we *spoon*."

OMG. Could he be any cuter?

He reached in the bag for the screw. "But most of all, what I love to do..."

Don't do it. Don't do it, Sam. Think of the children. The money! Marley prepared to apologize to the FCC and bid the battle bye-bye.

Sam cast a naughty glance at the camera and held up his last object, to the collective gasp of contestants and studio personnel alike.

"...is put together IKEA furniture with you."

Delaney

DELANEY BROOKS STARED AT THE STICK, WAITING. AND waiting. She was five days late—unusual for her—and had a sinking feeling what it meant.

Ready or not.

Her timer was about to go off when she heard a crash from the living room of their Cape May shore house, where she and her husband were spending two weeks on break from London.

"Son of a bitch!" Dalton yelled.

Forgetting her pressing concern, she dashed from the bathroom to see what was up.

Or down, as the case was.

Dalton, who'd been painting a wall last she saw him, now lay crumpled on the ground, the jaws of a ladder clasped around him like a hungry, hungry hippo. An upturned paint can on his chest oozed a gray blob across his Cape May t-shirt.

"It decided to close up and take me with it," he said, simultaneously laughing and wincing as he endeavored to lift the paint can without spilling more.

"Are you okay?" Delaney asked, choking back laughter as she pried open the legs of the ladder and took the can from him. She'd have been more concerned if the ladder were taller than three feet.

Dalton scrambled to a standing position, after barely escaping (unlikely) death.

"I think so," he said, holding his shirt out over the tarp, away from his body. "My shirt, not so much. Where've you been?"

"Just resting."

Delaney hadn't told him about her scare, not wanting to cause concern until she knew the results. Not that Dalton would be concerned—elated would better describe his likely reaction. He'd been pushing to start a family since they'd settled in London a couple of years ago, but she wasn't quite ready to start international family planning, hoping to wait until they were permanently back in the States. Things had been going well for them in London, where they'd moved after Dalton was offered the opportunity to open a new branch of his investment firm. As luck would have it, one of the partners at Delaney's law firm had a cousin who was a solicitor in London, and they struck an informal transatlantic merger to loan her to the British firm. She'd passed England's Solicitor Qualifying Exam, a herculean task, and wasn't about to give it all up to start a family just yet.

They'd only planned on staying a year but decided to extend it indefinitely. While they missed family, they loved London. To compromise, they purchased the Cape May house to give them a place to gather with friends and family when they returned to the States for visits, which was quite often. They were there for a couple weeks to flee London's end-of-June record-breaking heat and their non-air-conditioned flat.

Delaney was secretly happy to be away from work, a feeling to which she wasn't quite accustomed. She'd spent a lifetime building a legal career and, up until recently, had loved it. But lately it seemed...lacking. It wasn't that she didn't enjoy working with her UK firm mates or learning to navigate a whole new legal system. It just seemed like something was missing.

But it wasn't screaming babies, that was for sure.

Dalton carefully peeled off his shirt. Delaney took it and wiped some paint splatters from his mocha hair as she gave him a kiss.

"I'll take care of this while you wash up," she said as he headed to the bathroom.

After tossing his shirt in the washing machine, she pulled her long espresso hair into a messy bun and donned rubber gloves for the big clean-up. On her way back to the living room, Dalton nearly careened into her.

"What's this?" he yelled, waving the pregnancy test stick. He lifted her up and spun her around, laughing with joy. "Are you serious?"

Shit. Delaney had forgotten she'd left it on the bathroom counter. Her heart raced as she strained to see if the tiny window on the test stick bore two pink lines.

She chuckled at his exuberance. "I'm not sure. Let me see."

Dalton put her down and handed her the stick.

Negative.

Relief coursed through her. "Sorry, dude, not this time." Sorry, not sorry.

They hadn't been trying, but she'd missed a pill and was convinced the test was going to be positive.

"Bummer," Dalton said, his midnight blue eyes revealing his disappointment. But only for a moment.

Tossing the stick over his shoulder, he whisked Delaney into his arms and carried her to their bedroom. "You know, we can change that now."

Delaney chuckled with the confidence of a woman who'd remembered to take her pill.

This time.

Cleo

CLEO DUGGAN STOOD OUTSIDE IN THE SWELTERING heat, waiting for Gus to answer the door.

"What the hell do you want?" he barked from inside, likely peering through the peephole.

"I want to know if you've been saved by our Lord Jesus Christ," Cleo joked.

"I've been saved alright. By our Lord Jim Beam."

"Open the door, old man," Cleo said. "What the hell do you think I'm here for? Certainly not shits and giggles."

Despite their gruff exchange, Gus was one of her favorite people, and Cleo one of his. Her weekly visits were under the guise of selecting the fantasy baseball lineup they'd teamed up on—or so she wanted Gus to believe. In reality, it was Cleo's way of making sure her friend was eating and tending to his health after his cancer diagnosis three years ago. She was thrilled he'd beaten the odds after being told last year he had but months to live. Though he was still hanging in there, she knew he was on borrowed time and treasured every moment she had with him.

Cleo was shocked at his appearance when he opened the door. He was even thinner than the last time she saw him, if that was possible.

"Get in here." He ushered her in.

Cleo shoved a paper bag at him. "I brought your medicine."

If a six-pack of Pabst could be considered as such.

"About damn time."

So it was, between Cleo and the old goat. She'd met him on her first night bartending at Murphy's Tavern, a hole-in-the-wall dive bar in northeast Philly. He'd been looking for a place to hunker down on that blustery winter night when a snowstorm blew him in. Or maybe it was the flashing neon Yuengling Beer sign signaling him like a beacon as it lit up a snow-blanketed sky with the promise of a cheap buzz. Whatever it was, Gus had become more than a barfly who'd perched on the corner barstool every night from ten to two. He'd become the father she never had, the grandfather she'd always hoped for. Two for the price of one.

Cleo looked around the dingy apartment, better described as a bat cave. A TV tray next to a ratty old recliner held the remnants of a half-eaten Hungry Man dinner. Cleo scoffed at the irony that someone who'd basically lost all his appetite would eat something by that name. She picked up the plastic tray of leftovers and smushed it into the trashcan overflowing with a week of *Philly Inquirers*, *New York Times*, and old magazines.

"I was eating that," Gus said. "What are you now, my maid?"

"A maid wouldn't touch this place with a ten-foot pole."

Cleo was only joking. The pole would have to be twenty feet. Or longer.

She straightened up the place, throwing out discarded cups and empty food wrappers, relieved he'd been eating. On top of an empty pizza box was a copy of *Psychology Today*.

"Well played, Professor Shrinky-Dink." Cleo smirked, holding up the magazine. "I guess we're still on this?"

Gus chuckled. "I planted it there on purpose."

It was a running joke between them. For some reason, Gus refused to tell Cleo what he'd done for a living before he retired, instead joking about being a psychology professor at the University of Pennsylvania. With his crass sense of humor, blue-collar mentality, and love of drinking, he was the furthest thing from an academic—other than a study in how not to live one's life. He was a lonely old man who, like Cleo, had a penchant for pushing people away. She suspected it had something to do with his divorce, although her belief had never been fact-checked. He'd lost his only child, a daughter, when she was young.

Cleo figured the reason she and Gus were drawn to one another was because she lacked a strong male figure in her life, she reminded him of his late daughter, and they'd both lived pretty shitty lives. At least until recently, for Cleo.

"Do you need me to read this to you before bed?" she teased. Another running joke—the man claimed to hate reading anything that didn't have pictures. But that wasn't true, judging by the pounds of fully read newspapers and magazines Cleo dragged to his dumpster every week.

"How's your week been?"

"Good," Gus said. "Appetite's back."

"I see that."

"How's the new gallery coming along?" he asked.

"It's coming. Still lots to do, but I'm loving it. Can't wait to go from assistant director to the actual director."

She still couldn't believe how lucky she was to have the opportunity to move up so quickly, thanks to her boss's steadfast faith in her.

Gus thrust out his chin, and she prepared herself for an oncoming insult. In jest, of course—it's how they communicated.

"You'll be a great one. You know how I know that?"

"You're not just a shrink but also a fortune-teller?"

He ignored her. "Because, in addition to being a smart alec, you got moxie. You'll do just fine."

There was that word again. *Moxie.* Second time she'd heard it.

The first time was shortly after moving to New York with her boyfriend, Nigel, to pursue a career in art while he attended the culinary arts academy. They'd lucked into an affordable sublease through a friend of a friend, who also set them up with temporary bartending gigs in the same tavern.

Four months later, on a snowy December morning, Cleo had helped an older woman who'd fallen on the sidewalk outside the bar. She took the woman inside to tend to her and, after assessing her injuries and bandaging her knee, asked if she wanted a drink.

"Cognac. Straight up, double shot."

Cleo laughed out loud. It was only ten in the morning. She'd expected the woman to request something quaint to match her fragile appearance, like a spot of tea.

"Ah. Drinking before noon—a woman after my own heart," Cleo said as she poured.

"Someone has to keep the booze business thriving, but that's not the reason I fell. Damn ice got me."

"Hey, I'm not one to judge."

Despite looking as if she were ninety, the woman soon proved to be a quick-witted wise-ass. Just like Cleo. And Gus.

"Is this your fine dining establishment?" the woman asked, glancing around.

"Nah, I'm just the bartender. Moved here from Philly, hoping to make it as an artist. Just like every other damn person."

"What kind of art?"

"Painting and charcoal sketches. Mostly of people."

"Naked ones, I hope."

"I'm trying." Cleo smirked. "But I keep getting kicked out of the men's room."

"Get any good-looking guys in this joint?"

"Only the gay ones," Cleo reported. "Straight guys, not so much. But if you're looking to see if Bigfoot is real, do come for Monday Night Football."

"Shame. I like a good body, myself. Enjoy it now, because one day you won't be able to tell where boobs end and knees begin. Theirs, and yours."

Cleo loved this woman and was disappointed when she drained her drink.

"I best be going, young lady. Got a gallery to open up. I appreciate all you've done for me. Name's Daisy Kunkle. And you?"

"Wait—*the* Daisy Kunkle, owner of ImagineArt Gallery?"

"Who wants to know?"

"I'm Cleo Duggan. I just applied for a volunteer position."

"Is that so?"

The woman narrowed her eyes at Cleo, as if sizing her up. "I can do you one better, Cleo Duggan. One of our assistants just quit, and I have no time for that hiring bullshit. I like you—you remind me of my younger self. You got moxie."

Moxie. She'd had no idea what it meant at the time, having been born after World War II.

"Job's yours if you want it," she said.

Cleo's jaw dropped. "Absolutely, I'd be honored. What do you need from me? An interview? A résumé? A bribe?" She stumbled over her words, hoping the woman wouldn't retract her offer. "I'm legit, I swear. Got a Fine Arts degree from the University of the Arts. I'll be happy to show you some of my work."

Daisy shook her head. "I've seen all I need to see. Just be there tomorrow at nine a.m. Sharp."

As soon as the woman left, Cleo pulled out her phone and looked up the word.

Moxie [mok-see] - courageous spirit and determination; perseverance.

Perseverance was right. As the accidental product of two abusive alcoholics, Cleo had had to fight against all odds to slay her family's demons and survive, to learn how to love and be loved after a childhood of neglect and abandonment. She barely knew her father, mostly just through visits at the local jail. And her mom dropped her off at her grandmother's one day when she was six, never to return until Cleo was in her teens. Thank God for her grandmother, whose unconditional love had given Cleo a fighting chance, who'd told her she could do anything she put her mind to. As a result, no matter how many times Cleo was knocked down by life, she always landed on her feet. From the rubble of dysfunction and the ruins of a shattered childhood, Cleo had risen like a phoenix, somehow finding the grit and determination to get a college degree and move her sorry ass to Manhattan, where she was not only living, but thriving. Doing her art. Creating shit. And now, with any luck, becoming gainfully employed in an actual art gallery.

Bursting with an energy she'd never felt before, she'd arrived at ImagineArt studio at eighty-thirty the morning after meeting Daisy, and dove headfirst into a gallery assistant position, slowly working her way up in the year and a half that followed. She felt incredibly blessed for their chance encounter—even more so when, a couple months ago, Daisy announced she would be opening a second gallery in Chelsea and tagged Cleo as its new director. For some reason unbeknownst to her, she'd struck a chord in the crusty old heart of her mentor, who was willing to take such a huge chance on her. It was still months away from opening, but Cleo couldn't wait.

The upside: a shit ton more money. The downside: a shit ton more responsibility.

Unfortunately, that meant her own creative time would be compromised, but she banked on it being worth the sacrifice in the long run. Put in the hard work now to have more money and time to make shit later on.

"Do you have time to do your own art?" Gus now asked, as if reading her mind.

"Here and there." She shrugged. "I sketch on my commute when I can and paint on weekends."

"Got any recent pieces?"

She pulled a pad from her backpack and flipped to the page she'd started yesterday, a sketch of a woman whose eyes glimmered with hope despite her downtrodden posture.

"She was sitting across from me on the L train," Cleo explained. "Her hopeful sorrow spoke to me from across the aisle."

Looking at the woman was like looking into a reflection of her past, when her friends had been uprooting their lives to pursue new adventures, leaving Cleo in their dust. To avoid being abandoned again by the people she loved, she'd conjured a half-assed plan to move to New York City to "become an artist." And damn if that wasn't just what she did. She may have started out downtrodden, but hope's light led her to her own fabulous future.

She wanted the same for the woman on the train, to find whatever her hopefulness yearned for.

Gus smiled as he gazed at the sketch. "You have quite the talent, young lady."

Again, Cleo waited for a joke that didn't come. It was rare for him to give her such a compliment without a humorous kicker. Twice in the same day, no less.

"How 'bout you and Nigel?" he asked, handing her the pad. "You still carrying on, begging him to propose?"

"I see you've been smoking crack," Cleo deadpanned, having zero interest in legalized commitment. It was quite the other way around, with Nigel bringing up the subject of marriage more frequently.

Gus shook his head. "I don't know what you have against it."

"I saw what it did to my parents. Hard pass."

"Not every marriage is like theirs, thank God."

"Yeah, but it's still a form of possession. Marriage is a manmade institution designed to keep women in line."

Gus shook his head, chuckling. "Sometimes you're just too headstrong and distrusting for your own good. Marriage is what you make of it, child."

"And I'm choosing not to make anything of it."

"Well, you may want to consider it. Boy's not gonna wait forever."

"Well then, fuck him. Ain't no way I'm selling my soul to someone else. What's with you, anyway? I thought you hated marriage."

A flicker of emotion crossed the old man's face. Cleo wasn't exactly sure what that was all about, but damn if it didn't look something like grief. Which would be ridiculous.

She wasn't sure what had happened between Gus and his ex-wife—another thing he was closed-mouthed about, the secretive dick. She knew better than to press for details or he'd shut her right down. She assumed his marriage had ended badly; otherwise, why else would he have spent years trashing relationships?

That was, until Nigel had come along. Once Gus met her now live-in boyfriend, he'd flipped his usual script and wouldn't shut the hell up about them getting tied down. In truth, though, Cleo was happy her stand-in grandpa liked Nigel—the first guy to make Cleo feel loved for exactly who she was, no expectations for more. He made her feel chosen.

"Is he still wanting to leave the city?"

Cleo sighed. "Yeah, and he's on my last nerve about it. I don't want to leave. I'm about to become director of a new gallery and double my salary. And my volunteer work is crucial for my sanity, both with the mural project and the houseless youth with whom I've bonded. I can't leave. Them, or the city."

"Why does he want to go so bad?"

"Money's a biggie. You know his dream was to open a restaurant in the city, but he's realizing just how expensive it is and how hard it is to find investors. Beyond that, I think he's outgrowing New York. Claims he wants land to do a farm-to-table restaurant, but he can't do that living where we live. And then there's the noise, the pollution, the crowds... the complaints go on and on. I'm frankly sick of it."

"And you're good with staying?"

"Wouldn't want to be anywhere else. I love where I live and what I'm doing."

"But you also love him, right?"

"What's your point?"

"My point is, sometimes loving someone and being loved requires compromise."

"If we move from the city so he can start a new business, he'll be taking me away from mine. It's not a compromise on his part, it's flat-out asking me to change everything about my life."

Someone knocked on the door just then, interrupting Cleo's rant.

"There's my girlfriend," Gus announced.

"I'll be less surprised if it's Bradley Cooper asking you to play him his bio pic."

But damn if it wasn't a woman—Gus's friend, Charlotte, holding his cat formerly known as Rex (now Blinky, due to an unfortunate accident that nearly took out one of his eyes). They were sharing custody of the thing since Gus had landed in the hospital last year and Charlotte began caring for it.

"Hey, guys," Charlotte said as she set the cat down on his lap.

"How's my boy?" Gus sang.

"Missing you, that's for sure," Charlotte said as she turned to Cleo. "How's work going?"

"Great, thanks for asking. Getting closer to opening our new gallery. How about you?"

"Still gunning for partnership, but not sure how much longer I'll hang in there. It's exhausting."

"You're too young to be this miserable in your job," Cleo opined.

She didn't know how old Charlotte was, but guessed she, too, was in her young thirties, despite looking more like she was fifty. How she'd love to work her hair coloring magic on the woman, brighten her up a bit. Cleo, whose artistic talent stretched beyond the canvas, was once big into coloring her own hair, until she realized her natural burgundy shade was best suited to complement her hazel eyes. "Do you have any other options?"

Charlotte shrugged. "I did have one option last year, but it would've required a big move, which I'm not up for. I've been with this firm so long I need to give it one more shot." She turned for the door. "I'll let you two visit. I'll be back for Blinky tomorrow."

"I'll walk you out," Cleo offered.

Once outside, she asked Charlotte, who saw Gus on a more frequent basis, how he was really doing.

"He has his good days and bad," Charlotte said.

"I'm thankful you're doing this, bringing the cat over and keeping him company. It makes me feel good knowing someone else is looking out for him."

"It's been my pleasure," Charlotte said. "He's quite the conversationalist. I've enjoyed my chats with him. He knows a lot about the world and the people in it. Considering..."

Charlotte didn't have to say it. The man lived as if he were destitute, in a cramped apartment in a dilapidated building in a rough section of the city. Cleo had tried to get him to move, but he claimed to love his place and didn't want to deal with the hassle. There was no changing his mind. Rough around the edges, crinkled and bitter from a life of disappointment and grief, Gus was stubborn as fuck. But Charlotte was correct about his level of knowledge. While his outward appearance didn't suggest so, he was well-read and knew a lot about a lot. Perhaps that's what being alive on the planet for seventy-nine years did to a person.

After Charlotte left, Cleo returned to the apartment and resumed her tidying. She glanced around the corner to check on Gus, who was unusually quiet. The cat had not only crawled onto his lap but fallen asleep and taken Gus with it. Both looked at peace, content to be with one another.

Smiling, she reached for her coal pencils and began sketching what would soon become her most prized possession.

Charlotte

CHARLOTTE DRYSDALE WAS HAPPY TO SEE HER FRIEND having a good day. He always perked up a bit whenever she brought his beloved cat for a visit, but he seemed even perkier today. Perhaps because Cleo was there for her weekly visit.

Gus's closest family members, a niece and nephew, lived far away. She was glad to help Cleo tend to him. Charlotte liked the bartender-turned-artist, despite that they couldn't be any more different. Cleo was edgy, daring, while Charlotte was conservative, cautious.

Still, she admired Cleo's gumption, her ability to fly by the seat of her pants and land upright. She was in awe of Cleo's decision to uproot her life and move from Philadelphia to New

York to pursue a career in art. Whenever Charlotte shared her growing misery at her law firm, Cleo would encourage her to take a chance, move on to something different. Charlotte had briefly considered doing just that when her friend, Jake, introduced her to a lawyer in Cape May who was looking for someone to join his firm. But ultimately, she didn't feel bold enough to give up all she knew and start fresh somewhere else. Painfully introverted and risk-averse, she'd spent her whole life in Philadelphia and had worked hard to advance her position with her current firm. She wasn't about to flee her comfort zone for some small-town firm in Jersey.

After leaving Gus's, Charlotte waited on the corner for her Uber. She was anxious to get to work on the complicated mergers case she was handling, knowing the office would be empty. Saturdays were always her most productive day.

When the car was a minute away, her phone rang.

"What's shakin'?" her friend, Jake, asked. "Please tell me you're not working."

"I'm not working," she responded. "Yet."

Jake groaned. "Char, we've discussed this. You have to stop working so hard and live a little. Especially when I'm here in town. I was hoping we could hang before I head back tomorrow."

"You should've told me you were in town. I would've planned better."

"It was a last-minute thing. Are you free for dinner?"

"Ooh, sorry. I have a hot date tonight."

"Oh," Jake said, pausing. "Maybe next time."

Charlotte chuckled. As her good friend, who'd helped her climb out of her anti-social chrysalis and into a slightly *less* anti-social chrysalis, he should know better than to believe she'd have a date. Hot or otherwise.

"Kidding, of course. I'm free."

"Great," he said, his tone lightening. "Pizza at your place?"

"Perfect. How about seven? Hold on, my Uber just arrived."

She checked the app and circled behind the car, snapping a photo of the license plate.

"I'm sending you evidence, in case I get murdered."

Laughter wafted through the speaker as she hit send. Cradling the phone in the crook of her neck, she retrieved a Wet One from her purse.

"I still can't believe you've gotten over your fear of ride shares," he said.

It was true, for the most part. When they'd first met, Charlotte wouldn't even consider using the service, believing if the germs from the publicly utilized vehicle didn't kill her, the driver would.

"Only half my fear," she corrected, noting with relief the driver was familiar, one who knew of her need for a sanitized experience. His patient eyes regarded her through the rear-view mirror as she wiped down the seat.

"The only time my car gets cleaned," he said through a smile.

"Don't tell me that, or I'll need another wipe," she quipped, settling into the back seat.

"Good to see you, Miss Charlotte."

"You, too, Bungi."

"And you're on a first-name basis." Jake's incredulous tone came through the phone. "Wonders never cease."

In the two years they'd known each other, Jake had helped her overcome many of her fears, but not all of them. Especially where bacteria were concerned. Some habits lingered. Festered. Multiplied.

She settled into the plush leather seat, thankful she'd gotten the kind driver with whom she was often paired on weekends when traveling to her office. She far preferred the ride service to the Broad Street line, where derelicts and drunks frequented. One could never be sure about train commuters.

After putting in a few solid hours at the office, Charlotte emailed her boss, Tom Jervis, to share her achievements on the case. Not that he demanded it. As a senior associate, Charlotte deftly handled any case the firm took on, but she thought it extremely important to keep him informed about her hard work. As founding partner of Jervis Mahoney, he held the key to her future. The law firm was about to name its next partner. Charlotte, who'd been making a bid for two years now, was hopeful it was finally her time.

If not, she wasn't sure how much longer she'd stay. It had been brutal for Charlotte, after being told she had to socialize more to be considered for partnership. She'd tried like hell to prove she could be out in the community, schmoozing with potential clients, yet they'd promoted her insufferably boorish coworkers instead. Still smarting from that insulting blow, yet not one to give up easily, she'd decided to give it one more shot.

She found Jake waiting for her when she returned home, wearing jeans and a faded Avalon t-shirt that matched his indigo eyes. He'd made himself at home on her porch swing, a pizza next to him, gently rocking with outstretched legs. He raked a hand through his dark wavy hair as he stared at the porch ceiling, a big smile on his face. Charlotte paused, wondering if it was normal to go a bit breathless upon seeing a platonic friend.

"What's so funny?" she asked, to break the spell.

He jolted to attention and laughed. "I was thinking how funny it would be if I ate this whole pizza before you got here."

"Funny? More like a death wish."

"Tell me about it," he said, eyes twinkling. "I've never met someone who loved pizza so much. Were it not for the fact you'd probably kill me over one, I'd find your obsession kinda cute."

"Enough small talk," Charlotte said as she picked up the

box and headed for the door. "What brings you to town this fine weekend?"

Jake lived in Avalon, a little over an hour from Philadelphia, and often came to visit family who lived in nearby suburbs.

"I'll tell you over dinner," he said.

They settled in at Charlotte's kitchen table. Jake dished out their slices as Charlotte poured wine.

"Cheers," Jake said, offering a toast.

"What are we celebrating?"

"I have a date."

"Oh..." Charlotte hoped she didn't sound as disappointed as she felt. They were best friends and hung out whenever they could, despite living in different towns. The only exception was when Jake had a girlfriend, which, thankfully, wasn't too often. Charlotte didn't like taking a back seat in his life.

"Not that kind of date," he said. "A date for my trip. Finally. I'm leaving next month."

Shoot. Worse than a dating date.

Jake, an avid boater, had been preparing for a sailing trip around the world ever since they met. Up until then, it had only been a distant dream, a lingering possibility. She wished he wasn't serious about it. He was her only real friend, and she wasn't ready to lose him for the many months he'd be gone.

Charlotte faked a smile. "That's great."

"I know you'll miss me terribly," Jake teased, squeezing her hand. "As I will you. I promise we'll keep in touch."

"Like you did last time?" Charlotte asked, eyebrow raised.

Jake had taken off for the Caribbean last winter to practice for the bigger trip. Shortly after sailing into the tropical sunset, he'd met and started dating someone, virtually toppling off the edge of the planet like a pre-Columbus sailor.

"That was just me being weird," Jake reminded her.

"Very weird," she said, playfully tapping his foot with hers.

Charlotte had thought he'd stopped communicating with

her because he was dating someone else, but that was only part of it. Later, he'd admitted he wasn't sure how to handle the feelings that had threatened when things got a little too close between them one night prior to his trip. As platonic friends, they'd never shared an intimate moment before that.

"Please don't go MIA again. I don't think I can stand my life without Captain Brady."

"Ahoy, matey," he said, giving her a salute. "I promise I won't lose touch this time. So what's happening? Still trying to schmooze a partnership out of Jervis Mahoney?"

"Of course. Gotta give it one last try."

"When will you find out?"

"Hopefully, this week."

"What will you do if it doesn't work out again?"

"Stage a coup."

In all her years of practicing law, she'd never once thought she'd be thwarted in the advancement of her career by something as ridiculous as social engagement. Jake had suggested on more than one occasion she should consider another path if this one didn't work out, but that would feel too much like defeat. Charlotte didn't lose battles, especially one so important to her career. She couldn't imagine being beat out by any one of the other associates vying for partnership this round. She had seniority and more successful case resolutions than any of them. Combined.

She shrugged. "Nah. I'll probably just jump off the Ben Franklin Bridge and plummet headfirst into the Delaware."

"Or you could just call my friend Bob."

Bob Stevens was the Cape May attorney Jake had introduced her to last year. He was preparing to retire and looking for someone to take over his business. She'd given it some consideration after spending the day with him and seeing his firm in action but decided against it in favor of giving Jervis another try.

That's how confident she was that she'd be named their next partner.

Marley

MARLEY AND SAM WERE ENJOYING A LEISURELY WEEKend getaway as they sipped wine before a roaring fire at Willow Creek Winery.

"I can't believe you pulled that off," Marley said, laughing over Sam's last proposal line on the Battle of the Betrothed. "I seriously thought you were going to get our asses kicked out of the contest."

"Were you hoping for that?" Sam teased.

"At first, yes, but I'm all in now. If we win, we can have a nice wedding *and* buy our shore house."

Once she'd reclaimed her sense of adventure, her competitive nature kicked into high gear. The first round of the televised contest had been for practice, but from there on out, it was game on. Marley and Sam had won the practice voting round by a landslide, likely due to Sam working the camera, as well as his clever proposal.

"You're such a ham," she teased as she ran her fingers up and down his arm.

"Admit it. You kinda dig me."

"Meh, kinda."

"I see you undressing me with those emerald eyes of yours."

"Am I that obvious?"

"Embarrassingly transparent. So hey, what do you think is going on with Amanda and Eddie?"

"Oh, forgot to tell you," Marley said, chuckling over Amanda's snide Eddie comments on live TV. "We were all talking backstage when you went to the little boys' room and collectively decided, if anyone could get the facts, it would be you."

"Collectively?" Sam grinned.

"Yeah, we took a vote, and it was unanimous. You gotta get the scoop."

"Oh, don't tempt me, Maguire. You know how I love me some juicy gossip."

"That's what makes you the perfect man for the job, Jerry Springer."

"Do you think I should slide into their DMs?" he asked. "I bet Amanda would like that."

"Except Eddie wouldn't stand a chance then," Marley quipped, downplaying Sam's obvious attempt to make her jealous. She was accustomed to it, having served as his wing woman for years. "Someone suggested we bet on the likelihood of them getting engaged by the end of our contest. Maybe you could work your magic there as well."

"Like I did on you? Although it took me, what, seven years to get you to fold?"

"I just had to make sure no one better was going to come along."

Sam poured more wine and offered a toast. "To you, for finally saying yes. And to us, for the success of Maguire Adams."

She clinked her glass in celebration of their law firm's first year. Despite a modest staff of five—Marley's cousin, Kelly, as administrative assistant, two interns from Temple University, and the two of them—they were keeping pace with some of the bigger law firms.

"Do you realize what today is?" Sam asked.

"Of course. Exactly one year to our wedding day. Ready for it?"

"I was born ready. As if someone held newborn me up, fresh from the womb, and said, 'You're destined to marry

Marley Maguire one day.'"

Marley cracked up at his old lady tone, which sounded just like his grandmother.

"Twenty-eight years later, here we are. I just had to meet you first."

"And?"

"Oh, right. Make you fall for me."

"You're lucky I joined that bogus study group you invited me to, despite having written you off as a jock frat boy."

Sam had bounded into her life in their freshman year of college waving a huge red flag. He was so over-the-top with charisma and charm, Marley was certain he was an F boy (the F *not* standing for football). Especially once he began tagging along after class, trying to strike up conversations, not picking up the social cues of blatant disinterest she was laying down. For reasons Marley couldn't understand, he seemed to hone in on her while ignoring the gaggle of eager women who followed in his wake. He lured her in by asking her to join the study group of which, he later admitted, he was the only member. He hooked her by becoming a friend. She wasn't looking for a relationship at the time—her only goal was to get into law school. As it turned out, Sam was heading in the same direction. A mutual interest in criminal justice and similar goals laid the foundation upon which a great friendship, and later romance, was built. Enemies to friends to lovers, in the most classic sense.

"And so, it begins," Sam said of their wedding preparations. "What all do we have left to do?"

"All the things. Without breaking the bank and spending our shore house savings."

"We definitely need to win this contest. We should work on a strategy."

"As long as you keep making love to the camera, we should be good."

He gave her the same sultry look he'd given the audience. "Let the games begin."

Marley accepted his outstretched hand as they watched the crackling fire in silence. She couldn't wait to get started on the wedding planning, but for now, was content to spend a romantic weekend in Cape May with her partner in crime.

Cleo

CLEO RETURNED TO NEW YORK, ANXIOUS TO PAINT THE sketch she'd finished of Gus and his feline friend the night before. She'd stayed up late trying to capture as many details of his face as she could. The face that bore every emotion experienced by humankind, countless times during a life filled with joy and surprise, heartache and grief.

Born during World War II, he'd witnessed so much more than most generations. The birth of rock and roll, the death of an assassinated president. Mind-blowing advances in technology—the internet, portable phones that doubled as computers, mini-ovens that cooked food in seconds. He'd lived through several wars, even fought in one, and witnessed many firsts: the commercial jet, the moon landing, the Super Bowl. Above all, an Eagles Super Bowl win, the greatest miracle of his time on earth.

Tucked among the creases and folds of his nearly octogenarian face was the roadmap of a life lived hard.

Pulling the sketch from her bag, she marveled at her work. *Gus Sleeps*, she'd titled it.

"What have you got there, love?" Nigel asked as he came up behind Cleo and wrapped his arms around her waist, resting his chin on her shoulder. "That's a perfect Gus. Brilliant."

"He looks peaceful, doesn't he?"

"The only time I've seen him looking more so is when he's pissed."

"Your kind of pissed, not our kind," Cleo said, chuckling at her British boyfriend's term for *drunk*.

"Come here," he whispered, his voice husky as he yanked her close. Taking the sketch from her hand, he laid it on the counter. "I know it was only one night, but I missed you like crazy. I can't stay away from you that long."

She could tell he meant it by the soulful kiss he gave her before lifting her up onto the kitchen island. She wrapped her legs around his waist, and they continued playing tonsil hockey until he lifted her off the counter and carried her to the bedroom.

After a deliciously slow and passionate session of lovemaking, Cleo snuggled up against him. "How did it go with the investors?" she asked, linking her fingers with his in comfortable familiarity as she came back to earth, still trying to catch her breath. She felt bad for not asking him sooner, but in the throes of passion, she'd forgotten all about his meeting.

Nigel shook his head. "Another rejection. Looks like I won't be leasing space of my own anytime soon." He huffed, running a hand through tousled onyx hair, his dark eyes solemn. "Not in this damn city. Unless I sell body parts."

Nigel had been banging the "we can't afford this city" drum for a while, but Cleo tried to drown him out by tooting the horn of her own success. For the first time in her life, she was thriving, earning a grown-ass living as a respectable professional.

Quite the understatement to say it was a sticking point in their relationship. She wouldn't entertain the notion of moving, not even for a hot second. She knew it wasn't fair to Nigel, whose dream was being squeezed out by the financial burden of city dwelling, but—*whatev*. He'd been saving up for the past few years, but with astronomical rents, in addition to other start-up costs, the only way he'd be able to afford to open a restaurant in the city would be to convince investors. Win the lottery. Sell body parts. Or all the above.

"What about the partnership?" Cleo asked, wishing he'd consider his classmates' offers to join them on a multi-owner restaurant deal. They'd already scored a place in the Bronx.

"I'd rather sell used cars stark naked than climb into bed with that lot."

"Maybe it would be better to start off as a group, rather than doing it on your own. Less risky that way."

Nigel groaned. "That's not what I want, Cleo. I'm telling you, we gotta move out of this city if I'm ever gonna do this the way I want to."

They lay there in silence before Cleo got up, pulled on a tank top and shorts, and went to the kitchen to pour herself a glass of wine, hoping he'd move on to another subject and drop the whole moving routine.

He followed and poured a glass for himself. "How would you like to take a little romantic getaway this weekend?"

"Where?" Cleo asked, excited over the thought of a getaway.

"Not far. I was thinking Jersey."

Cleo nearly spit out her wine with her hearty guffaw. "Almost fell for it," she said, knowing what he was up to. It wasn't about a romantic getaway. It was to look for restaurant space.

"Come on, Clee," he begged. "Just the two of us. Think about it. You and me, chugging through the Lincoln Tunnel, the stench of Newark blowing through our hair. Nothing says romance like smokestacks on the horizon and miles-long traffic back-ups."

He could've done a better job selling it, knowing his real goal was to explore cheaper venues outside the city.

"Pass. But you can go."

Nigel looked as if she'd slapped him. "Why can't you

indulge me in this? I've been supportive of you. I'm not asking you to quit your job, just consider other options."

"Because indulging you means leaving the city if you find something. I'm not ready for that. My whole life is here—my job, my volunteer work, everything."

"Ever heard of commuting?"

"I'd ask the same of you. Why can't we live here, and you commute for work?"

"Because it's about finances all around. Why would we live in the most expensive place when we're both starting businesses? It makes more sense to go where rent is cheaper and do the commuting thing. Millions do it every day."

"Let 'em. Between the new gallery and volunteer work, I barely have time to create, let alone commute. There's no way I'm moving to Jersey."

He was pensive for a moment. "Will you ever be ready?"

"Maybe when I'm dead."

He winced. "A bit rude, don'tcha think?"

"Not rude, just real," Cleo said, an edge to her tone. "Remember all those conversations we had when we first met? How we shouldn't let someone hold us back from exploring our own goals? How the 'right person' won't make you change something about yourself?"

Nigel regarded her with a somber expression. "I do, but this is different."

"How?" Cleo demanded. "You're asking me to leave the city I love, all because it no longer suits your needs."

"I'm not asking you to change something about *you*, just asking you to relocate."

"But relocation means changing everything about my life. How I get around. How I spend my time. A commute will add hours to my day. I'll have to cut things out of my life that define me."

Cleo realized she was being stubborn but didn't care. It was more than just the inconvenience of commuting. Volunteering with the mural project and helping houseless youth find an outlet for their creative talents were activities she needed in her life. Bonding with the kids as they painted was cathartic, as she surreptitiously helped them brainstorm positive solutions for family and social matters so they didn't have to resort to gang membership, drugs, or guns to solve issues. It helped her resolve some of her own dark past. She knew how soul-crushing it was to be raised by parents with substance abuse issues. Parents who put themselves and their addiction first, not only creating a toxic environment for a child, but instilling toxic self-beliefs. It had taken Cleo thirty-two years to shake off the shit that had lived rent-free in her head since childhood, all thanks to the new life she'd created for herself. Living in the city made her feel strong, resilient. Pursuing an actual career made her feel successful and gave her a legit, income-producing outlet for her creative talent, something she didn't have before she'd moved here. Leaving it all to go live somewhere else felt like trashing that part of her newly discovered self. Going backward, returning to a lifestyle she now deplored. Defeat.

Finally, for the first time ever, she felt like she was 100 percent in control of her life and wasn't about to relinquish that for a man. Any man—even one as kind and loving as Nigel.

Charlotte

CHARLOTTE BUCKLED AT THE KNEES WHEN TOM JERVIS broke the news.

She could barely keep herself upright as she learned that the partnership she'd been practically killing herself over these past two years was once again being yanked from her. They were offering the partnership to another associate, one with fewer years and fewer successes than Charlotte. A female, no less, disproving Charlotte's suspicion of sexist practices.

Time to face facts. Charlotte just wasn't partner material.

"I'm sorry," Tom Jervis said.

She was accustomed to being overlooked. It seemed her mousy brown hair, glasses, and frumpy fashion served as in invitation for people to treat her poorly. She'd never cared much for her appearance, believing people should be rewarded for hard work, not looks or social status. Unfortunately, the rest of the world disagreed.

Accepting her fate, she mumbled that she understood and turned for the door.

Except—no. She didn't understand.

Something deep within the recesses of her soul cried out to her. Raw emotion from a lifetime of bad treatment toppled over the dam she'd built to stave off the memories. Bullied as a child. Ignored by salesclerks. Overlooked by men. Shoved aside so others could be promoted ahead of her. Years upon years of humiliation and devastation swirled within her to create the perfect storm.

She spun back around. "You know what, asshole? I *don't* understand. I've dedicated my life to this firm. I've worked most weekends over the past seven years, never took vacations, and stayed later every single night than any one of you fuckers. I've won case after case for you. I've worked my ass off and deserve to be made partner."

The venom spewing from within surprised her. Charlotte, who rarely swore, couldn't believe the words coming out of her mouth as her lips snarled and twisted and wove a maelstrom of obscenities that smacked Tom Jervis in his unsuspecting face.

Tears stung her eyes as her voice cracked with bitter

heartache. "I've loved working here and loved working for you, in particular. If you can't see my value, then consider this my resignation. Actually, I don't care if you can see it or not, because I can. I'm out."

She stormed from the room, not caring she'd just set ablaze the only real professional bridge she'd ever built.

It took precisely seven minutes to pack her belongings—a minute for each year she'd worked there. Years of hard work and dedication boiling down to mere minutes as she shoved her once-illustrious career into a tattered cardboard box and fled from the building before she could change her mind.

She found herself on the Broad Street line, clacking its way to her home in North Philly. Now that she was without a salary and disposable income, her Ubering days were over. She hugged the box containing the ruins of a promising professional life as it collected the tears tumbling from her cheeks.

Back at home, she paced her living room, still in a stupor over what had transpired. Disbelief turned to panic as she recalled the things she'd said to Tom Jervis, ruing her meltdown. Verbally ripping him a new one was tantamount to shredding any hope for a recommendation based upon her otherwise stellar reputation.

"I don't know what to do, Blinky," she said. The cat rubbed against her calf as if to calm her. She scooped him up and hugged him hard. "I've never been without a plan."

Blinky purred as Charlotte held him, until she hit the invisible wall of cat tolerance. He scrambled to get down, scratching her arm in the process. Great—that's all she needed was cat scratch fever.

He trotted to the desk and leaped onto her laptop.

"Scram! You can't sit on that," she said, swooshing Blinky aside. "It's my only lifeline to finding a job."

With no time to waste, she tapped her laptop to life, utterly dismayed over being reduced to this. As if socializing with people she hated hadn't been enough of a punishment with no reward, now she had to grovel for a job. She scrutinized recent emails from professional associates hoping to trigger an idea for a lead. One caught her attention.

The subject read, *Still Looking!* It was from Bob Stevens, Jake's friend, dated three weeks ago. They'd exchanged contact information last summer when she'd visited his office. How had she missed this? Hope sprung from the soft glow of her screen as she read his email.

Dear Charlotte,

I'm writing to let you to know I've selected a date for retirement and am still looking for someone take over my practice. Please let me know if you'd be interested in exploring this further.

Sincerely,
Bob Stevens

She closed her laptop to keep herself from leaping at the opportunity. Job insecurity or not, she wasn't one to act on a whim. She'd have to give this some thought. Fortunately, she'd taken and passed both the Pennsylvania and New Jersey bar exams after law school, so she was licensed to practice in both states.

She busied herself with her daily post-work rituals, but her heart and thoughts were racing. She recalled how enthralled she'd been by Bob's practice, the way his clients exuded appreciation for his personalized treatment of their legal cases. To pursue the opportunity, she'd have had to sell her house, move to Cape May, learn all new kinds of law. She hadn't been ready for that back then.

But now?

Before she could fully formulate a plan, she found herself responding.

Dear Bob,

Your email couldn't have come at a better time. I've decided to leave my firm and would love to explore options with you. Please call me at your convenience to discuss.

Yours truly,
Charlotte

A minute later, her phone rang.

By the end of their call, the trajectory of her career shifted southeast—to the coastal town of Cape May.

July

H AVING A NEW LEASE ON LIFE AFTER HER PREGNANCY scare, Delaney was excited about the weekend that lay ahead. Their friends were coming to Cape May for one last hurrah before she and Dalton returned to London.

Marley and Sam were first to arrive that morning with two bottles from her favorite Cape May winery.

"You guys know me well," Delaney said, giving them hugs.

"How's the London practice going?" Marley asked.

"Meh."

"Uh oh. What's up?"

Delaney sighed. "I dunno. Working in criminal law for so long has made me sour towards human behavior. Always seeing people at their worst is depressing. I was just assigned to an adoption case, and it's the most excited I've felt in a long time. Maybe using my law degree for something positive will make a difference."

"You always have a place in our firm," Marley said. "As you know, we handle all types of law. And we miss working with you."

"I miss you guys too. I'm still pissed at Howe and Clemson for how they treated you guys, even though it worked out in the end. I'm not sure I want to practice there when we return."

But that was the deal she'd made. She was only on loan to the London firm, still officially an employee of H+C. She resented the partners for forcing Marley and Sam out by cutting positions and pitting the two interns against one another in a sick competition over their bar results.

"Hey, it led us to having our own firm," Sam said.

Delaney was happy it had worked out for them but was still disillusioned by the firm.

Her sister and brother-in-law were next to arrive. Kate and Ryan entered bearing fresh corn on the cob and Jersey tomatoes.

"Stopped at Beach Plum Farm on the way," Kate said. "Cleo just texted to say they're hitting the liquor store if you need anything."

"I think we're pretty well stocked. Mimosas, anyone?"

Without waiting for her guests to answer, Delaney poured drinks and handed them out. Dalton dragged the guys into the living room to show off his new paint job, leaving the women alone.

As Delaney took a sip of her drink, Kate raised an eyebrow at her.

"What's that look?" Delaney asked.

"Nothing," Kate said.

It had to be something. She was about to press for more, but the sound of the guys' laughter filtered in from the other room. Peeking in, she saw Dalton lying on the floor, reenacting his painting fiasco. She couldn't help but smile at her good fortune, marrying a man who saw joy in everything.

"Sam just pushed me down," Dalton whined, fake accusation in his tone.

"Self-defense," Sam retorted. "I told him I hate the paint color, and he came at me."

"You better watch it, man," Dalton warned. "Delaney picked the color."

She chuckled. "I'll give you a pass this time, Adams. But if you ever criticize my décor again, you won't know what hit you."

"Marley! Did you catch that?" Sam cried out. "Our hosts just threatened me with physical harm. I need legal advice."

"Save it for the judge," Marley teased as she entered the room. "I'm off this weekend."

The guys headed to the backyard, where they prepared a

fire in a steel drum submerged in the sand. The backyard pit provided a cozy setting where they'd often spend summer nights lounging in Adirondak chairs, sipping wine, hosting their famous clambakes or roasting marshmallows.

Once Cleo and Nigel arrived, and the fire was covered and smoldering safely, the group headed to the beach.

"How's Battle of the Beleaguered coming along?" Cleo joked.

"Betrothed, you mean?" Sam chuckled. "Quite well."

"I think they're gonna win," Delaney predicted.

"From your mouth to voters' ears," Sam said. "We gotta win if we want to become your Cape May neighbors."

They set their chairs in a circle on the beach and caught up with each other's lives. Delaney and Dalton returned to the house a couple hours later to start the clambake, tossing lobster, mussels, crabs, and clams into the smoldering coals, topping the seafood feast with foil-wrapped potatoes and corn still in the husk.

"*Mmm, mmm,*" Dalton hummed. "My mouth is watering already."

Delaney bent over to cover the fire pit.

Dalton came up behind her and grabbed her waist. "And not just for the food." He spun her around and teased her with kisses. "You look too hot in this bikini. I think you better take it off."

"You're not so bad either," she said as she wove her fingers through his thick hair, his blue eyes drinking her in.

"What do you say we go for a quickie while the others are at the beach?" he asked between kisses.

"Don't dare me."

He looped his fingers into the waistband of her bikini and pulled her closer. "I double dog dare you."

She laughed as he scooped her up and carried her to their bedroom. The passion they'd shared over the years had never waned. It had ignited back when they were teens, that summer Delaney had finally been able to look at the shore-house-boy-next-door without feeling like she was crawling with cooties. She was seven when her family had purchased their Ocean City summer home, a beachfront duplex adjoined with Dalton's family's home. They started out as arch enemies and slowly became friends, spending their summers boogie boarding and building sandcastles together. Until they became even more during their seventeenth summer. Over the course of his sophomore year, Dalton had grown out of his scrawny preteen shell and into a ripped body, twelve inches taller. A body he still possessed, despite the passing years, much to Delaney's rapture.

Now here they were, making love, the thrill of getting caught only enhancing their desire.

When they returned to the beach, they were flushed from their impetuous rendezvous.

"You need to reapply your sunscreen," Kate said, tossing Delaney a tube. "Your face is getting red."

"Damn sun," Delaney said, giving her handsome hubs a teasing glance. "Gets me every time."

Before long, happy hour was upon them. Dalton doled out drinks and offered a toast.

"To a good weekend with great friends."

Kate gave Delaney a double take as she took a sip. There was that look again.

After a rousing game of volleyball and dips in the ocean, Dalton announced dinner would soon be ready. "Shall we eat here or back at the house?"

"I vote for here," Cleo said. "I'll help bring everything."

"Me too," Marley said, and the two women joined the guys in heading back to the house.

As soon as the group was out of earshot, Kate turned to Delaney and motioned to the glass of wine she'd refilled. "Should you be drinking that?"

"Is there a reason I shouldn't?"

"There's nothing you need to tell me?" Kate countered.

"No. Why do you ask?" Delaney knew exactly where her sister was going with her line of questioning.

"I noticed you weren't having drinks last week."

"Just wanted to cut down on empty calories."

Kate narrowed her eyes at her. "I don't believe it. You work out so often, you *need* the calories."

Delaney couldn't lie to her anymore. She told her about the pregnancy scare.

"Definitely negative?" Kate asked.

"Definitely."

"Remind me when we get back to the house, I have a little something for you."

The others returned with the clambake goodies simmering in a large pot. The group gathered under cabanas and dug in.

"Nothing like fresh seafood," Nigel said as they ate. "And fresh veggies. This corn is perfection, and I've never met a tomato so tasty."

"Jersey fresh is the only way," Dalton said.

"See, Cleo?" Nigel said. "Fresh food is the best food. I gotta get out of the city so I can grow this stuff myself."

Delaney noticed the frustrated look Cleo gave her boyfriend.

"Is that what you're hoping to do someday, Nigel?" Kate asked.

"Yes. Now that I've finished my culinary degree, my dream is to have a farm-to-table operation. Kinda hard to do in the middle of Manhattan."

Cleo rolled her eyes ever so slightly, but Delaney caught it. Obviously, her friend wasn't on board with his plans.

After returning to the house, Kate pulled Delaney into her room and handed her a box.

"It's a DNA test kit," she said. "When you weren't drinking, I figured you were pregnant, so I got this for you to learn more about your heritage."

Delaney was ten years old when her parents told her she'd been adopted. Their timing was perfect, as she was old enough to understand what it meant, yet young enough not to let it rock the foundation of her world. Instead, it became a fact of her life that she rarely pondered during the rest of her childhood and formative years. Due to Pennsylvania's closed adoption records, very little was known about the circumstances of her birth, and nothing about her biological family's history. She hadn't wanted to pursue it, anyway. She adored her family—the only family she'd ever known—and had no desire to discover what had happened before she was placed with them at five days old. She didn't want her parents thinking she didn't appreciate the life they'd given her. Even more so, she was afraid the circumstances of her birth were in some way tragic and wasn't in any hurry to learn as much. It was in the past, and none of that mattered now.

"Thanks," Delaney said, hesitatingly accepting the proffered gift. "I don't know that I'll need it anytime soon, but I appreciate it."

"You don't have to wait until you're pregnant," Kate said. "Maybe there's family out there you'd like to know about."

Delaney hugged Kate. "You're the only fam I need."

She put the kit aside, forgetting all about it as she enjoyed the rest of the weekend with their friends. But as they were packing to return to London, she shoved it into her carry-on at the last minute. She wasn't sure she wanted to do the test at all, but decided to take it with her, just in case.

Despite being in comfortable denial about her own roots, Delaney began second-guessing her original dismissal of the test, wondering if Kate might be right. Perhaps it was important to learn more about her heritage—if not for herself, then for her future children, who might need to know things about their heritage for health and other reasons.

A week later, having given the concept more thought, Delaney placed the completed kit in the mail. She'd opted in for the relative finder after curiosity got the best of her. It probably wouldn't reveal anything, but she couldn't help but wonder if someone out there could fill in some missing pieces. Even though she loved her adoptive family, there had always been something in the back of her mind—an inkling that some piece of her was somehow missing. Weird, considering how close she was with Kate and their younger brother, Jordan. It wasn't so much a loneliness, but a...disconnect. She'd always written it off as being a natural part of adoption—as if, upon learning one wasn't biologically connected to the family they'd known and loved, one would always feel a bit different.

There was no turning back now. One way or another, Delaney was going to learn more about herself.

Ready or not.

Cleo

RETURNING FROM WORK ONE EVENING, CLEO FOUND Nigel on the roof of their building, tending to his garden as steaks sizzled on the grill. She stepped over a pile of discarded junk to where he was plucking tomatoes from an overgrown bush.

"I'm still amazed you found a way to garden in the city," she said, giving her hot stud a hug from behind. Hot was no joke—his shirt was drenched in sweat.

To say they had a rooftop garden would make it sound as if they lived in luxury. Nothing was further from the truth. Their landlord, Ned, had granted Nigel the opportunity to create the garden in exchange for some of the produce it yielded.

He snaked a strong, sweaty arm around her waist, pulling her in. The scent of mint gum and aftershave tickled her senses as he gave her a soulful kiss.

"To be continued…" he teased.

A basket at his feet held several plump tomatoes, ripe green peppers, and crisp romaine hearts, hinting at the promise of a fresh summer salad.

"Is this for dinner?"

"This and those," he said, pointing to the steaks on the grill.

"Ooh. Doesn't get more farm-to-table than this. Well, except for the meat."

"Pretty sure Ned wouldn't appreciate me slaughtering livestock up here."

Cleo chuckled. Living with a chef with a sense of humor would never grow old, especially one that was so skilled in beds—garden, and otherwise.

"I'll take care of dessert," she said with a coy look.

He flashed his eyebrows at her, suggesting she'd be it.

"How'd your interview go today?" she asked.

Nigel had been gunning for a sous chef position at a new farm-to-table restaurant on the Upper West Side.

"I think it went okay."

"Just okay?"

"I should know soon. If they liked me, they'll have me back to cook."

Cleo waited for him to show some enthusiasm.

"Yay?" she suggested. "I mean, that sounds hopeful, right?"

He shrugged. "I guess. I mean, if I have to work in a restaurant, this would be the one. At least until I can afford my own place. Or you die. Whichever comes first."

"Hey—"

Oh. Right. Her joke about only moving to Jersey when she was dead.

"Here, take these down while I finish the steaks," he said, handing her the basket of produce.

"Don't be long, Chef Smith. Really looking forward to this. Especially dessert."

Later, over a delicious dinner, Cleo hummed with delight. "You definitely have the talent to make a living from this."

"I certainly have enough free time to cook nice dinners."

"When's your next shift?" Cleo asked.

"Not 'til Friday," he said, looking defeated. He'd been working in the same bar since they'd moved to New York. "I wish they'd give me more hours."

What was once a full-time job had been reduced to part-time to accommodate his class schedule. Now that he'd graduated, he both wanted, and needed, to work more. For his benefit, and their finances.

"Have you asked for more hours?"

"I have," Nigel said. "They're all staffed up. That's why I want to find another job. Or move."

Cleo chose to bypass those last two words. "Any other prospects, besides the place you interviewed at today?"

Nigel shook his head. "Not doing what I want to do."

Cleo took a gulp of wine to wash down her rising ire. She'd basically supported them in the last year of his schooling with the two jobs she'd been working—weekdays in the gallery, weekends in the bar. She wondered if his lack of motivation to find a new job was passive-aggressive in some way, knowing if he couldn't find a new job or increase his hours, they'd be *forced* to move from the city.

It was the first time in their relationship she'd felt a hint of distrust in him. She hoped she was wrong in her suspicion— because a suspicious Cleo wasn't a happy Cleo.

Charlotte

"I CAN'T BELIEVE YOU'RE ACTUALLY DOING IT," JAKE SAID as he loaded Charlotte's last box into his pickup truck. "Are you ready for a whole new life?"

Charlotte chuckled nervously. "I better be, now that I've sold my house."

She was overcome with fear. She'd never done anything so rash as quit a job in anger and accept a new one in a different state on the same day. The work of a fool, not someone as cautiously contemplative as she. But there she was, the physical remains of her entire life neatly stacked in the bed of a pickup truck.

From the back seat, another passenger gave an impassioned plea.

"It's okay, buddy," Charlotte said, turning to the cat who perched in his carrier.

At least she hoped he'd be okay. Gus had been elated for Charlotte when she'd told him about her move, and happy his cat would finally have free rein of the countryside. She felt guilty taking him away from the old man, but he'd insisted.

"Blinky's been a good friend to us both," Gus said. "He deserves to retire by the sea."

Charlotte was thankful for his response. Gus had even purchased him a carrier as a going-away gift.

"Are you ready for our new lives?" she asked her feline friend through the door of the carrier.

The bigger question—whether Charlotte was ready—still hung, unanswered, in the cab of Jake's truck as he pulled away from the curb. Ready or not, it was happening.

She watched her house, and the only life she'd ever known, grow smaller in the side view mirror. The house disappeared, engulfed by the past, as nostalgia gave way to hope. Opportunity. New beginnings.

She turned forward to meet her future head-on.

A little over an hour later, they pulled into a driveway leading to the small office where Bob's practice was located. He was out front to greet them.

"I bet you guys are tired from all that moving. Can I interest you in some fresh-squeezed lemonade? My son-in-law is somewhat of a connoisseur, making it from homegrown lemons."

"That sounds delightful," Charlotte said as she wiped a bead of July humidity from her forehead.

"Count me in." Jake shook Bob's hand.

"We should probably—" She gestured to the cat cage in the back.

"Oh, yeah." Jake pulled Blinky's cage from the back seat. "Do you mind if we let him out so he can explore?"

"Of course," Bob said. "I'm sure he'll find friends among the other critters."

Charlotte hoped the critters he referenced wouldn't harm Blinky. The last thing he needed was another scratched eye.

Blinky cautiously emerged from his open cage, stepping on the grass gingerly before flopping down and rolling onto his back.

"He'll be just fine here," Bob said, laughing as he led them into his office.

The tiny waiting room was tastefully decorated in white and navy, giving a nautical nod to its surroundings. Pictures of ocean scenes hung on the walls, complementing the coastal scheme. Charlotte loved its minimalistic look.

"So, this is our office. It's small, but it does the trick," Bob explained. He waved to a desk on one side of the room. "I haven't had a receptionist for a few years, but that's your call now."

Charlotte had never known a professional world without a full staff. The idea of working solo was refreshing.

Ice cubes clinked in tall glasses as Bob poured lemonade from a pitcher. He waved them to the couch, where they all sat. "Let's enjoy this, and then I'll give you another tour. Not sure if you remember much from when you were here last summer, Charlotte, but nothing's changed. In fact, not much has changed since I started this practice twenty-five years ago."

"I'm honored to become a part of it."

"And I'm grateful you're taking this on. I'm not retiring until the end of the year, but that'll give us a few months to work together so you can get acclimated before I head off into the wild blue yonder."

Panic swept through her as she realized his carefully crafted practice would soon rest solely on her shoulders.

"No worries," Bob added. "For me, the wild blue yonder is my back yard, right outside that window, where I'll be putzing around in my shed and spending time with my grandson. I'll be here for you for as long as you need me."

Whew. Having strictly been a business attorney for years, Charlotte had no idea how to handle the vast array of legal issues prospective clients would bring. She'd need those months with Bob to learn the ropes and brush up on other types of law. She hoped her new caseload would also include business matters, something she actually knew about.

He gave them a tour of the office, then led them out the back door, down a short path and through a white picket fence to another small cottage.

"Welcome to your new home."

The beachy cottage was like something from *Coastal Living* magazine—white with turquoise shutters and small window boxes featuring pink flowers. Beyond the cottage was a sprawling lawn, the rest of Bob's property, where a renovated farmhouse stood in the distance along a tree line. Charlotte recalled from her tour last summer it was Bob's family's home, where he and his wife lived.

"Jake, if you want to pull the truck around, we can help you unload," Bob offered.

We?

"Greetings!" someone called out.

Two men approached, holding the hands of a blonde curly-haired boy who they lifted and swung forward. The child's delighted giggles reached them before the trio did, and it instantly made Charlotte smile. Not that she liked children, but she'd been exposed to Jake's nieces and nephew for long enough now she'd grown accustomed to the tiny germ factories.

Bob turned to her. "Charlotte, this is my son, Owen, and his husband, Ben."

"Good to see you guys," Jake said. Turning to Charlotte, he explained, "I grew up with Owen and his brother, Peter."

As they greeted one another, Charlotte repeated their names to herself so she'd remember. Ben had the brown hair. Owen, red—more like orange. Ben brown. Owen orange. Okay, she'd remember that.

"And this big guy—" Bob bent over and picked up the child "—is my pride and joy. My grandson, Archie. Arch, say hi to these nice people. Ms. Charlotte is my new partner in crime."

Archie's expression grew serious. "Gramps, I thought we weren't supposed to do crime?"

Bob laughed. "You got me, Arch. And you're right. It's just a turn of phrase."

"What's a turnip phrase?" he asked, and the adults laughed.

Owen led them into the cottage. "It's a work in progress," he explained. "We've completed the living room and your bedroom, but there's still some work to do on the rest of the house."

Charlotte was surprised to hear him reference it as a "work in progress." The living room, which had its original hardwood flooring, was modestly decorated with new furniture. Her bedroom featured a wrought iron bed and art deco dressers, which instantly reminded Charlotte of her grandmother's furnishings she'd wistfully left behind after learning the cottage came fully furnished.

"These are gorgeous," she said, crossing to a dresser and running her hand along the top. Good, no dust.

"They belonged to our grandmother," Owen explained. "We'll happily upgrade with new furniture, if you prefer."

"Absolutely not," Charlotte said, giving the room a sweeping glance of approval. "It's perfect for me."

"The bathroom's a different story," Ben said as Owen opened the door to the tiny space. "We'll be replacing a lot of this."

"It's functional for now, just not very pretty. Owen and Peter will turn it into something fantastic." Ben smiled. "I'm just the supervisor."

"The kitchen needs some loving too," Owen explained as they turned a corner. "We'll be replacing the appliances and tearing down this hideous wallpaper."

Thank goodness. The dizzying floral pattern should've come with seizure warnings.

"The boys will work around your schedule to finish the renovations," Bob explained.

"No worries," Charlotte said, instantly worrying what this would mean for her inner peace. She'd never lived in a construction zone before, but that was part of the deal they'd made when she agreed to come on board. In exchange for ridiculously low rent, Charlotte would live in the old cottage while it was being renovated. In turn, she'd be responsible for its upkeep. Which was fine, because it also meant she'd enjoy the easiest commute to work, consisting of mere steps. No car service, no Ubers, no clackety-clacking Broad Street line.

As they turned to leave, her eyes darted around the room

for a cleanliness check. All seemed to be in good order.

"We good?" Jake asked as he squeezed her hand, likely knowing what she was doing.

"We good."

"Does this meet your expectations, Charlotte?" Bob asked.

"Absolutely. I appreciate all the work you've done here."

When Bob's eyes rested upon their clasped hands, she whisked hers away. They'd often held hands as friends, but she didn't want to give her new law partner the impression they were a couple. She had to admit, though, this time, Jake's hand in hers felt—different. Warmer. Tighter. Like it was more than just a friend holding her hand. Not that she'd know what that felt like, of course. No guy had ever held her hand as more than friends before.

The sea air had clearly gone to her head.

Once they'd unloaded the car, Jake announced he was leaving. "Big day ahead."

Charlotte felt a knife plunge into her heart.

"Oh, that's right—you're setting sail tomorrow," Owen recalled. "How long will you be away?"

"A year at least," Jake replied. "Maybe more."

And...twist.

"But we'll see." He gave Charlotte a smile that didn't quite reach his eyes, which looked sad. Or did she imagine that too?

"We'll take good care of your girlfriend while you're gone," Bob said.

"She's—"

"I'm—"

"Thanks, guys," Jake cut her off before she could explain. He wrapped his arm around her waist. "I appreciate that."

Charlotte felt a tingle go down her spine. She'd never been referred to as someone's girlfriend before. The title, while foreign and untrue, sounded nice. His arm felt comfortable, protective, around her waist. Until he playfully pinched her, bringing her back to reality. *Just friends*, the gesture reminded her.

"You're leaving Charlotte in good company," Bob assured Jake. "We promise to love her like you do."

Jake looked down at her. This time his eyes reflected his smile.

"I hope so."

Marley

MARLEY AND SAM REPORTED TO THE NEWSROOM FOR the first official challenge of Battle of the Betrothed.

"Sam," one of the contestants whispered. "Have you gotten the scoop on Amanda and Eddie?"

"Not yet, but I'm on it."

Sam beamed with pride that he'd been selected for this Very Important Task. Not that it was any of the contestants' business, but Amanda had made it so—along with the entire viewing public—when she went rogue and unleashed her snark on Eddie during the first round.

"What's this month's challenge?" Sam asked Marley.

"Who can read minds the best."

"Really?"

"No, Sam. I've been presented with the same information you have. How do you think I would just know what's happening next?"

"You're smarter than me," Sam said, pouting. "You just know things."

"One thing I do know—we're killing this challenge. Like we did the first one," now-competitive Marley announced, holding up her fist for him to bump. "Just don't embarrass me."

"I make no promises."

"Okay, guys, welcome back," the producer announced. "In a few minutes, you'll be boarding a shuttle to the location of your first challenge. We'll disclose the details once we go live. We're purposely keeping it a surprise, but I can give you a hint. You can expect an *amazing* experience that will make your heart *race*."

"Amazing race," Supersleuth Sam announced under his breath, on the off chance someone hadn't picked up on it.

"First, I want to go over the process you can expect for the next six months. On the first Friday of the month, you'll come to the studio, we'll introduce the challenge, and we'll dive right into it. Some challenges will be done in studio, some elsewhere. Each challenge will take less than one hour. A camera man will be assigned to each couple to record you during the challenge. We'll air the footage live to viewers, they'll cast their votes online, and we'll report results on the third Friday at the elimination round. Everyone good with that?"

The contestants nodded their consensus.

"We'll head to the shuttle in a minute. Questions? Comments?"

Sam raised his hand. "Where's Eddie?"

All eyes panned to an unattended Camera One.

"Who knows?" Amanda retorted, her tone suggesting the word *knows* could easily have been replaced with *cares*. Once again, not bothering to look up from her super-interesting fingernails. Probably still searching for Jimmy Hoffa. Perhaps Eddie as well.

"I'm here," a male voice came from the darkened portion of the studio. Eddie emerged a second later, shielding his eyes as he looked at Sam. "What's up, man? Can I help you with something?"

"Oh, um…" Sam shifted on his feet.

Marley smiled up at him in anticipation. This should be

good. Behold, Quick-On-His-Feet-Thinking Sam.

"I just feel like we kinda bonded last time, so I was hoping you'd be paired with us."

Wow. Sam definitely understood the assignment.

The producer consulted her notes. "You actually are paired."

Never knowing when to stop, Sam continued. "Great. I'd love some pointers on how I should look at the camera. Do I glance? Stare? Gaze? We should talk."

"Hey, man, you do you," an amused Eddie responded as the contestants tittered.

When the shuttle arrived, they were driven to the LOVE statue in Center City and lined up before it.

The producer counted Amanda down, and she turned on her smile as if someone flipped a switch.

"Hey, everyone, Amanda here with *PheelGoodPhilly*, the hap-hap-*happy* show brought to you by Channel Six news. We're here at the LOVE statue to learn the meaning of the word, since some of us haven't learned it yet, Eddie."

"Yes!" Sam said under his breath.

Marley shot him a look.

"I was hoping she'd do it again," he whispered, covering his mic. "Makes for good TV."

"I jest!" Amanda quickly added, probably because she'd been instructed not to air her Eddie grievances...well, on *air*. "We're here today to kick off the first Battle of the Betrothed challenge, in which these six *lucky* couples will compete to win an all-expenses-paid wedding and $10,000 cash. Everyone ready?"

The contestants gave a cheer.

"Okay, then. This first challenge is a cross between a scavenger hunt and the popular TV show, *The Amazing Race*. Everyone familiar with that?"

Heads nodded.

Sam whispered to Marley. "Told you so."

Thanks, Sam. Not sure how I'd navigate this puzzling world without you.

Amanda continued. "Each couple will be given fifteen minutes and five dollars to find the following objects." She paused for dramatic effect. "Something new, something old..."

A chorus of *aahs* rose from the contestants.

"Say it with me, guys...something..."

"Borrowed, something blue," they said in unison.

"Together with your partner, your five dollars, and your ingenuity, you'll find those four objects. You're confined to a two-block perimeter in any direction. The cameras will be following you. Anyone who goes outside that area will be disqualified. No splitting up, everything must be done as a team. You cannot add your own objects or money to the collection. Got it?"

Everyone nodded in agreement.

"The first ones back will receive *ten extra votes* to be applied when you're in danger of elimination. It may not sound like much, but in a close race, it could mean the difference between a free wedding or going into debt.

"Oh, I forgot one important piece," Amanda continued, cueing up a big surprise. "Each item has to relate in some way to the City of Brotherly Love. Any questions?"

Of course there were questions, but no one spoke up, lest they appear to be idiots on live TV.

"Okay. Good luck...and *go!*"

Marley and Sam took off in opposite directions.

"Where are you going?" Sam yelled, grabbing her arm, nearly yanking it from its socket.

"This way!" she yelled.

"No, this way!"

They played tug o' war for a couple precious seconds before Sam let go, causing Marley to fall over.

"Oh, for God's sake..."

Helping her up, he pointed to a bodega on the corner. "There has to be something there representing Philly."

They found it inside the beer cooler—a three-dollar can of Dock Street beer, Philly's microbrew.

"We have a couple bucks to spare," Sam noted as they ran from the place with their brown paper bag of something new. "What else can we use it for?"

Before she could answer, he grabbed her hand.

"Where are we going?" she asked.

"I'm getting a strong vibe in this direction."

A couple feet later, he stopped dead in his tracks.

"Something old...something blue..."

Marley followed his gaze and saw an older man with a young boy wearing a blue Phillies t-shirt.

Sam gave an evil victory laugh, walking toward the pair with steadfast determination.

"Excuse me," he said to the man. "Can we borrow your son?"

The man stepped between Sam and the kid. "He's my grandson, and what kind of dope are you on?" he asked, eyeing him and his brown paper bag with suspicion.

"Oh, geez." Marley turned away, pressing her fingers against her temple.

No more than thirty seconds later, Sam called her name. "They're in."

She turned to find the kid holding up two dollar bills, a huge smile on his face.

"Let's go win this thing!" the grandfather exclaimed.

"What did you say to them?" Marley whispered as the four hustled back to the LOVE statue, forever amazed at Sam's way with people.

"A magician never gives away his tricks."

"You bribed them."

"Basically. It's amazing what two bucks will get you these days." Sam started picking up his pace. "Mar, I don't see the others. Hurry!"

"Are we even done?"

"Yes!" He pushed her ahead of him. "Go! I'll follow with them."

Marley began a slow jog until she heard Sam yelling. "Faster! Faster!"

From her periphery, she saw a couple racing toward the statue. If racing could describe it—the bride was in the lead, while her broken-footed fiancé hobbled along behind her on crutches, his foot in a cast. Marley recognized them as the couple who'd announced they were pregnant.

Speeding up, Marley made it there first. Sam and company arrived a second later.

"Are we the first ones here?" the kid asked the producer, obviously clued in on the race.

"You are!"

Once everyone returned, Amanda went down the line and asked the couples to report their findings. When she got to Marley and Sam, standing with the old man and the boy, she laughed.

"I'm intrigued by some of the 'objects' you found."

Sam held up the beer. "Something new. Which I intend to make old as soon as this is over."

Amanda's eyes twinkled behind a hidden smile.

Sam pointed to the grandfather. "Something old."

The man flashed Rocky arms and the other couples laughed.

"Something blue," he pointed to the boy's Phillies shirt.

"I'm dying to hear what's been borrowed here," Amanda smirked.

"Me too," Sam joked, looking sheepish.

Marley wondered if he actually had a plan, or whether it was just dawning on him he needed something borrowed.

"These two are visiting Philly today for Blake's birthday," Sam explained. "Wave to the camera, Blake!"

The boy smiled and waved.

"They're from out of town, heading to a Phillies' game to-night. Grandpa wanted to show him around the city, give him a little history lesson. They have a busy agenda, so I asked if I could 'borrow' their time."

Amanda gave an impressive *hmm*. The other couples *aah*'ed. Marley was thankful it was a congenial group, and not a bunch of competitive crazed lunatics who would challenge their findings. The producer gave a thumbs up, signaling to Amanda it was acceptable.

She turned to the camera and encouraged the viewing public to vote for their favorite couple.

"And to those who inquired if they could vote for me and Eddie—the answer is no. He saw to it we'd never be a part of a competition like this."

She hooked an eyebrow at Camera One.

"Intriguing..." Sam whispered.

After the cameras stopped rolling, Amanda came over to them.

"You guys are my new favorite friends," she said. "We should go out for drinks someday."

"Sounds great," Marley said.

"So, what's with you and Eddie?" Sam came right out and asked.

Amanda shrugged. "He's a dick."

Marley waited for further explanation but that apparently was all she was willing to say on the matter.

Back at the studio, Sam reported their discovery to the group.

"That's it?" one of the contestants inquired. "No reason given?"

"That's what the woman said," Sam confirmed.

"One doesn't just achieve dickhood," another mused. "One earns it by doing something dickish."

"Gotta dig deeper, Sammy," the man with the broken foot said. Andy was his name.

"I may have to turn this one over to Marley. I don't see myself cavorting with a dick. I'm guessing Amanda has good reason to think it."

But later, he asked Marley if he should try to warm up to Eddie and get his side. "Let's divide and conquer. You work Amanda, I'll work him, and between the two of us we'll get the scoop."

"Sam, it was mostly a joke. Everyone's just curious about Amanda's snark, but it doesn't have to become an Olympic event," she said, knowing Sam made everything an Olympic event.

"Don't issue me a challenge and then expect me to back down, Mar. I'm fully invested in this and won't stop until I have facts."

So noted.

Charlotte

CHARLOTTE HEARD THE CRUNCH OF TIRES ON THE crushed-shell driveway from her bedroom. Grabbing her things, she let herself out into the cool dawn of morning where the headlights of Jake's pickup truck illuminated the way.

This was it. The moment she'd been dreading. For a second, she thought she might vomit.

"Howdy ho," Jake said, emerging from the truck. He hugged her. "You ready for this?"

"No," she said, her voice muffled by the fabric of his t-shirt. "I'm not ready to say goodbye."

"I meant your driving lesson," he said, pulling back and chuckling.

"Oh, that."

"Yeah, that. I know you have a license and all, but you haven't driven for quite a while, and I'm guessing never in a pickup truck. At the very least, I figured you should drive me to the dock so you can practice, and I can decide whether I'm okay leaving her with you."

Charlotte slugged his arm playfully. "Of course she's safe with me. I'm an excellent driver. And not to burst your bubble of distrust, but my dad had a pickup truck. It's what I learned to drive in."

"They had pickup trucks back then?" he teased as he climbed into the passenger seat.

"Hey, pal, watch it with the old jokes. You're older than me, anyway."

"By two months."

Charlotte handed him a bag. "A parting gift."

He gave her a half-smile. His eyes looked sad, his voice soft. "You didn't have to do that."

"Just a little something."

She and Jake had been strolling along Washington Street Mall on one of their earlier visits to Cape May when they saw a Polaroid camera in one of the shop windows.

"Oh, man—I had one of those when I was a kid," Jake had said, his face lighting up. "I thought it was magical, photos being printed right from the camera. I may have to get myself one. I had no idea they still made them."

Now, unwrapping the camera, Jake smiled. "Charlotte, this is awesome."

"I know you'll be memorializing your trip on social media, but I figured this might be fun, in case you ever want to put together a scrapbook." Charlotte thought for a moment. "Do people even do scrapbooks anymore?"

Jake laughed. "I don't know if 'people' do, but I will now. Thank you. This means the world to me."

He leaned across the cab of the truck and hugged her.

She sighed away her melancholy as they pulled apart, wanting to enjoy these last precious moments with him.

"Prepare to be amazed by my excellent driving skills," she joked as she put her foot on the gas and backed up.

Instead, the car lurched forward.

"Reverse, Char," Jake said, laughing as he grabbed onto the dashboard.

"Minor details."

Charlotte hit the gas a little too hard, and they lurched again, this time backwards, almost into a fence.

"Maybe I should cancel this trip until you learn to drive without killing someone. Namely, me."

"Shut up, I'm fine. I just have to get started."

Charlotte gritted her teeth as she pulled onto the road. Living in a city as she had, it had been years since she'd driven. As they traveled on, it came back to her.

"You're doing a great job," Jake assured her.

Tears sprung to her eyes. God, how she'd miss this man, his comforting presence, always ready with a compliment or words of encouragement. What was she going to do without him?

"Aww," he said, wiping a tear from her cheek.

"I'm gonna miss you." Her voice squeaked as she tried to contain her overwhelming despair. So much for treasuring the moment. "A whole lot."

"I'm gonna miss you a whole lot too," he said. "But I'm no more than a phone call, a text, a FaceTime away, most of the time."

"I know. It's just not the same." She chuckled, snorting through her tears. "This is the *last* thing you need, a weeping female clinging to you as you set off on an exciting adventure."

"Maybe not the last thing," he muttered, turning to look out his window.

They drove the rest of the way in silence, arriving at the dock much sooner than Charlotte wanted to. Fresh tears threatened, but she blinked them back.

She parked and they sat in silence.

Jake pulled out the Polaroid and aimed it at her. "Smile, beautiful," he whispered.

She instinctively removed her glasses and posed.

He took the glasses from her hand and put them back on her face. "I want to remember you just as you are."

The camera clicked and hummed as it expelled an undeveloped photo. He waved it, and an image emerged from murky white. Staring at it, he smiled. "My Char."

As they walked the dock, Charlotte willed herself not to beg him to stay.

"This is me," he said as they arrived at his sailboat.

She chuckled at the name emblazoned on its stern. *Diver~SEA~fied Investment.* Fitting, for a person who had once worked in finance as Jake had, before he gave up the corporate life for full-time seafaring.

Jake pulled her into an embrace. She breathed in his fresh scent as he held her for a long time. Slowly pulling back, their cheeks brushed together, lips close, foreheads touching. For a split second, she thought he was going to kiss her.

Instead, he kissed her on the nose.

"Okay, girl." His voice had taken on a husky tone. He cleared his throat. Taking both her hands in his, he squeezed hard. "Take good care of you."

"You, too, friend."

Jake climbed aboard and went about the business of readying for departure as Charlotte looked on, cracking up when he began "doot-dooting" the song from *Gilligan's Island.* They'd recently binge-watched the old sitcom, laughing over the cast's antics, hoping his tour didn't end like theirs.

"Until we meet again." Jake saluted her as the boat began drifting backward.

"Until then," she whispered, blowing him a kiss.

He caught it and blew one back.

Charlotte blinked her tears away as she watched her only friend drift toward the horizon. And then, just as he turned his boat toward the open sea, she heard him call out.

"I love you, Charlotte!"

His words echoed in her ears, making her tingle from head to toe. Had she heard that right? Did he mean it as a friend—or otherwise?

"I love you, too, Jake."

It may have been a whisper, but it was the loudest confession she'd ever made.

August

<h1 style="text-align:center">Charlotte</h1>

I LOVE YOU, CHARLOTTE.

It had been a month since she'd heard the words, but they'd been bouncing between her head and her heart ever since. In her head, it sounded as if Jake had meant it in a friendly way, but when the words made it to her heart, they sounded different. Hope-filled, as if maybe they were becoming more than friends.

But then her head took back over and convinced her otherwise. It was safer that way. Less likely to get her expectations up and be hurt if she was wrong about Jake's feelings.

But there was nothing uncertain about hers.

Despite her sadness over Jake's departure, Charlotte was beginning to settle into her new life. There was something cathartic about being so close to the ocean as the sea breeze swooshed away her anxiety and tension. After long days in the office, she'd settle into an old wooden rocker on the front porch of the cottage with a glass of wine, Blinky curled at her feet, rocking back and forth to the clittering of cicadas as the cool evening air teased her skin.

She was growing accustomed to small-town life as well. Awake at the crack of dawn, she'd walk along the Cape's back roads as the rising sun peered through foliage, lush with August, and sparkled on grass's morning dew. During her afternoon breaks, she'd wander down tree-lined streets seeking a cozy lunch spot or stopping to browse quaint boutique shops. She was in good company with the many well-known visitors who'd once strolled these same knobby, knurled brick sidewalks—from Ulysses S. Grant and Harriet

Tubman to, more recently, Oprah Winfrey, Anne Hathaway, and Taylor Swift.

On weekends, she loaded up with SPF 100 and headed to the beach, perching under the protective shade of both an umbrella and a safari hat, as one could never be too concerned about harmful UV rays. Latest beach read in hand, she'd occasionally glance up to watch the waves, wondering how Jake was doing.

She particularly enjoyed shopping in the town's tiny Acme Market. One day, while searching for her trusted brand of shampoo, she spotted rows of boxes featuring women with varying hair colors. Must be what her former coworkers were talking about when they discussed their "box dyes." Seeing the reasonable prices, she understood why it was such a thing.

Two years ago, her boss and his wife had given her a gift certificate to a hair salon. She'd nearly died from the experience—not at the hands of the staff or the nauseating odor of chemicals, but the exorbitant prices. Judging by the cost of the simple trim she'd received, she could only imagine how expensive a color job was. She vowed to never go back—certainly never spend that kind of money on hair care again.

Yet here she was now, standing in the beauty section of the grocery store of all places, like some sort of saucy singleton who cared about how she looked.

What had happened to her?

Actually, she didn't have to ask. For the first time ever, she did care. Even though the object of her growing affection wouldn't see her for quite some time, she knew they'd be sharing selfies and wanted to look her best.

Gazing at the dizzying array of shades, she decided to go for it. Quite a different Charlotte than the one Jake had come to know (and love?). With no plans for Friday night, she decided it would be a perfect time to do her hair. If it turned out hideously, she'd find a stylist on Saturday to fix it.

"Maybe I'll go blonde. See if they do have more fun," she said to herself, wondering if Jake would prefer her that way.

Ugh. That made her think of the flaxen-haired beauty who'd taken up residence on Jake's Instagram last year for a brief stint as his girlfriend. Tori was her name. According to Jake, she was a photographer, traveling the world to build her portfolio. They'd met at a barefoot bar when he was in the Caribbean doing his practice sail. Both from the Philly area, they discovered they had a lot in common—including the fact that one of Tori's close friends, Delaney, was married to Jake's cousin, Dalton.

It was around that time Jake stopped communicating with Charlotte. She thought it was because of his new girlfriend, until he explained his real reason for putting figurative distance between them. He admitted to having conflicted feelings about her and their friendship after they had a near-miss—or near-*kiss*, as the case was—one snowy January night before his departure. And yet, after he'd returned home from his practice trip, their friendship had corrected itself and continued on its familiar course.

She willed herself back to reality as her head took over where her heart left off. Jake would never pick someone like Charlotte—Tori was living proof of that. It made Charlotte nauseous to think of the many beautiful women he'd be meeting in each port. Dark-haired beauties browsing seaside boutiques in designer clothing. Tanned bleach-blondes perching on beach towels. Spunky redheads sporting cutesy ski gear, posing mountain top. Those were the types of women Jake could get, while she more closely resembled the random wildlife lurking beyond the photo frames of those beautiful, adventurous women.

But not for long. Enter New and Improved Charlotte.

"Chestnut Brown," she read aloud from the box that had drawn her eye with its warm tones. Perfect for a change without being too drastic. Or blonde. Even if that was Jake's preference, Charlotte refused to play that game, knowing there was no winning.

Next, she headed to the makeup section, calling in the big guns as she FaceTimed Jake's niece. Bella had been her twenty-first century mentor since she met the girl two years ago. Charlotte had to trust her, as a teen in today's society with her finger on the pulse of all things beauty.

"I want to invest in some makeup. What do you suggest?" she asked, flipping the screen to show Bella the options.

"Oh, I love that brand," Bella noted when Charlotte zoomed in on a mascara that promised lashes for days. "They're not kidding, your lashes will be so long you can practically braid 'em."

Charlotte giggled. "As long as they don't hamper my vision."

"You'll be fine. I'm so excited you're doing this! Way to start a whole new life with a whole new look. Now, what about foundation?"

Charlotte had to plead ignorance on that one, not even certain what it was. She'd only applied her own makeup once in her life.

Prom night. Senior year.

The memories came flooding back. Charlotte, an awkward, homely teen, had been overlooked throughout her high school years, ignored and passed by for all the school dances. She'd never been asked by a boy as his date, nor invited by the gaggles of girls who went together. Unwilling to miss out on what would be her last school dance, she decided to go solo in her senior year. She'd heard the boy she had a crush on—Garrett Bosley from physics class—was also going alone and hoped he'd ask her to dance.

Charlotte's mom had passed when she was an infant, and neither Charlotte, nor the grandmother who was raising her, knew anything about prom protocol of the 2000s. Grams had saved the dress her mom wore to her own prom, and although it gave '70s vibes, Charlotte felt pretty as she donned it. She found makeup in a bathroom drawer and decided to go all in.

She swept her lashes with the mascara and rubbed blush into her cheeks like she'd seen women do in the movies. She found a bright blue eyeshadow to complement the blue satin dress and dabbed it on her eyelids with a fingertip. Feeling elated, Charlotte twirled in the mirror, excited for the night that lay ahead.

What Charlotte didn't know was that makeup had expiration dates. These products had been in the drawer for years. A half hour into the dance, her face broke into a rash, and her eyes began swelling with a pus-like substance, rendering her unable to see well through her glasses. She took them off and accidentally careened into a body—belonging to none other than Garrett Bosley himself—crushing his plate of salsa and chips into his white-shirted chest. He got mad, she fainted, and spent the rest of the night in the ER.

Recalling the event now, she almost put the products back on the shelf.

"I'd be happy to give you a tutorial," Bella offered.

"Thanks, I'll need it."

"Have you heard from Uncle Jake?" Bella asked suddenly, sounding hopeful.

"No. How about you?"

"My mom said he texted last night to let her know he was good. He's in the Caribbean now. I'm sure he'll reach out soon."

She hoped so but didn't say as much, disappointed to learn Jake had texted Lisa but hadn't yet reached out to her. Then again, Bella's mom *was* Jake's sister. Of course he'd reach out to family first.

Charlotte felt excited for her new changes as they ended their call. She couldn't wait for Friday night to dabble in the world of beauty under the FaceTime guidance of a teenage makeup expert.

Charlotte was pleasantly surprised at the results of her first dye job. Gone were the grayish undertones of her understated brown hair which, upon reflection, made her look like she'd been dead for weeks. Instead, caramelly-reddish highlights now illuminated her skin to a healthy olive glow. Under Bella's tutoring, she learned how to properly apply makeup.

The following day, Charlotte went to the boutique in Stone Harbor where she'd purchased the dress she wore to Jake's brother's wedding two years ago—the dress that made his eyes pop out of his head. Deciding it was time for New and Improved Charlotte to snazz up her wardrobe, she spent over an hour trying on clothes and left the store with several new outfits. Carrying the fancy bags from the store, she felt like Julia Roberts in *Pretty Woman* after she went on her shopping spree.

Later that night, Charlotte 2.0 took herself out on a date. She'd read once that it was important to show yourself the love you were seeking. What better way of doing that than a romantic solo dinner? Okay, maybe the family restaurant in town wasn't the fanciest venue, but it was healthy, practical, and wouldn't set her back hundreds of dollars. The most important aspect of the night was treating herself to something special. Eating out—alone or with someone else—was something she rarely did. With no one beating down her door with invitations, it was up to her if she wanted a night out.

Charlotte's thoughts turned to Jake as she ate alone, wishing he was there to share the night, enjoy the meal, see her new look. She thought about his parting words and felt a tingle go through her once again.

Head: *Stop. He meant it as a friend.*

They'd been besties for two years now. Other than that one

close call over a year ago, their relationship had been strictly platonic, and she'd never wanted anything to change between them. But lately, he'd been getting more—something. Touchy-feely. Huggy. Glances lingering into gazes.

Heart: *But maybe...*

It was hard not to make something of it all, but Charlotte's insecurities got the best of her.

Head wins. *He meant it as a friend.*

Cleo

CLEO HAD JUST FINISHED A YOUTH MURAL PROJECT A few blocks from Nigel's workplace and decided to stop in. She made her way through the crowded restaurant and shimmied herself onto a bar stool, noting her boyfriend wasn't behind the bar where he'd usually be found on a Friday night.

"Hey, Frank. Where's Nigel?"

"He's on tables tonight," Frank said, nodding across the restaurant where Nigel stood talking to two men and a child.

Good. Tips from meals were often bigger than bar tips on a Friday night at the popular gastropub.

"What can I get you, fair lady?"

"Who you callin' lady?" she teased. "Shot of whiskey and a Pabst Blue."

It had been a shot-of-whiskey kind of day. Daisy had called a special meeting with Cleo to give her bad news.

"We're pulling out of the new space," her boss had reported. "The building owner just upped the rent, and I'm not crawling up his ass to beg him to lower it. Turns out city rents have tripled since I last checked, so to open something new, we've got to downsize first. That means cutting the recent hires."

Cleo's heart sank for those employees, until she realized this would affect her too. "What about the—"

"Directorship?" Daisy asked. "Unfortunately, until we find a space, you'll have to remain in your current position as assistant. But I'll warn you, there'll likely be more cuts, so you may want to consider your options."

"What other options?" Cleo asked, fear rising within her. Options meant change.

Daisy shrugged. "Maybe start your own? You have quite the talent, both for art and leadership. That moxie of yours will take you far, my dear. I don't want to be the one holding you back."

Even though owning her own gallery was her ultimate goal, Cleo hoped to work as a director under Daisy's seasoned tutelage first. Not to mention, she didn't have two wooden nickels to rub together, let alone open a gallery.

"It's what I did," Daisy declared with pride.

Must be nice. "Why do I suddenly feel like a baby bird being kicked from its nest?"

Daisy winked at her. "Am I that obvious?"

Well, fuck. Cleo felt bitch-slapped. Not only by the news itself, but the matter-of-fact way her boss let her know she may not have a future with ImagineArt.

One of the things Cleo loved most about working there was how Daisy had overlooked a pile of eligible candidates to cherry-pick her for the job, resume unseen. The way she'd chosen Cleo to rise through the ranks to lead the new gallery. It was the same way Cleo felt about Nigel—chosen, over all the other women he could have dated.

But now things were starting to feel different, between Daisy's news and Nigel choosing a path for his future that diverged from hers. It smacked of how it felt when Gus dropped his cancer bomb on her. When her best friends, Delaney and Tori, told her they were moving away from her to start new lives. Waiting at the window for her mom to pick her up from Grandma's, not knowing it would be years before she'd return.

After a lifetime of rejection, she'd finally felt chosen and in control of her destiny.

But now, like all those times before, Cleo felt the weight of impending doom. Things were about to change. When resulting from one's own choices, change was often a good thing. Not always the case when it was forced. It all smacked too closely of her past and her greatest fears. Rejection. Abandonment.

She threw back her shot, trying to wash down the creeping dread.

"Rough day in art land?" Frank asked.

"Yup."

Cleo noticed Nigel was still at the table, now sitting with the patrons.

"What's that all about?" she asked, swiveling back on her stool.

"Don't ask me. He's been talking to them like that for the past hour. Probably hustling for a good tip."

Yeah, but...sitting with patrons? Not usually done.

"He'll get one too," Frank continued. "Good guys. They own a few restaurants in Cape May."

Shit. That's why Nigel was sitting there. Not hustling for tips, but a job. In New Jersey. The very tip of New Jersey, which couldn't be farther from the city.

"You know them?" Cleo asked.

Frank nodded. "Friends of Gabriel," he said, referencing his boyfriend. "He went to high school with the red-headed dude. They often come in when they visit the city."

"Be right back," Cleo said, sliding off her barstool and weaving through tables to where Nigel was now getting up.

"Great meeting you guys," he said. "Come back again soon."

Nigel's eyes lit up as Cleo approached. "Hey, love!"

He turned to the guys. "Mates, this is my girlfriend, Cleo.

This is Ben and Owen."

"Nice to meet you," Cleo said. "Do you guys know each other?"

"Just met," the bearded one said. "We've been talking to Nigel about—"

"How I'm ruining their night," Nigel said, chuckling. "Off we go. Nice meeting you."

He led her from the table as if they were fleeing a crime scene. "To what do I owe the pleasure of your drop-in tonight?"

"We just finished the mural on 47th, and I wanted to surprise you. I also require drinks." She settled back onto her barstool. "Not a great day. I'll tell you about it later."

"Sounds good. I got some tables to check in with. Making serious bank tonight and don't want to piss anyone off."

Cleo waved him off and turned to Frank. "How is Gabriel doing? Is he coming up this weekend?"

"He's great. Loving being an assistant district attorney. He just finished up a trial in Philly today and should be here soon." A smile spread across his face. "Speak of the devil…"

Cleo turned to see the handsome attorney striding toward them.

"Hey, Clee." Leaning in, Gabriel kissed her cheek.

Cleo had befriended the former Philly detective years ago, before he'd become a lawyer, the night Gus was robbed leaving Murphy's Tavern. The two had become friendly, with Gabriel stopping in the bar every so often when he needed intel from one of the neighbors, or after his shift when he wanted to catch up with Cleo and Gus.

Cleo remembered the night Gabriel had stopped in to tell her he'd met someone special on a recent trip to New York. When he introduced them to Frank, she knew he'd met his match. Upon hearing she and Nigel were planning to move to New York, Frank helped get them jobs at the pub where he worked, as well as land their apartment.

Her curiosity over Nigel's sit-down with the Cape May guys dissipated now that her friend was here. She ordered another round, and they caught up. As he chatted on about his trial, Cleo couldn't keep her mind from wandering to Gabriel's boss. Wells Abernathy III was not only head of the trial division of the Philly DA's office where Gabriel worked as a prosecutor, he was also one of Cleo's pre-Nigel conquests.

"When are you gonna tell me what went down between you and Wells?" he inquired, as though reading her mind.

Cleo was shocked. She'd never told Gabriel about her former tryst.

"I have no idea what you're talking about. Wells who?"

Gabriel laughed and slid his empty beer mug for a refill. "Nice try, girl. The guy who asks about you every Friday when I'm coming up for the weekend."

Shit. The jig was up.

"Oh, you mean that prosecutor guy?" she teased.

"Yeah, that one. One of these days Imma get you good and drunk and hear all about it."

Cleo blinked innocently, then flashed him a smile. "But tonight's not that night."

Dang, though. Just hearing about Wells's inquiry made her heart skip a beat. Not that she was remotely interested in "that prosecutor guy" she'd once found so hot. Sexy. Sizzlingly irresistible; maddingly unsustainable. All that had changed when she met Nigel.

But still...sometimes she couldn't help but think about Wells. Especially when Nigel got on her nerves, which was happening more frequently. She chalked it up to the fact that, with Wells, it had all been fun and games, with none of the daily doldrums of coupledom: blankets stolen in the middle of the night, toothpaste caps gone missing, dirty dishes plunked in the sink and not the empty dishwasher right next to it. With Wells, she didn't have to worry about walking into the fart cloud he'd left in the kitchen or falling into the New York City sewer system because someone forgot to put the toilet seat down. What she and Nigel had was amazing, more than she'd ever imagined for herself, but her old commitment-phobe ways had a tendency to surface when things got tough. Old habits die hard.

Cleo chuckled at the word repeating in her head. Hard. Hard. *Haaaard.*

Grow the fuck up.

On top of all that, there were the bigger, more obvious things, like the fact she and Nigel were starting to drift apart when it came to the future. The more Nigel droned on about wanting to leave the city to pursue his dream, the more complicated it made things.

Cleo didn't do complicated. She'd always believed complications in a relationship signaled danger ahead, and her fear of getting hurt triggered a need to bail. Better to abandon ship than be abandoned.

"How did you know about us?" she asked, not necessarily wanting to talk about Wells, but unable to stop herself.

"Detective's intuition. I see how you both light up a bit when the other's name is mentioned. Now that you're with the beautiful Brit, I figured it was a thing of the past." He paused and raised his eyebrows. "It is, isn't it?"

"What happened in Philly stayed in Philly," she said. "He's nothing more than a friend now."

"Good," Gabriel said as he regarded her with skepticism. "Wells is hot, but Nigel's hotter. And way better for you. Don't fuck it up."

"Yessir, ADA Romero, sir. Shall I drop and give you twenty?"

"I'll let you slide tonight. Seriously, though...everything good there? Why do I get the feeling something's rotten in Washington Heights?"

Cleo sighed. She didn't want to be a downer but hey, he

asked. "I don't know if I'm getting the shits of being tied down, or...the shits of him."

"Oh no. Please don't tell me Old Cleo's coming back."

"No." She laughed. It felt good to talk to someone she'd known since before Nigel, back when Old Can't-Tie-Me-Down Cleo was in charge. Maybe he'd have some insight into how she could navigate this mess.

"It's just that I've finally made things happen for myself. I moved to NYC with a measly savings and a shitty bartending job, and I've worked my way up to almost running a gallery. I've forged great connections with the kids I've met through my volunteer work, and my heart beats to the pulse of this city. No matter how 'great' Nigel is for me, he'll never eclipse the new Cleo. No one, not even him, is going to make me give this up."

She wasn't sure if her headstrong statement was the result of stubbornness or drink, but it was how she felt in that moment.

Gabriel nodded. "Tough situation you're in. Not that you asked my opinion, but I believe the trick to a successful relationship is allowing space for both partners to grow in their independent ways. You need to be able to pursue your individual dreams without one asking the other to compromise to the point it's no longer the life you wanted for yourself."

Cleo nodded. "One of the first conversations Nigel and I had was about that very same thing. At our ages, we owe it to ourselves to fully explore our dreams without being tethered to someone else's. That no one else has the right to make you change to suit their needs. That's what happened to our friend Tori and her ex-asshole. Nigel and I agreed we'd never do that to each other."

"Sounds like you guys need to have some tough talks," Gabriel said.

Cleo glanced over to where Nigel was chatting with the two men from Cape May.

Again?

Gabriel was right—tough talks ahead.

She went home alone when midnight rolled around, as it would be a few more hours before Nigel closed up. But when her phone rang at four in the morning, jolting her awake, she noticed he wasn't beside her in bed where he should be. Instead, his name flashed on her screen.

She shot up in bed. "Are you okay?"

"No," he said. "I've been shot."

Marley

MARLEY AND SAM HAD NOT ONLY MADE IT TO THE NEXT round of the competition, they'd received the highest number of votes. Again. Which is how they found themselves on the first Friday in August standing at the front of a suburban Walmart with a shopping cart.

"Okay, guys, this week's challenge is a two-parter," Amanda informed the contestants as the cameras rolled. "From this hat, you'll pick a category. At the signal, you'll head to the appropriate section of the store and procure as many items within your category as you can before time's up. You won't know what these items will be used for until the second part of the challenge. This is another timed race. You'll have five minutes to fill your carts and make it back to the registers. Once everyone has returned, you'll be instructed on what you'll do with those items. The only hint I'm permitted to give you is...size *does* matter. In this case, the smaller, the better."

Amanda approached Marley and Sam first to pick their category.

"Health and Wellness," Sam announced, holding up the slip of paper. Then added under his breath, "*Boooor*-ing."

The host went down the line. After the last couple picked their category, Amanda gave the countdown. "And...*go!*"

Marley began pushing the cart, but Sam commandeered it.

"Where's the pharmacy?" he cried out as he swiveled the cart, nearly taking Marley out.

"Geez, Sam! Take it easy!"

"Can't, Mar. I'm on fire." He pointed to the sign. She took off, Sam hot on her trail. "Go! Go!"

She had to move fast to keep him from riding up the back of her heels with the cart. All's fair in love and competitive shopping.

"Okay, what's the plan?" Marley asked as Sam began pulling things off shelves and tossing them in the cart. She grabbed his wrist. "Hold up! We need a plan."

"Marley, don't stop me! She said as many things as we can fit!"

"Shouldn't we be strategic about this?" In their couple-dom, Marley was the thinker, Sam was the doer. "There's a second part to this, so we probably have to do something with the items we select."

Sam considered her suggestion for a split second. "Overruled!"

He continued throwing products into the basket. Toothpaste. Toothbrushes. Pain killer. And more.

"Duuuude!" he exclaimed as something further down the aisle caught his eye. Dashing away, he returned with several boxes.

"Really, Sam? Condoms?"

"What? Our category was Health and Wellness. Nothing wrong with promoting safe sex."

"Except maybe not on daytime TV?"

Sam flashed his eyebrows.

Oh God. She never should have said something. "Don't even—"

"You know how I love me a challenge."

"No. Big mistake. Huge!"

"You're right." He snickered. "These are too small."

He dashed down the aisle and returned a moment later, thrusting boxes of Magnum XXL into the cart.

She raised an inquisitive eyebrow at him.

He shrugged. "Hey, a little self-promotion never hurt anyone."

"Except for that pesky thing called truth in advertising," Marley teased as Sam made a mock laughing face.

She checked her phone. "Shit! Forty seconds left. We gotta go!"

Stations had been set up at the front of the store, each with three round cakes of varying sizes and tubs of frosting.

Amanda gave the instructions. "Okay, on the count of five, you'll construct your cake, add icing, and decorate it...using the objects in your baskets. Your goal is to use the most objects while still making your cake attractive. You'll have ten minutes to complete this task. And...go!"

Sam gave his evil laugh as he dove for the box of condoms.

"No," Marley said, slapping his hand like he was a toddler about to stick his finger in a socket. She grabbed for the icing. "This first."

Marley slathered icing on as fast as her OCD self would allow. She had a thing about crumbling cake into the frosting.

"Faster, Mar! They're winning!"

"Calm the fuck down," she muttered under her breath, forgetting once again they were mic'd. She took the time she needed to perfect her icing strategy. "Okay, I think we're good."

Sam grabbed a box of condoms. Before she knew it, he had one up against his lips and was blowing into it.

"What are you doing?" Marley hissed as she batted the

prophylactic from his hands. It went airborne, nearly hitting another contestant in the face.

"I'm gonna blow them up like balloons and attach them to the top."

"No." Marley's directive was firm, unyielding.

"Okay. How about this?"

He deftly unwrapped several packages and, keeping them in their circular shape, pushed them into the icing on the side of the cake.

Marley was about to object but realized she couldn't tell they were condoms the way Sam had placed them. Instead, they looked swirls of yellow frosting.

"Thirty-six in a box, five boxes, that's 180 objects on our cake. We got this."

Hyped by her own thrill of the win, Marley helped him unwrap while he shoved them into the icing around the perimeter of each layer.

"Five minutes left," Sam said. "Grab some other things!"

Marley shoved a bunch of toothbrushes in the top to resemble candles. She ripped open a pack of pastel razors and stuck them around the middle layer. Drizzling cough syrup around the edges with one hand, she grabbed for a tube of toothpaste with the other, piping a fancy border of blue gel around the edges of each layer like a cake boss. She sprinkled a fifty-count bottle of Advil tablets on top.

"Time!" yelled Amanda.

They gave each other a high five. Marley was impressed that Sam had somehow gotten all 180 condoms onto the sides of the cake.

Amanda made her way down the table, marveling at everyone's cakes, as Eddie followed her with the camera.

"Lastly, we have Marley and Sam's cake, and what a patriotic one it is!" She examined it from all angles. "Okay... looks like their category was Health and Wellness, and they creatively used red cough medicine and blue toothpaste as decorative icing on a white background. God bless America! What have we here?"

Amanda plucked one of the condoms out as Eddie zoomed in. "Oh, my, are these—"

Cut to black.

"I swear, you guys are fucking hilarious," Amanda later said to Marley. "I'm serious about grabbing a drink sometime."

"That'll be fun!"

Marley decided to cut right to the chase. She internally begged Sam's forgiveness for overtaking his Olympic quest and asked the question burning in everyone's mind. "How's things with Eddie? Will he be joining us?"

"Hell no. Not after *what he did.*"

She said it with such vitriol, Marley had to wonder what he'd done. Infidelity? Grand larceny? *Murder?* Marley was now as intrigued as Sam over their situation. But her opportunity for clarification went *poof!* as Amanda spun on her heels and marched away.

Marley shared their conversation with the others when they returned to the studio.

"I bet he cheated on her," one contestant guessed. "After all, in her words, 'he's a dick.' Cheating would earn him that title."

"Maybe he's on drugs," suggested another.

"Probably a voyeur."

All eyes swiveled to the speaker.

"I mean, he's into cameras and videotaping and shit," the guy reasoned.

"I'm hoping he's just dragging his feet on marriage, and they'll soon resolve it," Eternally Optimistic Olivia, a.k.a prego lady, said. "Maybe being around this competition, he'll see how fun it is to be engaged. Andy and I have been together since high school and had our kids first. This part is just icing on the cake."

"Speaking of icing..."

Everyone laughed over Marley and Sam's condom cake.

"How many kids do you have?" Marley asked Olivia to redirect their attention.

"Three," Olivia said, rolling her eyes. She pointed to her belly. "This one makes four."

"You guys deserve a lot of credit," another contestant said. "Must be hard doing this with three little ones at home."

"It's worth it, if we win," she said. "Andy and I are really just in it for the money. We're having a simple ceremony in our backyard with family, so we don't really need the wedding package."

Sam shot a look at Marley. She knew he was analyzing this set of facts. They'd agreed that, of all the competitors, Andy and Olivia posed the biggest threat. They were cute together, obviously in love, and consistently scored high votes. Competitive Sam was probably thinking, if they weren't planning an elaborate wedding, why should they win? Compassionate Sam probably reasoned they needed the money more than the others. Marley wondered if the other contestants had already figured this out and weren't trying so hard. Maybe she and Sam were the only competitive assholes in the group.

Then again, ten grand was ten grand. To the victor belong the spoils.

Charlotte

CHARLOTTE WAS IN HER OFFICE, BRUSHING UP ON CUStody law, when the door burst open, nearly causing her to jump from her skin.

"You must be Charlotte!" the man exclaimed.

He was tall with a solid build, sandy hair cropped short, and his smile seemed to take over his whole face in a Will Ferrell sort of way.

"I'm Peter, Bob's son," he said, offering a handshake.

Against her better judgment, Charlotte accepted it, promising herself she'd Purell as soon as he left.

"His *other* son, as I'm assuming you've already met my doltish brother."

Owen had told her that his brother, Peter, co-owner of several Cape May restaurants, had been on an extended vacation.

"I'm here to save the day as the better of Bob's sons, and not just in the looks department."

Charlotte laughed out loud, appreciating his exuberance. He instantly put her at ease.

"I'm not so sure. Owen's pretty handsome," she joked.

A first. Sharing humor within seconds of meeting someone was something she never did. In the past, if a man had burst into a room and startled her as he just did, he'd have met with a cloud of Mace to his face, a knee to his groin, and an oversized purse to the side of his head. In that precise order.

Must've been her Chestnut Brown hair talking. That or the Maybelline, as she certainly wasn't born with it.

"Yeah, but he's taken, and I'm not," Peter said, removing his suit jacket and flinging it over an armchair before settling into it. His legs were long, his shoes fancy, and his smile confident.

Charlotte found her heart fluttering as he smiled up at her. "It sounds like you're taken as well—with yourself," she teased.

Wait—was she actually flirting with a man she'd just met? There had to be something in the Cape May water, causing her to go rogue with whimsy, tossing her usual caution to the sea breeze.

Or...it could have to do with the fact she no longer lived in a gritty city, prepared to defend herself to the death each time she stepped off her front porch. The only thing to fend off here were midsummer mosquitos. Perhaps it was because she was no longer hustling for professional advancement in a law firm that refused to recognize her true value. Whatever the reason, Charlotte enjoyed peeling off a new layer of her old self to discover someone far more engaging. Adventurous. Even flirty.

They chatted for a few minutes before he got up.

"Well, Charlotte Drysdale. I just wanted to stop in and introduce myself. I hear you've been doing an awesome job, and I know how much my dad appreciates it. Maybe we can grab lunch one of these days, get to know each other? I'm always up for making new friends."

"That sounds lovely," she said. She could use a new friend.

Charlotte couldn't stop smiling after Peter left. She'd only been living in Cape May a month, but already she'd been fluttering her new wings like the colorful monarch butterflies that migrated through the Cape each fall.

New job. New hair. New friends. The possibilities were endless.

Charlotte Drysdale had finally emerged from her chrysalis.

Cleo

A WEEK HAD GONE BY SINCE NIGEL TOOK A BULLET IN protection of the pub—if getting grazed on the arm by passing ammo could be considered such. His wound wasn't nearly as dire as Cleo had envisioned as she'd raced to the hospital that morning, expecting to find his arm hanging on by a tendon. Or worse—completely disconnected from his body.

Struggling for oxygen, she'd decided she deserved the coronary she was about to suffer after bashing their relationship to Gabriel. She couldn't lose this man, her heart. Then again, she wouldn't need a heart if something happened to him.

She'd found him propped up in bed, eyes closed, a sling around his neck suspending his heavily bandaged right arm.

"Nigel." Her voice had wavered as a fat tear streamed down her face.

"Hey, Clee." He was pale, and his hair was a mess, but he looked no worse than a March 18 hangover.

"Thank God, you're okay," she'd said, gingerly leaning to give him a hug.

"You should see the other guy." He smirked. "Damn near had him, too, had his gun not gone off."

"You wrestled a guy with a gun?"

He gave her a lopsided smile. "Someone had to. Since your legislators can't seem to."

"The good detective wasn't there?" she'd asked.

"Nah, he and Frank had just left. Perfect timing. It was just me and the two new guys."

Nigel recounted how they'd closed the bar and were cleaning up when two masked men burst through the back door, weapons drawn.

"I jumped one of them from behind, not even considering they might shoot me. Impulsive and foolish, I know, but it was just my instinct. Fortunately, the other guy took off."

"You're lucky it wasn't worse. Does it hurt bad?"

"Yeah," he said, wincing. "Apparently, in the tussle, I broke my arm, too, the same one that took the bullet. So much for working anytime soon."

True. Hard to sling drinks when your good arm was out of commission.

But what hurt more, he reported, was his shaken faith in humanity.

"I hear ya, dude. It's fucked."

Cleo was heartbroken that someone as kind and gentle as Nigel had to deal with something so traumatic. Something he might never get over.

A week later, she watched as he packed for a trip back to the Mother Land. The stated purpose—to celebrate his great-grandmother's 100th birthday. The unstated purpose—absconding from the city he now doubly resented.

"Just ten days, right?" Cleo asked, confirming the length of his stay.

Nigel nodded.

"I'm going to miss you," she whined. "I could really use your support now that Daisy's pulled out of the new gallery space and I'm back to my old grind." She sighed in frustration. "She reiterated this morning I should decide what I want to do with my career. The old bitch doesn't sugarcoat, that's for sure."

"That sucks," Nigel said. "What do you think you'll do?"

"I want to advance my career, and if not at this gallery, then I need to hustle and find something else. We need the money—"

"And this trip isn't helping. I won't go if you don't want me to."

"No, go," Cleo said, sighing. "I'm just sorry I can't come too. I gotta stay and figure out my next move."

"Not to bring up a sore subject, but this could be a sign. Between your job and this—" he raised his casted arm, "—maybe the universe is telling you to look elsewhere, outside the city. There's so many cool places where we can both—"

"Nope."

He looked as if she'd spit in his face.

"Very well," he said, grabbing his carry-on. "I'm off. Sorry, but I need this, Clee. I need to get away for a little while."

But to Cleo, it seemed less about getting away and more like he was going toward something else. Was there something he wasn't telling her?

After she dropped Nigel off at the airport, Cleo drove to Philly for her weekly meeting with Gus. She'd brought hoagies, and they settled into their familiar banter.

"Come, have a drink with me," the old man said, settling into his recliner after they'd finished cleaning up.

"You sure that's a good idea? You barely touched your sandwich."

"I'd rather waste my calories on good ol' Jim Beam."

"Suit yourself."

His health seemed to have taken a turn for the worse over the past couple weeks. She was concerned about him consuming alcohol, but it was up to him how he wanted to spend whatever life he had left.

He poured drinks and offered a toast. "To life."

"To—" Cleo gulped a sob and blinked back tears. She clinked her glass with his. "Yeah."

"I'm guessing you can tell how mine's going," he joked half-heartedly. "How about yours?"

"Meh. Been better."

"Boy problems still?" he asked.

She told him about Nigel getting shot and how he was even more determined to leave the city.

"And you haven't changed your stance on it?"

"Hell no."

"So if he goes, it would be without you." It was more of a statement than a question.

"Yup."

She waited for the lecture that she should compromise, go with him, try to make it work. Instead, Gus was silent.

He reached out and squeezed her hand. "Cleo's a smart girl who'll figure out what's best for Cleo."

She felt the tears welling again. She thought she knew what his answer would be before she asked the question, but decided it was worth asking. "With Nigel...or without him?"

"You'll know it in your heart when you're ready to answer that for yourself."

That was it. No snarky tag line, like, *if he's willing to wait around for your reluctant ass.* Just a loving look.

She blinked rapidly again to keep her tears from going south. "But what if you're not here to—" She stopped abruptly. Shit! Why did she say that?

Gus just smiled. "I won't be. But that's okay. Hey, why don't you get yourself one of those Jesus bracelets, with the initials WWJD on it? Only a G instead of a J. That way, whatever life throws at you, it'll remind you to ask, 'What Would Gus Do?' My good old friend, handsome and wise beyond all his years."

"Handsome? Oh, for a second there I thought we were talking about you," Cleo teased before choking back another sob.

She didn't need a bracelet. She just needed her old friend.

Make that, friends. Gus and Nigel.

Both of them were slipping through her fingers faster than she could hold on.

Delaney

D ELANEY HAD FORGOTTEN ALL ABOUT HER DNA TEST UN-til the email came through, alerting her to a potential match. Not just any match...

A daughter.

She laughed out loud. What a scam.

"Oh well, I guess they're not all that accurate," Kate agreed when Delaney FaceTimed her. "No other matches came up?"

"Nope. It just says, 'You share 49% DNA with this person, who we predict is a daughter.'" Delaney paused for effect before shifting her tone to mock seriousness. "Do you think maybe I had a baby and just forgot?"

"Well, I suppose anything's possible, now that you like surprises and believe in destiny," Kate said, laughing. "I'm just glad you took the test. What else did you learn?"

"I'm mostly of Southern European descent, with some Northwest Asian. So, anything from Greek, Italian, Armenian, or a combination thereof."

"Very cool combos. Explains your dark hair."

"The lone brunette in a sea of blondes," Delaney said, referencing her fair-haired adoptive family.

"I've always been so envious of your dark hair and blue-gray eyes."

"You shouldn't be envious, brown-eyed blondie. My polar opposite. Hey, you should do a test too. Learn more about your origins."

"Already on it."

"Let me know if you find any illegitimate children," Delaney joked, "so we can invite them to our next family reunion."

Charlotte

IT HAD BEEN WEEKS, AND CHARLOTTE STILL HADN'T HEARD from Jake. She was beginning to worry.

Awaiting a client's arrival, she pulled up Jake's sailing route to check where he might be. He'd plotted a course through the Caribbean and planned to stop at a couple islands before heading southwest to traverse the Panama Canal. He should be approaching it soon.

The door opened and she tossed her phone in the drawer, wanting to make a good impression on her first official client, a local resident with a land dispute. For the past few weeks, she'd been shadowing Bob, meeting his clients and observing his process, but was excited to finally be set free on her own.

Excited, but also terrified. Funny, she never felt that way opening new cases for her old firm, but this was vastly different. Bob's practice offered a personalized, one-on-one style of lawyering. Now, her clients were people, not companies. She wielded the power to make or break lives with caution. Her primary goal this first year, in addition to learning new law, was to sustain the same level of integrity Bob's practice had provided the community with all these years.

But it wasn't the client she'd been expecting who burst through the door. It was Peter.

"Delivery for Ms. Charlotte!" He held up a box.

"I didn't know you worked for USPS," she teased.

"Only in my spare time."

She knew he was joking. She'd googled him and learned he and Owen had been modest about their success. The media had hailed them as award-winning restaurateurs.

"A gift," he said. "From me to you."

It was from Jake, the return label showed, but she played along.

"Why, Peter, I just couldn't accept. I barely know you." Clutching her hand to her chest in mock modesty, she felt her heart racing—from Jake's package, or the guy delivering it?

"I just hope whatever I sent is good."

"It better be, or you can take a big raincheck for that lunch you suggested."

"I'm guessing it's from a male suitor," Peter said. "I bet you have one in every port."

"You flatter me. Do I look like a woman who has a man in every port?"

Charlotte regretted her words the second she said them. She'd never viewed herself as attractive—certainly not enough to suggest she had men all over the world longing for her. But one of her goals this year was to stop being down on herself, limiting her potential with a fabricated prophecy that men wouldn't be interested in her. Jake always stopped her when she put herself down and made her feel attractive as she was—by commenting on the unique golden hue of her eyes, her dimples, the way her face lit up when she allowed herself to smile. He'd also taught her that attractiveness was more than just outward beauty, but instead had to do with personality and treatment of others. She was genuine, smart, and quick-witted, he'd said, traits he found attractive.

"I'm kidding," she said, hoping to do a bit of damage control.

Peter looked closer at the package. "Oh. Jake Brady, our mutual buddy. Your boyfriend?"

"Nah," Charlotte answered. "Just a friend."

I think?

Peter nodded. "I'm here to ask if we can start working on the house this week. We'd like to get started on the bathroom. We'll work during the day when you're here, since we tend to be busier in the evenings with the restaurants. Would that work?"

"Absolutely."

"Good. We'll start tomorrow."

Charlotte was relieved when he finally left so she could open Jake's package. She found a note tucked inside.

My dearest Charlotte,

I've decided to send you Christmas ornaments from every port, so you can collect them for this year's tree. (You WILL be getting a tree again, right? :) Here are the first three, in order of the ports I've visited so far, with a note on each to explain.

I miss you and hope all is going well with your new practice. Shoot me a text when you get this and keep me updated on your exciting new life!

All my love,
Jake

She gasped at his once-again liberal use of the L word. Maybe this was just the way people signed off on friendly letters. She wouldn't know, never having had a pen pal before.

The first gift was a glass pig ornament and a Polaroid picture of Jake in the ocean, floating among real-life swine. She grimaced at the potential health risks. He was far more adventurous than she'd ever be. On the back of the photo, he'd tacked a sticky note:

Here I am, swimming with the pigs in the Bahamas. I know what you're thinking, but they're super clean. Never be afraid to try new things!

She flipped the picture back over and looked closer at her friend. He looked so handsome—deeply bronzed, bathed in sunshine and sea, beads of water clinging to his long lashes. She stared for a second while her heart inflated with joy.

She shook herself back to reality before she started swimming herself. Not with pigs but with feels.

The second package contained a colorful paper mâché ornament resembling a fish head with fangs and horns. His note gave explanation:

During the Festival de Santiago Apóstol in Puerto Rico, vejigantes battle soldiers in a struggle between good and evil. Here I am wearing the traditional mask, and here's a smaller version for your tree. Always choose good, Charlotte!

She laughed out loud—not only at his picture with the hideous mask, but his suggestion she'd ever choose anything *but* good. She'd spent a lifetime being a goody two-shoes.

The third package was from his stop in Grenada—another glass ornament, this one of a spice bottle labeled *Mace*. Charlotte chuckled over his joke, which didn't need explanation. The Polaroid photo featured him next to a plant.

Grenada is known for mace—the spice, not your weapon of choice. I know how much you love the latter, so I thought you'd get a blast out of this. Stay spicy, Charlotte!

Charlotte delighted in his thoughtful, playful gifts. She would most certainly put these ornaments on a Christmas tree this year. After Grams died, she didn't bother with any of the holiday frivolities, unable to tolerate the falling needles from a fresh-cut tree or the possibility it could harbor spiders. But Jake insisted she get one, that year they became friends, and even helped pick one out. She'd forgotten how a lit tree created warmth and glow, something that had been missing in her life for so long.

She held up all three ornaments, snapped a selfie, and texted him.

> Dear Jake—I received your gifts and cannot wait to put them on my tree this year. I also appreciate your words of wisdom. I promise to try new things, choose good over evil, and stay spicy. Although the latter assumes I'm spicy in the first place. I'll work on it. Take care, my friend. Stay safe.

How should she sign off? Formal, or fun?
What the hell, Charlotte—loosen up.

She bit the bullet.

All my love, Char

Cleo

THE THIRD BAD THING HAPPENED THE DAY AFTER NIGEL returned from England.

It was just after midnight when Cleo got the call she'd been dreading. Gus's niece called to let her know her old friend had passed peacefully in his sleep, a day short of his eightieth birthday.

"Damn fool," she whispered as she eyed the birthday cake she'd baked him. She'd planned to take it the next day to celebrate his eight decades on the planet. "You couldn't have held on for one more day?"

Although she'd been bracing for this eventuality, she wasn't prepared for the torrent of tears that ensued.

Without having to ask, Nigel put his arms around her, holding her as she sobbed. "I'm sorry, sweetheart," was all he said. "He was such a good friend to you."

Gus was more than a friend. He was family, after her own had abandoned her. She often felt closer to him than Delaney and Tori, mostly because they both now lived overseas. With Gus gone, that left Nigel, who she now clung to for dear life, draining her tear ducts all over his Ramones t-shirt.

She heaved a sob-sigh and shared the funeral details with Nigel. The viewing would be on Friday, followed by a celebration of life on Saturday.

"I don't know about Cape May," Cleo said.

They'd planned to spend a long weekend away from the city at Delaney and Dalton's shore house.

"We don't have to leave Friday," Nigel said. "We can go Saturday if that's better."

"I'd rather not commit to anything right now. Gus didn't have much family, and I want to make sure I'm there for them if they need me."

"I get it."

As she said the words, she felt sorry for her old friend. His funeral wouldn't be a big one. Besides his long-lost wife and deceased daughter, the only family she knew about were his niece and nephew. His friends from the tavern would certainly be there, perhaps a friend or two from the veterans' organization. But that was about it.

"I doubt I'll be very good company that weekend," she added.

"No worries," Nigel said as he hugged her. "Let's just get through these next few days and you can decide later."

Cleo was grateful for her sweet boyfriend. She snuggled closer, resting her heavy heart on his, thankful he'd returned before she got this news. "Please don't ever leave me for good. I can deal with the occasional London trip, but that's as far as I want you to go. Having to say goodbye to Gus is hard enough. I don't think I could make it without you."

"You never have to worry about that. I'm not going anywhere."

September

Marley

ONCE AGAIN, MARLEY AND SAM FOUND THEMSELVES standing in a dwindling line of contestants, now one of four couples left. Entering the studio that morning, the men were told to select a picture of a dress from a bridal magazine that they'd like to see their bride wear on their wedding day.

"Look, Mar!" Sam sounded like a preschooler sharing a hideous, only-a-mother-could-love finger painting. "*Such* a pretty dress."

She stifled a guffaw upon realizing he was serious. "Oh, my."

To say the dress was full-on 1980s nightmare was an understatement. So huge, it not only took up the entire picture frame but looked as if someone had stuck a life-sized wedding dress on a Barbie doll. Yards upon foofy yards of tulle and ribbon were combined to create layers upon poofy layers of dress. It was long-sleeved with a vampire neckline, in case she needed to suck someone's blood. The train, while gorgeous, appeared to be a block long.

Good God. Wearing this wouldn't leave much room in the ballroom for her guests. Did he not know her? She was as simply stated as they came.

Marley had always known what the perfect-for-her dress would look like. She'd drawn it in college on the back of a notebook, next to a heart with the letters *M+S* inside. Despite being "just friends" at the time, she'd started developing crazy, crushing feelings for Sam even she couldn't explain. She remembered the day she drew the picture—her twenty-first birthday, as she waited for Sam to pick her up for their celebratory bar crawl.

Over the years, she'd misplaced the notebook with the dress sketch. While she remembered most of the details, she'd love to see the drawing now, to gauge whether it was still her chosen style or whether her tastes had changed.

Sam now gazed at his picture so lovingly, Marley wondered if he was considering trading her in for the model.

"She looks like a cream puff," he sighed.

"More like a dairy explosion."

As the cameras began rolling, the men were asked to explain why they selected their dresses. Marley prayed the viewing public wouldn't judge Sam too harshly for his questionable taste in women's wedding wear. Thank God he had a handle on tuxes.

"I chose this dress because it's so pretty," Sam said when it was his turn, staring at the picture with emoji heart eyes. "Marley's a simple, classy dresser, and she always looks great, but I think she'd look gorgeous in something like this."

Right. If my goal was to look like a parliament of snow owls had exploded in a cloud-filled sky during a blizzard.

Amanda raised an eyebrow at Marley, her smirk saying it all. *Poor you.*

I know, girl. He's otherwise harmless.

"Good choices, men." Amanda forced a smile into the camera. "Obviously, this month's theme is wedding dresses. The challenge? Your bride will make the dress you chose...out of toilet paper. The twist? You'll be the ones wearing the dresses."

A chorus of laughter (from the women) combined with groans of dismay (from the men).

"But that's not all. Once your groom is dressed, he'll be sent through a wedding day obstacle course. After all, as women, we go through an awful lot on that day. Or so I'm told." Amanda hooked an eyebrow at Eddie. "Anyway, the goal is to be the first man to cross the finish line with their dress still intact."

Carts stacked with toilet paper rolls were lined up before the contestants.

"We're gonna need a bigger cart," Marley said wryly as Sam shot her an apologetic look. "Couldn't have gone simple, could you?"

"I don't do simple," Sam muttered as he grabbed several rolls of toilet paper. Upon reconsideration, he rolled an entire cart over.

"There goes the planet."

He held up the picture so Marley could see it as she wrapped and wrapped and wrapped him until he was about a foot fatter. She tucked yards of TP into one of the folds to create a long-ass train while cursing him under her breath.

Marley noticed that the other men, fully cloaked in their toilet paper dresses, were starting the obstacle course.

"Go!" she yelled.

The first leg required the men to don high heels. Marley laughed as she watched Sam teeter-run to the next station, where he was challenged to put on lipstick and mascara while trying to balance on six-inch heels. Epic fail, as the makeup ended up on every part of his face *other* than his lips and lashes, making him look like a deranged clown. By the time he got to the third station, where he had to affix a veil, two of the men had already finished the course.

The next task had Marley almost peeing her pants when he was required to do three rounds of the Macarena. How someone could look utterly ridiculous yet so adorable at the same time was beyond her. Clown-faced, he nailed the moves, even added a few sexy hip sways, his wobbling ankles threatening to take him down.

Sam was the last to finish the course with the required bouquet toss. He threw it over his shoulder at the pretend line of bridesmaids. At the last second, Amanda leaped into the air and caught it.

"Got the most important thing!" she exclaimed. "Now I just need a groom."

Marley waited for a snarky comment, but Amanda remained silent. Eddie looked relieved.

Sam's over-the-top dress selection may have cost them votes, but Marley hadn't had that much fun or laughed that hard in a long time. Her heart swelled over his good sportsmanship and beauty—even dressed to the toilet paper nines, makeup smeared all over his face, wobbling in a pair of pumps as he gyrated his hips. She thanked her lucky stars this was the man she'd spend her life with.

IT WAS ONLY THE BEGINNING OF SEPTEMBER, BUT THE chilly air took Cleo's breath away as she stepped from the Uber.

"Ready for this?" Nigel said, taking her hand in his.

"No. Never."

"I got you, girl."

He wrapped an arm around her and she laid her head on his shoulder. She was so lucky to have this man, this rock of hers, at a time like this. If it weren't for Nigel's strength holding her upright, she may have drowned in a puddle of her own tears.

When he guided them around the corner, Cleo stopped dead in her tracks.

"Um..."

"Whoa," Nigel said.

Snaked around the building was a line to get in.

"What is this?" Cleo asked in amazement. Clearly not the

viewing of the Augustus James Rourke she knew. He had lots of friends at the tavern, but not enough to form a *line*. "We must have the wrong place."

"'Scuse me," Nigel said, tapping the shoulder of the last person queued up. "Whose viewing are you here for?"

"And old friend and mentor," the man said, a tear in his eye.

"What's he called?" Nigel probed.

"Gus Rourke."

If the man had said King Charles, Cleo would have been less blown away. She loved her old pal but couldn't fathom how in fuck's sake he'd touched all these souls. Unless he'd been some sort of rampant pervert.

"Did you guys have him too?" the man asked.

"Have him for what?" Cleo asked.

Before he could answer, they were interrupted by an approaching woman.

"Miles Granrath, is that you?" the woman asked, chuckling as she gave him a hug. "Good to see you! Sorry about the circumstances, though."

Nigel waved the woman into the line ahead of them, and the old friends turned away to catch up.

"What do you think he meant, 'have him?'" Cleo whispered.

"Hell if I know. I'm still in shock over this line."

"Must be people from his past. Maybe distant family? Other than his niece, he's never mentioned any relatives." Cleo began to wonder if her friend had withheld some details of his life.

When they finally stepped inside, it took a minute for her eyes to adjust to the darkened foyer, lit by only one small light affixed to the top of a sign bearing a photo of a much-younger, surprisingly handsome, Gus. Cleo's Gus.

Bearing the caption *Dr. Augustus James Rourke, PhD.*

Cleo stumbled into Nigel. "Oh, my God..." she whimpered, her voice cracking. "It was true."

Tears cascaded down her face as she recalled the many times Gus had joked—or so she'd thought—about having been a professor.

"That son of a bitch," she muttered, in utter shock. "He wasn't lying. I can't believe this."

She looked at Nigel, who wore the same surprised expression.

"Here's a card," he said, holding it so they both could read the brief details of his life. "Wow," Nigel exclaimed. "Quite an accomplished educator, at that."

A woman in a black dress and strappy sandals approached them. "Cleo?"

She instantly recognized her from the dusty picture frames on Gus's shelves. Gus's niece, Beverly.

"I knew that had to be you from all the photos Uncle Gus showed me," she said, hugging Cleo. "My God, he wasn't joking. You are the spitting image of Susan. His daughter, my cousin."

"He's told me so much about her throughout the years," Cleo said, tears welling. If only he'd told her more about himself.

"Sounds like you two had similar personalities. I hope you know, he absolutely adored you, as if you were his own daughter."

Cleo clutched her chest. "I'm honored." Her tears tumbled as she tried to hide the shock waves still passing through her.

"We're in town for a few days after this," Beverly said. "I'm hoping we can get together. Maybe for dinner after the service. You and...Nigel, is it?" She took his hand. "I recall when you two met. Uncle Gus gushed about you, so happy Cleo had finally met someone worthy of her."

Cleo laughed out loud at the visual of Gus "gushing." In all the years of their friendship, she'd never seen Gus gush, but would've enjoyed it.

"We'd love to join you for dinner," Cleo said.

"I must be off, lots of people to greet," Beverly said, giving her a hug. "Will you be at the service tomorrow?"

"Of course."

After Beverly walked away, Nigel turned to her. "So, I guess we're not going to Cape May?"

Cleo had hoped she'd be able to rally for their weekend away, but with this shocking turn of events, she couldn't bear to leave. "I have a lot of questions, obviously, and I want to get to know his family better."

Nigel looked crestfallen.

"You can still go," she said. "I think you should. After all, we promised Delaney we'd check on their house. I'll join you down there Saturday night when this is all over."

As they inched closer to the open casket, a slideshow came into view on a nearby projector screen. Cleo teared up again as she watched the photos flip through the stages of Gus's life. A rich and full life that had been kept a secret by the old goat. Photos of him as a young lad, playing in the streets of a much different-looking Philadelphia. Photos of him in an old-time UPenn football uniform, then later, his army uniform. Gus with a beautiful woman.

"Ahh, look how pretty Bonnie was," a woman behind them said. "The love of his life."

Cleo choked back a guffaw. Love of his life, her ass. Maybe before she'd taken off, leaving him to raise their only child. While Cleo didn't know the details, she assumed they'd divorced, and not amicably, by the way he'd always bad-mouthed the institution of marriage and the idea of happily ever after.

"Shame she died so young," the woman continued.

That stopped her short. Cleo had no idea his ex-wife had died. "How old was she when she passed?" she asked the woman.

"Thirty-five. Same age as their daughter when she later died. Same kind of cancer too. That family has some bad genes."

"Except for Gus, who almost made it to eighty," Nigel mused.

"A long life to live with two soul-crushing heartbreaks. Susan was only four when Bonnie passed, so Gus basically raised her."

Cleo shook her head, trying to make sense of it. She'd always assumed divorce had separated them, not death.

"He was seven years her senior, and absolutely idolized her," the woman continued. "I don't know if he ever got over her death. He definitely became a lot more cynical about life after that. Especially after Susan also died."

"They were...happy?" Cleo asked.

"*So* in love," the woman said, "until death did they part."

Cleo felt her knees weaken again.

Nigel wrapped his arm around her. "You okay?" he whispered.

She shook her head. "How many years have I known him, and I never knew this? I had no idea he lost his wife to cancer. I just assumed... He was always so bitter about marriage."

"Maybe because his wife was taken from him at such a young age."

"Then why not just say that?"

Nigel shrugged. "All I know is he didn't want to see you end up with the wrong person, settling for less than what you deserved. He pulled me aside once and told me not to even think about dating you if I wasn't all in. He was very protective of you. I knew then I had to commit, or it would be off with my head."

Cleo recalled something Gus had said when they were discussing relationships one day.

It's not love I hate. It's loss.

His comment now made sense. Here, she'd thought it was love that was the problem. No wonder loss was the thing he despised, after losing the purported love of his life and his daughter, both so young. She'd just always assumed he was bitter about relationships because his had been bad.

"Everyone should be loved the way Gus loved Bonnie," the woman said.

Nigel squeezed Cleo tighter. Leaning down, he whispered in her ear, "The way I love you. I'm just glad Gus convinced you to give me a chance."

Charlotte

IF SOMEONE HAD TOLD CHARLOTTE A YEAR AGO SHE'D BE here now, working in a sole practitioner's law firm, interviewing a client with a neighbor dispute, she would have told them they were batshit crazy. And she would have been right.

Yet here she was, as Agatha Krancks spewed her latest complaint about her neighbor. Agatha was a frequent flier, Bob had warned the first time Charlotte met the woman.

"Part of being a small-town attorney is learning how to grease the squeaky wheels," Bob had said, standing by the window watching Agatha march up the driveway wearing a housecoat and a scowl. "I present to you Agatha Krancks, a lonely old woman."

"So, her name is fitting?" Charlotte had asked.

Bob chuckled. "You could say that. She never had kids and hates animals, so pets aren't an option to soften her up. She spends most of her life being disgusted by everyone around her, particularly her neighbor, Len. You can count on her storming in on a weekly basis and complaining about him. I've found the best way to handle her is to let her blow off steam. I don't bill her because, more than anything, she needs a friend."

"Weird," Charlotte said. Although she wasn't sure what was

weirder—the woman's behavior or the fact that Bob let her drop in, taking up valuable lawyer time, without compensation.

"You haven't seen weird yet," he said, stepping away from the door as it flung open. "But you're about to."

Charlotte sat in on their meeting, which lasted all of two minutes, and consisted of the woman complaining about Len parking his car in his yard.

"It's blocking my view of the street," she said.

"It's his property," Bob explained. "He's permitted to do that. But I'll give him a call and ask him to move it, if it'll make you feel better."

She nodded. "It will."

And, like that, she was gone.

"See? She's a pain in the ass, but she'll only take up a few minutes of your time."

We'll see about that. Charlotte wasn't prone to trivial nonsense. And seriously, if the woman thought someone parking their own car in their own yard was unneighborly, she should come to Charlotte's old neighborhood where residents greeted one another with flipped middle fingers and occasional gunfire.

"Are you really going to call Len and ask him to move his car?" she'd asked Bob after Krancks left.

"Hell, no. He only parks there on Sundays. Don't ask me why, or how I know that. Small-town life means knowing your neighbors' habits. Agatha's memory is bad, and this is the fifth time she's made this complaint. I just tell her what I think she wants to hear and let it go at that."

Since that first meeting with Agatha, Bob had found a way to conveniently disappear when the disgruntled woman stormed their driveway, leaving her in Charlotte's hands. She couldn't help a creeping sensation in the woman's presence. There was something oddly familiar about her.

"He's it again," Agatha now said.

"At what?" Charlotte asked, taking a deep breath for patience, only half-listening as the woman recounted her latest run-in with Len.

"Indecent exposure. This time with his robe wide open, only boxers underneath, taking his trash out. It was—"

"Wait. By trash do you mean—"

"His garbage bag," Agatha clarified. "What did you—*ohh.*"

The women chuckled over their near misunderstanding.

"No, *that* junk he left in his trunk," Agatha clarified. "Thank the good Lord. Anyway, it was all I could do to keep from calling the cops and having him arrested."

"Other than taking out his trash—his garbage bag—did he do anything else?"

"He gave me the finger."

"What time was this?" Charlotte asked, pretending to take notes.

"Midnight."

"So it was completely dark outside?"

"Yes. I had to use my binoculars to see him."

Charlotte stifled a giggle. "It sounds as if he was dressed, maybe not as much as you'd like, but I see nothing criminal about his actions."

"Not even giving me the finger?"

"No."

The woman clutched her purse in her lap. "Well, that's not helpful."

"But it is the law."

As Agatha stormed away, Charlotte realized why the woman creeped her out. Listening to her rants was like glimpsing into what might have been Charlotte's own future. She, too, had been a consummate complainer about others' behavior until she loosened up. All thanks to a friend who'd shown her that the world, and the people in it, weren't all that awful.

God, how she missed Jake. He'd probably delight in teasing Charlotte about how much she was once like Agatha.

Other than Agatha's occasional visits, Charlotte loved working with Bob. In the two months she'd been at the practice, she'd handled land disputes, minor criminal charges, zoning issues, and had been mentored on a divorce and custody case. All new, all exciting, all more fulfilling than business law.

The other thing she loved was the ability to close down shop at five o'clock. It was Bob's rule: no working after-hours.

"This law stuff can eat you alive if you let it," Bob had warned. "Work-life balance is critical to living a good life."

The term *work-life balance* was so foreign to Charlotte, she'd had to look it up. Work was the only life she'd known.

Charlotte was happy to discover the brothers were still at the cottage when she returned home that day. It was becoming commonplace, and she enjoyed having someone to chat with each evening.

She followed the sounds of banging and found them in the bathroom, installing her new countertop.

"Hey, Charlotte," Peter greeted her. "We'll be outta here in a few. Just want to finish this."

"No worries," Charlotte said, running her fingers along the smooth granite countertop. "This is beautiful."

"Thanks," Owen said. "My good tastes, coming through."

"Except this was the result of *my* good tastes. Nice try, though, Owe." Turning to Charlotte, Peter fake-whispered, "I'm the one who brings the beauty."

"Is that what you call it?" Owen teased.

She chuckled, enjoying the playful banter of the brothers. "Let me cook for you guys, if you don't have plans."

"Bummer. Ben and I are having dinner with his parents tonight," Owen said. "Can we take a raincheck?"

His words were barely out of his mouth when Peter piped up. "I'm available."

Charlotte caught the glint in Owen's eyes. "You kids have fun."

"Great. How does seven sound?" she asked.

"Sounds like I'll have a chance to take a much-needed shower. What can I bring?"

"Just yourself."

Peter returned at seven on the dot with a bottle of wine. He poured two glasses as Charlotte removed a lasagna from the oven.

"This is delicious," Peter said as they dug in. "I haven't had someone else cook for me in ages."

Charlotte cocked her head. "Not even your restaurant chefs?"

Peter laughed. "This is different. Deliciously homemade. You could have a career in this if you wanted."

She was touched but couldn't take credit. It was her grandmother's recipe. When she told him that, they launched into a discussion about family recipes, discovering they both had several worth sharing.

"That's it," Peter announced. "Once a month, we'll take turns cooking for one another, sharing our family secrets."

Charlotte agreed, happy to have something social to look forward to. Hanging out with Peter that night made her realize how much she missed having a companion. With Jake gone, Peter could be a nice replacement.

After they cleaned up, he wandered over to a shelf where Charlotte's favorite photos were displayed.

"That's me as an infant with my mom," she said, pointing to a photo. "Taken right before she passed."

"I'm sorry to hear that." He picked up a framed photo of her at age five, sitting on the couch with her dad as he read to her.

"He raised me through my formative years," Charlotte explained. "We weren't very close, but one thing he loved to do on his day off was read to me. The man worked two jobs, six days a week, counting down the days until he could retire." Charlotte felt a wave of sadness pass over her. "He never got there. Died at work, actually."

She shuddered, realizing she'd been heading in the same direction. Not necessarily for retirement, but for a promotion.

"That sucks. Good reminder to keep work in perspective."

"Anyway, on Sunday, we'd read. Probably why I became an avid reader."

"Big reader myself," Peter said.

Charlotte was surprised. She didn't take him for a bookish guy. "What's your favorite genre?" she asked, testing his knowledge.

"Everything from literary fiction to romcoms. Love me some historical romance as well. And the classics, of course."

"Me too," Charlotte said. She was impressed. "Somewhere around here is a box filled with my collection. I just haven't unpacked them yet."

"I'd love to see your books someday." He picked up the next photo, one of a much-younger Charlotte with Grams, standing in front of the Cape May lighthouse. "Hey, I know that place." He chuckled.

"Yeah. I spent a lot of my summers down here as a kid. My great-aunt had a place."

"Even more we have in common."

"We'll always have Cape May," she joked. "You know, like the line from—"

"*Casablanca*," he said. "That's one of my—"

"Favorite movies? Me too!"

Charlotte was thrilled to learn her new friend was just as into books and movies as she was. They launched into a discussion of their favorite films, agreeing their top three were *Casablanca*, *An Affair to Remember*, and *When Harry Met Sally*.

"We'll have to watch a movie together some night," Peter suggested.

Her thoughts instantly turned to Jake, how they'd spent last New Year's Eve watching movies all afternoon before *Dick Clark's Rockin' New Years Eve* ball drop. That was the night she'd introduced him to *An Affair to Remember*. She loved how the two main characters agreed to meet at the top of the Empire State Building if they were finally free to pursue a romance.

"We should do that, Char," Jake had joked. "If we're not married to other people by the time we're forty, we should meet at the top of the Empire State Building. No, make that the Cape May lighthouse."

Charlotte giggled. "What makes you think I want to be married by the time I'm forty? And to you, of all people?"

"Fifty then. And why me? Because I make you laugh. I bring out your dimples like no one else can."

Charlotte gave him a big smile to showcase them. "Fifty it is. Unless Ryan Seacrest comes knocking on my door first."

"As I'm sure he will."

"What's so funny?" Peter now asked, bringing her back to the present.

"Oh, nothing. Just remembering a funny conversation with a friend."

"Who's this?" Peter asked, pointing to a photo of Charlotte taken years ago for the Philadelphia Bar Association website.

She smiled looking at it. "That's me."

"You?" he said, incredulously. "I thought you were going to say it was your great-aunt or something."

She slugged his arm. "I've changed a bit."

"I'll say."

Charlotte peered at the image of her past self—kitchen shear-cut dull brown hair, thick-framed glasses, and a frown. Agatha Krancks-like. It had been taken back when her only goal in life was to become partner at Jervis Mahoney. Before she met Jake. Seeing it made her realize how miserable she'd been.

If someone had told three years ago she'd end up here in a charming Cape May cottage with a handsome man standing so close their arms were touching, laughing over Old Charlotte, she would have told them they were batshit crazy. And she would have been right.

Marley

MARLEY WAS RUNNING LATE, HOPING SHE HADN'T KEPT her friends and family waiting too long. She burst through the door of the bridal gown shop.

"She's here!" someone cried out and everyone clapped.

Her mom was the first to greet her, followed by Sam's mom.

"With three sons, I never thought I'd be invited to shop for wedding dresses," she said. "It means the world to me to be included."

"I wouldn't have it any other way," Marley assured her future mother-in-law with a hug.

"Hey, girl!" Matron of honor Kate was next to greet her, followed by Kelly, the administrative assistant at Sam and Marley's law firm and the closest of her cousins. She knew she could count on Kelly's honest (at times brutal) input when she tried on dresses. Her four other bridesmaids, which included two cousins and two childhood friends, greeted her next. Followed by...oh geez. Several aunts and cousins.

Par for the course as it was, Marley was dismayed her mom had included her extended family. But this was a monumental event for the Maguires, being that she was the first of her many female cousins to be married. She'd looked forward to this day and wasn't about to let a few extra attendees get her down. She just hoped her outspoken aunts weren't too forthcoming with their opinions.

After a champagne toast, it was time to start the search. Marley wished she still had the sketch she'd done back in college, even though most of the dress's features were forever etched in her brain—off-the-shoulder, scooping back, long train. Simple yet elegant. With Kate by her side, Marley selected the dresses that appeared to be close to her dream dress as the other women milled about, *oohing* and *aahing* over their favorites.

Suddenly, her mom called everyone's attention. "Okay, ladies, let's have some fun! You've all been a huge part of Marley's life, and you know her so well. Why don't you each pick out a dress you think fits Marley's style, one you'd like to see her wear."

"Mom," Marley whispered, trying to be diplomatic, "we don't have all day. Also, you see how some of them dress?"

"I know, but relax, Marley," her mom whispered back. "It should be fun. Not to mention funny when you see the ridiculous taste my sisters have."

She already had a pretty good idea, but decided to just go along with it, mostly to appease her mom. Marley was her firstborn child, and the only daughter in a family of boys, so her mom deserved to have some fun on this special day.

She tried on her own dress choices first, finding each had something slightly wrong with it. Too plain. Too tight. Too revealing. Her squad's lackluster response with each reveal confirmed her belief that none she'd selected were "the one."

"You'll know it's the right dress if you cry," an aunt offered. "At least I did."

"You cried because of who you were marrying," another aunt said.

The Maguire women all cracked up, knowing the skank Marley's former uncle turned out to be after he cheated with his twenty-years-younger secretary.

"Ugh, don't remind me," the aunt said, rolling her eyes. "You'll never have to worry about that with Sam. He adores you."

"I remember how Marley used to talk about her 'good friend' Sam, back before they started dating," Kelly said. "She had such a raging crush on him."

"My son was a changed man after he met Marley," Sam's mom offered. "He always spoke about this friend of his, how funny, cute, and smart she was. I knew, probably before he did, she'd end up being much more than a friend." She turned to Marley. "I've never seen a man so in love, and I'm over the moon it's with you. And now I get to be your mother-in-law!"

"Aww!" Marley exclaimed, taken aback by her comments. She'd always worried, coming from the other side of the SEPTA tracks, his family wouldn't accept her. Not that they'd ever made her feel that way—it was just her own insecurity. She gave his mom a hug. "I'm so honored to be your daughter-in-law."

"If that's the last of the dresses you selected, why don't you try on some of ours?" Marley's mom suggested. "Just for fun."

Although certain none would work, she didn't want to let her mom down.

The first dress, selected by one of her more clothing-adverse cousins, was a bit too revealing. Another, chosen by a middle-aged aunt, was a Victorian nightmare.

When she emerged from the dressing room in the third dress, everyone burst into laughter. It was the exact dress Sam had chosen for their challenge.

"Hideous!" Kelly cried out.

Kate giggled. "I chose that for you as a joke. Let's get a picture and send it to Sammy."

Marley struck a silly pose.

"I should have instilled better fashion sense in him," Sam's mom said, chuckling. "Just don't let him dress your baby girls, Marley."

"He definitely has it when it comes to men's clothing, though," Marley said. Boy couldn't look any hotter in whatever he wore, unless he wore nothing. Marley blushed at the vision of her sexy hubs-to-be, hoping his mom couldn't read her thought bubble. She couldn't wait to see him tonight and do tawdry things with him.

Kate laughed out loud as she read Sam's text response. "'I thought the groom wasn't supposed to see the dress until the wedding day?' Followed by laughing emojis, so *whew*. He knew it was a joke."

Of the dresses left to try on, one in particular caught Marley's eye. It looked similar to her sketch. She pulled the dress from the hanger, wondering who'd selected it. It slid on effortlessly. After adjusting it, she glanced up into the mirror, and her eyes instantly welled with tears. It was a perfect replica of the dress she's sketched—off-the-shoulder with a long train and a scooping back. It made her feel gorgeous. It was everything she'd ever hoped for in her wedding gown.

The collective gasp of her friends and family when she emerged from the dressing room confirmed her belief. She'd found The One.

"My God," Kelly whimpered, clasping her hand over her mouth. "It was made for you."

Marley smiled through her tears as she watched the women passing around the tissue box, each dabbing at their eyes.

"That was the dress I picked out for you," her mom said as tears streamed down her face. "There was a drawing you once did—"

"On the back of a notebook?" Marley asked, in awe she even knew about it.

Her mom nodded as she reached into her bag and pulled

out the notebook. "I found it when I was cleaning out your room after you moved out. I kept it all these years and brought it with me in case it was still what you hoped to find."

"Oh, Mom." Marley wept as she gazed at it.

She turned to Sam's mother. "I drew this the day I realized I was in love with your son, hoping we'd have a future together."

She held it up and pointed to the M+S heart.

There wasn't one dry eye in the room after that. Not even the dress shop staff. The women poured another round of champagne and did a toast as Marley gazed at the vision of beauty in the mirror.

It finally hit her. She was a bride, and she was about to spend the rest of her life with Sam. Her best friend. The beautiful, silly, super-competitive, sexy, Magnum XXL-wearing* love of her life.

$$\mathcal{Cleo}$$

CLEO WAS STILL REELING FROM HER DISCOVERY ABOUT Gus's secret life as she said goodbye to Nigel the following day, promising to join him in Cape May after dinner.

As anxious as she was to get to know Gus's family better, she wasn't sure what to do with the anger she'd been feeling over his lies. She certainly didn't want to show it around his grieving family.

Although...had he really lied? She'd thought he was just joking the few times he referenced being a psych professor at UPenn. Cleo, too thick-headed to give the idea credibility, merely laughed it off, having judged him as the furthest thing from an academic. Some friend she was. She wished she'd

---

* Marley takes the fifth on the accuracy of this statement.

believed him, learned more about him. It had to take a person of amazing skill and reputation to achieve tenure at an Ivy League university.

Now that she knew the truth about his marriage, she saw his bitterness toward relationships in a new light. His had been yanked from him upon the death of his young wife and mother of their only child. Again, if only Cleo had asked questions, probed a bit—cared more—she may have learned the truth from the man himself. She would have loved to hear his tales of teaching. What it was like to raise a child after the death of a spouse. Why he was so adamant that Cleo not tie herself down to someone—until the last couple years of his life, when suddenly he was all "give some guy a chance." Maybe he'd realized he didn't have much time left on this planet and wanted to make sure she didn't end up alone. His constant reminders she was worthy of love had opened her heart to Nigel, who'd come along just in time.

Instead, her relationship with Gus had consisted mostly of dark humor and teasing insults. Whiskey and wit. Secrets.

When she entered the restaurant, Beverly rose to give Cleo a hug and introduced her to the family.

"We've heard so much about you, Cleo," Beverly's husband, James, said as he pulled out her chair. "You made an old man quite happy with your companionship. We thank you for that."

"Living as far away as we all do, the family is grateful to you. Not only for your years of friendship but checking on him and making sure he was okay," Beverly added.

"It was my pleasure," Cleo said.

Whatever she'd expected of Gus's family, she didn't find it. Instead of a sobbing, sorrowful lot, she found a large Irish clan of warm, friendly people with great senses of humor. It was certainly a gathering to celebrate Gus's life, not wallow in grief, as the family members took turns roasting the old man and telling stories about his impact on them. Cleo found herself crying with cathartic laughter.

"To Cleo," Gus's nephew Mike suddenly said, taking her by surprise as he raised his glass.

Everyone followed suit. Cleo's cheeks flushed with embarrassment.

"You stayed by our uncle's side in his time of need, stepping in when we couldn't. You deserve everything he's left you."

"Mike!" Beverly exclaimed, laughing nervously. "I thought we were going to be more formal with our presentation?" She turned to Cleo. "We have some news to share. Uncle Gus had a long time to think about what he'd do with his estate prior to his passing."

Cleo laughed, certain she was pulling her leg. Estate? The man barely had two nickels to his name, living in a dingy apartment in a shitty section of town. What could he have bequeathed—his ratty old BarcaLounger?

"Uncle Gus didn't appear to have money, we know." Beverly smiled upon seeing Cleo's reaction. "That was by design. As a psych professor and consummate student of human behavior, he made a point of living 'where the people lived,' as he put it. He grew up on that same street, never wanting to leave, despite being able to afford a much nicer place."

"*Much* nicer," Mike added.

Cleo, incredulous, raised an eyebrow. "This is *my* Gus you're talking about?"

"The same." Mike shrugged in obvious agreement of the preposterousness.

"He cared very much for you, Cleo," Beverly went on. "As I said yesterday, he saw you as his own daughter. As much as you looked out for him, he looked out for you as well. Which is why he's left you a token of his appreciation." Beverly glanced at Mike, a gleam in her eye. "Of *our* appreciation. He spoke to us about it months ago, and we wholeheartedly agreed."

Cleo tried to keep the smile from spreading across her face. That son of a bitch probably left her that mangy cat. It would be his parting practical joke on her. Or maybe his collection of vintage Phillies bobblehead dolls that nodded maniacally as she walked by the shelf where they'd collected dust for years. Or his tattered Eagles cap, which he wore every night as he perched on his stool at Murphy's, the one she threatened to burn when he left this earth.

"It represents a small portion of his overall estate. He hoped you'd put it to good use."

"In fact, he left explicit instructions on how you must use it," Mike said. "I helped him with the language in his will." He pulled an envelope from the breast pocket of his designer suit jacket.

She opened it with suspicion, glancing between the smiling siblings. This was some level of formality for a practical joke.

Except it wasn't a joke. It was a letter.

My dearest Cleo,

By now you've learned I wasn't completely honest about who I was. It wasn't my intention to mislead you, I just wanted to live simply and among good, honest people such as yourself. The kind of people I found at Murphy's, the ones who put in a hard day's work and came to the ugliest bar on the East Coast (don't tell Murph I said that) to find escape from the harsh reality of life, but also kinship and compassion. I came for a drink but stayed for the people.

That includes you. Because, among those bunch of drunks, I found this beautiful, sparkling diamond in the rough. My Cleo. A brilliant young woman, who, like my dear daughter, is too good for this earth and the people in it. I saw an angel with broken wings, and I made it my mission to repair that damage with love, friendship, and humor. I thought I was going to be the one to teach you how to move forward and leave the past where it belonged. The thing is, I was wrong about you. You weren't broken, you'd simply been thrown off course by the people who should have loved you the most, who instilled in you destructive self-beliefs and, in so doing, had you convinced you were unlovable. Nothing could be further from the truth. In the end, you didn't need my help—you had within you all the strength, resilience, and self-assuredness you need. "Moxie" is truly your middle name.

Turns out, I was the one who needed your help, in a classic case of teacher becoming student. I am forever grateful for the monumental role you played in my life. You were my pal when I was lonely, an inspiration when I was lost, a caregiver when I needed one the most. You've filled my life with your vibrant colors, your outrageous humor, your unique ability to make people feel special. You have and will always be my fam (as you younguns call it), so much like the daughter I lost and the granddaughter I never had.

As such, I'm leaving you a small token of my enormous gratitude for everything you've done for me. I wish for you to use this gift to open your own gallery so you will never again have to work for some schmuck (don't tell Murphy I said that).

And for God's sake, woman, marry that Nigel already. I know I promised not to tell you what to do about him, but now I will. You'll never find a partner who equals all your many strengths, or a man who loves you more. Other than me, of course. Failure to follow this prescription will result in my haunting your skinny ass for the rest of fucking eternity, and if you think I'm joking, try me.

I love you, Moxie, to the Schuylkill River and back.

Yours truly,
Dr. Augustus James Rourke, Psychology Professor (no joke
*   this time)*
A.k.a. your pal
A.k.a....Dad/Granddad

A sobbing Cleo clutched the letter to her chest as the enormous weight of regret descended upon her. She wished she'd given Gus the benefit of her doubt, so she could have known more about him and his life. Hell, known herself better. It isn't every day someone befriends a psychologist.

But in the back of her mind, she knew why Gus hadn't pushed the truth. Wise beyond her wildest imagination, he knew she wouldn't open up to him, share the shit she had with him, if she believed his vocation would cause him to judge her. Instead, he'd used his knowledge and experience to help her without her knowing it.

Cleo was brought back to the present by Mike clearing his throat.

"This is for you," he said, handing her another envelope.

She opened it and pulled out a check. Her mouth flew open when she saw the amount.

A hundred grand.

"What the *fuck!*" she yelled before she could stop herself.

Everyone laughed.

"I can't," she blurted out, thrusting the check toward Mike, a fresh round of tears pooling in her eyes. "This can't be for me. It's too much."

"It's what he wanted to give you," Beverly said, squeezing her hand. "He—we—feel it's what you deserve after caring for him."

This had to be a huge part of his estate.

"You wouldn't know it to look at him, but our uncle comes from old money."

"Lots of it," Mike said, laughing.

"He said you'd refuse to take this. That you'd worry you were taking something from us," Beverly said. "Rest assured, we've all been well taken care of, and on top of it all, he gifted a large donation to UPenn."

Cleo, still flabbergasted, felt an unexpected wave of joy—of hope—wash over her, sending chills down her spine. The money would be enough to kickstart her dream—to find space in a decent part of the city and give herself a small salary while she built her business. If it was true the old buzzard could speak to her from the grave, he just had.

Cleo hugged Mike and Beverly, thanking them profusely for the generous gift.

"I promise to put this to the use Gus intended," she said.

"Keep us posted so we can visit once you open your gallery," Beverly said.

Your gallery.

The words tingled in her ears as she felt the wave of hope pass through her again. She owed it to Gus and his family—and to herself and Nigel—to make this happen. Nothing would stop them now from reaching their dreams.

Cleo raced to Cape May after dinner, excited to share her news.

"You're not going to believe this," she said, thrusting the letter at Nigel the moment she walked in the door. "You have to read it for yourself."

As he read through it, he teared up. "Wow," he whispered when he got to the end.

Without speaking a word, Cleo laid the check in his hands.

His eyes shot up at her. "Are you kidding me?" he exclaimed, slamming the palm of his hand to his forehead. "Cleo...I'm *literally* without words."

"Me too. I still don't think it's set in. But do you know what this means?"

"You're rich as fuck."

"*We're* rich, Nigel. You can use some to open a restaurant in the city."

Still staring at the letter, he shook his head.

"What do you mean 'no?'" Cleo laughed. "Okay, so after my start-up costs, there probably won't be a whole lot left, but maybe enough—"

Nigel's silence cut her to the core. His eyes slowly rose to meet hers. A tear tumbled down his stubbled cheek. "I can't go back to the city," he whispered, his words barely intelligible.

"What do you mean, you can't go back? We live there, for Christ's sake."

"I mean, I can go back, but...I can't stay."

She was shocked, yet somehow not surprised. Ever since the robbery, she had a feeling this was coming. Still...

"I've...found something else," he continued. "A place for me to start my business."

What? This was news. "Where?"

He paused. "Here. In Cape May."

Cleo was flabbergasted, uncertain how to respond. It was one thing to look immediately outside of the city, but Cape May was three hours away. "When did this happen?"

"Today. I viewed a property and...well, it's exactly what I'm looking for."

"You did this without consulting me?"

"Nothing official's happened yet."

"What about owning a restaurant in the city? What happened to that?"

"My goals have changed. Owning a restaurant is no longer what I'm passionate about. I want to create the food, grow it, build recipes. Work *with* restaurants, not *in* them. Certainly not run them."

"Then find something like that in New York! I mean, you can't swing a dead rat without hitting a food service business. I'm sure there's tons of opportunities."

"Not really. Produce is what I'm interested in sourcing. I need to be in a rural place for that. I've also dreamed of owning my own winery, but Manhattan doesn't lend itself to grape-growing like Cape May does."

Her heart was racing. "So that's it? You're gonna leave the city? Leave me and move three hours away?"

"Absolutely not you. I'm thinking maybe we can do our own things, you there and me here, but stay together as a couple. Like Frank and Gabriel. They make it work."

Gabriel. Just the mention of his name brought her back to the conversation they'd had at the bar, about how a successful relationship is one where you're free to pursue your dreams without being asked to compromise to the point it's no longer the life you wanted for yourself. The same conversation she and Nigel had had before they joined forces and moved to New York to pursue their individual, yet at the time parallel, dreams. Then, brought together by a roadmap that had them traveling in the same direction. Now, pulled apart by meandering career paths.

"Do you remember how we talked about this before we got together?" Nigel continued. "How we're too young to have someone else derail us from our dreams?"

Cleo grimaced. "Is that what I'm doing? Derailing you from your dreams?"

"No! That's...that's not...what I meant," he stammered. "I used the wrong words."

"But that's how you feel."

He sighed and raked a hand through his moppy strands. "How I feel is that my goals have changed since we first moved here. I simply cannot achieve what I want to achieve for myself living in the city. I've asked you for a compromise, to move to a place where I can start my business, but you won't even consider it."

"Because that scenario allows you to live where you work, but I'm the one who'd have to do all the traveling. Compromise is just another way of saying change my whole life for you."

He threw his hands in the air. "Okay, yeah," he exclaimed in agreement. "You're right. But guess what? We can't afford to do it the other way around."

"What's to say your goals won't change again? Newsflash: I'm not giving up my life to follow you around, hoping you someday figure out what you want to do when you grow up."

He grew quiet. "I know what I want, Cleo. I have grown up, unlike some of us."

"What's that supposed to mean?" she demanded through clenched teeth, blood boiling.

"You're so focused on the here and now, you never stop to think about the future. What's it gonna be? Is your plan to stay in the city forever, living like we're single, struggling to make ends meet just so we can say we're doing what we love to do? Or are we going to map out a future together so we can both achieve our dreams in a reasonable, fiscally responsible way? If anyone has to figure shit out, it's you. Stop being a spendthrift party girl and grow the fuck up already."

"I'm about to be the director of a fucking art gallery in New York City!" she bellowed. "That's not grown-up enough for you?"

What in the fucking fuck.

There was no middle ground for Cleo's extreme version of the fight-or-flight response—it was either fight to the death or bail completely—two classic responses she'd learned at an early age from her parents. She couldn't help it; destructive behavior was in her blood.

"Well, don't let me derail you any longer," she spat. "Go do whatever the hell you want to do, I don't care. But I'm not giving up my dream so you can have yours. Especially now that I have *this*." She waved Gus's check in the air.

Whoever said money is power wasn't kidding. The check may as well have been a sword for all the domination it wielded. And she carried that powerful weapon with her as she stormed away and took off for the city. Alone.

Delaney

TRUE TO HIS NATURE, DALTON HAD SURPRISED DELANEY with a romantic getaway to New York for a long weekend to celebrate the five-year anniversary of rekindling their teenage love affair. He'd made reservations at a swanky new restaurant and arranged for tickets to see the show Delaney had skipped that night after unexpectedly running into Dalton.

They were getting dressed for their night out when Dalton suggested going somewhere nice for a pre-dinner cocktail. Emerging from their hotel, he strode toward a black stretch limo parked out front.

"What are you doing?" Delaney asked.

"Taking you for a drink somewhere nice," he said as he opened the door.

"Oh my God." Delaney giggled. "Always full of surprises."

Dalton gave the driver an address and popped a bottle of champagne. "A toast, to being back where it all began."

She clinked her glass with his and took a sip. "We should try to find that corner where we first ran into each other. I wish I could remember where it was."

"Me too," Dalton said, grinning.

Delaney's heart filled with joy as she recalled that special day five years ago. She'd been in Manhattan for a conference and was heading to a museum one evening when she'd turned a corner and literally bumped into a man. They both immediately jumped back and apologized.

"Oh my gosh," Dalton exclaimed. "Delaney? Are you serious right now?"

Delaney, equally shocked, gazed into the handsome face of her grown-up childhood crush. Her real-life boy next door. "Oh, my! What are the chances, right?"

"Unbelievable."

Gazing at one another, they'd laughed in amazement. They hadn't seen much of each other since they'd broken up the summer before college. They'd been heading off in different directions—Delaney to the Midwest and Dalton to Boston—and she didn't want to start college with a long-distance relationship. It had been heart-wrenching for both of them, but always-practical Delaney reasoned there was no sense in being tied down when they both had their whole lives ahead of them. Throughout college and grad school—which brought her back to Philly but landed Dalton in Chicago—they'd only seen each other at the shore when visits to their respective houses overlapped, which wasn't too often.

But there they stood that day, nearly a decade after their sizzling teenage romance, staring into each other's eyes. If her racing heart and his twinkling eyes were any indication, the sizzle hadn't fizzled.

They quickly caught up, Dalton explaining he worked for an investment firm in Chicago and was on a business trip. Delaney told him about her work in a Philly law firm.

"So...where are you headed now?" he'd asked.

"MOMA."

"Can I walk with you?"

Delaney smiled. "I'd love that."

As they walked to the museum, she felt breathless with anticipation, just like she had when she was seventeen and he showed up unannounced at the Kohr Brothers stand on the boardwalk where she worked to walk her home. It was the first night they'd realized they had feelings for one another after a lifetime of friendship. The first night they kissed, in the lifeguard stand in front of their houses.

When they reached MOMA, Dalton had asked if he could join her. "I've been wanting to visit but haven't had a chance."

"I insist," Delaney said, giddy to have more time with him.

Strolling through the exhibits, Delaney could barely focus on the art. In fact, she wasn't even sure she was in a museum, that's how focused she was on Dalton—the finest piece of art she'd seen in a long time.

"Would it be too forward of me to inquire what you're doing after this?" Dalton asked as they exited the last display. Facing her, he took her hands. "Truth is, I'm really enjoying catching up with you, and I don't want it to end. Are free for dinner?"

"Of course," Delaney said, even though she had a ticket to a Broadway musical—a hot new show called *Hamilton*. Founding Fathers, be damned.

Dalton leaned over and gave her a kiss now, bringing her back to the present. "It was one of the best days of my life, running into you on the streets of New York. It was like we were meant to reconnect at that exact moment of our lives."

"Some would say destiny," Delaney said.

"Some, being Kate?"

Delaney rested her head on his shoulder. "I think I'm Team Kate on this one. We were meant to be together. Destiny knew we weren't gonna make it happen for ourselves, so she presented us with a chance encounter so we could get the ball rolling again."

Dalton cupped her face and kissed her, long and slow. "Thank God for destiny."

A few minutes later, the limo pulled up to a familiar corner where a man stood holding a balloon bouquet bearing the words *Welcome Home*. Another man next to him held a dozen red roses, as a third man strummed a guitar.

"No way!" Delaney exclaimed as she shot him a look. "Is this it? The actual corner?"

"It is, my lady."

Delaney was incredulous, although nothing this man ever did should surprise her.

"As I said, I've never forgotten a detail about our chance meeting that fateful day on this random corner," he said as he helped her from the limo.

The man with the guitar began singing an acoustic version of "On the Way to Cape May." Their song, the one Dalton had arranged a singing flash mob to serenade her with on their wedding day.

Suddenly, he was on one knee, holding open a ring box.

"Delaney Brooks, you are the love of my life. I never should have let you go back when we were teens, but I'm elated that destiny brought us together on this very corner. Will you accept this anniversary ring as a token of my lifelong passion, friendship, and love for you?"

Delaney blinked through tears to see a sparkling ruby, her favorite gemstone, shaped like a heart, set on a simple gold band. "I will," she said as the guitarist began playing their first wedding dance song.

Dalton slid the ring on her finger and swept her into an embrace, swaying to the music. And there they danced, on the very corner where their lifelong love affair had reignited.

After dinner and the show, Dalton turned down the lights of their hotel room and put on a playlist of songs he'd made for her on their first anniversary. He led her to the window overlooking Times Square, where he danced with her again, this time basked in the glow of Manhattan lights.

"Love of my life," he whispered as he nuzzled her neck.

Woozy from drinks and romance, Delaney's heart fluttered over the undeniable love this beautiful man showed her every day.

He swooped her up and carried her to the bed, kissing her tenderly, then with mounting passion. "You rock my world."

And then he proceeded to rock hers. Twice.

Cleo

TWO DAYS AFTER THEIR FIGHT, COOLER HEADS FINALLY prevailed. Cleo and Nigel migrated from their respective corners of the ring to discuss their situation.

Pulling her into a hug, Nigel held her for a long time before he spoke. "I'm sorry for saying you were derailing me from my dreams. I want both of us to achieve our goals."

"Me too," she said, humbled by his apology.

They stood silently facing one another. Cleo wasn't sure how they would resolve the situation but was relieved they were back to talking. A step in the right direction, hopefully.

"Anyway, I guess we have to talk this out, but...what time are we meeting for brunch?" Nigel asked.

"Noon. We better head out."

Delaney and Dalton were in town for a brief visit, and they'd made plans to meet up before they headed back to London. Cleo was thankful for the outing, as it gave her and Nigel a reason to step away from the battleground and focus on something else instead.

They met up in the restaurant. After a round of hugs, Cleo turned to Delaney. "Got kids yet?" she teased.

"Zero, and not counting," Delaney said.

It was their inside joke—Cleo guessing Delaney was

pregnant every time she saw her, knowing one of these times she'd be right.

"How 'bout you guys?" Dalton asked. "Any plans for a wedding soon?"

"Hell no," Cleo said.

While Cleo often joked about wanting to avoid the trappings of marriage, she usually said it in a more jovial way. She felt bad after seeing the look on Nigel's face, so she tried to make light of it. "I'm still looking to trade up."

"Me too," Nigel said, straight-faced, not missing a beat. In fact, he was so deadpan, Cleo wondered if he was serious. "Statistics show women outnumber men in this city. I'd be a bloody fool not to keep my options open."

The tension swirling around them was palpable. She hoped their friends didn't notice.

Once they were seated, a waitress approached their table. She gave Delaney a big smile as she poured coffee. "I see you brought friends this time. Good to see you again."

"Oh." Delaney chuckled. "This is actually my first time here."

She squinted at her. "Weren't you here yesterday with your daughter?"

"Not me. I don't have a daughter."

"Yet," Cleo added.

Delaney glared at her.

After the waitress took their order, Delaney patted her hand. "You hanging in there?"

They hadn't spoken since Gus's funeral. Knowing they'd be meeting up today, Cleo had decided to wait and share her big news in person.

"Well, there's a lot to catch you up on, actually..."

She told them about Gus's secret past and the inheritance he'd left her.

"Cleo, that's amazing," Delaney exclaimed. "How about you, Nigel? I bet this will help jumpstart both your goals."

Cleo smacked her lips together and gazed at her lap as Nigel, coughing, waved for the server.

"More coffee, please?" he indicated with his raised cup. Changing the subject, he asked, "How was the show last night?"

Delaney looked from Cleo to Nigel. She must have sensed their tension, but Cleo wasn't about to get into it right now. This conversation was better left for a wine night between the BFFs over Zoom.

October

<h1 style="text-align:center">Marley</h1>

MARLEY AND SAM BARELY MANAGED TO SQUEAK BY October's challenge—making centerpieces with produce from a local market. They'd been proud of their pineapple-leek-eggplant-inspired conglomeration, until they saw Andy and Olivia had carved roses from apples, securing their place as clear frontrunners.

"We suck," Sam announced. Fortunately, another uninspired couple was sent home.

On their way out of the studio, Sam and Marley congratulated their triumphant competitors, as Olivia rested her hand on her pregnant belly.

"When's your due date?" Marley asked.

"April first," Olivia said, laughing. "Hopefully, this little guy won't be a fool."

"If so, he'll just join the other three fools," Andy said, rolling his eyes.

Marley shook her head. "I can't believe you're about to have four kids under four."

"Don't remind me," Andy said. "All boys."

"This one too?" Sam asked, pointing at her belly. Marley was relieved he knew better than to touch it.

"Yep. Which means we're looking for a new house. Our duplex is already too small."

Marley asked what neighborhoods they were considering.

"The cheapest we can find. I don't know how people afford single-family homes," Andy said. "Even the side-by-sides are out of our price range."

"Did you hear that?" Sam whispered after they walked away. "He's playing the poor card so we'll feel badly about beating them."

"I do feel badly about it. They need that money more than we do."

"Except we need it for the Cape May house."

"First world problems," Marley said, grimacing. "I feel awful going after this money."

Sam shook his head. "You're a much better person than I am."

"Don't be a competitive ass. We should throw the last challenge. Let them win."

"Mar, I can't hold back. Put me in a competition, and I'm in it to the death."

"No shit, Cutthroat Curtis."

He didn't have to tell her, the way he'd fan his Monopoly money in her face, laughing maniacally when she'd land on a Sam-owned Boardwalk crowded with hotels. How he'd proclaim they were racing to the corner when he was already halfway there, or *in your face* her when he won a friendly (or so she thought) game of Uno. Competitive juices flowed more readily through Sam's veins than actual blood.

"Just promise me you'll think about it before the next challenge," Marley said.

"Okay, I will." And then he held up two sets of crossed fingers. "Not."

Delaney

THEY APPEARED SO QUICKLY. THERE WAS NO MISTAKING it this time.

Two pink lines on a plastic strip, and suddenly Delaney's entire life changed.

She stared at the pregnancy test, trying to calculate how

far along she was. It had to have happened during their New York trip, as she had been so swept up after they'd returned from the show and danced under the stars before making love that she'd forgotten to take her pill again.

It wasn't the news she was hoping for, but the longer she sat and stared, the more she felt a stirring within her. A tiny spark of joy ignited in her belly, starting as a tiny trickle, rising up and toppling from her in giggles.

Ready or not, motherhood was upon her.

The joy soon turned to nausea. Was morning sickness possible at this early stage? By her calculations, she was probably around four weeks pregnant, too soon to even think about telling anyone. Except Dalton, of course. She smiled, anticipating his reaction, knowing how badly he'd been wanting to start a family. Elated wouldn't begin to describe it.

She had to find a creative way to tell him. She guesstimated she had thirty minutes to come up with a plan before he returned from the grocery store. Searching for inspiration in the kitchen, her sweeping glance rested on a plate of fortune cookies from the previous night's takeout. Perfect.

With the precision of a skilled surgeon, Delaney used a needle to extract the tiny strip of paper through a gap in the cookie's seam. She wrote a message on an equally small strip of paper and carefully inserted it back inside. She'd just have to remember which one it was.

After Dalton returned and they put away the groceries, Delaney offered him the cookie.

"No thanks. I was just thinking I need to cut down on carbs."

Damn.

"Come on. Just one. These cookies don't have many carbs."

A total lie, but she had to get him to bite. Literally.

"Maybe after lunch," he said.

She didn't want to act too suspicious, so she bided her

time. By the time they'd finished eating, she was practically bursting from the news.

"Here," she said, hoping he'd play along.

"I'm too full," he said. "You have it."

"You're no fun," she said.

She needed a Plan B.

"How 'bout we just do it for the messages? I feel like good fortune awaits," she said, hoping that would do the trick. "Plus, I wouldn't want them sitting here tempting you, oh Carb-less Wonder."

"Okay, but I want this one," he said, grabbing the wrong one.

Oh, geez. Hopefully his child wouldn't prove to be as challenging as he could sometimes be.

"Let's read our messages to ourselves, then switch," she suggested.

Dalton opened the cookie, read the message, and handed it to Delaney.

"'You will live long and prosper,'" she read aloud.

She pretended to read her cookie's message, expressionless, before handing it to him. "Read it aloud." She tried to keep the smile from spreading across her face, knowing the tiny fortune was about to change his entire life.

"'You're gonna make a great dad.'" He furrowed his brow at Delaney. "Why is mine handwritten?"

"Why do you think?"

He stared down at the message. He read it aloud again, then shot her a look. "Did you write this?"

"I did." Delaney nodded, tears welling in her eyes. "You're gonna make a great dad. Starting now."

"Are you serious?"

"As serious as two pink lines on a pregnancy test."

Leaping up from the couch, he screamed, "I'm going to make a great dad!"

"The best dad ever!" she exclaimed, joining in his revelry.

They clasped hands and jumped up and down like they did as kids when the ice cream man came around.

"We're pregnant!" he cried out as he picked her up and spun her around. "We're gonna be parents!"

She delighted in his reaction. Simultaneously laughing and crying, he set her down and cupped her face before giving her a passionate kiss, his lips salty with tears. She was happy she'd set her iPhone to record this precious moment.

"Oh my God. You just made me the happiest man on earth. How far along are you? When is the baby due? When can we tell people?" His questions tumbled out over one another.

Delaney laughed. "Not sure how long, but I'm pretty sure you knocked me up in New York."

"Ooh, why does that sound so sexy?" Dalton said, pulling her in, his voice lowering. "I guess I knocked you up good."

"Nice and good. That was late September, which means the baby should be due in..." Her fingers flew out in rapid succession as she counted the months. "June."

"Oh, my God," Dalton said, eyes wide as he raked his hand through his hair. "That means the next time we go to the beach, we'll be parents!"

"That's right, friend. No more taking just a chair and a book."

"Oh, I can't wait to Seuss the place up!"

Delaney cracked up, recalling Dalton's observation of what he referred to as Dr. Seuss Dads—guys lugging wagons stacked high with every beach accoutrement known to mankind, like the Cat in the Hat's Thinga-ma-jigger.

He laid his hand on her belly and leaned down to kiss it. "Hi, little guy," he said to her stomach. "I can't wait to meet you!" He looked up at Delaney. "How big is he now?"

Delaney cocked an eyebrow. "*She* is probably the size of a poppy seed."

"Oh my gosh. We should name him/her Poppy."

She smiled. "That's actually a really cute name. We should start a list."

"When can we tell everyone?" he asked.

"Let's get it confirmed with a doc first. I'd like to wait three months, just in case."

"Three months! I can't wait that long. I want the whole world to know."

"They will, in good time. It's just that the first trimester is the most vulnerable time in a pregnancy, so I'd rather get beyond that first." She laughed at his crestfallen expression, patting his hand. "Calm down, Daddy-O. We'll get there."

He pulled her hand to his lips and kissed it before embracing her. Then he leaned down to communicate again with his unborn child. "I love you, little poppy seed. I don't care if you're a boy or a girl. But if you're a boy, I'm taking you to every Phillies and Eagles home game. And if you're a girl—"

"You'll take her to every Phillies and Eagles home game."

"Right. I was gonna say that."

Cleo

"I PROMISE, YOU'RE GONNA LOVE THIS PLACE," NIGEL said as he turned the car down a long country lane off one of the Cape's back roads.

"I'm sure I will," Cleo said, sure she wouldn't. She was already getting the heebie-jeebies being in the middle of the boonies, so far away from modern amenities. Would there even be running water out here?

In the weeks that had followed their fight, Nigel proposed a geographical split so they could both pursue their dreams. But Cleo didn't have much faith in long-distance relationships.

What was the point? Two people clinging to one another just to say they were in a relationship?

Yet she agreed to accompany Nigel on this field trip after he explained how special the property was that he'd viewed that day when she was at Gus's service. Situated in a gorgeous rural setting in the middle of the Cape was a farm that sourced the restaurants owned by the men Nigel had met in the bar. The property was on the market after its owner had fallen ill. So far, no one had been interested in the land, largely because it came with the contingency it would continue to source the restaurants.

"It's like a dream come true, Cleo," Nigel explained. "All the stars aligned for me to find something already established, rather than starting from the ground up. It's exactly what I'd hope to build years from now, just waiting for me to come along."

She was mesmerized by the light in his eyes, the smile on his face. He hadn't looked this happy in over a year. She paused, nodding. "Okay then. You have to do it."

"You mean it?" he exclaimed.

"Yes."

"What about us?" he asked softly.

What choice did she have? She wasn't about to stand in the way of him achieving his dream, any more than she wanted him standing in her way. Nor was she interested in joining him full-time in Cape May with her gallery now underway. But she wasn't ready to let him go, either.

She found herself reluctantly agreeing to the long-distance thing, even though she had little faith in the concept. She wasn't sure why, other than she was a physical person who craved touch. Being apart from Nigel would be challenging in that regard. But if she dug deeper, she wondered if the idea of physical separation triggered a fear in her, like when her mom dropped her off at her grandmother's.

Okay, maybe that was too deep. Because, on the other hand, there was something alluring about having the time and space to focus on her business and reconnect with herself, outside of a daily, constantly connected arrangement. Perhaps that's why they'd been fighting a lot lately. Maybe space was just what they needed. The more she thought about it, the more she warmed up to the idea.

As they drove further into the property, Cleo had to admit it was beautiful. More green space than she'd seen in forever. Nigel parked the car next to the farmhouse he'd soon call home. He showed her the greenhouses where he'd grow vegetables and the space where he planned to grow grapes for a future winery. Off to one side was a tiny cottage in disrepair.

"This could be your studio," he said. "I'll fix it up so you can do your art when you're here."

Cleo's heart warmed to hear that, but dismay niggled in the back of her mind. She doubted she'd be here much to "do art." She was already up to her neck in her own business start-up and didn't see herself having a lot of time to get away in the near future.

She kept these thoughts to herself as her gaze swept across the property. It was beautiful. Nigel was lucky to have found it.

As she turned, she almost tripped over Nigel, kneeling before her on one knee.

Oh God. Oh no...

"Marry me," he said, holding up a ring.

Cleo knees buckled beneath her. "What?"

Not the most romantic response to a proposal, but her mind was spinning. This was the last thing she expected.

"Marry me, Cleo," he said, his voice thick with emotion. "I love you so much, and I'm thankful you're giving me the space to follow my dream. My life won't be complete without you in it."

"But...but..." she stammered. "I'm already in it. I'm here—I mean, not *here* here—but I'm still gonna be a part of your life. We don't need to—"

"I want to marry you, so I know we'll stay together." His voice was now firmer.

She felt the strings of commitment tightening around her neck. And just like that, Old Cleo returned. He must have sensed she was waiting just below the surface, ready to reappear. This must be his way of keeping her in his reins.

"We don't have to have a wedding right away," he added. "Or, hell, ever. I just want to know we're staying together through this separation."

"You don't have to do that by—" *Branding me* were the words going through her head. She softened them. "By giving me a ring."

Nigel deflated before her. "Got it," he said, head down as he thrust the ring box back in his pocket and walked away.

"Wait, Nigel! I didn't mean to—"

"To what, Cleo?" He turned back to face her. "Break my heart?"

"I didn't mean we can't be together. I just don't see the need to go...that far."

"*That far?* We've lived together for three years now. We're in love. I thought we were planning a future together. Doesn't this seem like the next step?"

She shuddered at his use of the words *next step*. It reminded her of the days when her friend Tori couldn't wait for the next step in her relationship with her awful ex. As if being in a relationship meant you could never be fine with the status quo, always striving for the next thing. Don't just date, get engaged. Don't just be engaged, get married. Don't just get married, have a kid. Don't just have one...and so on.

"Nigel, I love you. But things happened so fast between us in the beginning, moving to a new city and living with each other two months after we met. And now we come to find, after all this time, we want different things out of life. The only way for me to know whether there's a future for us is to follow our own paths and find out where they lead us as individuals before we put a ring on it. Not the other way around."

"I thought we were on the same page about trying to make the long-distance thing work?"

Cleo was silent for a moment, searching for the right words. She didn't want to hurt him any more than she already had, but marriage was the last thing on her mind right now. The first...her dream. So close to coming true, she could taste it.

"I don't know, Nigel," she said, backpedaling on her earlier resolve. "Can't we just give it a rest and see what happens?"

"A rest?"

"That's not what I meant—"

"Forget it, Cleo. You know what? If a rest is what you want, you got it."

She scoffed. "Are you breaking up with me?"

"I don't have to," he said quietly. "You already did."

Three days later, Cleo stood speechless as Nigel taped up his last box, still in shock over his reaction.

He'd taken a stand. They were done.

She asked him to reconsider.

"Remember how we used to say we shouldn't settle for less than what we want?" he asked. "What I want is a future with you, but you're obviously not ready to commit to that now. Or ever."

"I never said never," she reminded him meekly. "Just not now."

"Well, I know what I want. Whenever you figure it out, let me know." His soulful brown eyes now swept the room. "I guess that's everything."

The clingy part of Cleo, which she never realized she had until she'd started dating Nigel, wanted to scream, *No!* He didn't have everything, because he didn't have her. But the fiercely independent, ambitious part of her told her inner wuss to shut the fuck up.

Humbled by the reality of their impending split, all she could say was, "I still can't believe this is happening."

"Me neither." Nigel hauled his last rolling suitcase to the door.

And with that, Nigel closed the door on their relationship.

Charlotte

"GOOD MORNING, CHARLOTTE," BOB GREETED HER one Monday morning. "I think I've finally found you a business case."

Music to Charlotte's ears. As much as she loved learning new areas of law, she was ready to do something familiar.

"Someone's just purchased the old Hoover farm. The one near Willow Creek Winery."

Charlotte was familiar with the farm—she passed it every day on her morning walk.

"A guy from New York," Bob continued. "Friend of the boys. It's his first business, so I thought he'd do well in your hands."

"What kind of business?" Charlotte asked.

"He'll be taking over the farm-to-table operation for the restaurants, eventually starting a winery. Should be interesting, being a city boy."

An hour later, her new client arrived.

"Nigel Smith," he said, shaking her hand.

She was too charmed by his British accent to think about

hand sanitizer. "Charlotte Drysdale, pleased to meet you. Come sit, tell me all about your new business."

Nigel laughed. "I was hoping you'd tell *me* about it."

She instantly liked him. He wasn't the New York businessman prototype she'd envisioned. He had a cool, laid-back vibe, like he belonged in a boy band. She liked the way his dark eyes twinkled as he explained his business plan. Which was also impressive—he'd clearly done his research and had a firm grasp on business concepts. After explaining the process for setting up a business in New Jersey, she had him fill out forms.

"So, are you from here?" he asked as he finished signing.

"I'm a transplant. Moved here three months ago from Philly."

"My girlfriend's originally from Philadelphia." He shook his head and corrected himself. "Ex, that is."

"I'm sorry to hear that. About the ex part."

"Yeah, it sucks," he said. "So you like living here in Cape May?"

"Love it," she said without hesitation. "I'm sure you will too."

"I already do."

If that was true, why didn't his smile didn't reach his eyes?

Whatever the reason, Charlotte hoped he'd find the same peace she'd found here in this quaint little village by the sea.

Peter kept his promise to meet up with Charlotte monthly for what he called "Favorite Family Recipe Night." Since she'd kicked them off with Grams's lasagna in September, Peter hosted October with a backyard clambake on his dad's property.

After devouring the delectable seafood feast, they settled into Adirondak chairs by a firepit. Conversation flowed easily as they covered a variety of topics—from childhood memories to their current lives.

"I hope you don't mind my asking, but...what's up with you and Jake?" he said.

"What do you mean, what's up?"

"Are you guys dating? I know I asked before, but for some reason, my dad thinks he's your boyfriend."

Charlotte laughed. "No tea to spill here. We're just friends."

"Is there any other special person in your life?"

"No. I'm single as the day is long," she said, borrowing a phrase Jake once used.

Peter nodded, smiling. "I'm glad to hear that."

The gleam in his eye gave her confidence, made her feel flirtatious.

"How about you, Mr. Stevens? Anyone special in your life?"

"No. I haven't had a serious relationship in five years."

"Wow, that's a long time," said Charlotte, the woman who'd never had a serious relationship.

"Yeah, she was really special. I thought she was my person. It was the only time I experienced love at first sight, not to mention crushing heartbreak."

"What happened?"

"We met through work and started dating. Casually, at first. Before I met her, I was pretty much a serial dater. Lots of women, but never getting too close. Until I met her. I was so smitten, I decided I didn't want to be that swinging single anymore. But I didn't want to scare her away either, so I came on soft. Probably too soft, because shortly thereafter, she met a guy who swept her off her feet."

"Ouch."

"Yeah. Good-looking, smooth-talking politician. Not a very nice guy, from what I've heard. Made her quit her career, one she loved and was good at, to cater to his schedule."

Charlotte grimaced. She couldn't imagine someone forcing

her to stop doing what she loved. "I'm sorry it didn't work out. Are they still together?"

"Don't know. We lost touch after she started dating him. He didn't like her having male friends."

"Sounds like a classic narcissist. Is that why you haven't dated anyone recently?"

"You got it," he said. "I know it sounds ridiculous, it being so long ago, but I just haven't met anyone I feel strongly enough about to open up my heart again. I think I'm better off as a professional friend. Plus, the restaurant business keeps me busy, not leaving much time for relationships. At least right now, with a new one opening in months."

Charlotte wondered if he'd said that in warning, so she wouldn't make more of their friendship. So noted. Besides, she was too busy making more of her friendship with Jake.

She'd just received his latest gifts, all ornaments. Two toasting coffee mugs from Columbia, inscribed with each of their names. One from Panama featuring a sunrise over the Pacific and sunset over the Atlantic—apparently, the only place on the planet where that happens in the same day. A fuzzy sloth, her favorite animal, hanging from a branch with one hand, holding a sign with the other that read *Don't Hurry...Be Happy* was from Costa Rica. The ornaments were accompanied by another heartfelt note and Polaroid photos of him in each of the places. She especially loved the one from Costa Rica where he held a real-life sloth. With each gift, she grew more and more fond of him.

"How's the new restaurant coming along?" Charlotte asked, bringing herself back to their conversation.

"Great, now that we have Nigel on board. Pretty pumped about it."

"He seems passionate about the project," Charlotte noted.

"I don't know if he told you, but we're shooting for the second weekend in June for the grand opening of my new restaurant, when we'll announce our partnership with Nigel's farm."

"That sounds wonderful. Don't forget to invite me."

"You'll be the first on our list."

Another first for Charlotte, being the first on anyone's list. For anything.

Cleo

A WEEK LATER, CLEO STILL HADN'T HEARD FROM NIGEL. For some reason, she thought he'd change his mind, come back begging for another chance, suggest something other than all-out marriage to keep them together. But...nothing.

She missed him like hell. Missed everything about him, even the feeling of her butt cheeks hitting the thin, cold band of porcelain in the middle of the night. She found herself tossing off covers—they were suffocating with no one there to steal them. She even threw the toothpaste cap in the trashcan, sick of seeing it consistently attached to the tube.

To keep from being swallowed by sadness, she dove into her gallery opening with gusto. Thanks to Gus's generous gift, she'd secured the same space in Chelsea once intended as ImagineArt's second location. Unlike her former boss, Cleo *was* willing to "crawl up his ass and beg him" to lower his asking price. Especially after he'd divided the space into two, which meant a smaller, cheaper space for Cleo's gallery, but one that would work for her purposes.

Every once in a while, as she curled up with a glass of wine late at night, she'd pull out the sketch she'd made of Gus. The paper, now curled and worn at the ends, went everywhere she did as a constant reminder to stay strong, keep going. Just like a guardian angel would.

But on that night, she was hit with profound sadness as she stared at his picture, feeling his loss. Wondering if he'd be proud of her for making her dream come true.

Or...would he be disappointed she'd let Nigel go in order to achieve it?

She recalled their last conversation, about her getting a WWGD bracelet. Inspired by their talk, and maybe the wine, she opened up her laptop and ordered a customized bracelet with just that inscription. In addition to his picture, it would hopefully be a reminder of the sage advice her old friend had given her over the years and would help guide her decision-making in the future. She goddamn well needed it.

She closed her laptop to keep the tears from flooding her keyboard. Now wasn't the time to get all weepy. She had a business to start, a gallery to run, and a star to reach for.

November

Marley

A ND THEN THERE WERE TWO. MARLEY AND SAM HAD made it to the final round.

"For your last challenge, we're giving you homework," Amanda announced. "Your task is to create a video of your relationship. Think movie trailer, as if your love story is the next romcom. You'll have one month to make it, and our viewing public will have two weeks to vote after we play it. Our ultimate winner will be announced in January. Good luck!"

"Oh, we got this," Sam said under his breath as they left the stage.

Marley wasn't so certain. They'd never made a movie before and had no idea where they'd begin. "I think we're screwed. Isn't Andy an IT guy? He strikes me as the kind of guy who has mad video skills."

"You haven't seen what I got," Sam said, waving her off. "I'll put something together and see what you think."

Marley was happy for Sam's uber-confidence in everything he touched. No one had bothered to tell him about imposter syndrome, that maybe he shouldn't be so self-assured about *absolutely everything*. Then again, that was part of his charm.

As they were leaving the studio, they ran into Amanda. She was red-faced, as if she'd been crying.

"Hey, is everything okay?" Marley asked.

Amanda nodded, a fresh round of tears breaking free. "Yeah, I'm— No. I'm not fine."

"Do you want to talk about it?"

"No," Amanda said, shaking her head vigorously. "It's too humiliating."

"Well, I'm here for you," Marley offered. "Anytime you need to talk. Maybe we can grab that drink we've been talking about."

Amanda gave her a weak smile as she swiped at her tears. "That sounds nice. I'll reach out soon."

Marley and Sam gave her hugs.

As they walked away, Sam whispered, "I wonder what's going on?"

"My money's on something with Eddie," she said under her breath. "Did you notice? He wasn't here today."

"I did notice that."

Two weeks later, Sam announced he was finished with the video and cued it up to show her.

The first shot was of Temple University's campus accompanied by Sam's voiceover.

"Sam Adams had no idea when he walked into his criminal law class that day, just how much his life was about to change."

The video showed Sam walking into the actual room where their criminal law class was held, as two super-imposed heart eyes popped from his head. The camera cut to the seats where Sam, now wearing a curly auburn wig, sat.

"No way!" Marley cracked up as she watched Sam play her.

The music faded so they could hear the dialogue.

"Hi, I'm Sam Adams," Sam-playing-himself said. *"And you're?"*

"Not named after a beer," Sam-playing-Marley responded.

Marley had to admit, his impersonation of her was pretty good.

"You didn't have to play both parts," she said. "I could have acted this out with you."

"This is funnier. Besides, I make a better Marley than you do. No worries...the real you will show up eventually. How do you like the wig, though? Not as nice as your actual hair, but close."

"Love it, RuPaul."

The video continued, showing Sam-playing-himself ap-proaching the library table where they used to study. His voiceover resumed.

"Marley didn't know it at the time, but our boy was crushing on her big time. Fortunately, he'd come up with the brilliant idea to invite her to a study session."

"Where's everyone else?" Sam-playing-Marley asked.

"They'll be here. Tell me, do you have a boyfriend?" Sam-playing-himself asked.

"You're the only man for me."

The voiceover resumed. *"Okay, so maybe this isn't exactly how it happened, but they soon became friends."*

The video then became a montage of photos from their actual lives. The first selfie they'd taken together in their fa-vorite café, toasting with coffee cups. One of Marley studying, unaware Sam was taking a picture. Flanking a snowman they'd built on campus instead of going to class. Scenes of them at parties, dances, on college graduation day. Each photo showed the two becoming closer but still obviously just friends.

Sam's voiceover continued. *"They attended the same law school, and their friendship continued to build."*

The next photos showed them standing outside the law school building, during a moot court competition, and on the beach with friends.

"And then—"

The video shook to the sound of a loud crash.

"She met someone else. Poor Sam was heartbroken, wondering how he'd ever win the woman of his dreams."

Sam walked along the beach, head hung low, Charlie Brown's big head photoshopped over his own.

Marley laughed out loud.

"He had to find a way to win her heart, hoping her boyfriend would go on to greener pastures."

The next photo was of her ex-boyfriend Rick on the cover

of *People* magazine with the headline, "The Most Genuine Bachelor," after he became a national sensation from the reality show.

"You're too much," Marley said, shaking her head in disbelief.

"And then, Sam had an idea."

New footage began playing, showing Marley standing by the water's edge in the distance, staring out at the ocean.

Sam spoke from behind the camera. *"I'm here on our beach in Strathmere,"* he whispered. *"Marley has no idea, but I'm about to tell her I'm in love with her. I've loved her since the moment I met her six years ago. I just hope she feels the same. Wish me luck!"*

Marley, wide-eyed, hit the pause button. "I've never seen this video! Is this for real? The actual day?"

"The actual day," Sam said, smiling. "Right before I talked to you. I'd completely forgotten I'd taken it. I was so nervous."

Marley cupped his face and gave him a slow, passionate kiss. "What an incredible memory you made for us. I had no idea. I'm so happy you did that."

"I just wish I had footage of the good part."

"It's okay," she said, chuckling as she pointed to her head. "It's all in here. And here," she added, hand over heart.

It was the best day of her whole life. She'd just broken up with her boyfriend, Rick, after realizing she was in love with her best friend. She'd gone to the shore, thinking Sam was getting back together with his ex that day. Instead, he was racing to the shore to give his heart to Marley.

She unpaused the video.

The song Sam had written, the one that got them into the contest in the first place, began playing in the background, accompanied by another montage of photos of them as a couple. Dancing at Delaney's wedding, cuddled up before a Christmas tree. Posing on the beach in the Maldives, standing in front of the law firm they'd created.

Marley was crying as another real video began playing—the one taken by Delaney during Sam's surprise proposal. Marley had thought she and her friends were witnessing someone else's engagement, but the couple were actually actors hired by Sam to surprise her. When they turned and began singing Sam's song, the camera panned to show Sam going down on one knee before Marley, giving a beautiful speech before asking if he could "finally marry the hell outta her."

The last photos on Sam's video were of their engagement photo session on the dock at their favorite shore watering hole, the Deauville Inn, on the beach in Strathmere where they rented houses for summers, and the dunes on the Cape near their wedding venue. It ended with their wedding invitation.

Sam's voiceover completed the video. *"From classmates to friends, to partners in love and partners in law. This is the classic story of how two best friends became lovers. A Cape May kind of love. Coming soon, to a beach wedding near you."*

As the video ended, Marley sat there, mouth agape, tears streaming down her face. She was awestruck.

"That is the most beautiful thing I've ever seen," she said. "You're amazing."

She hugged him as he whispered in her ear. "I don't care anymore if we win this thing. I've already won. I got you, for the rest of my life. There's nothing more I need in this world."

Cleo

"HEY," CLEO SAID SOFTLY, TRYING NOT TO SLUR HER words. Three glasses into her wine and suddenly she'd felt the need to drunk dial Nigel. She wanted to hear his British accent, always stronger (and sexier) when he was half-awake. Assuming he was half-awake in bed, not half-pissed in some bar.

"Cleo! Is everything okay?"

"Yeah, it's all good," she said. Lying, of course, because why else would she be calling her ex at two in the morning?

"You scared me. Were you out tonight?"

"Yeah," she lied. She hadn't gone out; she just didn't want him knowing she was drinking alone. Well, not alone exactly—she'd spent the night in with Josh.

A bottle of Josh Cellars rich red blend, that is.

"Everything going well with the gallery?"

"Yeah. Looks like I'm on track to open New Year's Eve. Just in the nick of time." She laughed, because it struck her as hilarious that she'd be hosting her grand opening party mere hours before her self-imposed deadline of year's end. She was crafty that way.

"*Imissyousomuch,*" she slurred.

He paused. "I miss you too," he said, not sounding convincing.

"How's your farm coming along? Meet any hot women lately?"

Wait, what? *Shut up, Josh. You and your tastebud-tingling notes of blackberry and chocolate have no right to speak for me.*

"Farm's great. No women."

Good. "What are you doing for Thanksgiving?"

This was the real purpose for her call. She tried to make it sound inquisitive, not invitational. Cool, not desperate.

Nigel had always wanted to watch the Macy's Thanksgiving Day Parade, and not just on TV. He thought it would be fun to stand among throngs of losers in freezing temps, no bathroom in sight. Cleo had shot down the idea the first time he'd mentioned it.

"I'm not hanging out with a bunch of drunk assholes on Thanksgiving," she'd announced, despite the fact she'd spent years among a bunch of drunk assholes tending bar. And at

Thanksgiving. At times was even one herself.

But now, this year, it seemed like an excellent idea. Could've been Josh talking, but going to a parade actually sounded fun. Especially if it meant spending the weekend with Nigel.

"I've been invited to the Stevenses'," he said.

"Oh. Is that what you wanna do?"

"Why? Shouldn't I?"

She paused. "I dunno."

Suddenly, Josh stopped making sense. Of course, he should go to the Stevens house. What was she thinking? Cleo was relieved she hadn't proposed her preposterous idea, suddenly remembering she'd rather swim across the East River naked than go to a stinking parade.

I really need to stop drinking.

Nigel announced he had to be up early in the morning. After they hung up, she randomly began sobbing. Her tears served as an epiphany: her true heart only came out when someone was strong enough to knock down the guard she'd built to keep from getting hurt, the wall that kept her from getting too close to someone. So far, only a handful of people had been able to knock it down. Gus. Nigel. Now, Josh.

She grabbed her pad and sketched a wine bottle with a heart trapped inside. Across the top, she wrote, *bottled (up) he*art.*

The following day, she picked it up and stared at it, wondering what in the hell Drunken Cleo meant.

She really needed to stop drinking.

Delaney

PREGNANCY HAD NOT BEEN EASY ON DELANEY. NOW AP-proximately nine weeks along, she'd been sick almost every day. She was sad about their decision to wait out the first trimester before telling everyone, wishing she had the comfort of friends and family when she needed it the most. She was counting the days until Christmas when they'd share their big news. Assuming she made it that far. She couldn't wait for her eleven-week ultrasound, which was scheduled right before they'd leave to spend the holidays in the States. If only she could go one day without puking.

"Hey, girl," Dalton called out as he entered the room with her favorite craving, Nando's Peri-Peri Chicken—the hotter the better. It was one of the few foods she could actually tolerate. "Spicy hot chicken for a spicy hot mama," Dalton said, presenting her with the bag. "I still can't believe you can eat this."

"Pregnancy does strange things to a body."

That was another thing. If she wasn't puking, she was ravenously hungry.

"Okay, Poppy, get ready for your crazy meal. Just don't blame Daddy-O," Dalton said to her tiny baby bump. He swore it was starting to become noticeable, but she chalked it up to bloating. And his wishful thinking.

Delaney dug into her meal just as Kate FaceTimed her.

Her sister scrunched her face as Delaney shoved a forkful of chicken into her mouth. "Why are you eating so early?"

Oops. Delaney and Dalton were late eaters, something Kate often teased her about. She had to stave off her inquiry with something plausible. "Big workout this afternoon. Combo late lunch, early dinner."

A lie, but she didn't want Kate getting suspicious.

"Just wanna say, the invite for Thanksgiving is still open."

"I'm sorry we can't make it. Work's a little crazy right now."

More lies. It wasn't her job that kept Delaney from making the transatlantic trip. It was pregnancy sickness and not wanting to be couped up in a plane for seven hours. They'd be heading home for Christmas in a few weeks anyway, when they could finally share their secret with family.

Instead, Delaney and Dalton enjoyed a cozy holiday just the two of them.

Dalton poured Delaney sparkling grape juice and offered a toast. "To us, and our little family," he said. "I'm so thankful for you and Poppy, I can't put it into words."

He didn't have to. He let her know every day.

"I'm thankful for you, sweet boy," she said. "And this delicious meal."

It was a good day, and she was thrilled to be able to eat without feeling sick.

"Wanna start on our Christmas movie watch list?" Dalton asked as they finished doing dishes.

"Sure," she said, picking up her phone. "Let me check my email first, in case someone sent a holiday greeting. Don't wanna be rude."

And that's when she saw it. The email that changed her life.

Charlotte

BY MID-NOVEMBER, MOST OF THE INDOOR RENOVATIONS to Charlotte's cottage had been completed. She returned home one evening to find Peter packing up his tools.

"Well, Ms. Charlotte, this'll be the last time you'll see me here for a while. We're taking a break for the holidays, but we'll be back in January for the final touches."

Charlotte was disappointed she wouldn't be seeing her new friends every day. She'd grown accustomed to coming home at night to find either Owen or Peter, often both, working away. Sometimes Ben and Archie would join them. It felt less lonely having the guys around. She'd often cook dinner for them, or they'd take her to one of their restaurants.

"Got any plans for Thanksgiving?" Peter asked as he washed up.

"Oh, you know me," Charlotte said. "They've been beating down my door for months. Just not sure which invite to accept."

Peter seemed to believe her, but then smiled when he caught her teasing look. "You're funny, Charlotte."

She refrained from adding *looking*, in line with her new strategy to stop putting herself down.

"Well, I'd be honored if, among your many offers, you'd consider mine. Please join me at my parents' house. We'd love to have you."

Charlotte had never spent Thanksgiving with anyone, much less a handsome man. She was delighted, even if it was a sympathy invite for the new girl in town who didn't have anywhere else to go.

"I'd love to attend. Thank you."

"That'll make my mom happy. She's always telling me to bring a date to family gatherings—she's grown tired of my singlehood."

Charlotte was shocked he'd remained single for so long. He was too good-looking and accomplished to still be single. Even with a broken heart.

"Nigel will be joining us too," he added.

"Great. I look forward to seeing him again."

Between Charlotte pining away for her long-distance best

friend, Nigel with a recent breakup, and Peter still nursing a broken heart five years later, Thanksgiving was shaping up to be a gathering of the lonely hearts club. She'd feel right at home.

Cleo

DESPITE VOWING TO NEVER DO IT, CLEO FOUND HERSELF standing along the parade route on Thanksgiving morning. Even without Nigel here, it made her feel closer to him for some reason. It also gave her something to do since she'd otherwise be spending the holiday alone.

She'd arrived before the ass crack of dawn, lucky to find an opening in the crowd. Before long, the pushing and jostling of people around her landed her in the front row. It was an absolute spectacle to see, nothing like how it appeared on TV. The enormity of the balloons floating above her, the vivid colors of the floats and fancy costumes, the synchronized sound of the bands marching by, was like nothing she'd ever witnessed. She reveled in the revelry, gathering inspiration for future art projects.

"Smile at the camera!" someone in the crowd yelled as Cleo looked up to see a float with a camera crew.

Cleo smiled, less for the camera than the funny thought she had—that if anyone she knew could see her now, they'd never fucking believe it.

Charlotte

CHARLOTTE CROSSED THE LAWN TO THE FARMHOUSE with her Thanksgiving offering, a warm pecan pie fresh from the oven. Everyone was gathered around the big screen TV, watching the Macy's Thanksgiving Day Parade.

"Is that still going on?" she asked Peter as he took her coat. "I thought it was a morning thing."

"We recorded it. One of the local school bands is performing. What's your pleasure?"

"Clarinet."

Peter laughed out loud. "I mean, your drink of choice."

"Oh," she said, chuckling as she turned as red as her impending drink order. "I thought you meant what instrument I played in marching band. Well, now you know. And thanks, Cabernet is fine."

"One Cabernet coming up," he said, a twinkle in his eye. "With a clarinet on the side. We're still looking for après-dinner entertainment, so please give it some thought."

"Oh, trust me, you'll be entertained, for sure. As long as the sound of mating barn animals tickles your auditory fancy."

Peter cracked up and told her to make herself at home as he went to hang her coat.

"Hey, Charlotte," someone sounding like a Mayflower passenger greeted her.

She turned to find Nigel. They shook hands, followed by an awkward hug as they laughed, acknowledging there was no need for attorney-client formalities, it being a holiday and all.

"Come sit with me," Nigel said, leading her to the oversized sectional where members of the Stevens family chatted as they enjoyed adult beverages.

"Have you ever been to this parade?" Nigel asked, pointing

at the screen.

She shook her head. "No desire. I heard people urinate in the streets because they can't get to a bathroom."

Nigel almost spit out his beer. "Thanks for the warning. Always wanted to go, myself, but maybe not now."

"Sorry. I'm a little blunt at times."

"No worries. Big fan of brutal honesty, myself. As a matter of fact—" Nigel's eyes darted to the TV. "*Fuck. Me.*"

"But, Nigel, I hardly know you," Charlotte yucked, until she saw the color drain from his face. She followed his gaze to the screen. "What is it?"

"My girlfriend...my ex..." He appeared dumbfounded. "She's...in the crowd."

The camera focused on a group of spectators standing along the parade route. Charlotte instantly recognized the redhead wearing a beret and matching scarf.

"That's my friend Cleo!" she exclaimed, clasping Nigel's hand. "Which one is your girlfriend?"

"Cleo," he whispered.

It took a second for it to register. "Wait. *Cleo* is your *girl*friend?"

The camera swung back to the floats. "Was my girlfriend. You know her?"

"Yes, I know her!"

Charlotte was blown away. The only thing Cleo had shared about her boyfriend was that they lived together, and he was British. There was no way of knowing the man who'd strolled into her office that day was one and the same. Looking at him now, seeing his pained expression, her heart went out to him. And to Cleo—for losing Gus, then Nigel. It was times like this Charlotte was glad she didn't have a significant other to lose.

Speaking of which...her phone buzzed with a call. It was from Jake.

"I have to take this," she said, squeezing Nigel's hand as she got up. "Talk later?"

He nodded and she stepped outside to answer the call.

"Charlotte! It's so good to hear your voice. Happy Thanksgiving!"

She smiled, feeling the same way. "Happy Thanksgiving, Jake. Where are you?"

"French Polynesia," he said. "I've been sailing around these gorgeous islands for a couple weeks now, but the sunshine and crystal blue waters are starting to get to me. I'm ready to come back for some frigid temps."

She laughed, feeling joyful to hear him joke around. It had been too long.

"Have you received all my gifts?"

Had she ever. Jake had kept his promise, sending her a package every week or so with unique ornaments from his stops and corresponding Polaroids of his adventures. He'd sent so many, her tree would have to be a big one this year. Fortunately, her living room had a huge bay window next to the stone fireplace, as if it had been built to showcase a large Christmas tree. She'd started a scrapbook using the Polaroids he'd sent and planned to give it to him when he returned next summer.

"I wasn't kidding about missing cold weather. And other things." His voice took on a softer tone. "I miss ya, girl."

Charlotte's breath caught in her throat. "I miss you too," she said, trying hard not to sound like she had a thing for him.

"Good, because I'll be flying home for Christmas," he announced.

"What?" Charlotte jumped up and down, her face in a silent scream. "Are you *serious*?"

"Yes. I'll arrive on the 23rd."

"What about your boat?"

"I haven't figured out how to make it fly yet, and they won't let me check it, so it's staying here."

She grinned, imagining his white smile set against his tan, handsome face. "Very funny, Captain Brady." She hugged herself to keep warm from November's chilly air, even though the thought of him coming home toasted her from the inside out. "I can't believe you'll be home for the holidays."

"I can't stay away. I really miss my girl."

My girl. Charlotte's heart almost leaped from her chest. She was about to tell him how much she missed *her boy*, but he began laughing.

"My truck, that is."

"Oh," she said, blowing a raspberry. "Of course."

"Did you think I meant something else?" he teased, his voice dropping even lower.

She cleared her throat. "Don't be ridiculous. Of course not. I know how much you love that truck."

Charlotte all but skipped back into the farmhouse after their call. She encountered Nigel in the hallway, who looked as if he'd been crying.

"Hey," she said. "I didn't realize you were Cleo's boyfriend."

"How do you know her?"

She told him how she'd met Cleo through Blinky and Gus. "Small world, right?"

Nigel laughed. "So, you're the one who'd been taking care of Gus's ugly cat?"

"Hey, he's not ugly," Charlotte said in defense of her furry friend. "Well, not that ugly."

"I'm just kidding, although I saw him once and...well. Let's just say he's not winning any calendar contests any time soon."

"Just for that, I'm gonna enter him into one," Charlotte teased. "And I'll put your name down as owner."

Charlotte was pleased to make him laugh. They refreshed their drinks and found a cozy spot in an adjoining sunroom to talk. He told her all about the issues he and Cleo had, how he wanted to move from the city, and how she wanted to stay to open her own gallery.

"Our goals are at complete odds right now," he said. "Shitty timing, all the way around."

"It's tough when our dreams take us in different directions," Charlotte noted, sounding sage. What was she now, some sort of relationship expert? It just sounded like the right thing to say. Yet, she understood. Her dreams had brought her to Cape May right as Jake was leaving to sail the world. She would never have asked him not to go but was happy he was temporarily stepping away from his dream even for a quick visit.

"She's my person, Charlotte. I'm not doing too good without her. I mean, my business start-up is going well, but I just feel...I dunno. Lost without her."

"Have you told her how you're feeling?"

"No," he said, giving a sardonic chuckle. "There's more to it than that." He took a deep breath. "Truth is, I asked her to marry me, and she said no."

"Ouch," Charlotte grimaced. "Is that why you broke up?"

"Yeah. I made a mistake, though. I don't think she saw it coming, and I was a hot-headed fool in the moment, telling her she'd ended our relationship when she said no."

"Oh boy. And you regret that now?"

"Yes and no. I knew going into it she was afraid of commitment, so asking her to marry me like that was bloody stupid. I'd been thinking about it for a while but wasn't planning on doing it until I knew she felt better about the whole idea of marriage. When I had to jump on the opportunity to purchase this land, I let my now-or-never attitude bleed into our relationship. I wanted her to know that, even though I was moving, I wasn't leaving her. She took it as me trying to possess her. I know that sounds weird, but if you knew Cleo—"

Charlotte stifled a giggle. Oh, she knew Cleo alright. While Charlotte wasn't the most perceptive person when it came to human behavior, she knew Cleo wasn't looking for marriage after she heard her joking with Gus about it.

"It sounds like you guys need to talk it out."

Nigel shook his head. "There's no point. She basically said she wanted a break, and I'm trying to honor that, at least until her gallery is up and running. I get it, she wants to focus all her energy on that, and neither one of us has time to commute back and forth. But even though cutting it off has been heartbreaking, I think it would be worse to hang in there with her, knowing she can't commit to us like I'm ready to."

Charlotte didn't know what to say. She felt bad for Nigel.

He apologized for ruining her holiday with his sob story, then hugged her, thanking her for listening. "There's really no solution, but it felt good to talk to someone."

"I'm here for you. Not just as an attorney, but as a friend. Please remember that."

Later, as Charlotte joined everyone around the table, she said a silent thanks to the universe for bringing Jake into her life. If it weren't for that fateful work cruise, she wouldn't be here now, breaking bread with a great group of people. It was the first time she'd spent Thanksgiving with friends. What a far cry from two years ago, when her only dinner date was a mangy cat.

Okay, maybe Nigel was right. Blinky was pretty ugly, with a face only a cat mom could love. But he was all hers, the only man to have ever loved her. Possibly forever.

Cleo

HIS CALL CAME AS CLEO WAS ON THE WAY BACK TO HER apartment.

"Never in a million years would I expect to watch the Macy's parade on TV and see standing you there."

"Wells!" she exclaimed as she stopped dead in her tracks, laughing. Never in a million years would she expect to answer her phone and hear his voice on the other end. Especially on a holiday, and most especially when he was an ex.

She hadn't spoken to him since she'd moved from Philly. It was good to hear his voice.

"How are you doing, girl?"

"I'm good," she said, uncertain whether her breathlessness was the result of walking up miles of subway steps, or the butterflies she felt upon hearing his soothing voice. "How 'bout you?"

"Pretty good, pretty good. Looks like New York's treating you well. I hear from Delaney you've been with a gallery for a couple years now."

"Wells, you're not going to believe this." She paused before delivering her news, knowing how excited he'd be for her. "I'm about to open my own."

"Clee! That's amazing! Okay, that does it. I've been wanting to visit, and now I have to. When's it opening?"

"New Year's Eve."

"Wow. Amazing. I wish I didn't have a party that night or I'd come. Assuming I'd be invited," he added.

"Of course," she said.

"Hey, I'm heading to Connecticut to visit my family for the holidays. I'll be passing right through Penn Station on the 23rd. Any chance you could meet me for a drink?"

"I'd love to," Cleo said.

"Great. I got some big news to share."

Probably his engagement to the bombshell, Sabrina. The one he'd moved on to, after Cleo kicked him by the wayside. They were still dating, last she heard.

Cleo was excited at the prospect of seeing her old friend. They'd had a lot of fun together, until he'd told her he was catching feelings for her. Nigel, who'd come along shortly thereafter, had inspired a totally different reaction from her. In fact, many of her commitment-phobic idiosyncrasies had dissipated upon meeting Nigel—until recently, when they'd reared their ugly heads again.

Which begged the question: if Nigel was truly the one for her, why wasn't she ready for the next step?

December

<h1 style="text-align:center">Charlotte</h1>

"**A**RE YOU SURE YOU CAN HANDLE THIS?" CHARLOTTE asked as she watched Peter drop down on one knee, saw in hand. "It's huge."

"I worked on this Christmas tree farm as a kid," he said, referencing the acres of wooded land situated next to his family's property. He'd borrowed his neighbor's horse-drawn wagon to help Charlotte find The Perfect Tree. "Cutting down Christmas trees is in my blood."

"Wait!" Feeling guilty, she stopped him. "We should thank this tree for giving me its life. I feel like a murderer."

Peter stood and held his hands in prayer. "Dear tree," he began. "Thank you for giving your life for Charlotte, the ax murderer, for her holiday folly. She is a wretched, wicked woman, and my only wish is that I could have saved you. Instead, I shall now put you out of your misery."

Charlotte laughed out loud but couldn't help feeling sad as she watched the tree topple to the side, defeated, as the last threads of its trunk snapped in surrender. She and Peter pulled the nine-foot victim to the waiting wagon, grunting all the way.

"Dear Stevens family," she said as Peter hauled the thick trunk into the wagon. "I shall require a retainer for representing your son in his murder case against this poor tree."

"Very funny," Peter said, clasping her cheeks with his sap-soaked gloves. "That'll be a Franklin."

"A hundred bucks? You don't even own this farm."

He shrugged. "Finder's fee. But it's okay. I'll settle for a lasagna dinner."

Owen, Ben, and Archie met them at the cottage with a tree stand and lights. Together, the group lugged the tree inside and set it up. Peter lit a fire in the fireplace while Owen and Ben unpacked the food they'd picked up from one of the restaurants.

After dinner, the guys helped Charlotte pull Grams's old Christmas decorations from the attic. Together they strung lights and hung the few unbroken ornaments she'd saved. Later, they stood back and admired their work. More like, criticized it.

"Needs more ornaments," Owen said.

"Lots more," Ben added. "Maybe we can pick some up tomorrow. There's a cool Christmas shop in town."

"That's okay. I like it like this," Charlotte lied. She hadn't told the guys about the many ornaments Jake had sent, now totaling close to thirty. She planned to wait for him to come home, hoping they could put them on the tree together. Just two more weeks...

Delaney

"YOU SURE YOU GOT THE GIFTS?" DALTON ASKED HER for the hundredth time that morning as he loaded their luggage into the taxi.

She held up her carry-on. "Got 'em right here."

It was the week before Christmas and they were on their way to Heathrow for their flight to the States, excited to be spending the holidays with family. They planned to stay until mid-January, to allow plenty of time to see everyone.

"Got Poppy?" he teased as he placed his hand on her tiny baby bump.

"Oh, I got Poppy alright" She chuckled. "And extra barf bags, just in case."

Delaney had been feeling much better since her eleven-week ultrasound, the difference between night and day. She wasn't as exhausted, could eat anything she wanted, and hadn't been sick for days. She just hoped it would last throughout their visit. The irony wasn't lost on her—when she'd felt the worst is when she could have used the love and comfort of her family.

Delaney's parents picked them up at the Philly airport to take them to Ocean City, where their adjoined houses provided the perfect setting for the Ross and Brooks families to mix and mingle in holiday cheer. They planned to do their big reveal on Christmas Eve, when both sets of parents and siblings would be in town. Delaney hoped they could keep their secret until then. The person she most worried about was Kate, who saw right through her whenever she tried to keep things from her. Fortunately, Kate and Ryan wouldn't be arriving until the 23rd.

They somehow made it through the first few days without spilling the tea. Delaney was surprised she was able to keep it from her own mom, as they spent a lot of time together shopping, visiting cafés, and hanging out. There was only one time she worried her mom was suspicious.

"Since when do you do decaf tea?" she inquired after their third visit to a café. "I thought caffeine was your lifeline."

"Oh, it's a big thing in London," Delaney lied. "Decaf is the new caffeine. Healthier for your heart."

Thankfully, her mom accepted her zany explanation.

When Kate and Ryan arrived, Delaney tried her best to avoid looking directly at her sister, as if she'd know immediately something was up. She was still able to fit into non-pregnancy clothing, but it was getting tighter, so she opted for two sizes up.

"Hey, sis," Kate said, giving her a hug. "I love your comfy outfit. Is this a London brand?"

"Yeah, you know me...always on the cutting edge of international fashion!"

International pregnancy fashion, that is.

"I can't wait to catch up over a glass of wine," Kate said, looping her arm with Delaney's and leading her to the kitchen.

Shit. It had been so long since she'd had one, she didn't stop to think about drinks. Kate would definitely sense something was up if Delaney wasn't drinking. Fortunately, enough buzz had been created with everyone's arrival, nobody seemed to notice Delaney didn't drink the wine offered her. She caught a break when, after the meal, her mom brought out her famous hot chocolate bar for the family to enjoy as they hunkered around the fireplace and played games.

One more day and she wouldn't have to lie to her family or mask her excitement any longer.

Marley

TO THANK THEIR STAFF FOR THE INCREDIBLE JOBS THEY'D done throughout the year, Marley and Sam decided to close the office Christmas week. They took themselves out to dinner on the night of the 22nd to celebrate their holiday break.

"To us," Sam said, raising his wineglass in a toast. "We totally killed it this year."

He was right. Not only had they grown their firm to a respectable business, but they were getting married in six months. They were also hopeful this was the year they'd own a piece of the shore. They'd scheduled a couple house viewings the following day in Cape May, just to tease themselves with hope over winning the contest and scoring a shore house. Perhaps prematurely, as they still wanted to save more for a down payment, but a few houses had come on the market in their projected price range, and they were anxious to start looking.

They'd just placed their dinner order when Sam's eyes bugged out of his head.

"Jesus," he muttered, staring at something going on behind Marley.

"What?" She swiveled in her seat to see what had him so bothered.

"It's Eddie."

Marley spun back around and thumbed in his direction. "Should we go say hi?"

"He's with a woman who's not Amanda. And he just kissed her."

Marley began to stand to get a better look when Sam grasped her arm.

"You're being obvious."

"I guess this means they broke up," Marley surmised. "Sure didn't take long for him to move on."

Sam grimaced. "Eww."

"What's happening?"

"He's feeding her something. Chicken fingers?"

"Classy. I wonder if it's a first date?" she asked.

"I dunno, Mar. Seems a little too cozy for a first date. Now they're kissing again. I'm wondering if—"

"Eddie was cheating on her?" Marley guessed, stating the obvious.

"Oh, he's heading to the bathroom," Sam announced.

Marley jumped from her chair and tossed her napkin on the table.

"What are you doing?" Sam asked.

"Getting to the bottom of this. Asking for a friend, of course."

Marley sidled up to the bar next to the woman and flagged down the bartender. "I'll have a G and T."

As the bartender turned to make her drink, Marley glanced at the woman. "How are the chicken fingers here?" she asked.

"Pretty good."

"Hey, question. The guy you're with, he looks really familiar. Sorry if I'm being too forward, but is he a local celeb or something?"

Marley waited for her to say no, he was just a regular guy, someone she'd met on Tinder, and it was their first date.

The woman laughed. "You mean Eddie? My husband?"

Charlotte

CHARLOTTE AND NIGEL MET FOR COFFEE ON THE MORNing of the 23rd. She agreed to the business meeting to help pass time while she waited for Jake to arrive in Cape May. After they discussed business, talk turned personal.

"What are you doing for the holidays?" she asked him.

"I'm flying home tonight and returning on the 30th."

"So you'll be back for New Year's Eve?"

"Yeah. I was thinking about going to Times Square for the ball drop, but after your toilet warning, I thought better of it," he joked.

Charlotte laughed. "Yeah, that's supposedly a nightmare too. Actually, I'm having a dinner party. If you don't have plans, I'd love for you to join us."

Nigel's face broke into a smile. "That sounds nice. I appreciate the offer, but I actually do have plans. Cleo's gallery is opening that afternoon, and I'm going to go show my support."

"What a nice gesture," she said. "And maybe an opportunity to open up a much-needed conversation."

"I guess," Nigel said, looking pensive. "Either way, it's a monumental achievement. I couldn't miss it for the world. If she's not happy to see me there, I'll take the first train out and come to your party, if you don't mind me dropping in."

"You always have a place to land. No offense, but I hope not to see you."

"Me as well."

Charlotte was excited to host her new friends in her freshly renovated, decorated-to-the-gills cottage. She couldn't help herself from going a little crazy with holiday décor, making up for all the years she hadn't celebrated the season. She wanted the cottage to look cozy and festive when Jake visited. His Avalon house was being occupied by long-term renters while he was away, so he'd be staying with his family in an Airbnb they'd rented for the holidays. She hoped he'd also want to spend some time at her place.

"I'm famished," Nigel said. "Let me treat you to brunch."

Charlotte hesitated, checking the time. Even if Jake had landed and made the hour-plus drive to the Cape, he probably wouldn't be free right away.

They were perusing the menu when the bell on the café door tinkled.

A blast of arctic air ushered in a swirl of snowflakes along with a dark-haired man and a blonde woman. From her periphery, she saw him rub the snow from his hair as he said something to the woman that made her laugh. Charlotte casually glanced over. When the man's face came into focus, she jolted upright.

It was Jake. And with him, the illustrious Tori.

Tori—the woman who'd been featured heavily on his Insta last year when he was in the Caribbean. The one partially responsible for him going incommunicado from their friendship. The one he insisted was just a friend now.

So why, a year later, were they together here in Cape May?

Charlotte instinctively ducked behind her oversized menu. Nigel shot her a look.

"Long story," she whispered, wishing there were more patrons in the café to obscure her. She didn't want him seeing her here. She wasn't prepared to hear that he and Tori were dating again.

Too late.

"Charlotte?" he called out.

"Fuck," she hissed. It was rare for her to be so crass, but the occasion called for it.

"Look at you!" Jake exclaimed.

She lowered her menu. "Jake!" she feigned surprise as she stood on legs as shaky as her voice. "I didn't know you were home."

"I almost didn't recognize you," he said, grinning as he held her at arm's length. "You look...amazing. How are you?"

He seemed nervous. He pulled her into a hug, but it felt quick and cold, and not just because of his frosty, snow-speckled coat. More like he was hugging his matronly aunt. She felt like she was in a dream with someone she knew but couldn't name. He was acting distant, as if he hadn't just sent her nearly thirty gifts with heartfelt notes from every port he'd visited. Must be for Tori's sake, Charlotte's intuition deduced.

Why? Were they back together?

"Hello, Nigel," Tori said in a chilly tone of her own.

Wait—How did she know Nigel?

"He used to date my friend," Tori explained, her glance darting between Charlotte and Nigel as if to decipher their connection.

Nigel looked like he wanted to dash out of there, but Jake extended his hand.

"I'm Jake, Charlotte's good friend. And you are?"

"Nigel. Also Charlotte's good friend."

Oof. Did he have to load it with innuendo? Even though he probably didn't mean to.

Jake's brow furrowed. "Well, we'll leave you two alone then." He turned to leave.

Really? Charlotte felt whiplashed. They hadn't seen each other for five months, and this is how he was going to act?

Her heart sunk into her snow boots. Not that she expected Jake would come home and profess undying love for her, but she was put off by his strange behavior, not to mention Tori's presence. Were they an item now?

"Thank fuck," Nigel said as they slunk out the door.

"Why are you acting like you've just seen a ghost?" Charlotte asked.

"Tori's one of Cleo's best friends," Nigel said, looking nervous. "She's a great gal, but she tends to gravitate toward drama and gossip. I can see this going right back to Cleo that I'm already on to someone else. I mean, not that I would care, right? Why should I?"

"We're just having lunch," Charlotte said defensively. "But maybe it wouldn't be so bad if it got back to Cleo that you were seen out with a woman. According to the movies, jealousy can go a long way in helping nudge someone's feelings in the right direction."

Nigel gave her a half-smile. "And you say you're not a relationship expert."

"That was just...so weird," Charlotte said as she shook her head, still flummoxed about Jake's behavior.

"Who's Jake to you?"

"He's just—"

Not that into me, apparently.

"—a friend. Returning for the holidays from a world sailing cruise."

"He and Tori must have hooked up along the way," Nigel surmised. "Cleo often gets postcards from her. Apparently, she's dating someone. That must be her new guy."

Suddenly, Charlotte had no appetite.

He regarded her. "Or maybe that's just foolish thinking," he quickly added, as if he could see her heart break. "I mean, what do I know?"

No, Nigel. I'm the fool.

Cleo

CLEO WAS STANDING OUTSIDE PENN STATION WAITING for Wells's arrival when her phone dinged with an incoming text from Tori.

> Hey girl. Made it to Cape May. Ran into Nigel having brunch with a woman. Waah. I guess you guys are already seeing other people :(

> I'm not. But I guess he is.

Cleo's heart sank to her knees. It had been two months since Nigel had knelt before her, asking her to marry him. He'd seemed so serious, so committed. How could he have already moved on to someone new?

Thank God she hadn't accepted his proposal.

Before she had a chance to obsess over Tori's news, Wells emerged from a sea of commuters. She shoved her phone in her pocket and swiped away a tear.

If anyone could lift her spirits, it was Wells. Her old squeeze. At the base of everything that had happened between them was a good friendship. She was thankful their "thing" had ended amicably. It was good to see him.

His blonde hair, still in the same Ivy League cut, was a winter shade darker than when she'd last seen him. His sea green eyes never left hers as he jostled through the crowd, finally grabbing her in a silent embrace, slowly spinning her around.

"God, I've missed you," he whispered as he pulled back to look at her. "You're stunning."

She giggled (yes, giggled!) at his expression. The last time he'd seen her, she had a jet-black pixie cut. Now back to her natural shade, her hair brushed her shoulders in a long, sophisticated bob. She wore a long red coat over black dress pants and a cropped black turtleneck—something a respectable adult would wear. Since moving to New York, she'd retired Old Cleo's wardrobe of mini-skirts and fuck-me-boots, opting instead for slightly boring but more respect-garnering Grown-Ass Women's Wear. She'd even donned a matching beret and scarf. It just seemed very Holiday in New York, and she'd wanted to give less gritty bartender and more Hallmark movie cast member. Not that she'd ever watched one.

She gazed up at him, and memories of their times together flashed through her mind. Bantering at the bar as she served him drinks. Racing to his apartment in Society Hill to get tangled up in Egyptian cotton sheets together. How good he was in bed as he shot her to the moon. Every. Single. Time.

He was even more handsome than she remembered. Great. She was hoping he'd become less attractive—sprout some facial hair or a beer belly—just so she wasn't tempted to go back in time. But here he was, looking fine and fit as ever.

"You're not so bad yourself," she said, punching him in the arm, hoping that would stop her thought process and keep it platonic. She didn't want to go there with him but...

Damn.

"How 'bout that drink?" he said, his eyes twinkling. "The

last train out is in a couple hours. I want to make the most of the time we have together."

They found a pub not far from the station and settled into a booth.

"Cheers to old friends and new beginnings," he said, raising a glass. "I'm so excited to hear all about your gallery."

Cleo filled him in on the details—about Gus's generous gift and how it allowed her to find a small space to get things started. She rattled off all she'd accomplished in a very short time frame, ready to open on the 31st. Not having a significant other in her life had certainly freed up her time, but she didn't share that with him.

"What kind of art will you be featuring? Just your work, or others?"

"A little of both. I'll have a few pieces of my own on display, but I'll mostly feature the art of other female artists who've overcome hardship to get to where they are today. It's kinda the theme of the gallery."

His eyes gleamed. "I'm so happy for you. You've really made your dreams come true."

"Speaking of dreams, what's this big news you have?" she asked. "I'm assuming it involves a wedding?"

He laughed out loud, furrowing his brow in confusion. "Wedding?"

"Yeah. I'm assuming Sabrina is the unlucky girl?"

"Sorry to disappoint," he said, "but you won't be getting a Save the Date anytime soon."

She felt ridiculous. Of course he wouldn't invite Cleo, presumably the last person he'd slept with before he got together with his future wife.

"Because we broke up."

"Oh!" Not what she was expecting to hear. "I'm sorry. That sucks."

Was she sorry?

Girl, get ahold of your damn self. This man here, while fine with a capital F, is no longer yours for consumption.

"I'm not sorry," he said, giving her a look. "It ran its course. How about you and your dude—what's his name? Nelson?"

Cleo smirked. "You know his name's Nigel. And I wouldn't know either because we, too, are...on a break."

"*Mmm,*" Wells said (or was it a moan?) His mouth slid into a suggestive half-smile as he took a slow, sultry sip of his gin martini, licking his lips, never letting his eyes drift from hers. If that wasn't the biggest come-on, she didn't know what was.

"I wish my fam wasn't waiting for me, or I'd be so rude as to ask if I could stay over. Maybe do some of that holiday stuff you always see in the movies."

"Aww, Wells. When did you become such a romantic?"

"Always been one," he said. "You were just too busy using me to notice."

Ouch.

Was that true? Had she been using him back then? She recalled the night he'd told her he was falling for her, and she took off running from his condo like she was being chased by killer bees. Killer bees, commitment—both equally dangerous to a relationship-phobe like Cleo. It was Nigel who tamed her, made her feel like she didn't have to bolt when the L word came into play.

"So, then, what's this big news you have to share?"

He raised his eyebrows and gave her a smile. "I'm running for district attorney."

"Oh my God, Wells. That's great!" Cleo exclaimed. He'd had his eye on the prize for a long time.

They talked about his campaign and shot the shit about other things until he checked the time and announced his train would soon be leaving. She walked him back to the station.

"It's been great seeing you and catching up," she said.

But the best part of their reunion was realizing the grass wasn't always greener on the other side. Maybe Wells didn't leave the seat up or the toothpaste uncapped, but there was more to a relationship than that. More than just lust or ease or thrill of the chase. She wasn't exactly sure what it *was* that made a relationship great, but suspected a lot of it was what she and Nigel had shared.

The thought made her sad.

"Bye, Clee," he said, leaning in to give her a peck on the cheek. With a shake of his head, he added, "Damn. What kind of a fool lets something so good slip away?"

She wondered the same thing as she watched Wells disappear into the crowd. But it wasn't him she was thinking about. It was the sweet man who went down on a knee for her. The one who'd already moved on, according to Tori.

She was the fool for letting someone like Nigel get away.

Waving her past goodbye, she turned to her future. As she rounded the corner to her gallery, she stopped in her tracks. Two men on a lift were affixing a sign above a large picture window. Her sign.

Moxi Art Gallery.

Cleo had decided to keep the "e" off the end to give it a little distinction from the word, even though it's exactly what the gallery would offer to the public. Art created by women like Cleo, who had overcome heartbreak, tragedy, or other life challenges, yet persevered to find the ability to create. She'd gathered similarly situated artists over the past couple years and made it her mission to find others, giving them a safe space to showcase their work along with hers. In the back, she'd created a small studio for artists who had no other place to create, including the teens with whom she volunteered.

The sign, now attached, reflected the sunlight pouring between the buildings as if it were a beacon. All she could think was, *Bring us your tired, your poor...*

As the lift went down, one of the sign-hanging men called out to her.

"You the owner?" he asked.

She nodded, unable to believe the word coming out of her mouth. "Yes."

"Beautiful space you got here. My girlfriend's an artist. Can't wait to bring her once you're open so she can get inspired."

"Please, be my guest," she said as she pulled an invitation from her bag. She carried them around for just these occasions. "I look forward to meeting your girlfriend and seeing you here."

He read the invitation. "New Year's Eve, huh? What a perfect way to end a tough year. You can count on us being there."

The men pulled away in their truck, leaving Cleo standing on the sidewalk gazing up at the sign. A single tear rolled down her cheek as she realized this was it. Her dream had finally come true.

All thanks to Gus. And a side of moxie.

Charlotte

CHARLOTTE COULDN'T HELP BUT CHECK HER PHONE EVery few minutes, hoping for a text from Jake with a plausible explanation for his bizarre behavior earlier that day.

It never came.

Her original plan had been to invite him over that night. She'd purchased an expensive wine, made cookies, and put together a jazzy Christmas playlist for them to enjoy as they decorated the tree and caught up. But when the clock struck ten and she still hadn't heard from him, she gave up hope.

Her suspicions must be factual. Jake and Tori were dating again, and Charlotte had misread every gesture, letter, and gift he'd given her over the past few months.

She was heading to bed, heart heavy, when someone rang her doorbell. Racing to the door, she expected to see an apologetic Jake. But it was Peter instead.

"Beware of geeks bearing gifts," he said as he held a bottle of wine. "For you, my lady. How's your day been?"

"Meh," she said, ushering him in.

"I've had a day myself. Let's indulge."

Relieved for his company, she retrieved two glasses from the cabinet as Peter opened the bottle.

"I heard Jake's back in town for the holidays."

"Yeah, I ran into him in town." She tried to sound nonchalant but didn't pull it off too well, judging by the look Peter gave her as he poured.

"Tomorrow is another day," he said as he handed her a glass. Just as another knock came at the door.

"Are you expecting someone?" he asked.

No, but her racing heart apparently was. She opened the door and, sure enough, there stood Captain Jake Brady in all his glory.

"Hey, Charlotte," he said as he leaned against the doorframe, hands in his pocket, sheepish grin on his face. He looked so handsome—hell, make that sexy—her tongue almost rolled out of her mouth and smacked him in the leg.

"I'm so sorry for—" His eyes darted behind her. "Peter?"

"Welcome home, my man," Peter said as he strode toward Jake, giving him a man hug. "Looks like sailing's been treating you well."

"It has," Jake said, looking from Peter to Charlotte, his eyes finally resting upon the two full glasses of wine. "Sorry if I'm interrupting something."

"Not at all. I was just heading out." Peter gave Charlotte

another knowing look, confirming he'd seen through her woeful attempt at nonchalance.

After he left, Jake turned to her. "Look at you," he sighed as he gave her a hug, this one much longer—and warmer—than the one in the café. There was a teasing tone to his voice as he pulled back. "Two dates in one day? What's become of you, Charlotte?"

"Must be something in the water. I've had to beat them off with sticks," Charlotte said, going along with his joke. "What about you? Looks like you've had no problems picking up international women."

She regretted the words once they left her mouth. She didn't want him thinking she was jealous over Tori. She couldn't let him know she cared.

"Tori's just a friend," he explained.

"Who you brought home for the holidays."

"I didn't bring her anywhere. Her grandmother has a house in Cape May, and she's spending the holidays here."

Somehow that made Charlotte feel better. But still, how did they—

"I ran into her at LAX where I had a stopover. She'd just finished a photo shoot in Hawaii. We were on the same flight to Philly, so we shared an Uber here. My parents' rental doesn't start until later today, so I dropped my bags at her grandmother's. She invited me to lunch, and that's when we saw you guys."

Charlotte was thankful to hear they hadn't originated in the same place, or else she would have reason not to believe his "just friends" assertion. Still...

"You ran out," she reminded him. "What was that all about?"

"Sorry for that," he said, giving her a conciliatory smile. "And for my weirdness. When I saw you with that dude, I thought maybe it was a date or something and didn't want to interrupt."

Charlotte wondered if he'd felt the same snippet of jealousy seeing her with a guy as she felt upon seeing him with Tori. She wanted to assure him Nigel was just a friend but held off, recalling the positive effect jealousy could have. According to the movies.

"Anyway, I wanted to stop by to apologize, and give you a proper greeting."

"Come, sit. Have a drink," Charlotte offered.

"I'd love to, but I have to run."

"So soon?" The words flew out of her mouth without warning.

"Yeah," he said, sighing. He looked genuinely sorry. "My siblings just got into town, and my parents are due a little later—they're flying into Philly after a trip to the Bahamas. I'm heading over to our Airbnb now. I just didn't want today to end without saying a proper hello."

Charlotte nodded, trying not to feel let down. Also wondering where he'd been all day. And with whom.

"I got a call from my renters just after I saw you," he said, as if reading her mind. "They were having problems with the heater, so I spent the day troubleshooting, trying to figure out how to get the house warm."

Okay. She could accept that.

"I'm bummed, too, because I'd hoped to spend the day with you," he continued. "My family's having an early Christmas Eve celebration tomorrow, but I'll be free afterwards, if you'd be up for hanging out."

"That sounds nice."

"Great," he said. "I'll text you when I'm on my way."

After another hug, this one even longer than the first, he let himself out. Charlotte sighed to ward off her sadness. It wasn't the reunion she'd hoped for. But...

As Peter had said, tomorrow was another day.

Marley

MARLEY AND SAM HEADED TO CAPE MAY EARLY THAT morning to do their house tours. Naturally, much of their ride was consumed with talk of Amanda and Married Eddie.

"Do you think Amanda knows?" Sam asked.

"I'm guessing that's why she was crying."

"What if she doesn't know?" he inquired. "We should probably tell her. Right?"

Marley shook her head. "Let's assume she knows, unless we find out otherwise. Then I guess I have to tell her."

"The wife must not watch the show," Sam mused. "Otherwise, she'd have caught Amanda's comments, and instead of being fed chicken fingers, I'm guessing she'd be telling him where to shove 'em."

Before long, they arrived at the first house in North Cape May. It was a little above budget, and while they liked the house, they didn't love it. Which made it easy to walk away, especially since they'd just begun their house search.

The second house, better described as a cute bungalow, was just a little too far from both the town and beaches.

But the third house was another story.

Located on the same street as Delaney and Dalton's house in Cape May Point, and half a block from the beach, the sprawling six-bedroom house featured multiple decks and floor-to-ceiling views. It was much larger than they needed at that point in their lives, but as a bank foreclosure, it was at an attractive price point. It had been renovated by the bank for resale and was in great physical shape, with new appliances, laminate flooring, and a fresh coat of paint throughout. It was like they'd stepped into a gold mine.

"Wow," Marley said as they entered the house. "The pictures don't begin to do this place justice."

As they went from room to room in awed silence. Marley sensed Sam's mounting excitement matching her own. She was trying to keep herself in check, reminding herself they weren't quite ready to be finding "the one," but couldn't help feeling hopeful. It reminded her of their earlier days in college, when she'd met the most fascinating person at a time she wasn't looking, or ready, for romance—but found him nonetheless.

Climbing the stairs to the top-floor living room, they were treated to floor-to-ceiling panoramic views of the dunes and, beyond, the vast sparkling ocean.

Sam spun on his heels and grabbed her face, scaring the bejesus out of her. He peered into her eyes. Her soul.

"Standing here in this space, gazing into your beautiful eyes, all I see is our future. Growing our family here. You and me lugging a wagon to the beach, our four little kids in tow."

"Only four?" she teased.

Back in college, when they were still just friends, they'd talked about how many kids they'd wanted. Sam had insisted he wanted ten.

"And they're all gonna have some variation of 'Sam' in their names," he'd said, sounding serious.

"Okay, George Foreman."

She'd said she wanted four.

"Four, like you've always wanted," he now confirmed. "Two boys, two girls, the perfect fam. I see us teaching them how to surf from the time they can walk. Searching for seashells at sunrise, playing beach games at sunset. You know all those family photos with everyone wearing matching outfits? I can picture one every year and know what each of our kids will look like. Two blonde boys. A little ginger girl. And one with dark hair like your mom."

His words took her breath away. She could see his vision as if it were her own. In fact...

"I know where we'll put our Christmas tree when we come here for the holidays," he continued. "How we'll celebrate birthdays, graduations, our kids' weddings. I see us retiring here, taking beach walks hand in hand as we boast about our grandkids and our hip replacements."

"That's beautiful," she whispered as a tear slid down her cheek.

The visual he painted wasn't far from a dream she'd had years ago. The dream where she realized she was in love with Sam. He was on the beach, playing with two little blonde boys and a toddler girl. Maybe she'd been pregnant with their fourth in the dream, or—

She recalled they'd made love on the beach in her dream, perhaps that's when they'd conceived their fourth. Even though the images had only been conjured in a dream, it gave her chills to think that maybe, just maybe, the dream had been a glimpse into the future Sam had just described.

"I see it all, Marley. And I see it in this house. I feel it in my soul. We're home."

Marley blinked back her tears. "I see it too."

"We've got to make an offer," Sam said as he took his phone from his pocket.

"Are you sure?" Marley asked nervously as she grasped his wrist. "We still have a lot more money to save. We don't even know if we'll win this contest. I think we should think about this..."

Sam wrapped his arms around her. "Trust me, Mar. We'll make it work. I can't pass up the opportunity to make all those dreams of ours come true. Here, in this house."

"Sam, this is crazy..."

He held her by the elbows as he gazed at her once again. "What's crazy is me walking into a college class and seeing the most beautiful woman in the world, a woman who simultaneously took my breath away and rocked my world, knowing she was my person before I even knew her name. Crazy is spending the next six years hiding my mounting feelings for her so I wouldn't scare her away, and now, in 185 days, I'm going to make her my wife. You think I'm not nervous to do this? You don't know nervous until you've driven eighty miles an hour, dodging weekend shore traffic, to tell your best friend you're in love with her and have been since the moment you met her. But that's what you do when something is so right. It may not be the timing we wanted, but we can't pass this up. And I always have my parents' offer of assistance to fall back on if we don't win the contest."

"But I thought we didn't want to—"

She was about to say "rely on his parents' money," but he cut her off.

"I'll swallow my pride and a whole lot more so I can spend my life with you in this house, making love to you, making babies, watching them grow."

Wiping her tears, she gazed up at him. She bit her lip as she stood on the edge uncertainty. It was where she often found herself, afraid to take a risky leap as she weighed all the possible crash landings, while Sam dove in headfirst and figured out the landing later. It was how they both naturally existed. Fortunately, their opposing attitudes toward new adventures had served them well so far.

He thrust his chin out. "Just like I had to have you, I have to make this dream come true. And just like us, I'm not giving up until we make it a reality."

His words stirred up a cocktail of joy, passion, fear. She met the determined gaze of her handsome fiancé, filled with such hunger—for adventure, for love, for the future.

For her.

So palpable, she had no choice but to relent.

"Go for it," she whispered, a fresh tear rolling down her cheek as she stepped off the figurative ledge.

Sam made the call and put in their offer.

Delaney

CHRISTMAS EVE WAS FINALLY UPON THEM. TIME FOR THE big reveal.

It was Dalton's idea to play upon the Seuss theme. The first step was wearing the "Thing One" and "Thing Two" t-shirts they'd purchased—the nicknames the two had earned growing up as summer neighbors.

It wasn't unusual for the daring duo to be banished to their rooms throughout much of their childhood summers after they engaged in shenanigans, like throwing baloney slices off the deck at boardwalk passersby and hiding crab parts in the adults' shoes. The kids loved their nicknames so much that when they spotted shirts in a boardwalk shop bearing the names, they saved their allowances to purchase them. Having outgrown the originals, Dalton found the throwback shirts in adult sizes for this special occasion.

Their family members laughed when they emerged for breakfast that morning.

"Laugh now, but you're all getting one," Delaney joked.

"As long as I'm Thing Twelve," said her brother JJ—or Jordan, as he preferred the family to call him now that he was in college. It was his football jersey number.

Later that evening, Delaney's mom assembled her family-famous Italian pasta bar, along with a salad, garlic bread, and an array of desserts. Jordan had invited his girlfriend, Bella, whose family was also spending the holidays in Ocean

City. Dalton's parents and siblings arrived, and the two families enjoyed the feast.

After dessert, Delaney announced she had gifts.

"Aren't we exchanging them tomorrow?" her mom asked.

"This is just a little something special for immediate fam. Once everyone else gets here tomorrow, it'll be complete bedlam," she said, referencing their Christmas Day tradition, when both sets of extended families gathered for their annual gift exchange.

Delaney handed a box to her parents and a matching one to Dalton's. "Mom, why don't you go first?"

"Oh my God!" her mom cried out upon opening the gift. "Is this what I think it is?" She held up a baby onesie that read, "Thing Three."

"Yes!" Delaney exclaimed, as her tears began flowing. "You're going to be grandparents."

The family erupted in cheers, hugging and congratulating the couple.

Kate began sobbing. "I had a feeling there was something you weren't telling me!"

"When's the baby due?" her dad asked.

"June 25th," Delaney answered.

"So close to your anniversary!" her mom exclaimed, laughing as more tears spilled. "That's amazing!"

"Destiny," Kate whispered.

"But wait, there's something else," Dalton said. "Mom, go ahead and open yours."

"I hope this is a babysitting invitation. I'm free anytime now!" his newly retired mom said.

Dalton laughed. "You may change your mind when you see what it is."

His mom lifted the lid from the box and clasped her hand over her mouth as she broke into sobs.

"What is it?" Delaney's dad asked.

She paused, shaking her head in disbelief, before raising another onesie bearing the words, "Thing Four."

The family leaped to their feet with a roaring cheer, like Eagles fans upon a last-minute game-winning touchdown.

"Twins?" the grandmothers-to-be yelled in unison as they ran to each other and embraced before turning to hug their respective children.

After excitement of the double baby announcement died down, a discussion ensued about whether twins ran in either of their families.

"They do on our side, as you know. Dalton's cousin Amy has identical twin daughters," his mom said.

"The cutest flower girls a bride could ask for," Kate added. "What about our side, Mom?"

Their mother shook her head. "Not that I'm aware of."

"It wouldn't matter anyway, being as I'm adopted," Delaney said, raising an eyebrow at her sister, who should know better than to ask that question.

They both cracked up.

Kate gave her a squeeze. "I always forget we're sisters from another miss and mister."

Delaney smiled, thinking of the other news she had to share with Kate, which would have to wait until later that night. She wanted her sister to be the first to know.

"That was more fun than I thought it would be," Dalton said later that night as they prepared for bed. "I still can't wrap my head around it. Two babies." He shook his head, smiling. "Tell me again...how we gonna do this?"

"We take it one day at a time. That's all we can do," she said. "But if any man is up to being a twin dad, it's you."

"Twin dad. I love that."

After changing into her pajamas, she kissed Dalton on the forehead. "Do you mind if Kate and I have a little late-night girl talk? I'd love to catch up with her before everyone descends upon us tomorrow."

"Not at all, as long as you return with my babies."

"I hope I remember," she teased, before joining Kate at the kitchen table.

Good. They were the only ones still awake.

"Thanks for staying up with me," Delaney said as she took a seat and opened her laptop.

"I'm elated for you," Kate said, her eyes beginning to water again. "I can't believe I'm gonna be an aunt for the first time on my family's side. And not just to one Brooks baby, but two! Will you return to the States to have them?"

"Absolutely," Delaney said. "Not only to have them, but we'll be returning permanently and settling in Cape May. Probably late March, early April at the latest."

She and Dalton had discussed it at length over the past few weeks. Wanting to raise their children near their families, they'd made the decision to pack in London for good.

"Wee!" Kate exclaimed, clapping her hands. "That means I get to be with you for some of this pregnancy. I was starting to feel sad, thinking I'd miss it all!"

"Oh, you'll be there for the best part. Not to mention all the babysitting," Delaney said with a wink. Even though Kate and Ryan lived in DC, Delaney assumed they'd be happy to come north more often for babysitting stints.

"I'm your number one auntie," Kate said, beaming. "Maybe we'll save our pennies and think about looking for a house in Cape May too, so we can be with you guys."

"That would be amazing," Delaney said, clasping her hand. "I couldn't imagine doing this motherhood thing without you close by."

"Maybe Ryan and I should speed up our timeline for parenthood, so our kids can all grow up together, like we did with our cousins. And like Ryan and Jake with Dalton and Alex, who are more like brothers than cousins."

"Yes! I'd love it if our kids could all be around the same age."
She paused before bringing up the next topic.

"There's something I need to show you. Something I haven't told anyone about, even Dalton."

"Wow, this sounds intriguing," Kate said. "Should I be worried?"

"No. At least, I hope not."

Delaney couldn't believe she'd kept not one secret but two—the second from her own husband, no less. It just felt too personal, something she wasn't sure what to do about. She wanted to give herself time to process the news before sharing it with anyone.

Delaney opened her laptop to the email she received on Thanksgiving night and turned it to face Kate.

Dear Delaney -

You don't know me, but my name is Frannie, and I am 10 years old. For my birthday this year, I begged my mom to do 23andMe tests to learn more about our heritage, because my mom is adopted. She hasn't taken her test yet, but they said I was a match with you, and that you may be one of our family members. If you would like to meet me and my mom, please email me...

Kate looked up from the email, eyes wide, voice hushed. "Is she the 'daughter' they said you matched with?"

"It looks that way."

"Delaney, this is huge!" Kate exclaimed. "You could be on the verge of finding your birth family. Have you responded to her?"

"No."

"Why not? This is exciting—I'd be all over it."

Delaney was relieved to see Kate's reaction. She'd been afraid her sister would be jealous for some reason, especially if the girl's mom turned out to be Delaney's biological sibling.

Despite having different birth parents, she and Kate were very close—the only sister each of them had growing up. The only sister Delaney had ever wanted to know.

"She's probably just a cousin or something," Delaney mused. "Right?" She was still in denial about learning she'd matched with someone and didn't want to get her hopes up. For someone who'd never really cared to learn about her birth family, she was simultaneously intrigued and terrified, wanting to know more but not wanting to be let down.

"There's only one way to find out," Kate said.

"I'm nervous." Her eyes met Kate's before voicing what she'd been afraid to consider. "What if the girl's mom is a sister?"

"That'd be even better. Remember how we always wanted another sister? Wished Jordan was a girl?"

Delaney laughed, recalling how, as young teens, they used to paint their much-younger brother's nails and do his hair. He made a cute girl, with his curly blonde locks and big brown eyes. He now made a much cuter boy, judging by how his girlfriend Bella gazed at him with emoji heart eyes.

"I feel blessed to have him, now that I'm older," Kate said. "Plus, if he ends up marrying Bella, we'll finally get that sweet little sister we hoped for."

Delaney placed her hand on Kate's. "You won't be upset if I pursue this?"

"No!" Kate exclaimed, squeezing her sister's hand. "Gosh, Delaney, why would I? I've always hoped you'd learn more about where you came from."

Delaney appreciated Kate's enthusiasm, but still wondered if it was the right thing to do. What if the test was wrong, and it wasn't a match? What if her birth situation was tragic? What if her mom was a drug addict or died during childbirth? Or worse...she was the product of an intact family, but for some reason, they opted to give her, and only her, up? She certainly didn't need to know any of that. Further exploration could create a fresh wound where she'd never had one before.

Charlotte

JAKE TEXTED CHARLOTTE TO LET HER KNOW HE WAS ON his way. She put on her jazzy Christmas playlist and stoked the fire she'd built earlier that day. She set out a tray of cookies in case he hadn't had dessert.

He arrived looking as handsome as ever, wearing the sweater she'd given him last year for Christmas. He laughed when he saw she, too, was wearing his gift from last year, a light pink cashmere sweater. She'd paired it with black leggings, a fashion item she'd never have been caught dead in before, but had become one of her wardrobe staples. Her selection was purposeful; she liked how she looked in them. She noticed his double take and lingering gaze as she turned to hang his coat on the rack, and his shy half-smile as she caught him looking. His cheeks, already crimson from December's frigid air, turned a shade darker as she smiled back at him.

"Did you have a nice dinner with your family?" Charlotte asked.

"If you're asking whether I had a nice takeout with my siblings while my parents' plane was diverted, then yes." He went on to explain that his parents' plane couldn't land in Philly last night as planned. "They've been on standby in Charlotte all day. How's that for coincidence?" he joked. "They're pretty sure they're getting on the next flight to Philly and will be here tonight, so I'll have to leave earlier than expected, unfortunately. I just didn't want to keep you waiting."

"Oh..."

"Or keep *me* waiting," he said, smiling as he clasped his hand with hers. "I'm anxious to finally hang with you and catch up."

She refused to let his anticipated departure detract from the fact that he was here now. Feeling bold, she squeezed his hand and ushered him into the living room, cast in a cozy glow from tree lights and smoldering embers. Perry Como crooned in the background about being home for the holidays as Blinky rubbed up against his leg, marking Jake as his own. Charlotte chuckled, imagining herself doing the same.

"Hey, little man," Jake said as he scooped up the purring cat before turning to Charlotte. "The tree looks great. Did you set it up yourself?"

"The guys helped," Charlotte said.

"Guys?"

"Peter, Ben, and Owen."

"Ah, yes."

She noticed he was checking out the sparse decorations, her cue to bring out his ornaments. "I was waiting for you to come home so you could help me with these."

His face lit up. "I was hoping you'd do that."

"Great minds think alike."

Their hands brushed against one another as they went to lift the same ornament from the box. Laughing, Charlotte pulled back, feeling a decided *zing!*

Jake laughed too. "Sorry for my haste. I've been looking forward to doing this with you. You pick."

As she lifted each ornament from the box, Jake told her more stories about his travels in the countries from which they came. After they hung the last one, he crossed the room to where his jacket hung and pulled a box from his pocket.

"To complete your set, at least for now," he said.

Inside the box were two small glass ornaments—a sailboat and a lighthouse. The Cape May lighthouse, to be exact. On the sailboat, he'd written the name of his boat in tiny letters.

"That day when we sailed to Cape May and climbed the lighthouse was one of the best times I've ever had here," he said.

"This is so sweet." She was elated to hear the day was as special for him as it had been for her. She hung the lighthouse ornament on the tree and handed him the sailboat. "Why don't you do this one?"

Jake hung the boat with its bow facing the lighthouse. "So I'll always remember where my home port is."

Thank God she was sitting, or she might have just passed out right then and there.

They sat on the couch and admired their work. He was so close, his leg was almost touching hers.

"I've been eyeing these up since I got here." As he slid the cookies over, his leg rested against hers, where it stayed.

They chatted away, catching up in the glow of the tree, eating cookies and drinking wine. Jake told her about the many people he'd met over his trip so far, and Charlotte entertained him with stories of her clients, particularly Agatha Krancks.

"You know what's the scariest thing about her?" she asked, getting tipsy from the wine. "She was future me, if I hadn't met you. I was constantly in a state of pissy-ness over everything and everyone. Thank God, you got me off that path."

"How's that?" Jake asked, his tone soft as he rested his arm along the back of the couch, squeezing her shoulder.

"You helped me see the world as a fun place, full of adventure, not as scary as I once saw it. Although," she paused to laugh, "germs continue to exist. I just handle them better."

"You have loosened up quite a bit, and I appreciate you giving me credit, but that was all you, Char."

He squeezed her shoulder again and she felt a jolt travel through her entire being. She wasn't sure if it was his soft touch, or the huskiness in his voice, but she'd never felt such electricity before. She wondered if he felt it too.

Suddenly, Jake looked beyond Charlotte to the picture window. "It's snowing." He gave her a half-smile. "Wanna play?"

She giggled, recalling that January night when she'd cooked dinner for Jake. It had snowed, and they'd ended up outside, making snow angels. At one point, he went to help her up but fell alongside her instead. She couldn't stop recalling that moment, caught up in the intimate gaze of a man who looked at her with what felt like longing. For the first time in her life.

But then he went to the Caribbean and—record scratch—met Tori.

"Let's go enjoy this snowfall. Tropical weather is great, but I really miss winter."

They dressed for warmth and headed out. Charlotte stuck her tongue out to catch a snowflake and caught Jake looking at her. He brushed one off her cheek with his thumb. They crunched through snow down the long driveway, discussing their favorite snow day memories as kids. When Charlotte almost slipped, Jake steadied her. Moments later, she was in the middle of a story when she realized Jake was no longer by her side. She turned, just in time for a snowball to slam into the middle of her chest.

"You're lucky you didn't hit me in the face!" she called out, laughing as she scooped up snow and quickly made it into a ball, racing against time and Jake's snowballing prowess to launch hers. Too late—the next one smacked her in the arm.

"Just for that..." she called out, taking aim at a retreating Jake and nailing him in the leg.

They spent the next couple minutes romping through snow, pummeling each other with snowballs, until Charlotte fell to the ground, spent and out of breath from laughing. Jake trudged toward her and flopped down next to her. They began making snow angels. Charlotte's leggings were completely snow-coated, and her legs were starting to feel numb from the frigid cold, but there was no place else she'd rather be.

Looking up into the snow-lit sky, blanketed in a white cloud cover as it sprinkled its frosty contents on them, she wished the night would never end. They laid there silently for several minutes until Jake rolled over and took her hand, pulling himself to a standing position and hoisting her up with his strong arm—history repeating itself as they ended up face to face, inches apart.

He stared at her like he had that snowy night. Only this time, he didn't look away.

Instinctively, Charlotte bit her bottom lip.

"Charlotte..." he breathed, his voice husky. He linked his gloved fingers through hers and squeezed.

An animalistic instinct took over her entire being, and she leaned into him, hungry with desire, gazing up into his beautiful eyes.

"Kiss me," she tried to say, but it came out more like a moan.

Embarrassed by her raw emotion, she began to pull away, but he yanked her back, his arm snaking around her waist, holding her tightly. Before she knew what was happening, he ran the fingers of his free hand up the back of her neck, his lips slowly descending toward hers. Her heart was beating so hard she wondered if he could feel it vibrating against his chest.

But it wasn't her heart. It was his phone, tucked into the chest pocket of his coat.

He gave a frustrated groan.

"That's probably my sister, texting to say my parents are there." He pulled it out and read the message. "Yup, they're here." He sighed. "I'm so sorry—"

"It's okay," she said, crestfallen. If she had loving parents like his, she'd want to go see them too.

But that near-kiss...was like nothing she'd ever experienced before. Even more so than the first time it almost happened.

He held her hand as they walked back to the cottage. By the time they got to the front door, her teeth were chattering from the cold. And nerves.

He pulled his phone from his pocket again and ordered an Uber.

"Do you want to come in and warm up while you wait?" She bit her lip, hoping he'd say yes. Hoping they could finish what they'd started. Just one kiss, to let her know he was feeling everything she was feeling.

His eyes softened, and his head began to tilt toward hers. He stopped himself, but his heavy-lidded gaze never shifted. "I'd love to, but..." His throatiness drifted off as he consulted his phone. "The Uber's two minutes away."

They stood there caught up in each other's gaze as snowflakes tumbled around them.

Jake reached out and tucked a strand of her hair behind her ear. "I forgot to tell you earlier. I love your hair." He trailed a finger along her cheek. "Such a pretty color on you."

"Thanks," she said, hugging herself to get warm.

Jake rubbed her arms before wrapping his around her.

Two minutes came and went, but no Uber.

"We could go in and get warm..." she whispered into his chest once again,

He hesitated. "I honestly don't know if I can trust myself to do the right thing."

That sent a chill through Charlotte from head to toe, wondering what *not* doing the right thing meant. What it would look like. Feel like.

"What do you mean, the right thing?" she dared to ask, just as a set of headlights appeared at the end of the driveway.

He didn't answer, so she silently filled in the blanks for him. *The right thing for our friendship.*

"Thank you for tonight," he said, giving her a shy smile as he pulled back. "I'm so sorry I have to leave, but my parents..."

"No, I get it," she said, even though there was a part of her that didn't.

He held her hands for a moment before letting go. As he was about to climb into the back seat, he turned to her. "And I also may never leave."

She watched, dumbfounded, as he closed the door behind him and the car pulled away.

There she remained, frozen in space and time. Never in her wildest dreams did she imagine something feeling so good, so right. Even if it was only a *near*-kiss. She couldn't help but play the moment over and over in her mind, her heart soaring with hope and elation that maybe, just maybe, his words that early morning in July meant more than friendship. Perhaps his *I love you* meant more.

Lying in bed that night, Charlotte imagined what it would have felt like to have Jake's soft lips on hers, his tongue probing as their kiss deepened. She'd never been kissed before but had seen enough of it in the movies to have a fairly good understanding of what went on there. Although, in typical Charlotte 1.0 fashion, she could only watch on-screen couples kiss for so long before her thoughts turned to mouth germs and communicable diseases. Then she'd start wondering about the rampant spread of germs among actors who had to kiss through multiple takes, then kiss their significant others. She could only imagine what the CDC stats looked like for all the random diseases the Hollywood crowd inherited from one another.

Banishing concerns of hygiene from her mind, she tried to conjure the image of Jake's lips hovering above hers, the look of passion in his eyes, the way he held his breath. But...

Somehow, her mood had changed.

She recalled the first conversation she ever had with him. It was during her firm's annual work retreat, when Tom Jervis had arranged for a sunset cruise on the boat where

Jake worked. After her coworkers left without her, she and the handsome sailor struck up a conversation. A pretty intimate one at that, considering they'd just met. Before that night, Charlotte had never trusted anyone enough to open up. But open up she did—a wide, gaping hole of raw truth. As had he.

When talk turned to relationships, Jake described himself as being "thirty-one and single as the day is long." Like Charlotte, he'd admitted to being lonely. He'd also shared his big dreams to sail the globe.

"My family doesn't understand why I don't want to settle down. Why I want to see the world, meet new people, experience life. Maybe it's because I just haven't met the right person yet—one who wants to join me on my journey, or causes me to want to stray from it."

It wasn't until later that Charlotte discovered he had a habit of picking the wrong women. She'd noticed they were always beautiful, often blonde, and not anyone she'd have picked out for the guy who'd, over time, become her best friend. The women were nice, but they didn't seem to meet Jake at a level he seemed to be seeking. Jake would then bail—always around the three-month mark—when things got too close.

"Why?" she'd asked once, after he'd broken up with a woman Charlotte had actually liked.

He just shrugged. "No chemistry, I guess."

"Bullshit." She couldn't help but call him out on it. She'd seen the chemistry, up close and in person. "You two were all over each other that time we met for coffee. I was nauseated the entire time."

He chuckled. "Physically, yes, but not in the brain department. Or the heart. Like I told you when we first met, I seem to attract people who want to dwell in the shallows, but the older I get, the deeper I wanna go with someone. You know, beyond the physical stuff."

Charlotte had no earthly idea what he'd been talking about, having never been in a relationship herself. She nodded like some sort of love guru.

"But then you never do go deeper," she'd challenged. "What is it with you and intimacy? Why do you back off?"

He smiled. "Am I that obvious?" He thought for a moment before giving her a look of sheer vulnerability. "Actually…I've never told this to anyone. Promise you won't laugh?"

"I promise."

He paused. "I've always felt like…like I'm somehow lacking in something. Like I'm a fraud. I'm afraid to give my heart to someone and have her discover I'm not worth it."

"Good God, Jake," Charlotte said. She was flabbergasted that someone who appeared so confident, so gorgeous and successful and larger than life on the outside, could feel so small on the inside. "How can you feel like that about yourself when none of it is true?"

"I guess that's one of the reasons this sailing trip means so much to me. I need to do it, to prove to myself I have the physical strength, the mental fortitude, the ability to survive everything Mother Nature—and life—will throw at me. I know that probably sounds ridiculous, but I've kind of made it my benchmark. To learn how to believe in myself. I feel like I need to do that before I let someone else in, or bailing on relationships will be a pattern I repeat forever."

"That's not at all ridiculous," she said, laying her hand on his. "You need to do it to prove it to yourself. I get it. That's why I need to make partner. To prove to myself I'm worth it."

He squeezed her hand. "You do get it."

It was the first time she understood the drive behind his sailing trip.

Charlotte recalled another conversation they'd had back in February. It was after his most recent breakup, which is why she found him sitting on her couch on Valentine's Day, legs propped on her coffee table, a bucket of popcorn between them as they watched old movies. Among them, *Somewhere in Time.*

"Do you ever feel like you've done this before? Lived a life before the current one?" he'd asked.

Charlotte pondered his question for a moment. If she had, it was hopefully better than the one she was living at the time. Alone, with no close relatives, friends she could count on one hand, working her ass off at a law firm that didn't value her, living with a mangy cat in a small duplex in a semi-rough section of Philly. Fun. *Please. Sign me up for this again.*

Before she could answer, he continued. "I'm convinced I'll just know it when I meet my person, like Richard in the movie. Maybe that's what I'm holding out for, an instant feeling of familiarity, because we've been through other lives together. A feeling she can see right through me, through my bullshit, and find something in me I can't see. I know that sounds batshit crazy."

"That's not crazy," Charlotte had assured him.

She'd considered telling him there were times she felt that way about him. She felt an unexplained connection with him that seemed timeless. It went beyond the surface, something even she couldn't understand. She often wondered if he felt the same way.

But she hadn't wanted to be suggestive, so she opted for humor instead.

"I kinda feel the same way, like I'll know it when I see him. In fact..." She lowered her voice. "I think I've already met him."

Jake leaned in. "Who is it?" he asked with a flirtatious whisper.

"Ryan Seacrest."

He laughed out loud. "Okay, I can see it."

Now, as she lay there piecing together remnants of their previous discussions, a feeling of foreboding came upon her. She'd be ill-advised to continue down this path, savoring the near-kiss moment, wondering if his feelings for her were changing. By his own accounts, Jake believed he'd know his person when he met her, which, after two-plus years of platonic friendship, meant Charlotte wasn't it—then, or now. He could say he loved her all he wanted, but she'd be a fool to believe it meant anything more than friendship.

Then again, she could just ask him...

Oh, hell no. She'd never put her heart on the line like that. Nor would she lay burden on their friendship in that way. Putting him on the spot, introducing the idea, wasn't a risk she was willing to take. Because if his honest answer was no...

Charlotte felt her stomach roil at the thought. *Nope! Not gonna do it.*

Rolling over, she bunched her pillow under her head and tried to slam the brakes on this crazy thought train before it derailed her into heartbreak. A single tear rolled down her cheek as she came to terms with the truth. She had to cease and desist with this ridiculousness if she wanted to keep her self-respect and heart intact. And their friendship. The last thing she wanted was to make things weird between them. Even if he did have romantic feelings for her, he could change his mind as he had with the others, suddenly deciding she wasn't it. If he bailed on her after she opened her heart to him, it would destroy their friendship. Destroy her.

She chalked up their near-kiss to the romantic setting—Christmas Eve, hanging ornaments on the tree, cozying up on the couch with cookies and wine, playing in the snow. The last time they'd come that close, they'd been out in the snow, which could only mean one thing.

They should stop hanging out in the snow.

But ah, what a change of heart she had when, two hours later and still wide awake, Jake called.

"Hey."

"Hey."

Silence fell between them. Charlotte snuggled further into her flannel sheets, wondering why he sounded so shy. Maybe she'd been wrong trying to shut down her feelings. Maybe she needed to listen to what the man had to say.

"How are you doing after...you know," he finally said.

"After what?" she asked.

"That whole thing..."

"I have no idea what you're talking about," she teased.

She could hear the smile in his voice. "You're gonna make me say it, aren't you?"

"Yeah," she said, getting sucked down the rabbit hole against her will. This was a pivotal moment in their whatev-ership. Despite her earlier resolve not to go there, the teasing tone of his voice opened up possibilities.

"The almost-kiss?" he asked, sounding tentative.

"Oh," she said, as if she'd just recalled it. "That."

"Yeah, that." His voice now sounded sultry, like he was ready to grab her hand and jump in the hole with her.

"I'm...good. And you?"

"Good," he said, clearing his throat. "I'm just—I don't know."

Yes, you do, Jake. Say it.

Hope flooded her heart, washing away all her carefully placed caution signs.

He sighed. "I'm just sorry about...you know...that whole thing tonight."

She heard the cartoonish *womp-womp* as the tone of conversation turned from ripe with hope to rotten with disappointment.

"No worries," she said, quickly leaping away from the edge of the hole and resetting herself. Once again. She opted for a shield of dismissiveness after hearing he was "sorry" it had happened.

She could not, under any circumstances, let this go any further.

"No. *I'm* sorry we ended up in that situation," she said, taking responsibility for her part. "It won't happen again. I promise."

He paused for a long while before whispering his response. "'Kay."

Delaney

AFTER THE CHRISTMAS GIFT EXCHANGE WITH EXTENDED family members, a celebratory meal, and lots of congratulations over their big news, Delaney had a change of heart about contacting Frannie. While her fears about incorrect test results or tragic birth stories remained, she realized how important family was—regardless of the place they occupied in your life, or for how long. She felt herself growing more and more curious about her origins.

After mulling over Kate's positive response, and feeling the warmth and love of family for the past couple weeks, Delaney had made up her mind. She was going to pursue this.

She stole away to her room and opened her laptop, pressing Reply on the girl's message.

Dear Frannie -

Thank you so much for your email. I hope you're having a great Christmas and got everything you asked for! I'd love to meet you and your mom someday. I live in London now, but I'm in the States until mid-January. Please let me know if you'd like to talk on the phone or meet over FaceTime.

Within minutes, Frannie responded.

Dear Delaney,

Yay! Thank you for getting back to me. I'm having a great Christmas, especially now, because the only thing I wished for was my mom to find out more about her family. We live in Delaware. Where are you staying in the States? I'm sure my mom won't mind if you wanted to stay with us. I can ask her!

Delaney laughed out loud. She liked this kid. But the eagerness of her response gave her pause. Was she ready to do this? It terrified her to jump into things without knowing the result. Once a consummate control freak, she'd only recently allowed life to just happen, thanks to her spontaneous groom and his love for life's little surprises. Like a pregnancy when it wasn't planned. Multiple fetuses when they'd only expected one. She'd come a long way and was learning to roll with the changes.

Finding out about her birth family was another one of those changes. Scary, yes, but the rewards could far outweigh the risks.

She responded:

Dear Frannie,

Thank you for your invitation, but I'm staying with my family in Ocean City for the holidays. What's your mom's name? How old is she?

Two minutes later, Frannie responded.

Her name is Daphne, and she's 32. She's excited to meet you. Maybe we can meet you in Cape May? We take the ferry there a lot.

She was shocked to learn they were the same age. Daphne had to be a cousin.

Delaney sat on this news for a couple days before sharing it with Dalton. It's not that she was trying to keep it from him, she just wanted to determine for herself how she felt about the situation before inviting his opinion.

"That's amazing, Laney," he exclaimed when she told him. "I'm so excited for you. When are you going to meet up with them?"

Delaney shook her head. "Not sure I want to."

As curious as she was to learn more about Daphne, her propensity for control began to sneak back in. She couldn't help it. Her college roommate, a psych major, had suggested her type A tendencies may have resulted from being adopted. Delaney's instinct was to dismiss that diagnosis, although it could be that something happened during her birth or adoption experience that left her feeling out of control, thus the need for her to gain it at any opportunity. But she'd come a long way since her college days, thanks to Kate and her dad, who'd taught her the importance of letting go and being in the moment. Most of all, Dalton had helped her to loosen up in recent years and find joy in the unknown. Despite all that, she wasn't sure she was ready for this surprise of a lifetime.

"I can go with you, if it would help," Dalton offered.

"I think I'm afraid to find out it's some sort of hoax or something."

"Pretty elaborate hoax for a ten-year-old."

"True," Delaney said, chuckling. "I've always been fine not knowing about that part of my life. Safe, almost, not allowing myself to wonder why I was put up for adoption. I love my parents and siblings. This feels like I'd be cheating on them, even though I know that sounds ridiculous."

"I've never gotten the impression your family didn't want you to discover more about yourself. Your dad, in particular, has always encouraged you to do DNA testing to learn about your heritage."

"What if I discover my birth, my very existence, was the result of something horribly tragic? Maybe what's in the past needs to stay in the past."

"The past *will* stay in the past. Nothing you do or discover today will change that. As you've said, you've been blessed with your adoptive family. They're not going away, no matter what secrets your past holds."

Delaney nodded, knowing they'd encourage and support her in any decision she made.

"Besides," he said, laying a hand on her belly, "it may be important to learn about your biological family for the Poppies' sake."

Of course, Dalton was right.

"Okay," Delaney agreed. "But I'd like to tell my fam and gauge their reaction before I make any plans."

Charlotte

CHARLOTTE SPENT CHRISTMAS DAY WITH THE STEVENS family, this time at Ben and Owen's place. Jake called her that night just as she arrived home.

"I feel like I should clarify what I meant when I said I was sorry about last night," Jake said, jumping right into it. "I'm not at all sorry I almost kissed you. What I'm sorry about is—"

Not actually kissing me?

"—making 'us' more complicated. The thing I love the most about our friendship is just how uncomplicated it is."

She wasn't sure what to say to that. So she went with, "Okay."

"I suck at relationships, Charlotte. I know that's not a good excuse, but I don't want to suck at us and fuck everything up."

She sighed. "I understand."

And she did. Spending the day with Owen and Ben, two people so obviously in love with each other, had made her re-assess the slippery slope of her feelings for Jake. Charlotte had witnessed several intimate moments between the couple—the look they gave one another from across the table, snapping dishtowels at each other as they did the dishes. Later, how they gazed lovingly at their son as he opened presents. There was no question they were deeply in love, no obvious feelings of vacillation.

It was the kind of love she wanted for herself. A deep, un-ending connection, one that could withstand the twists and turns life would throw at them. A relationship that would forge on unapologetically and without reservation, mixed sig-nals, false starts. Anything less just wouldn't do.

Jake's buzzing phone last night was just the wake-up call she'd needed. Not only to stop the kiss from happening, but to drive home the reality of his feelings toward her. The fact that he could let an incoming non-urgent text stop a near-kiss in progress (maybe even years in the making) could only mean one thing—he wasn't developing the same feelings for her as she'd been for him. Had it been her phone, she would've tossed it into a snowbank and went for it.

But what would have been the point? Anything more than a friendship simply wasn't plausible between them, given his worldwide travels, expected to last several more months. They'd long ago shared their observations of others' long-distance relationships, mocking the point of it all. A kiss would've just made it, as he said, more complicated. She re-fused to lose his friendship over misplaced feelings.

"I fly back on the 27th. I'd like to see you before I leave," he said, interrupting her thoughts.

She tried not to feel disappointed. She'd assumed he'd be staying through the New Year. But she'd take what she could get, knowing how much she'd miss him when he took off again.

"Not if I see you first," she joked.

His hearty laughter made her smile. This was how they should be interacting—as good friends. Nothing more.

Marley

MARLEY AND SAM WAITED ANXIOUSLY TO HEAR FROM the real estate agent after tendering their offer. Due to the holidays, it took days to hear back. Sam's face was full of hope as he answered the phone, but it didn't take long for it to melt into disappointment. The news, apparently, wasn't good.

"I see," he said quietly. "No, I understand how it works. We'll keep looking."

"Oh no," Marley said as he hung up.

"Someone made an offer an hour before ours and the bank accepted it."

"Why did it take so long for them to let us know?"

Sam shrugged. "The holidays. So much for our Christmas miracle. I loved that house."

Marley's heart broke for Sam. He looked crestfallen.

She wrapped her arms around him. "We'll find one we like just as much, if not more. And then we'll get to work on making the rest of your dreams come true."

Charlotte

ACCORDING TO THE TEXT JAKE HAD JUST SENT, HE WAS on his way to her office to say goodbye. It was all Charlotte could do to refrain from pushing Agatha Krancks out the front door. She didn't want the drop-in client taking up what precious little time she'd have with Jake, but the woman wouldn't shut up.

Her issue this time: Len had put up too many Christmas lights. They were keeping her awake at night. And didn't he know? It was the 26th—time for them to come down.

"I swear, Ms. Charlotte, one of these days I'm gonna kill that man," she was saying.

"Agatha, we can't go killing our neighbors. Unless you mean with kindness. Have you ever given that a thought?"

Agatha narrowed her eyes at Charlotte. "What's that supposed to mean?"

"It means, maybe if you address him kindly when you have an issue, you'll get a better response. You catch more flies with honey than with vinegar."

She should know. It was a lesson Charlotte herself had to learn.

Agatha regarded her with interest. "Go on," she urged.

"If his lights are bothering you, simply ask him to turn them off earlier. Or offer to help take them down. Make it worth his while—tell him you'll give him one of your famous pies if he does so."

"I'm not wasting a pie on him," she said, her eyes darting to something outside the window. "Now who's this fine young man coming up your walk? 'Zat your boyfriend?"

Charlotte peered out to see Jake strolling toward the door, looking fine indeed, in worn jeans and a fleece jacket.

"He's not my boyfriend. Just a friend," she said, willing the butterflies in her belly to cease.

"*Mmm-mmm-mmm*," the old woman emoted, as if he were decadent chocolate. "You're a fool not to make him more."

She ignored that comment as the door burst open and Jake walked in. He did a double take, obviously not expecting anyone else to be there.

"Jake," Charlotte said, "meet Agatha Krancks. Agatha, this is my friend Jake."

"Ooh," Jake said, his eyes twinkling as he gave Charlotte a knowing smile.

"Well, I best be going," Agatha said, heading to the door. "Gonna try some of that honey stuff you speak of." As she passed Jake, she wagged her finger at him. "Ask this girl on a date, already. I don't want her ending up an old hag like me."

As soon as the door closed behind her, the two of them burst out laughing.

"You didn't tell me she was a psychic," Jake teased.

"Hey, I represent that!" she said, giving him a slug. She was happy to see him and relieved their easy banter had replaced their earlier awkwardness.

"I'm kidding, of course. And I'm sorry this has been such a quick visit."

"Yeah, me too." She was disappointed she hadn't seen more of him, but then she recalled a great quote she'd once read: *replace expectations with gratitude, and it changes everything.* He hadn't intended to return for the holidays at all, so she was thankful for the time they did have.

"Got time for a hot chocolate?" she asked.

"Always got time for that," he said.

They went to her cottage, where she put on the kettle and lit the tree lights. A sunbeam poured in from her front window, casting a poignant spotlight on the sailboat orna-ment, a cruel reminder of what was about to transpire.

As they settled on the couch with their cocoa, Jake asked what she was doing New Year's Eve.

"I'm actually hosting a party," she said proudly.

"Look at you, being all sosh and shit," he said. "You've re-ally expanded your horizons, Charlotte. I'm impressed."

As he should be. A few years ago, friendless Charlotte had hated the thought of being social. Now, here she was, hosting a holiday party where she'd be surrounded by good friends.

"Who all is coming?" he asked.

"Just some locals. And the Stevens boys."

"Stevens boys, meaning Owen and Ben?"

Charlotte nodded. "And Peter."

"Of course. Peter." Jake stared at the tree.

Charlotte followed his gaze and noticed the sunbeam had shifted to the lighthouse.

He rested his head on the back of the couch and turned to look at her, clasping her hand. "Be careful there."

"Where? With Peter?"

"Yeah."

"Why?"

He shrugged. "I grew up with him. He was kinda a player back in the day. Maybe he's changed, but...just be careful. I don't want to see you get hurt."

Trust me, buddy. You're the only one with the power to do that.

"Funny, Peter doesn't strike me as a player," she responded, even though he'd referred to his past self as one. "He certainly hasn't tried to play me."

Or maybe she just wasn't play-worthy.

"Good," was all he said.

"Besides, you don't have to worry about me," Charlotte added, tapping him on the chest assuredly with her free hand. "Don't forget, I've got that natural man repellent thing going."

Jake shot her a look—a mixture of guilt, sadness, and something else. She instantly regretted her words.

"I'm joking," she said, even though she wasn't really. "Got plans for New Year's Eve?"

"Meeting up with some sailing mates for a party in Tahiti," he explained, giving her details about the party, as if he felt he needed to account for his whereabouts. Perhaps because they'd spent the past two New Year's Eves together—the first year at Congress Hall's gala with his family, and last year on her couch, flipping back and forth between holiday movies and the ball drop.

After they finished their cocoa, Jake got up to leave. She took their mugs to the sink, turned back and nearly jumped out of her skin. He was standing right behind her. She backed up into the counter, but he wrapped his arms around her shoulders in a bear hug, like a friend would, holding her tightly as he gently swayed back and forth.

"You're making it hard for me to leave," he whispered.

Her tone was hushed. "As I suspected."

"What's that?"

"My cocoa brings all the boys to the yard."

He laughed out loud. "You're not wrong about that."

She had to make a joke; otherwise, she would have grabbed his face and kissed him. Fully, this time. The scent of his aftershave and pheromones acted in concert to almost change her mind about her *just friends* resolve.

She walked him to the door and held his jacket for him as he put it on.

He turned and pulled her into his chest again, wrapping his jacket around her. "How 'bout I shrink you down and take you with me?"

"I'm all in," she said, nuzzling inside his North Face and snaking her arms around his back, her cheek resting on his chest.

He held her like that for a long while. They said nothing, enjoying each other's warm proximity for what would be the last time in months.

He finally broke away. Charlotte could see the tears in his eyes before he quickly swiped at them.

"Alright, enough," he said. "I'll be in touch." Just as he was about to shut the door behind him, he leaned back in. "I meant it when I said I love you, Charlotte."

He didn't have to say the rest of the sentence because she knew what he was thinking.

As a friend.

Cleo

NEW YEAR'S EVE. THE DAY OF THE GALLERY'S GRAND opening. Cleo vacillated between feeling over the moon and under the wheels of a speeding locomotive.

Ready or not, her dream was about to become a reality.

She purposely scheduled the open house from 4:00 to 8:00 p.m. to give invited guests a chance to observe the art and mingle while they enjoyed catered hors d'oeuvres and champagne before heading to their New Year's Eve festivities. She'd invited a hundred or so guests, including former coworkers, artist friends and their families, and a few people from her past. She'd sent an invite to Nigel via text, and he'd responded that he was invited to a party but would try to make it (don't knock yourself out). She presumed he'd be spending the evening with whatever side dish he'd recently been spotted with. Otherwise, the Nigel she knew wouldn't miss it for the world, whether they were together or not. But, in case he did come, she purposely didn't invite Wells, who'd been a sore spot for

Nigel. She didn't want to tempt fate.

She'd also refrained from making plans with anyone after the opening. Knowing she'd be exhausted by gala's end, she wanted to spend the remaining hours of the landmark year by herself, reflecting on where she'd been and where she was going. She planned to pop the bottle of Dom Pérignon she'd stashed away in the small fridge in the back after the last guest left and sit in her darkened gallery to celebrate in her own way. Then she'd head home to watch Ryan Seacrest hype up the Times Square crowd for the impending ball drop.

T minus two minutes. Standing before the mirror in the back of the gallery, she smoothed out the bodice of her simple black cocktail dress. She gazed at the sketch of Gus she'd taped to the mirror just for that night—her reminder he was there with her in spirit.

"This is it, old man," she said to his charcoal rendering. "Thank you for all the gifts you've given me. The humor, the friendship, the money. Most of all, the belief you instilled in me. Thanks to you, I have full faith in myself and my abilities. I've come a long way, baby. At long last."

She gave her reflection a double high five in the mirror. It was go time.

"Let's do this."

Cleo was surprised to see a small crowd already gathering outside and was overwhelmed by the turnout as guests steadily streamed in. The sign-hanging man and his girlfriend were among the first, followed by Gus's niece and nephew and their families.

"I'm so glad you could come," Cleo said as she hugged them, blown away by the fact they'd made the trip to New York for this.

"We're here because he couldn't be," Beverly said, wiping a tear rolling down her cheek. "He'd be so proud of you."

Cleo felt joyful as she wandered through the crowd,

discussing her art and her vision for the gallery.

Thirty minutes later, while talking with a former co-worker, she saw the door open out of the corner of her eye. A familiar dark-haired guy dressed in black entered, taking her breath away.

The British Invasion had arrived.

His chocolate eyes searched the room, finally finding hers. A shy smile spread across his face. Her heart leaped at the sight of him as he made his way through the crowd.

"Cleo, my love," he said, likely out of habit, as he hugged her. "So good to see you."

"You, too, Nigel." She breathed in his woodsy scent and allowed herself to linger just a little longer in his embrace than a friend would. "I wasn't sure you'd come."

"I wouldn't miss it for the world," he said, sounding hella more determined than he had in his text.

She was thrilled he'd made the trip from Cape May for her. Maybe this meant she'd end up with someone to spend the evening with, after all.

"Come, let's get you a drink," she said, leading him to the bar. "What's your fancy?"

"If I say 'you,' would that be too cliché?" he teased. "You look gorgeous tonight."

As he leaned in to kiss her cheek, she felt a zing go straight to her lady parts. His voice was lighthearted and flirtatious, but she heard the underscore in his tone. Despite all the weirdness they'd been through, he still made her feel more desirable than anyone ever had.

"How long are you here for?" she asked.

"That depends."

"On what?"

"On whether you can quit ending your sentences with prepositions." The twinkle in his eye infused her with joy. "I jest. It depends on how long you want me here—assuming you don't have a hot date tonight."

"Who, me?" Cleo teased, hand on heart.

Nigel's brow furrowed as he looked behind her toward the door. His voice suddenly took on a tone she didn't like. "Yeah. You."

She turned to see what he was looking at, but the crowd blocked her view.

"Is something going on with you and Wells?" he asked, eyebrow raised.

"No. Nothing," she protested, because there wasn't. Nigel didn't need to know about his quick visit last week. He'd never been Wells's biggest fan, considering she'd still been embroiled with him when Nigel had first come into the picture. Bringing up the subject of Wells now would only upset the delicate balance between them.

"Then why is he here?"

Sure enough, Wells was making his way toward them.

Shit.

She spun back to Nigel. "I didn't invite him—"

"Right," he said, his jaw tightening.

She felt a hand on her elbow and a kiss on her cheek.

"Hey, beautiful." Followed by, "Oh—Nigel. Nice to see you."

"Wish I could say the same," Nigel said under his breath.

She was surprised by her ex's bitterness. Nigel was normally a happy and upbeat sort of chap, but apparently, Wells still had the power to stoke jealousy in him.

Wells looked like he couldn't decide between suiting up for battle or running from the place like it was on fire. Cleo was about to tell Nigel to cut the shit when one of her featured artists approached.

"Cleo, I'm sorry to bother you, but I'd like to introduce you to someone..."

She was relieved to get away from the dueling dudes as they stood there awkwardly, staring daggers through each other. Hopefully, they'd find some common ground to talk about, and she wouldn't return to find one of them mauled to death by the other.

When she returned, Wells was chatting away with an attractive older woman, and Nigel was off with Beverly and her family. Good. Relieved her two exes seemed to be coexisting in this space, at least for now, she wandered off to talk with some of her artist friends. She wasn't up for boy drama tonight, the biggest night of her life.

Ten minutes later, Nigel approached and told her he was leaving.

"So soon?" she asked, trying to mask her disappointment.

"Got a party to get to in Cape May," he said.

"But what about—"

"About what?"

"You're all 'what are you doing tonight,' but then Wells walks in and your panties get bunched. Is it because of him, or did you just now decide there's something else in Cape May you'd rather do?"

There. It was the perfect out for him to come clean if there was a new woman. But he said nothing.

"Wells is just a friend," she assured him.

Nigel sighed and gave her a sad look. "But I'm not. I can't just be friends with you, Cleo. I thought I could. Hoped I could. But seeing him here tonight..." He shook his head. "I just can't do it. I hope you'll respect that."

She wasn't sure what to say. She didn't want to see him go, but she wasn't about to beg him to stay, especially if he was heading back to some waiting woman.

"Congrats on all this," he said, then headed to the door and slipped out.

Cleo stood there, dumbfounded, as he disappeared into the night.

She turned back to the party in progress, expecting to feel

sad that Nigel was leaving so early. But the sultry notes from the jazz ensemble warmed her as she gave a sweeping glance around the crowded gallery, filled with happy people, there to support her in the space she'd created all by herself. She'd painted the walls, built the displays, designed the layout and lighting. She'd hired the musicians, caterer, and bartender (all friends, who's counting). She'd created a beautiful home for the art she'd created from her heart, hung next to the creations of other enduring women, who, like her, fought an uphill battle to get where they were today. This was a full-blown, classy-as-fuck event in *her* honor.

This was her night, and she wasn't going to let Nigel ruin it with his disappearing act. It was nice enough that he'd come. She'd settle for that for now.

Glancing around the room once more, her eyes met with those of a waiting, worried Wells.

"I'm so sorry if I screwed something up for you guys," he said.

"He's the one who screwed up," Cleo insisted as she snatched a glass of champagne from the tray of a passing server.

"Don't let either one of us ruin your night. You've worked too hard to achieve this. I'll be happy to scram if you don't want me here."

She was grateful Wells got it. Still...

"What *are* you doing here, anyway?"

"I was on my way home from Connecticut, heading to a party in Philly. But as the train pulled into the station, I couldn't help myself—I had to stop in and see how it was going. There's another train at 8:30, I can just catch that one."

"There must be scads of alluring women waiting back in Philly," she teased. "Hoping to kiss the sexy future DA at midnight."

"If there are scads, or even one, I'm completely unaware of it."

Cleo narrowed her eyes at him, trying to ascertain whether he came by his uber-hotness naturally, and without pretense, or whether he knew *Just. How. Fucking. Hot.* he actually was.

"Screw them," she decided. "You're here now, and you've officially become the date I didn't know I needed."

He smiled.

"But I do have a gallery to run, if you don't mind." She took him by the hand. "I want to introduce you to some people, and then I'll make sure you get back to the train station on time."

She introduced him to Daisy and some of her former co-workers, delighting in the coquettish smile Daisy instantly pulled on Wells. He took her hand and kissed it, the ultimate Rico Suave move. She noted the spark in Daisy's eyes, the teasing glance she gave him as she made a trademark bawdy comment, which was met with Wells's own raunchy comeback. It was entertaining, like watching two professional flirts, even if Daisy was old enough to be his great-grandmother.

Cleo couldn't help but feel that familiar pull toward the dashing district attorney-to-be. Not a good sign. The last thing she needed was to get sucked back into their "thing" just when the rest of her life was coming together.

Charlotte

CHARLOTTE DIDN'T THINK IT WAS POSSIBLE, BUT SHE missed Jake even more than the first time he'd left. Thankfully, party preparations helped keep her mind off his absence.

Her New Year's Eve gathering turned out to be a nice, intimate affair. She'd cooked dinner for everyone—once again, her favorite lasagna. Ben and Owen brought Archie, already in his pajamas and excited to be staying up late. Bob and his wife brought a case of wine, and Peter brought an array of desserts from one of his restaurants. A few other friends showed up as the night wore on, including Nigel, who arrived close to midnight.

"How'd your visit go?" she asked.

"Not great," he said, giving her a straight-lipped smile. "Can we talk, maybe tomorrow?"

"Sure, buddy," she said, patting his arm. After their talk on Thanksgiving, he felt more like a friend than a client. Maybe that's what being a small-town lawyer was like.

Her heart swelled upon that realization. It was all she'd ever wanted from being a lawyer—to help people using her education and skill and to gain their respect in return. Not just in the courtroom, but in other walks of life.

Charlotte was having a great time surrounded by her new friends, but as the clock crept closer to midnight, she couldn't help but think about Jake. About that first awkward, accidental kiss they'd shared two years ago as they rang in the New Year at the Congress Hall gala. About the friendly kiss on the cheek he'd given her last year on her couch, over the popcorn bucket. And, of course, the steamy almost-kiss that almost-happened a week ago. That was the one she couldn't stop thinking about as she wondered how his New Year's Eve was going. Tahiti was six hours behind East Coast time, which meant he was probably just getting ready for his night. Was he alone? Or with someone else? Someone "uncomplicated," unlike her?

She tried to distract herself by basking in the glow of Ryan Seacrest's uber-hotness as she and her guests gathered around the TV, but even his handsome looks and peppy personality couldn't get her excited about the turn of the calendar page.

With a minute left of the year, Peter sauntered over, placed a party hat on her head, and handed her a glass of champagne. "For the prettiest girl in the room," he said.

"I bet you say that to all the girls," Charlotte teased.

When midnight struck, he put his arm around her and kissed her on the cheek.

"Happy New Year, Charlotte." Clinking his glass with hers, he added, "To our new friendship."

"Yes, to friendship," she said, smiling. It may not have been as good as having Jake there, but she was happy to have someone take his place.

Speak of the devil. Her phone buzzed as Jake's name scrolled across the screen.

"Excuse me."

Her heart fluttered as she slipped away to her bedroom to answer the call.

"Happy New Year, Charlotte," Jake said. She could hear the din of a party going on in the background.

"Jake!" she exclaimed. "Happy New Year to you too. Where are you?"

"At the marina party in Tahiti. They start early here with dinner. How's your shindig going?"

"It's lots of fun. Turns out, being social's kinda cool," she said. "How about yours?"

"It's...nice. Fun." He paused. "Then again, I was more excited to call you at your midnight than to be inside, drinking with my pals. If that means anything."

It did mean something. She got a chill, picturing him standing by the water, all his attention focused on her while, behind him, a party raged on.

"To be honest, all I could think about all day was last year, snuggled up on your couch under one of Grams's afghans, watching movies. Not to mention you salivating over Ryan Seacrest. I'm assuming he hasn't asked you out yet?"

"Nah, he's playing it cool," Charlotte quipped. "He doesn't want me to know just how much I mean to him."

"Don't worry," Jake said, the background noise lessening

as Charlotte imagined him clutching the phone to his ear and walking farther away from the crowd. "He'll get there."

Ryan? Or you, Jake?

Cleo

CLEO AND WELLS SAT ON THE FLOOR OF HER GALLERY AS the clock struck midnight, a half-consumed bottle of Dom Pérignon between them as they chatted about her gallery, his cases, her volunteer work, his campaign. Wells had decided to skip the Philly party and hang with Cleo instead. They drained the last of the bottle of Dom into their glasses and raised a toast.

"To old friends," Cleo said.

"And new beginnings."

They drank in silence, and then Wells stood and extended a hand to help her up. She came face to face with him as she rose, his hands tightening on her waist as he steadied her.

"I didn't have much of a chance to see all your art, with Daisy all over me. I'm guessing she'll be sliding into my DMs soon."

Cleo giggled from too much champagne and the vision of her octogenarian boss flirting it up with Wells earlier that night.

"Then let's remedy that."

Wells took his time walking around as he looked at paintings. He stopped before one she'd painted back when they were still doing their thing. A smiling moon among sleeping stars.

"I remember this," he said softly.

One featured star had two sets of opposing trails—one suggesting it was rising, the other, falling. Atop the star was a small figure, representing Cleo at that time of her life. Losing the life she knew as her friends moved on (falling), hopeful for the new life she'd have to forge (rising). It was also a nod to the song "Fly Me to the Moon," which she and Wells often danced to back in the day.

He took her hand. "Play among the stars with me," he said, his voice raspy with desire. He wrapped his arm around her waist and held her hand to his chest as he slowly swayed, softly singing the lyrics to their song.

Don't look up. Don't look up.

Too late. She looked up. Looked into his jade eyes, which were staring directly into her soul. He sucked in his bottom lip, and it was all Cleo could do to keep herself from crushing her mouth against his.

But then, she thought of Nigel, the way he'd looked so hopeful and happy when he first came in. The way their eyes had locked. The look of devastation on his face upon seeing Wells.

Regardless of her self-doubt, Cleo had changed. She was no longer the commitment-phobe she'd been when she and Nigel met. Because look at her now—she'd committed to her goals and made them happen. The reason: she'd committed to herself.

Nor was she still the risk-seeking person who'd throw caution to the wind and hook up with a guy for the sheer sake of sex. After being with Nigel, she knew she could never go back to meaningless passion. This night with Wells—the champagne, the dance, the comforting familiarity of his embrace—all felt like a prelude to more. But as sexy and charming as Wells was, he was part of her past. Where he belonged.

"I'm good for a friendship, but nothing more," she said just as he began to lean in for a kiss. "I hope you understand."

He backed off, smiling through seeming disappointment. "I'm sorry. Old habits and all."

"They do die hard, I guess," she said, giving him a sad smile.

His expression became solemn. "I sense you guys aren't completely over each other."

"You think?" Cleo teased, recalling how Nigel had reacted to Wells's surprise appearance.

"I can tell by the way you looked at him that you still care about him. I don't believe you ever looked at me that way."

Cleo felt bad. She wasn't sure what to say.

He chuckled. "It's okay. I'm over it now, but I can say from experience you're not easy to get over. What happened between you guys, if you don't mind me asking?"

She hesitated, not really wanting to talk about it, but Wells knew Old Cleo well. He'd even been the brunt of her bailing ways. Maybe he'd have some insight.

"He wanted to move out of the city but I didn't, and then he went and asked me to marry him. You know me, I'm not about that ball-and-chain shit. At least not at this point in my life."

"Is that why you broke up with him?"

"He actually broke up with me. I was cautiously willing to give the long-distance thing a chance, but for him, it was marriage or nothing."

"So, it's nothing." Wells was quiet for a moment. "Yet still, he came today. Gotta give him credit for that."

"He said he couldn't be my friend. And I don't know if that's even what I want. I miss him."

"He may still be looking at it from a too-close vantage point. Maybe distance will allow him to see things more clearly. There's more than one way to be together. Marriage isn't always the answer."

"Since when did you become a relationship guru?"

He shrugged. "I guess I've grown up a bit, too. The surface-level thing doesn't cut it anymore. You brought that out in me, actually. The desire for more. As I'm sure you've done with him as well. He may be locked into this idea of marriage from a traditional mindset, but there are many ways of being in a committed relationship, even with distance. Married or not. He seems like a good guy, even if he doesn't like me very much. I have a feeling you guys are gonna work things out."

She appreciated Wells's vote of confidence. If only she had one of her own.

January

Delaney

DELANEY GLANCED AROUND THE DINING ROOM TABLE on New Year's Day as the family finished breakfast. Everyone who mattered was at the table. It seemed like the right time.

"I have news," she said, taking a breath, preparing for their reactions. "Kate gave me a DNA test a few months ago. I've received the results, and apparently there's someone out there I may be related to."

"Wonderful!" her dad exclaimed.

"What kind of relative?" her mom asked excitedly.

"The match suggested she was my daughter." She chuckled as her family gave a collective gasp. "And before you ask...no. There's nothing I've been hiding."

"So what does that mean?" her dad inquired.

"It means our DNA, me and this other person, is so similar, we're likely close blood relatives."

"How can you find out more?" her dad asked. "It would be great for you to know a relative. If there's one, there might be more."

"More family members to love!" her mom exclaimed.

Delaney was thrilled her parents seemed supportive of exploring her biological roots.

"I already heard from the girl I've matched with. She's ten. She told me she did a DNA test because her mom was adopted. The daughter wanted to learn more about her mom's past."

"Oh my gosh, Delaney. The mom could be a sister," her mom said.

"Oh man, another sister? I'll be even more outnumbered!" Jordan said.

"I hate to burst all your bubbles, but I'm thinking more along the lines of a cousin." She didn't tell them about them being the same age. Didn't want to get ahead of herself.

"Are you going to meet her?" her mom asked.

"Well, I pose that question to you guys. What do you think?"

"Yes!" they all answered in unison.

"Why wouldn't you?" her dad asked. "You should never stop discovering who you are and where you came from. We got you. We'll always be here, no matter what your past uncovers."

Delaney's eyes watered. She was so thankful for her family's unwavering support.

"Any relative of yours will also be related to us. Not by blood, but definitely by love," her mom said.

"I love you guys so much. Your support means everything to me."

Wiping her tears, she exhaled and took a deep breath. Out with old fears, in with new wonder. She decided right then she didn't want to meet her alleged relatives virtually or on the phone. She wanted it to be in person.

"I guess I have an email to return."

Delaney stole away to her bedroom and opened her laptop.

Dear Frannie,

I'd love to meet up with you and your mom wherever it's convenient for you. I'm heading to Cape May, where I'll be staying for the next two weeks.

Frannie's response came a few hours later.

Dear Delaney,

I'm sorry I didn't write sooner, but I had to ask my mom. She's right here with me and said we can take the ferry and meet you in Cape May for lunch next Thursday if you're free. That's her day off.

Dear Frannie,

Thursday's perfect. Let's meet at the Blue Pig in Congress Hall Resort. Just tell me what time and I'll be there!

And hello, Daphne! I'm looking forward to meeting you.

After hitting send, Delaney wondered if she should've asked for a picture, but part of her wanted to be surprised.

Another email came through a minute later.

Dear Delaney,

Daphne here! Thank you so much for agreeing to meet us. We're excited to make your acquaintance. Nervous, but excited!

Delaney responded to the email to assure Daphne she, too, was nervous but couldn't wait to meet her.

In fact, the closer she got to Thursday, the more excited she became.

Charlotte

CHARLOTTE CALLED NIGEL ON NEW YEAR'S DAY AS promised.

"So. Tell me all about it," she said. Recalling his forlorn look, she suspected things didn't go well for him at Cleo's opening.

"The gallery is great. Things between Cleo and me, not so much," he reported.

"What happened?"

Nigel proceeded to tell her how he'd arrived at the gala moments before one of Cleo's exes showed up.

"I left shortly thereafter. Probably an overreaction on my

part, but it was a big step for me, going there. I was hoping to have some time to talk about us, but with him there, I knew it wouldn't happen."

"I'm sorry, Nigel."

"Me too. She really did break my heart when she turned down my proposal, but I've missed her so much, I needed to see if there was a chance we could—I dunno. Maybe get back together, or at least be friends. But seeing her ex there made me realize I'm not quite ready to be friends. Maybe someday."

"Is she still involved with him?"

"Who knows. It's the guy she was dating when I met her. I don't know why he else he'd be there, but I didn't stick around long enough to find out. I obviously need time to process everything before I can get to a place where we can move forward, in whatever capacity."

It reminded Charlotte of the movie *When Harry Met Sally*, when Harry insisted men and women could never be friends because sex always gets in the way, especially if the man finds the woman attractive. She wondered if it was possible for people like Cleo and Nigel to be platonic friends after having been together. It seemed it would be easier if they hadn't gone there before, like her and Jake. *He* seemed to be doing a fine job disproving Harry's theory.

Whatever. It didn't matter whether Jake was attracted to her. For the first time in her life, she felt attractive, and that's all that mattered. Even if no one else could see it.

Charlotte had willed herself not to check Jake's social media pages in the weeks following his departure. It was part of her plan to reset herself, to rid herself of expectations. It was her most important New Year's resolution.

Until, one night, curiosity got the best of her as she pulled up his Insta account. She scrolled his most recent postings in reverse order, starting with him snorkeling in Tonga, hiking a rainforest in Fiji, lounging on a beach in Bora Bora. A few photos of Jake with a group of guys at the New Year's Eve party he'd attended in Tahiti.

Then there were photos of a family holiday gathering at his cousin Dalton's house where he'd spent Christmas Day. One photo featured Delaney and Dalton in shirts that read "Thing One" and "Thing Two," holding up two onesies. Charlotte and Delaney were acquaintances from their Philly law practice days. She smiled as it dawned on her that *two* tiny onesies meant they were expecting twins. Another photo showed the extended family in front of a Christmas tree, Jake's arm around his brother Ryan's shoulders. The last photo was a closeup of Jake and—

Gut. Punch.

Tori.

Charlotte's heart sank. What was Tori doing at Jake's family's Christmas celebration?

That was the last of the photos from his visit to Cape May. No photos of him and Charlotte—not the one they took in front of her tree, or making snow angels, or toasting hot cocoa mugs. Why did she expect anything different?

Just another piece of evidence that she was doing the right thing, putting an end to silly thoughts of her and Jake being more. She wanted to believe he and Tori were nothing more than friends whose travel paths occasionally crossed. But it was becoming harder to ignore the fact that Tori had taken up far more real estate on his social media platforms than Charlotte ever had. In fact, he'd never posted one photo of the two of them, despite hanging out as friends for the past couple years and taking many photos together.

Okay, Jake. Message received. Their friendship wasn't Instaworthy in his eyes.

Nor, apparently, was she.

Marley

MARLEY AND AMANDA MET UP FOR DRINKS AT A TINY South Street hole-in-the-wall after Amanda reached out to let her know she was in need of girl talk. Marley was nervous, wondering if she'd have to be the one to tell her that Eddie was married—or if Amanda already knew.

"I know we hardly know each other, but I feel a kindred spirit with you," Amanda said after they ordered their drinks. "Like you're someone I know I can trust."

"Of course you can," Marley assured her.

"That's good to know," Amanda said, giving her a shy smile. "I don't know if you figured this out, but when the contest started, Eddie and I were dating."

Marley chuckled. "I had a feeling."

"We'd just celebrated our third anniversary." Tears welled as she gave a heavy sigh. "Everything was going great. I felt like I'd met my person, you know?" She dabbed a finger under each lash line to stop her tears from flowing. "We were talking marriage. Even went to *look for rings* one day. A week later, he told me he couldn't do it."

"Do what?" Marley hedged. "Shop for rings? Or—"

"Marry me."

"Oh."

"Yep. His excuse at the time was he couldn't take my late hours. He gaslighted me into thinking it was my fault we weren't getting married. We'd just had an argument about it the week before the contest started. I hoped that maybe filming the segment, being surrounded by happy couples, he'd come around. Until—"

Marley held her breath, hoping the truth was next.

"He got arrested."

Wait, what? Not the plot twist she was expecting. "For what, do you mind me asking?"

Amanda sighed. "He'd been on long-term probation for possession of pot, which he claimed he was 'holding for a friend.'" She rolled her eyes as she made air quotes. "But then he decided it would be a good idea to send dick pics to a woman he'd been flirting with online. While he was dating me."

"*What?*" Talk about a curveball. It was everything the contestants had collectively guessed. Cheating. Drugs. Voyeurism...or at least creepy-ism.

"I'm so sorry to hear this."

"But all good deeds deserve another..." Amanda's mouth turned upward into a smile. The gleam in her eyes gave Marley permission to do the same. "Turns out, she was an undercover officer."

Marley hesitated, then followed Amanda's lead as they both burst out laughing.

"Apparently, engaging in 'lewd and lascivious' behavior was against his rules of probation," Amanda cried out with hilarity. "Who knew?"

"I'm sorry things ended like that." Marley was relieved she didn't have to share Eddie's other truth.

"Oh, it doesn't end there. Like a complete asshole, I took pity on him when he called me from jail to let me know they were keeping him until bail was posted. And like an idiot, I agreed to bail him out." She shook her head in disbelief. "I don't deserve to find happiness after that bonehead move."

"That's not true," Marley said. "You were just being a nice person. It must have been awful going through all that after dating for so long. Not gonna judge."

Even though, yeah, she felt some judgment coming on. Wanting to bail out a guy who'd sent dick pics to another woman? Rot in hell, is what Marley would've told him. You and your cheating tallywacker.

"Well, grab your gavel and don the robe," Amanda announced, her eyes lighting with the juiciness of gossip. "Because it gets better."

"Oh no..."

"I show up at the jail to post his fucking bond, and who's there at the desk also trying to pay it? Some woman who tells them she's his *fucking wife*. Now, don't you think I'd know it if I was dating a guy who was already married?"

Oh, boy. Moment of truth. The pit in Marley's stomach grew as she prepared to confirm the woman's assertions.

Before she could speak, Amanda started laughing again. "So I go, 'You're not his wife. I am.'"

Marley laughed nervously, wondering where she was going with this.

"I know, a lie, but I'm not quite ready to give up on this loser. But then she goes, 'I got proof.' Doesn't she pull a picture from her wallet of her and Eddie the Scumbag on their *fucking wedding day*. Tux, gown, and all." Amanda raises both hands in mic drop gestures. "So, there you have it. I was dating a fucking married-ass man for the last three years. Piece of total shit."

Whew. The relief Marley felt coursing through her veins was indescribable, now that she didn't have to be the bearer of such bad news.

"It gets better," Amanda said.

Better? Oh, how she wished gossipmonger Sam was here for all of this. He would've been on the edge of his seat, begging for more.

"She says to me, 'Why did you tell me *you* were his wife?' and I say, 'Because I've been fucking your husband for the last three years.' She calls me a big fat liar, and then hauls off and comes at me. Takes a swing at me like we're on one of those trashy 'who's the baby daddy' shows. Thank God I took martial arts as a kid. I ducked, just in time for her to clock the deputy sheriff standing behind me. Right in his unsuspecting face."

Marley burst out laughing over Amanda's theatrics.

"Right?" Amanda said, eyes wide. "The first thing that came to my mind as the guy went down was 'how is this my life?' I mean, I'm Ivy League educated. I have a private driver. I live in an upscale part of the city with panoramic views of the BFB, for Christ's sake. Not me standing in jail, preparing to defend my life over some lying loser." She laughed. "Then again, I was born and raised in South Philly, so I guess anything's possible. Especially when you have the shit-for-brains taste in men I've carefully crafted over the years."

Marley was without words. She just sat there, shaking her head.

"Needless to say, they're now both wards of the Philadelphia jail system." Amanda looked skyward and raised her hands like a worship leader, proclaiming, "God is good!"

After their laughter subsided, Marley sighed. "I'm so sorry it didn't work out for you, but you clearly dodged a huge bullet, finding out when you did. You know what they say—when God closes a jail cell, he opens a window. Hopefully, the next guy won't be such a—"

"Bite your tongue, woman," Amanda chastised. "I'm done. Done. With. Men. Over it. I'm happy to live in perpetuity as the *PhuckingPheelGoodPhilly* host, celebrating others' successes and all that happy horseshit, but count me out of the dating scene."

"That's exactly when you're likely to meet the man of your dreams."

She shook her head. "Not this woman."

Cleo

NOW THAT THE EXCITEMENT OVER THE GRAND OPENING was behind her, it was time for the real work. Cleo had seriously underestimated just how much energy it would take to run a gallery—managing daily operations, marketing, attending art shows, and more. When she added it to her volunteer work, it left little time for creating. Make that, *no* time.

Once she'd created enough buzz and had consistent sales, she'd hire staff to handle some of the menial tasks. She couldn't wait for that day, because here she was at ten at night, still in the gallery, poring over financial details. For the first time since her dream took shape, she allowed herself to ask the question that had been burning in the back of her mind: is this really what she wanted?

She called it a night and was heading to the subway station when an aggressive wind gust tore the portfolio from her hands, taking with it several looseleaf drawings. Among them, her treasured sketch of Gus—the one she carried everywhere.

"Nooo!" she cried, lunging for it before it caught an updraft. All she could do was watch as it swirled above the buildings and vanished into the night air.

She was crushed to see the last remnant of Gus ripped from her. Just as he'd been. She sunk to her knees and wailed—not only over the loss of the drawing, but the man himself.

As weeks passed, more bad luck came her way. A pipe burst in the back studio of the gallery, causing just enough damage to keep her from renting the space out to other creatives as she'd planned. Then, one night on her way home from work, she slipped on ice and sprained her ankle, making it challenging to get around and tend to her tasks.

To top it off, she still hadn't heard from Nigel since the gallery opening.

There was one bright spot in the otherwise dreary month—Tori was coming for a visit before she headed out for her next trip. Cleo could hardly wait for the weekend, anxious to catch up with her dear friend.

And get some intel on Nigel.

"She's cute, I hate to say," Tori reported about the woman she'd seen Nigel with over the holidays. "Chestnut hair, dimples, beautiful eyes, I think they were hazel or golden or something."

"Don't spare any details on my account," Cleo said wryly, as her heart took a swan dive into her Uggs. She was hoping for reports of a gargoyle but reminded herself she's the one who drove him into the arms of someone else. She had no right to sulk over the fact he sought company with someone else, even though it tore at her heart.

"She's a friend of Jake's," Tori added.

"Oooh! Jake, the hot sailor you once dated? He's still in the picture?"

"Don't wet yourself. He's just a friend now."

"Friend with benefits?" Cleo waggled her brows.

Tori didn't bite. She was no fun.

"Do you think it's a serious thing?" Cleo asked. "Nigel and the chick."

Tori shrugged. "Not serious like you guys. Who knows, maybe she was just a friend, but he seemed nervous to see me, so I figured it wasn't just an innocent thing."

It made Cleo sick to think of Nigel with someone else. Then again, what did she think would happen when she turned down his proposal? That he'd stay chaste forever? She wished it didn't have to be all or nothing. She might not be ready for marriage, but couldn't they find some happy medium? As Wells had pointed out, there were more paths to commitment than just through marriage. She'd have to give this some thought.

Marley

MARLEY AND SAM HAD JUST REPORTED TO THE STUDIO for the final results of the contest when she turned a corner and almost careened into a man. Not just any man. Her former boss, who'd recently announced his candidacy for District Attorney of Philadelphia.

"Wells!" Marley exclaimed at the same time he cried out her name. "What are you doing at here?"

"I'm being interviewed about my campaign," Wells said as he hugged Marley. "I wondered if I'd see you guys. Is today the big reveal?"

"It is," Sam said, giving him a back-slapping man hug. "Congrats on your campaign. You've got our votes."

"Speak for yourself," Marley teased.

"Thanks, guys. Did you guys enjoy the competition? I watched some and it looks like you killed it."

"It's been fun," Sam said, smiling down at Marley. "We'll see what today's results bring."

"My money's on you to win," he said. "True love beats all. That's—"

Something behind them suddenly caught Wells's attention. His eyes widened as a smile spread across his face.

"Wow," Wells breathed. "Is that...?"

Marley heard Amanda's voice behind her. "Oh good, Marley. You're here. I have— *Oh!*"

Marley turned to see Amanda's eyes dart to Wells. "Wow, Mr. Aber—*Whoa.* You're so much more handsome in person."

As soon as the words were out, Amanda clamped her hand over her mouth. "I can't believe I just said that," she mumbled between her fingers.

Wells laughed out loud. "The pleasure's all mine. I want—I mean, I think, I have—"

"Amazing command of the English language?" Amanda teased.

"I guess you can say that," he said, his eyes twinkling with undeniable interest, "since I obviously can't."

"I didn't mean to put words in your mouth," she said coquettishly as she batted her fake lashes at him.

Marley filled in the veritable thought bubble above Amanda's head: *Words, no...but how about my tongue?*

Wells stood there, wordless, gazing at the beautiful host. Marley knew him to be such a quick thinker on his feet, he could make Sam look like an amateur. Though not now, in the captivating presence of Philly's accomplished newscaster. And she regarded him with such admiration, another thought bubble may as well have popped above her head. *Eddie, who?*

Marley shot a look at Sam, and she could tell he was thinking the same thing—they were witnessing a spark. An instant connection. Possibly love at first sight.

"I've been looking forward to this interview with you," Amanda said.

"Me too," Wells said. It looked like he was blushing.

"We'll be going live for your interview after the contest results are announced," she told him. "Let me show you to the dressing room so we can get you ready."

Amanda turned away and sashayed down the hall with the confidence of a woman who was Done. With. Men.

Wells watched her, mouth hanging open, before turning back to Marley and Sam. "What just happened?"

"Don't keep her waiting—go!" Marley said, laughing as she ushered him to follow the retreating woman.

"I have a feeling we just witnessed the end of Wells's single days," Sam said as Wells scurried to catch up. "I know that look. It's the same one I had the first time I met you."

"She claims she's done with men, but judging by that interaction, I'm not so certain. Maybe meeting a nice, law-abiding, non-cheating asshole will change her mind."

An hour later, Marley and Sam stood shoulder to shoulder with Andy and Olivia, awaiting the final vote tally.

"Okay, is everyone excited?" Amanda cried out with what sounded like renewed vigor. "The Battle of the Betrothed started with six couples six months ago. After a series of challenges, you, the viewing public, whittled it down to our final two. We showed you their videos a couple of weeks ago and your votes have been tallied. Who will win the grand prize? Let's view our couples' videos one last time before we announce our winners."

They played Marley and Sam's first, then Andy and Olivia's. They'd created an equally heartwarming video, showing the births of their three boys and the gender reveal for the last child. Instead of acting disappointed about yet another boy, they seemed joyful, with Andy in the background of the video crying, "We'll almost have our own basketball team!"

Their final message: their love story took a nontraditional route, but starting a family before marriage was a guarantee of their success.

"There'll be no surprises here, because we've already done it all," a smiling Olivia said to the camera as three little boys ran around in the background.

Marley was choked up by their video. She'd never tell Sam, but she lowkey hoped they'd win. They deserved the money.

"Okay, everyone, it's time to find out who our winner is," Amanda said.

A drum roll sounded.

"The winners...of the first Battle of the Betrothed...are..."

Sam squeezed her hand.

"Marley and Sam!"

"Yes!" Sam exclaimed, grabbing Marley in a hug. "I told you we were gonna win this thing!"

Marley shot a look at Andy and Olivia, who were clapping and smiling along with the news crew. They looked genuinely happy for them. Andy stepped out of line to shake Sam's hand as Olivia gave Marley a hug.

"You guys deserve this," Andy said. "That was an awesome video. Congrats."

"We're so happy for you," Olivia gushed.

Marley felt as small and heartless as a Lego person.

Sam beamed. "Thanks. You guys gave us a great run for the money."

"You're not going to believe this," Amanda continued. "But the votes were equally split between the two of you. An absolute, honest-to-God tie. But, if you recall from our first competition in Center City, the couple who crossed the finish line first would earn an extra ten votes. That was Marley and Sam, and that pushed them over the edge. Congratulations, guys."

Marley's heart sank further for Andy and Olivia upon hearing that. She recalled broken-footed Andy hustling to return to the LOVE statue. Parents of three, dealing with what Olivia described as a challenging pregnancy, it was likely the exhausted pair hadn't had a good night's sleep in years. It seemed inherently unfair to be standing here now, victors in a game with odds so stacked against their competitors. Didn't feel much like a win at all.

As the couples parted, they wished the expectant couple luck with the new baby.

"Sam's a great name, just sayin'," Sam teased.

Andy and Olivia laughed. "We'll keep that in mind."

"What do you say we celebrate with a nice dinner tonight?"

Sam asked as he wrapped his arm around Marley on the way out.

"Sure," she said, even though she didn't feel much like celebrating. Instead, she felt as if they'd taken candy from a baby—or a down payment from a baby and his family. Even though they needed the money themselves, it wasn't lost on Marley how indulgent it was that they'd been competing to purchase a second home, when Andy and Olivia were simply trying to buy their first.

Despite the nice dinner they enjoyed later that night, Marley couldn't shake the guilt.

"Don't," Sam said as he reached across the table. "We were all consenting adults, knowing what we were getting into. Besides, Andy and Oliva were genuinely happy for us. As their video suggested, they already have everything they need."

"And so do we," she said.

It had started snowing during dinner. When they emerged from the restaurant, they delighted in the tumbling snowflakes. Marley turned in the direction of their condo when Sam nailed her in the back with a snowball.

"Just for that, Adams," Marley said as she scooped a handful of snow and wound up.

But Sam slip-slid to her and grabbed her arm before she could let loose.

"Kiss me," he said, lowering his lips to hers as snow rested on his long lashes.

She said a silent prayer their kids would get his eyes. Beautiful, like glacier ice, surrounded by sweeping lashes.

"I know what we're doing when we get home," Sam said, his voice husky with desire.

"You have to catch me first!"

They teased each other the whole way home, pretending to race, throwing snowballs, stopping for kisses—the perfect playful prelude to a steamy lovemaking session.

Afterward, as she drifted off to sleep in Sam's arms, his warm, muscular torso pressed up against hers, he moved his lips to her ear. "Marley?"

"Hmm?" she hummed, half asleep.

"You're right. That money belongs to Andy and Olivia. We only won by a little and they need it more than we do."

Relief washed through her. She rolled over to face him. "What made you change your mind?"

"Laughing with you like that on the way home made me realize just how blessed our lives are. That we can even think about purchasing a second home makes us the luckiest people. Let's take our time and find the house right for us. That'll give us more time to build up our savings. For now, though, the money should go to a couple struggling to afford their primary home."

"It's ten grand, Sam. Way more with wedding expenses. Are you sure?"

"Absolutely. It's the right thing to do."

Marley was so moved by his generosity, his kind heart, she climbed on top of him. Straddling him, she kissed him slowly, passionately, and proceeded to show him in other ways just how much she appreciated him.

Delaney

THE DAY WAS FINALLY HERE.

Delaney had received another email from Frannie and Daphne the day before, confirming their meeting at the Blue Pig. She arrived at the restaurant thirty minutes early to be there first—probably a control thing. She was seated at a table by the roaring fireplace, under a large oil painting of the restaurant's namesake, when she saw two people enter from her periphery.

Glancing up, she almost fell out of her chair when she saw the spitting image of her younger self enter with a dark-haired woman who looked just like—

"Delaney!" Frannie exclaimed. Within seconds her mini-version was in Delaney's arms.

Laughing at her exuberant greeting, Delaney turned to Daphne and was met with the same steel blue eyes she saw every time she looked in the mirror. Same espresso hair. Same wide smile framed by dimples. The only thing noticeably different was that Daphne's hair was shorter and she wore glasses.

It was uncanny. Scary even.

"Oh, my gosh," Frannie exclaimed, looking from one to the other. "You have to be sisters."

Delaney and Daphne laughed, both covering their mouths with their left hands.

"Sorry I'm staring," Daphne said. "It's like looking in the mirror."

So taken aback, Delaney could only nod as her tears began flowing.

"I'm so glad you wanted to meet in person," Daphne continued. "As Frannie told you, I'm adopted. I was raised by a great family, so I never cared to know much about my origins."

"I felt the same way," Delaney said, clasping her hand. "I took the test months ago after a pregnancy scare. I figured I should probably know my health history."

"I never even thought about that when I had Frannie, but that was smart. She's the one who pushed me. I was uncertain I wanted to go there myself—too afraid I'd learn something bad about my birth."

"Me too. I was also afraid I'd insult my adopted family. But they're the ones who encouraged me to learn more about myself."

"I have this brave girl to thank," Daphne said, hugging Frannie. "It's all she wanted for her birthday, and you know how expensive the tests are. But I couldn't deny her the right to find out about our heritage, just because I was hesitant. Once she told me she matched with you, I figured I had to take one too. I'm currently awaiting my results."

Delaney smiled. "I'm happy to hear that, although I think it's fair to say we're related."

Daphne giggled. "I agree."

They both sighed at the same time.

"This is...just..."

They began giggling, both waving their hands in front of their eyes to stop the tears.

"You even act the same!" Frannie said.

Delaney had to agree, noting Daphne had similar mannerisms: the way she talked with her hands, how she lifted her eyebrows when she smiled, the fact that she nodded when someone else spoke.

"It's like you're twins," Frannie noted.

"You're 32?" Delaney asked for clarification.

Daphne nodded and confirmed her birth year was the same as Delaney's. "What do you know about your birth?"

"I was born at Brentworth Hospital in Philadelphia on June 6."

Daphne gasped.

"OMG," Frannie exclaimed.

Daphne pressed her fingers against her temples. "I was born June 7. Also at Brentworth."

"We have to be cousins, right?" Daphne hedged. "That's the only plausible explanation. I mean, we can't be sisters, born one day apart. Unless..."

"Maybe one of your birthdays is wrong?" Frannie offered. "You guys really look like you could be twins."

Delaney flipped open the folder she'd brought containing

her records. She looked at the time of her birth on the certificate, surprised she'd never known it.

"Eleven fifty-two." It was barely a whisper as her world began swirling. She slowly looked up to meet Daphne's widened eyes. "P.m."

Tears cascaded down Daphne's face as she choked back a sob. "I was born at 12:08 a.m."

"Sixteen minutes apart," Delaney said as their eyes met.

They looked at each other in utter shock before both spoke at the same time.

"Twins."

Marley

AFTER MUCH DISCUSSION AND DRAWING OF DOCUments, Marley and Sam met with the *PheelGoodPhilly* producer and presented their idea for splitting the prize.

"We can do that, if it's what you guys want to do," she said, looking from one to the other. "Are you certain?"

"Absolutely," Marley answered quickly so Sam didn't have a chance to change his mind.

"Okay. I wonder if we should have you sign something releasing the funds—"

"Already on it," Sam said, handing her a folder.

The producer laughed. "Of course. Two attorneys, I should have known you guys would be on top of this."

She read over the document, which set forth their terms. They would split the prize—Marley and Sam would keep the wedding package and gift the $10,000 to Andy and Olivia.

"Okay, then, I'll make the transfer. This is really decent of you guys. What would you say to doing this on live TV?"

Sam shook his head. "No. We don't want to let our voters down."

Marley rolled her eyes. "What he means is, we don't want to take credit, or in any way embarrass Andy and Olivia. We'd like to visit them privately and let them know about our decision. No cameras."

Amanda came into the office just then. "Hey, what are you guys doing here?"

The producer filled Amanda in.

"Wow, that's awesome. You guys truly are winners." She turned to Marley. "Are we still on for drinks tonight?"

"Absolutely." She and Amanda had been texting and had become quite friendly.

Later, sitting at The Clink with her, Marley couldn't help but notice there was a sparkle in Amanda's eyes that hadn't been there before.

"Wells asked me out," she blurted out after they'd ordered their drinks. "I know I swore off men, but he seems like such a decent guy. I can't believe he's still single. I feel like I have to give him a chance. Am I being an idiot?"

"Of course not," Marley assured her. "You're being human."

"You worked with him, right? Any red flags I should be aware of?"

Marley gave it serious thought. She adored Wells but didn't want to give Amanda misleading information. Yet as hard as she tried, she couldn't come up with one warning about her former boss.

"Not at all. As long as you don't mind a guy who puts in a shit ton of hours at work."

"Sounds like my kinda man," Amanda said. "He'll be a good match for my crazy hours."

Marley recalled a statement Wells had made once about the importance of not losing someone you love over a job. She'd guessed at the time he was talking about his ex-fling,

Cleo. She felt hopeful for both Amanda and Wells—one broken heart finding another, making both whole again.

"Anyway, wish me luck. I hope it works out better than it did with Eddie."

"I'm sure it will. Wells is an awesome guy who deserves to find love as much as you do."

Amanda gave a little shimmy. "I hope you're right. I know we just met, but I've never felt this way before."

Marley hoped theirs would be the next great love story, while Eddie would be relegated to feeding his wife chicken fingers between the bars of a jail cell.

Delaney

DELANEY AND DAPHNE SOBBED AS THEY MELTED INTO each other in an embrace thirty-two years in the making. Rocking back and forth, Delaney stroked Daphne's hair, compelled by her older-sister instincts. Frannie wrapped her arms around them.

It all made sense now. The disconnect she'd felt throughout her life, despite feeling loved and accepted by her adoptive family. The unexplained need for control and order in her life, most likely due to the trauma of being separated from a twin. It was like finding a piece of her that was missing. She didn't try to hold back her tears. She'd spent a lifetime dealing in facts, being practical. It felt good just to *feel* in this life-changing moment.

Delaney became aware that the lunchtime chatter of other diners had subsided, but she didn't care if they were making a scene. She had a sister. A twin. The place could have burst into flames and she wouldn't have cared.

She was found. Rekindled with her first love. Her womb-mate.

"I've always felt like there was a piece of me missing," Daphne said, voicing what Delaney was feeling. "It makes sense now."

"Is this real?" Delaney asked, her joyful heart thudding away in her chest.

"It's real."

She suddenly deflated into sadness, then anger, over their situation, as Daphne asked the same question burning in her mind.

"Who separates twins?"

"I know." It seemed almost criminal. Delaney's older sister instinct kicked in once again. "But you have me now. That's never gonna change."

For the next two hours, they chatted excitedly, getting to know each other, trying to jam three decades into one conversation. Delaney broke into attorney mode, questioning Daphne about her life. She discovered she'd been raised in Collegeville, a town not too far from Doylestown where Delaney grew up. She'd married and moved to Delaware ten years ago and worked as librarian. Her husband was killed in the line of military duty when Frannie, their only child, was two.

Delaney's eyes welled with tears to hear of her brother-in-law's passing. "I'm so sorry to hear that."

"It was horrific—still is—but I have to move forward, you know? I have a little girl who needs me. But enough about me. Tell me all about you."

Delaney told her she was married and currently practicing law in London.

"Very impressive," Daphne added. "Do you enjoy it?"

She hesitated. "I do...at least, I did. I think I'm ready to do something different."

"Like what?"

Delaney shrugged. "I have no idea, but I'm working on it."

"Any children?" Daphne asked.

Delaney smiled and placed a hand on her belly, still somewhat hidden under loose clothing. "I guess you could say that. I'm pregnant, due in June."

"Congratulations!" Daphne said, giving a little clap.

"This means I'm gonna have a cousin!" Frannie exclaimed as she jumped up and hugged her. "I thought I'd never have one. Mom's an only child."

"Her dad was an only child too," Daphne explained.

"You're actually going to have two cousins," Delaney said.

"Twins?"

She nodded, her voice wavering as fresh tears welled. "Twins."

Daphne clamped a hand over her mouth, her eyes flooding too.

"Two girls, or two boys? Or one of each? Can I babysit them?" Frannie asked in rapid succession.

The women laughed.

"Fran, don't jump the gun," Daphne warned, swiping at her tears. "It may be a couple years before you can babysit. And we just met Delaney. Who knows if she even likes us?"

"That's true. I don't like you," Delaney said, giving them both a teasing glance, "because I already know I love you. That includes you, my niece." She gave Frannie's hand a squeeze.

"I'm someone's niece, for the first time ever!" Frannie exclaimed. "And I'm gonna have two baby cousins!"

"To answer your other questions, we won't know their gender until my next ultrasound, after we return to London. That also means they don't have names yet. I'd love to have you as a babysitter—maybe you can keep them entertained while I'm home at first, until you're old enough and I can leave you alone with them."

Delaney was amazed at her own laissez-faire attitude toward leaving her unborn children with someone she didn't even know. A child, yet. But a blood relative was something she'd never had before.

"Yes!" Frannie gave a victory pump.

Daphne, sighing, reached for Delaney's hand. "Twins. Just like us."

"Dalton's cousin also has twins," she said, then turned to Frannie. "You'll really like them. Two little girls, Violet and Petunia. They're almost four."

"Oooh, I love their names!" she said, squealing. "Are there any other kids in your family?"

"Dalton's sister has three boys, and his other cousin has a teen girl and a boy who's about your age."

"I hope the girls like me, but I don't care if the boys do. I don't like boys."

"What about Logan?" Daphne teased.

"Gross, Mom. Stop!" Frannie's tone was annoyed, despite her half-smile. "He's just my friend. We're in fourth grade. Stop trying to marry me off."

"No one said anything about marriage," Daphne said, holding up her hands up.

"Yeah, be careful there," Delaney told her new niece. "That's what happened to me and Dalton. We met when we were seven, became friends a year later, and now look at us."

After they finished their meal, Daphne suggested taking a walk before heading back to the ferry to return home.

"I've spent a lifetime not knowing I had a twin sister. I don't want to leave you so soon. Birth separation was bad enough, but this somehow feels worse."

Delaney and Dalton weren't due to return to the UK for another week. Delaney suggested meeting up again, so she could introduce them to her family.

"How about this weekend?" they both asked simultaneously.

"Now you're even talking alike," Frannie said.

"We'll take the Friday afternoon ferry, after Frannie gets out of school."

They made plans and said their tearful goodbyes. Delaney hurried home to share her news with Dalton.

She found him in the living room, watching football. He hit pause on the remote and jumped from the couch when she entered the room.

"So?" he asked, expectantly.

Tears were already flowing before she could get the words out. "I have a sister."

Dalton gave a loud whoop and scooped her into his arms. "That's amazing! I can't believe it. Tell me all about her!"

She gave him the basic details about Daphne and Frannie but withheld the most incredible part of their discovery. She wanted to surprise everyone when they met her in person. After all, they'd spent a lifetime being robbed of twin-she-nanigans and had a lot to make up for.

"When will you tell the family?" Dalton asked.

"Let's Zoom with everyone tonight. I know they're dying to know how it went."

Everyone had gone back home for the week but would be returning to Cape May that weekend for a farewell gathering before she and Dalton returned to London.

An hour later, Delaney and Dalton started the call.

"Well?" her mom asked. "What did you learn?"

"I have a sister!" Afraid they'd ask who was older and younger, she added, "A younger sister."

By a few minutes, but who's counting? They'd know soon enough.

"That's fantastic!" her dad exclaimed as he high-fived her mom.

Jordan gave a whoop and Kate squealed.

"Tell us all about her!" her mom said. "What's her name, where does she live, and when do we get to meet her?"

"Her name's Daphne, she lives in Bethany Beach, Delaware, and she's coming to visit this weekend. Can you guys be here Friday afternoon?"

Jordan responded first. "I can't think of a better way to spend a Friday, surrounded by sisters."

Delaney loved that about Jordan. He was just a happy kid, sister overload aside.

"Bring Bella, too, so she can meet her future sister-in-law," Delaney teased.

He was only nineteen, but the family was certain Bella would be his one-and-only, ride-or-die, person for life.

He blushed. "She'll love that."

The rest of the family gave their all-in.

Later that night, Daphne texted to say she'd received her DNA test results and was notified she had a perfect sibling match. With Delaney Brooks.

"Look what I made, Aunt Delaney!" Frannie exclaimed as she disembarked from the ferry on Friday afternoon. She unzipped her jacket to reveal a hand-painted sweatshirt with the word "NIECE" in bold letters.

"I've never been someone's niece before, so I decided to wear my new title proudly."

Delaney's heart melted. "That's awesome!" she said, hugging her.

On the ride to her house, Delaney explained who they'd be meeting: her husband, Dalton; parents, Faye and Joe; her sister Kate and brother-in-law Ryan; and her brother, Jordan, and girlfriend, Bella. She'd decided to keep it small, limited to just immediate family for their first introduction.

The twin sisters decided to have a little fun. Delaney stepped aside to let Daphne enter first. She'd worn contacts instead of glasses today, so the only difference they'd notice was Daphne's much shorter hair.

"Hello!" Daphne called out as she breezed into the living room where everyone was gathered. "We're here!"

Delaney and Frannie held back on the front step, giggling.

"Your hair!" her mom exclaimed.

"You like?" Daphne asked. "I decided to stop off for a haircut on my way to the ferry."

Delaney was amazed at Daphne's acting chops. They all seemed to be buying it. Unable to wait any longer, she took Frannie's hand and entered the house.

They were met with a collective gasp.

"Um...is anyone else seeing double?" Jordan was the first to speak.

Delaney put her arms around Daphne and Frannie. "Everyone, I'd like you to meet Daphne, my sister. And this is Frannie, my niece."

Nobody spoke for a moment as her family members looked at Daphne, then Delaney, comparing their similarities.

Kate's mouth hit the floor. "Oh. My. God..."

"As you can probably tell, we're pretty related. Go ahead, tell them your birthday."

When Daphne told them, her mom gasped, her eyes filling with tears as she clasped her hands over her mouth. "So that means you're..."

"Twins," they said, simultaneously.

"Oh my God!" Kate exclaimed, nearly tackling them with a hug. "I knew it the second I saw you!"

Dalton was next. "I can't believe you kept this from me!"

"Well, I know how much you love surprises, so...surprise!"

Dalton laughed. "I guess we know now how we ended up with two poppy seeds!"

"Wait, how can you guys be twins if you were born on different days?" Jordan asked.

Delaney spoke first. "Sixteen minutes apart, before—"

"And after—" Daphne added.

"Midnight," they said together.

"You guys even finish each other's sentences!" Kate exclaimed.

Jordan slapped his forehead. "Yeah, I probably would've come up with that had I given it a little thought."

"Frannie, show them the sweatshirt you made," Delaney said.

The girl unzipped her jacket.

"'Niece!'" Delaney's mom said as she hugged Frannie. "That's a beautiful shirt. Did you make it yourself?"

"Yes. With puffy paint."

"It's awesome," Jordan said, giving Frannie a fist bump. "Can you make me one that says 'UNCLE'?"

"Absolutely!"

"Frannie, do you know you're the first kid to join our immediate family?" Kate asked, wrapping her arm around the girl. "Which makes you my niece too."

"And mine," Jordan added.

"Wow, I not only get two aunts, but an uncle too?" Frannie asked excitedly. "I shoulda taken that test a long time ago!"

The family members laughed, and Frannie gave her new aunt and uncle high fives.

"Twins..." Her dad shook his head, voice hushed. "How did we not know this?"

"We didn't know. I swear," her mom insisted, choking back a sob. "We were told a baby girl was up for adoption. They never said anything about twins. We wouldn't have allowed you to be separated, had we known."

Daphne reached over and took her hand. "It's okay. My parents didn't know, either."

"Well, I guess you made two families happy."

Daphne smiled. "That's exactly what my mom said. I was an only child, so if not for adopting me, they wouldn't have become parents."

"We're not going to think about what may have been, be-cause we have each other now, and we're never letting go," Delaney said, smiling at Daphne. "We have a lot of time to make up. Starting now."

February

Marley

MARLEY AND SAM STOOD ON THE WEATHERED FRONT porch of a duplex in a run-down Philly neighborhood.

"We definitely did the right thing," Sam whispered, looking around as he knocked on the door.

A surprised Andy ushered them in. Two toddler boys darted around the room while another sat by himself on the couch watching TV, his features hinting of Down syndrome.

Andy called to Olivia to join them in the living room.

"Hey, guys! What brings you here?" She waddled over, looking pale and drawn. "I was just napping, although I don't know how anyone can sleep with these monkeys running around."

"Where are my manners?" Andy asked, chuckling. "Let me get you guys something to drink. What's your pleasure?"

"Oh, no bother, we'll just be a minute—"

"Nonsense. I take you both for beer drinkers. Amiright?"

They laughed. "We're that obvious?" Sam asked.

"Takes one to know one. Honey? Can I bring you a water?"

Olivia nodded as Andy helped her into a chair.

"First, a toast," he said after returning with drinks. "We had such a blast with you guys. We'll always have these videos to show the kids. I think they'll love seeing how Mom and Dad competed with the coolest people to buy a house." He glanced over at Olivia, a sad expression on his face as he chuckled. "Ah well, that's what they make mortgages for, right?"

"That's why we're here," Marley said, looking at Sam.

He nodded for her to go ahead, for once not insisting on being the talker.

Marley proceeded to tell them of their decision. Olivia burst into tears.

"Oh, man," Andy said, giving them each a hug. "You really don't have to do that."

"We want to. It's our pleasure."

"Andy, this means we'll have enough for a down payment on the Drexel Hill house."

He smiled and clasped his wife's hand as he turned to them. "We finally decided we needed to look outside the city. We found a house in a nice neighborhood we really like. A suburb with good schools that's also convenient for me to take the train into work."

"And it has a fenced-in back yard for the boys to play in," Olivia added, a huge grin on her face.

"Have you made an offer yet?" Sam asked.

"No, we weren't sure we could afford it. But now—"

"We should do it, Andy," Olivia said.

He nodded. "If you're sure. I'll call the real estate agent later. I don't want to be rude to our guests."

"Do it now, man," Sam urged. "Don't let it get away if you think it's the right one. We learned that the hard way."

Andy looked from Olivia to Sam. "We haven't figured out the closing costs—"

"We can help with that, pro bono," Sam offered. "We've done a few real estate transactions in the past and that'll help offset some of the costs."

Marley beamed at her beautiful fiancé, moved by his generosity.

"If you're sure..." Andy got up, phone in hand.

"Do it!" Olivia giggled.

A few minutes later, Andy returned. "The agent's on it. He thinks they'll accept. It's been on the market for a while, and the sellers are motivated."

"That's fantastic!" Marley exclaimed.

The couples enjoyed another round of drinks in celebration of the anticipated good news. Just before Marley and Sam left,

Andy received a phone call that their offer had been accepted.

Marley was ecstatic. Not only had they done the right thing and made new friends in the process, they'd helped a family find a new home.

Delaney

"HEY, GIRLS," DELANEY COOED AS THE IMAGES OF HER BFFs, Cleo and Tori, popped up on her laptop screen from New York and the Caribbean, respectively. She'd arranged for a Zoom call to share her latest big news.

"Are the babies okay?" Tori blurted, a hint of fear in her voice.

"They're great," Delaney assured them.

"Whew," Tori breathed. "I was afraid when you said you wanted to chat and it was important, there was something wrong."

"There *is* something wrong," Cleo piped in, sounding serious.

"What?" Delaney and Tori asked in unison.

"I'm stuck here in snowy New York while *dis bitch* sits outside, basking under a palm tree."

"Well, let's change that!" Tori said, laughing. "It's a two-hour flight, Clee. You could be here in time for happy hour."

"I'd love to, but I'm too busy with the gallery," Cleo said.

That was a first—Cleo turning down an impromptu trip involving palm trees and piña coladas in favor of work? Who was this version of her friend?

"What's your news, Laney?"

"Remember how I told you guys Kate gave me a DNA test?"

"Yes!" Tori exclaimed, jumping up. "Did you get a match?"

Delaney grinned. "I did. Turns out, I have a sister."

Her friends erupted in joy, firing questions at her.

"What's her name?"

"Where does she live?"

"Have you met her in person?"

"Daphne, Delaware, and yes, I've met her in person. In fact, she's in the Zoom waiting room now. She's dying to meet you guys."

"Fuck yeah!" Cleo exclaimed as Tori clapped.

"Hold on..." Delaney clicked the Admit button, and Daphne's image appeared.

"Hi, everyone," she said, waving into the camera.

Dead silence. Eyes widened. Jaws dropped. Somewhere, a pin fell with a thunderous clap.

Tori responded first. "Holy shit..."

Cleo followed. "No. Fucking. Way."

"Are you guys—" Tori began when the sisters cried out in unison.

"Twins!"

Tori gave a blood-curling scream as she jumped up, nearly dropping her laptop. Cleo erupted in a slew of obscenities, the proceeded to fake-faint.

"See? I told you they're fun," Delaney said.

Daphne laughed. "Amazing. You guys remind me exactly of my two besties."

The four women chatted and got to know each other for the next hour, until Tori reported her laptop was losing its charge and Cleo announced she had to get back to work.

"Great meeting you both. I can tell we're all gonna be great friends," Daphne said as they signed off.

Delaney and Daphne had kept their promise to make up for lost time. In the month since connecting, they'd sent hundreds of texts and emails, engaging in several FaceTime chats and Zoom parties, sharing information about their lives and photos from their pasts. Photos bearing uncanny likenesses—first day of school outfits, prom dresses, barhopping outfits from their single years. Even their wedding dresses were similar.

In addition to similar mannerisms and styles of dress, the twins discovered they shared similar tastes in food, music, and more. Both had four wisdom teeth removed in March of their fifteenth year; both dated a boy named Bill in their sophomore year of college; both refused to eat broccoli when they were kids because they looked like "little trees."

When talk turned to travel, the twins discovered they'd not only been to many of the same places, but eerily within months of each other. Including New York.

"We found the cutest brunch place on 51st," Daphne said. "I forget the name, but I highly recommend, next time you visit."

"On 51st?" Delaney recalled that the place they'd met Cleo and Nigel for brunch was on 51st. "Wait—when were you there?"

"Last September."

"Dude," she whispered, getting goosebumps. "We were there in September too. The waitress even welcomed me back and mentioned my daughter."

Checking receipts, they realized they'd been in the same restaurant, a day apart.

Meeting Daphne helped fill a hole in Delaney's heart she hadn't even known existed. She vacillated between feeling angry they'd been separated, that she'd been robbed of time with her twin, and simply feeling grateful to have reconnected when they did, instead of going a whole lifetime without knowing each other. When virtual meetings weren't enough, Daphne and Frannie decided to spend their mid-winter break in London.

Delaney, now five months pregnant, was feeling energetic and excited to show them around town. She'd offered to pick them up at Heathrow after their daytime flight from Newark, but Frannie was excited to ride in one of London's black cabs.

Delaney waited on the sidewalk in front of their flat as the cab arrived.

"Aunt Delaney!" an excited Frannie cried as she burst out of the car and ran toward her. After throwing her arms around her, she pulled back and unzipped her jacket.

"Check this out." She was wearing a puffy paint sweatshirt boasting the title "COUSIN." "Mom says I'm extra, but I've never been someone's niece or cousin. I want the world to know."

"Extra sweet, that is," Daphne corrected with a teasing smile.

Delaney chuckled as she hugged her little niece, amazed at how a child she'd only met a couple times had stolen her heart. Dalton brought their bags inside, where the foursome caught up over cups of tea before settling in for the night.

As they were about to leave for their tour of London the following morning, Delaney handed Daphne and Frannie two gift bags.

"Just a little something from the babies. Go ahead, Frannie, you open first," Delaney said.

Frannie pulled out a pink onesie with the words "Jersey Girl" printed on the front.

"Yay! I'm gonna have girl cousins!" she exclaimed, hugging Delaney and laying two soft hands on her belly. "High five, girls! I got a lot to teach you."

Delaney and Dalton shared a glance.

"Your turn, Daph," Dalton said.

But it wasn't a pink one she pulled out.

"Beach Boy!" Daphne laughed as she read the inscription on the tiny blue onesie, her eyes welling with tears. "Oh my gosh, you guys! One of each! What a special gift!"

After a round of congratulatory hugs, Frannie leaned in and whispered to Delaney's belly. "Sorry, boy baby. I assumed you were a girl, but I love you just the same." She turned to Delaney. "Do they have names yet?"

"The girl baby is Emma," Delaney said.

"And the boy is Everett," Dalton added.

Frannie rested her cheek on prayer hands, looking like the heart-eye emoji. "I love you, baby Emma and baby Everett."

After Dalton left for work, the women went off to sightsee. It was an unseasonably warm day for London, so they rode on the rooftop of a double-decker bus to get the best views of the city. The first stop was Buckingham Palace to see the changing of the guard, after which they toured Westminster Abbey. Laughing, they made silly faces and snapped selfies on the bridge before Big Ben and Parliament.

Next up was the London Eye. Looking down on the city from the pod of the skyscraping wheel, Delaney felt a pang of sadness. It was such a beautiful city, and she was going to miss it terribly when they moved back home. Later, they met Dalton for dinner at Passyunk Avenue, a Philadelphia-inspired restaurant created by ex-pats from the City of Brotherly Love.

"Thank you so much for today," Frannie said, taking her aunt and uncle's hands as they strolled back to the flat. "If I haven't told you yet, I'm having the time of my life."

Delaney smiled at Dalton over the bouncing child, a glimpse into their future as parents. In this perfect moment, the thought of parenthood didn't seem so scary, especially knowing her twin sister could help her navigate the once-daunting prospect of raising children.

They spent the rest of their visit striking a good balance between doing touristy things and simply hanging out. On Friday night, they watched the movie *Notting Hill* in anticipation of their trip to the Portobello Market the following day. They ate at Delaney and Dalton's favorite restaurants, including Nando's, where Delaney succeeded in converting them into fans, just as she had Kate when she'd visited after the holidays.

As if knowing Delaney was thinking about her, Kate sent a

picture of her and Ryan standing at the Great Wall of China, where they'd been visiting that week.

"Aww, look," she said, sharing the photo with Daphne and Frannie. "They're in China."

"Beautiful," Daphne said. "I've always wanted to go there."

"Me too," Frannie said. "A girl in my class is from China, and she gave us a presentation after she went for a visit. Let's make that our next trip, Mom."

Daphne laughed. "I'll add it to your ever-growing bucket list."

"What can I say?" Frannie shrugged. "I'm an adventurer."

"Frannie, do you know what you'd like to be when you grow up?" Delaney asked.

"A pediatrician. I want to help little sick children."

"That's a great goal."

"What about you, Aunt Delaney?" Frannie asked. "Do you have other dreams besides being a lawyer and a mom, since you've already accomplished both?"

"Funny you should ask," Delaney said, chuckling. "I've been giving that some thought lately."

She still couldn't shake the feeling there was something else she'd rather do. The adoption case she'd been working on had wrapped up to a happy ending, but now that she'd experienced her own messed-up adoption story, she couldn't help but feel there was more she could do to ensure what had happened to her and Daphne would never happen to another sibling set. She just wasn't sure that the legal aspect—which was the final stage of the process—was where she wanted to focus. It seemed there was more to be done to improve the process earlier on. Even as early as the DNA testing stage. For starters, test kits should be made more accessible and less costly.

"It's good to always have goals," Frannie said. "My mom accomplished hers, becoming a librarian and a mom. And now she has another goal. Go ahead, tell her, Mom."

Daphne gave a shy smile. "It's just a little pipedream. I'm kind of embarrassed to say."

"Don't be embarrassed," Delaney said. "There are no wrong answers when it comes to pipedreams, as long as it doesn't involve breaking the law."

"I want to be an author."

"That's great! What kind of author?"

"Fiction. Romance, to be exact. What can I say, I'm a hopeless romantic."

"Just like Kate," Delaney said. "She'll be your first fan. After me of course."

"And me," Frannie said. "Mom's an excellent writer. Wait till you see her work!"

On their last night, to take advantage of London's unseasonably balmy temps, Delaney lit candles, and the sisters settled in at the bistro table on their balcony with tea and digestives while Dalton and Frannie played a video game inside.

Daphne handed Delaney her iPad. "Here's a sample of my writing. Not my best, but it's what I wrote after meeting you."

Delaney read the short story her sister had written, titled "Rekindled." It told the tale of twins discovering each other after being separated at birth. She read Daphne's heartfelt description of meeting her twin for the first time as she blinked back tears.

"That's beautiful," Delaney sighed, tears streaming down her face. "You really have a gift. I hope you do pursue your dreams of becoming a writer. Actually," she paused as she looked back over the writing, "you already are one."

"Thank you. That means a lot to me. But my ultimate goal is to be published."

"No worries, Aunt Delaney," Frannie said as she joined them on the balcony. "I'll make sure she pursues it."

Their conversation sparked something in Delaney. If her twin could conjure a goal beyond her wildest dreams and take steps to achieve it, so could Delaney. Maybe a complete career pivot was in order. Life was too short to no longer enjoy what she was doing for a living.

"I'm gonna hold you to that, Fran," Delaney said. "I believe we have an award-winning author in our midst."

"We also have a grown man inside, crying like a baby after I beat him at racing," Frannie told Delaney. "You better tend to your husband."

"He cries when I beat him too." Delaney waved her off. "He'll get over it eventually."

The following day, after loading their bags into the cab, Frannie hugged Delaney. "Did you have a chance to think about your next goal?"

She laughed. "Yes. To be a wonderful aunt to the most amazing niece."

Frannie shook her head. "Doesn't count. You've already accomplished that. You have to come up with something new. Just make sure it's something that matters to you."

"I promise I'll come up with something," Delaney said, blowing her niece a kiss.

Tears flooded her eyes as she waved goodbye to the retreating cab. Separated once again, but not for long this time.

Cleo

THE WINDS OF FEBRUARY BROUGHT WARMER TEMPS, AND with them, better luck.

Cleo was in the gallery one day when a man came in and asked for her by name.

"I believe I have something of yours," he said, pulling a paper from his pocket.

"Gus!" she exclaimed. It was the sketch that had blown away. The page was a bit more tattered, with a few blotches of dirt, but still intact. "I lost it in a windstorm. Where did you find it? And how did you find me?"

"I was looking for my cat one night after he got out. Found him lying next to a trash can on top of that drawing. I found *you* because of your signature on the bottom. I did a Google search, looking for New York artists with those initials. Your website popped up pretty high up in the search. I'm guessing you've recently opened?"

"Little over a month ago. Good to know my website is ranking high in searches."

"I'm glad too. It made it easier to find you." He glanced around. "Nice place you got here. I'll have to bring my wife sometime. She really loved your rendering of Gus. Who is he to you? Your dad? Grandfather?"

Cleo smiled. "Both."

The man gave her a puzzled look. "Wanna know the funniest thing about this?" He pointed to the top of the paper, where she'd written *Gus Sleeps*. "My cat's name is Gus, and he was sleeping on this when I found it. How coincidental is that?"

Cleo laughed. If he knew the real Gus, he wouldn't find it coincidental. The old goat must be looking out for her. At least he wasn't "haunting her skinny ass" as promised, if she didn't end up with Nigel.

Knowing Gus, it was only a matter of time. She'd better figure her shit out and stop fugging around. And soon, before it was too late.

Ah, Valentine's Day. Cleo's least favorite day of the year. A contrived holiday designed to make people feel bad if they weren't in a relationship. She'd never personally found sin-glehood to be a detriment, but it was hard when stores began hustling heart-shaped shit literally the day after Christmas, along with fat-ass flying babies taking archery lessons on un-suspecting passersby. And it would go on for months, until the entire length of the Ben Franklin Bridge was aligned with desperate singletons ready to jump because they weren't part of a couple.

Up until two years ago, Cleo had never been in a commit-ted relationship long enough to give two flying fucks about it. When she and Nigel had started dating, she refused to cele-brate the pointless holiday unless it was in an anti-establish-ment sort of way.

She'd just finished hanging the piece she'd titled *bottled (up) he*art*. Standing back to admire it, she still wasn't sure what message she was trying to relay. She was pretty shitfaced the night she dreamed it up. Nonetheless, it was apropos for this wretched month.

Her phone vibrated as Nigel's face popped up on the screen. Her brain wondered why he'd be calling her. Her heart did a jig.

"I know it's not your favorite day, so I'm calling to wish you Unhappy Valentine's Day," Nigel said, a teasing tone to his voice.

Her heart skipped a beat. "Aww! You remembered!"

"How could I forget? You only allowed me to send you black roses each year, and insisted I couldn't give you heart-shaped sweets unless I'd taken a bite from each one."

"In case they'd been shot up with cyanide."

"Always happy to fall on the sword for you, my lady," he said.

Cleo smiled and snuggled the phone closer to her, as if it would bring her closer to Nigel. She was missing him some-thing fierce, especially the inside jokes they'd shared over the years. In fact, she missed everything about what they had together.

They caught up for a few minutes, each inquiring about the other's business. It felt good to be talking with him and not fighting.

"So here we are, both living our dreams," he said after a long period of silence. "I guess."

"Yep."

But for some reason, she still felt unfulfilled. She wondered if he felt the same way.

"I'm sorry about how I left your gallery opening," he blurted out. "I was just jealous seeing him there. I know you and he had a thing in the past, and it brought up a lot of feelings."

"I wish you would've stayed longer so I could explain. Wells is just a friend. He was headed home from visiting family in Connecticut and decided—*on his own*—to stop in to see how my opening was going."

"There's nothing going on there?"

"Absolutely not." She paused before showing her own cards. "How 'bout you and your *new friend*?"

"What friend?"

"Tori said she saw you out with a woman." *Ack.* As soon as she said the words, she regretted them. She didn't want to rat out Tori or have him think she was checking up on him.

"A woman?" he asked, then gave a nervous chuckle. "Oh! When I ran into Tori in December? That was my lawyer. We were meeting about the business."

Relief flooded Cleo. She took a breath and prepared to swallow some of her commitment-fearing pride.

"Listen. I'm sorry about my reaction to your proposal. I never wanted to break up." Cleo's heart raced. Admitting feelings never came easy for her.

"But that was the result," he said after a moment.

"Because you said it was. You know how I feel about

marriage. I can't go there, at least not now. But...I really miss you. And I wish we could be in each other's lives, in some capacity."

His pause gave her hope. Until he spoke.

"I'm sorry, Cleo. If you're saying 'let's be friends,' I can't. I love you too much for that. If you ever want this to be something more, let me know."

"And by more you mean..."

"Marriage. I'm too far gone over you for anything less than that."

"Are you giving me an ultimatum?"

"Call it what you will."

"Whatever. I gotta go," she said sharply. Classic Cleo, cutting off convos when they got uncomfortable. Maybe she hadn't changed as much as she'd thought.

"Alright," he sighed. "Just wanted to touch base and let you know I'm thinking of you today. Love you."

She stared at her phone for a long while after they hung up. She so badly wanted to call him back. The way he said "love you" at the end was how one would say it to a friend. And he'd called to let her know he was thinking of her...as would a friend. So where was this I-can't-be-friends-with-you bullshit coming from?

She grunted and tossed her phone down on a display counter, pressing her fingertips to her temples as she tried to make sense of their situation.

Nigel was right. They were well on their way to making their individual dreams come true. Thriving, yet separate, with no workable solution, no contemplative middle ground. She should be happy for herself and for him, achieving what they both wanted so badly.

Then why did she feel so empty?

Charlotte

CHARLOTTE HAD NEVER GIVEN FEBRUARY 14 A SECOND thought. It was just another calendar day to those for whom Cupid's arrow wasn't intended (*read:* her). But she vowed this year would be different. Fueled by another New Year's resolution, she intended to use the occasion to give herself the love she wasn't receiving from someone else.

To accomplish her goal, she'd made a Valentine's Day Bucket List. First thing on the list: take the day off. Second: treat herself to a leisurely brunch. Third: buy a new outfit to celebrate newfound appreciation of her own attractiveness.

Funny, because Charlotte 1.0 was never interested in fashion beyond having fabric (lots of it) to completely cover herself. Back then, she cared not whether her chosen outfits were in vogue or even of this century. She just needed clothing to do its job. Keep her decent. Covered.

But here was the new Charlotte, standing once again in a clothing boutique. After trying on several items, she selected a pair of brown (leather!) pants and a fuzzy tan sweater, pairing them with knee-high boots to complete the outfit.

Successful shopping trip: check.

Next, Charlotte popped into her favorite coffee shop for an energizing iced latte. She sat down with her drink to consult her list when a FaceTime call came through. She was surprised to see Delaney's name flashing across her screen.

"Hey, Charlotte," Delaney said. "I'm calling to congratulate you. I heard you've taken over Bob Stevens's practice. That's fantastic!"

Charlotte thanked her.

"I was surprised. I never saw you leaving Jervis."

She chuckled. "Me either, but the firm had different plans for me."

Charlotte told her about her multiple failed bids for partner.

Delaney sighed. "I hear you girl. I myself am getting the shits of big law firm life. How does it feel, going out on your own? I'm starting to consider other options for myself as well."

Charlotte told her how liberating it was to run a law practice solo, and how interesting it was to learn new law and help people. "That's the part I like the most. Helping people, not just making rich companies richer."

Delaney sighed. "That's exactly what I needed to hear. It helps to know a fellow attorney who's worked for a similar type of firm has found something good on the other side."

"What are you thinking of doing?" Charlotte asked.

She laughed. "I'm not sure, but I promise you it'll be a lot more rewarding than dealing in crime."

Talk turned to more personal matters as she congratulated Delaney on her pregnancy.

"I'm good friends with Jake Brady," Charlotte said. "I saw the photos after your announcement."

"Yes, at our Christmas party. I'm sorry I didn't know you were in town, or I would have invited you," Delaney said.

"No worries. He was with his girlfriend, I think?"

She knew she was taking a risk, pretending not to know whether her "good friend" had a girlfriend or not, but she wanted to gauge Delaney's understanding of the situation.

Delaney crinkled her brow. "No, I don't think he has one. If he does, she wasn't there."

"That's funny. I assumed the blonde woman in his Insta photos was—"

"You mean Tori?" Delaney asked, before waving her off. "Oh my God, no. Tori's one of my best friends. They're not dating."

Charlotte felt massive relief to learn that Tori was there that day for Delaney, not Jake.

"Listen, I gotta run," Delaney said. "Congrats again. Let's keep in touch and plan to meet up after we move back to the Cape."

After they ended their call, Charlotte consulted her list. The fourth item required a spa visit, where she got her nails done and indulged in a ninety-minute massage.

Her phone rang again as she was leaving the spa. Charlotte chuckled at her newfound popularity.

"Happy V-Day, Char," Jake's voice came over the line, instantly warming her core. A Valentine's greeting! Not the same as a date, but she'd take it.

"Same to you, Jake."

"I made it to Australia. It's gorgeous here, just as beautiful as New Zealand. I thought of you as soon as I stepped foot in both countries. The offer's still open. I'll be in Australia for another week."

"Oh, that's sweet, Jake. Thank you. But..."

"I know. The flight. Just keep it in mind." His tone dropped. "I really miss you, girl."

A few simple words, but there was just something about his intonation. Deep. Throaty. She tried to stifle her Pavlovian response, without luck.

"I miss you too."

"Did anyone ask you to be their Valentine?" he asked, his tone lightening.

"No, unless Blinky counts."

His laughter was music to her ears. "He counts."

They chatted for a few more minutes until he signed off. Charlotte held her phone to her heart after their call, uncertain whether the heat radiating through her was from the device, or an internal response to the person who'd just called.

She consulted her list and smirked at the last item, which

was not only ironic, but something that would be a lot tougher after the call she'd just received.

Her final task: *Find someone to get your mind off Jake.*

Good luck with that.

Yet, she found him—at the humane society. He had long hair and the cutest face.

"You're precious," she said, rubbing noses with the tiny shih tzu. Surprising, given Charlotte was once grossed out by animals. In fact, if someone had told her back then this was how she'd spend Valentine's Day, she would've assumed it was because she'd died and gone to hell.

"You guys make a cute couple," a familiar voice came from behind her.

She turned to find Peter standing there, holding her puppy's twin.

"What are you doing here?" She was tickled to see her handsome friend snuggling a tiny furball.

"Holding puppies on Valentine's Day isn't just for women, you know," he said teasingly. "I'm embarrassed to admit it, but this is how I often spend the holiday."

She was flabbergasted. She had no idea Peter had a romantic side.

"I also volunteer here in my spare time."

Charlotte laughed. "Wow, between the restaurants, home renovations and this, when do you sleep?"

"I manage. This work is far more rewarding than running a restaurant, that's for sure."

The two continued talking as they snuggled their puppies, then traded off.

"I know it's Valentine's Day and all," Peter said, giving her a shy smile. "I'm assuming you have plans, but if not...would you care to join me for dinner tonight?"

His invitation caught her off guard. But what better way to continue fulfilling the final task on her list?

"Why, yes," she said demurely. "That sounds lovely."

With that, Charlotte Drysdale, Singleton Extraordinaire, scored a date on Valentine's Day. With an actual man. Would wonders ever cease?

Back at her house, she began getting ready for her date with Peter when her phone rang. It was Nigel.

"I fucked up," were the first words out of his mouth. "Again."

"Oh, no." She put him on speaker to do her mascara. "What happened?"

He proceeded to tell her how he'd called Cleo to wish her an Unhappy Valentine's Day (which might sound insulting but was actually sweet if you knew Cleo) when things went south. She'd suggested staying connected as friends, and he basically gave her an ultimatum: marriage or nothing.

"Oh my." She winced as she accidentally poked her eyeball with the wand. "But is that how you feel?"

He sighed. "I dunno, Charlotte. I miss her like hell, and would love to stay connected, but it would kill me if I ever found out she was dating someone else. At least when we're not connected, outright rejection isn't staring me in the face. Like I can almost put it—her—out of my mind."

"But do you?"

"Not for a second." He sighed. "It just feels safer this way. Emotionally."

"Nigel, you have the right to feel how you feel, and nobody can blame you for it. It sounds like the situation is layered and complicated, which means there probably isn't a magic answer. But don't beat yourself up for how you feel. Be true to you, take it a day at a time, and you'll figure something out that works for both of you."

"What if she moves on by the time I figure it out?"

"What if you settle for less than what you want and end up hurt?"

"Good point."

"Expect the best, and you often get it. Or so they say."

Charlotte stared wide-eyed at her reflection. Where the hell was all this love advice coming from?

"Look, I don't know Cleo that well, but I do know she doesn't give up on things—on people—very easily," Charlotte continued. "She strikes me as a fighter. You're someone worth fighting for."

"Thanks. That actually makes me feel better."

"And about the friends thing...I kind of agree with you. Some would even say it's impossible for men and women to 'just be friends,' especially when sex is involved."

He chuckled. "*When Harry Met Sally*, right?"

She grinned at her reflection in the mirror. "You got it. You may not know this, but I obtained my degree in human relationships from Netflix."

"With honors, apparently." He laughed. "Listen, I'm sorry to bother you with this on Valentine's Day. I hope you have something nice to do tonight."

"I do, thank you. And hang in there. I feel like there's more coming for you and Cleo. Maybe she'll change her mind."

"Or maybe mine is the one that needs to change. Until then, thanks for your wisdom and friendship."

Peter arrived ten minutes later to pick her up. She gave herself a final inspection, running her fingertips along the buttery leather pants and adjusting the fuzzy sweater—the neckline of which was off-the-shoulder. She was tempted to hike it up, but if her new sweater wanted her to look sexy, who was she to argue? She pulled on her knee-high boots and ran lip gloss over her lips.

Thanking her lucky stars for finding such a nice outfit, Charlotte blew a kiss at her reflection. "You saucy minx, you."

She assumed they'd be dining at one of his restaurants, but Peter steered the car away from the center of town.

"A friend of mine just opened a new restaurant. I thought we'd give it a try."

They were seated at a cozy table in the front window of a fancy Italian bistro.

"Best spot in the house," the owner announced. "And a bottle of red, on me, coming up."

"Wow," Charlotte said, impressed by the royal treatment. "It's good to know people in high places."

"Only the best for you, my Valentine date."

That gave her chills. While she and Peter had dined out together before, this time it felt like an official date, not just a dinner between friends.

Charlotte delighted in hearing about Peter's latest trip, this time to Indonesia.

"I take it you travel a lot?" she asked.

"Absolutely." Peter nodded enthusiastically. "I get away every chance I get. A little tough to do in summer with the restaurants operating at full capacity, but it's my off-season stress-reliever. Not only do I get to see new places, but I get to try exotic dishes. It's how I came up with the theme for the new restaurant, which will feature global cuisines from places I've traveled."

"That's so cool," Charlotte said, wishing she was more adventurous. Maybe someday.

After a lovely dinner, they returned to the cottage. Charlotte wondered if he would try to kiss her, but he was a perfect gentleman, walking her to the door and only hugging her goodnight. Which only intrigued her more.

It was the most romantic dinner date she'd ever had. Make that the only one she'd ever had. On Valentine's Day, no less—even if they were only friends.

But maybe, just maybe, the winds of luck were changing for Charlotte.

March

Charlotte

P ETER HAD BEEN TRAVELING FOR TWO WEEKS. THE NIGHT he got home, he called Charlotte and asked if she had plans that Saturday night.

"We're doing a fundraiser for the humane society. It's a full moon lighthouse climb called 'Howl at the Moon.' Would you be interested?"

"Do I have to howl?"

"Only if the spirit moves you."

Normally, Charlotte wouldn't be caught dead outside after ten p.m., and certainly not climbing a lighthouse (howling optional). But she wasn't Normally Charlotte anymore and wanted to support the humane society.

"Count me in."

But that night, staring up at the lighthouse, Charlotte wondered if she'd lost her mind. Climbing a lighthouse in the dark? What had gotten into her? Yet once she got into a rhythm counting its 199 steps, it became easier. At the top, she was filled with adrenaline from combined fear and exhilaration. All her trepidation swooshed away in a cool sea breeze as she stepped into the night.

Grasping the deck railing, she stared out at the black waters of the Atlantic and instantly thought of Jake, wondering where in the world he was just then. Were the stars out, or was he bathed in sunlight? Was he thinking of her, as she was him just then?

She couldn't help her thoughts—lighthouses always made her think of him. She wished Peter were here to keep her mind off Jake, but he'd already done his climb and was volunteering at the base of the lighthouse to greet people as they descended. Alone in the silent darkness, she decided to let her thoughts of Jake drift into the clouds. Just for tonight. Ever since her Valentine's Day reset, she'd done a good job keeping them at bay and was confident she'd successfully do so again once her feet were planted firmly on the ground.

As she gazed up into the sky, ablaze with stars, a flash of light streaked across the night, its long tail seeming to last forever. Would Jake have been looking up just then? Would he have seen the same falling star?

"Stars fell on Cape May," an older man next to her commented. "My favorite song, only it's Alabama. Beautiful story, though. A man kisses the woman of his dreams, then wonders if it really happened."

Was his message a sign? Was Jake somewhere out there, reliving their near-kiss, as she had a million times, wondering if the moment had really happened? *Stars Fell on Cape May* sounded like it should be the title of a romance movie. Starring her and Jake. Except—record scratch—that's right. Stars never fell where Charlotte was concerned.

"Make a wish if you see another," the man said in parting. "May stars fall on you, my dear."

Shortly after he left, another streak of light fell from the star-studded sky. Charlotte made her wish.

Whether it be Jake, Peter, or someone else, she was ready to finally experience romantic love. Bring it on.

Charlotte and Peter continued spending time together, having dinner at least once a week and often doing something on Sundays.

"I feel like climbing a lighthouse," Charlotte said one day when he picked her up. "What do you say?"

"Again?" Peter laughed. "I thought you hated heights?"

She nodded. "I do. That's why we have to do it."

Ever since the full moon climb, Charlotte had decided to experience things that gave her life meaning. Like the thrill of climbing a lighthouse and peering out over the sea, watching as the rhythm of the waves matched the beating of her heart. She was ready to open her mind to new experiences. New people. New possibilities.

Instead of heading to Cape May Point, Peter steered the car north on the Garden State Parkway. "I know just the one."

Not long after, she found herself atop the Absecon Lighthouse in Atlantic City.

"You've just climbed the tallest lighthouse in New Jersey," Peter informed her as he gave her two high fives.

She reciprocated without thinking about germ transmission.

"That was amazing!" she huffed, trying to catch her breath.

"What is it about climbing lighthouses you like so much?" Peter asked as they looked out at Atlantic City, over the line of casinos dotting the coast, beyond the iconic boardwalk to the vast ocean.

"I've spent most of my life fearful of everything. But I finally decided to open up my world, try new things. Now, I get a rush doing things that used to terrify me. And look how worthwhile it is." She made a Vanna White motion, indicating the beauty around them.

She looked up at Peter, who was gazing at her.

"Very well said." He cleared his throat. "Hey, speaking of trying new things, I was wondering if I could purchase the rights to your lasagna recipe? I'd love to include it on our menu at the new place. With your Grams being from Italy, I thought it would be a perfect match."

"You can have it," she blurted out. "I'm honored. My grandmother is whooping it up right now in heaven. She loved making that dish as much as she loved the compliments it garnered."

"Thank you. I'll reimburse you in some way."

"You already have, fixing up the cottage. Not to mention your friendship. I'm happy to give it to you."

"Thanks, Char. It means a lot to me to have you and your grandmother represented in our restaurant," Peter said as he gave her a hug. "You mean a lot to me."

Their hug lasted longer than usual. She lingered there, breathing in his scent. Different from Jake's, but alluring nonetheless.

Although they never discussed their relationship, things between them were starting to feel coupley. The more time they spent together, the more her feelings for him grew. Every once in a while, she'd wonder whether he was feeling the same way, but didn't want to ask and make things weird between them. Nor did she want to repeat the mistake she made with Jake—making more of a friendship than was warranted.

Having a few months after their near-kiss to reset her feelings with the facts, she was pretty certain she'd resolved her waffling feelings about Jake.

Fact: Jake said he'd know his person when he met her, and, after more than two years of friendship, had never indicated she was it.

Fact: They were both too afraid of getting hurt, not to mention ruining their friendship, to take things any further.

Fact: Jake was bobbing around in the ocean, still trying to prove something to himself, while Charlotte's feet were planted firmly on the ground. Standing before a man who suddenly looked like he wanted to kiss her.

"Container ship!" Charlotte blurted out, pointing toward the horizon. "Big."

"Yes." Peter chuckled, as if sensing her discomfort. "Come on, let's grab lunch."

She was thankful for the easy out he'd given her. She may have been starting to fancy him, but if Charlotte Drysdale was anything, she was a slow burn. Apparently.

A few days later, it dawned on her she hadn't seen Agatha Krancks in a couple weeks. Concerned she might have been having health issues, Charlotte decided to make a house call.

She knocked on the door of the old clapboard house and a man answered. Clad in an open robe, he had nothing but boxers on underneath.

Behold, Len in the flesh. She'd never met the man before, but Agatha had done a grand job describing him.

"I'm sorry, I must have knocked on the wrong door." Confused, Charlotte added, "I'm looking for Agatha."

"This is her place. Come in," he said, stepping aside.

She hesitated, wondering if she was about to stumble upon Agatha's lifeless body after he'd bludgeoned her to death.

"What are you doing here?" Charlotte demanded, fearing for her client.

He smiled. "Netflix and chilling."

"Don't listen to him!" a woman's laughing voice called out from behind him. "He has no idea what that means."

It was Agatha, wearing a housecoat.

"We're just binge-watching our favorite show. No chill."

Charlotte did a double take when she saw the smile on Agatha's face. A first.

"I took your advice and killed him with kindness," she explained. "I brought him one of my peach pies. Turns out, it's his favorite. He invited me in, we got to talking, and discovered we're both fans of *Law and Order*."

"Your advice helped us discover a mutual passion," Len said. "We've decided to watch all twenty-three seasons together. We're on seven now. Long way to go."

Charlotte saw the gleam in both their eyes as they gazed at one another.

"Thanks for helping us become friends," he said as he took Agatha's hand.

"My pleasure," Charlotte said as she turned to leave, wide-eyed over this turn of events.

She was still in shock over her discovery when she met up with Peter for dinner that night.

"I don't know how it happened, I'm just happy it did," she said.

"It's because you gave her great advice," Peter pointed out. "You've also been helpful with other folks, and word's getting out. People have been genuinely pleased with your services."

It warmed Charlotte to hear that. "Thanks, but I'm just doing my job. I just wish I'd taken Jake's advice and joined your dad sooner."

"Well, you're here now, and you're killing it. Making people whole again, regardless of their situation. Think about all the different cases you've handled since you arrived here, everything ranging from adoption to divorce, traffic stops to business start-ups. Nigel, for one, can't stop singing your praises. When he came here, he knew nothing about American business law, but you helped him succeed."

Charlotte was thrilled to receive such accolades. While she never got this from her previous job, it sounded vaguely familiar—it was the way Bob's clients regaled his handling of their legal affairs. Up until she'd met Bob, her ultimate goal in life was to become partner so she could gain her coworkers' respect. Now, instead of commanding respect, she earned it.

"How's Nigel's business coming along, by the way?" she asked.

"Fantastic. He's all set up to source our restaurants. His greenhouses are going strong, summer veggies are coming in, and he's experimenting with some grape varieties, hoping to get a winery started."

"That's good to hear," Charlotte said, beaming.

"Speaking of restaurants, I'd like to check in on one of my new chefs. Up for a walk?"

It was a chilly night, but Charlotte agreed a little fresh air would do her good. They decided to walk by way of the promenade. She tightened her scarf to guard against March's roaring cross-cape winds.

Before long, Peter stopped walking and leaned up against the railing of the promenade. "Here, let me warm you up."

He embraced her, rubbing his hands up and down her back, smiling as he pulled away.

"I really enjoy our time together. It's been so long since I've felt like this."

"Me, too, Peter," she said, feeling a rush of endorphins. Finally, someone who wasn't afraid to share feelings.

"You sure there's nothing going on with you and Jake?" he asked.

She sniggered. "Why do you keep asking me that?"

"Sorry, it's just that when he showed up at your place that night, I sensed something was going on between you. And your face lights up whenever you talk about him."

Charlotte blushed. She had no idea she was so transparent.

"No," she assured him once again. "We're just friends. So stop asking."

Peter smiled and nodded. "Okay. I just wanted to make sure I wasn't stepping into something. Jake's a good guy, a friend, and I don't want to...you know..."

"You have nothing to worry about," Charlotte said, for the first time feeling confident in that assessment.

Because here was a guy who, for the first time in her life, seemed genuinely interested in her. Someone who didn't appear to be hesitant. Someone who wouldn't opt to look at a text instead of kiss her. A guy who seemed ready to give her the romantic love she wished for at the top of a lighthouse.

Then why did her heart only race upon the mention of Jake's name?

Delaney

AFTER WEEKS OF PACKING AND TEARFUL GOODBYES TO the city they'd grown to love, Delaney and Dalton boarded their final flight to the US, where they were permanently relocating.

The flight was long and brutal, especially once the babies decided to strike up a soccer match in the middle of the Atlantic. By the time they landed, got through customs, and met up with her parents at baggage claim, Delaney was exhausted. She slept the entire way to their Cape May home, awakening only as they pulled up.

"Are we here already?" she asked, yawning.

"We are," Dalton said, putting his arm around her. "Home."

Delaney and Dalton enjoyed several days of solitude as they adjusted to the time difference and got accustomed to being in their forever home. Delaney was anxious to get the babies' room ready, not wanting to wait until the last minute.

Her mom called her that Friday after they'd finished painting.

"I know you're trying to get the nursery ready, but people are dying to see you. I've asked them to give you space, but I'm wondering if you could join us for brunch tomorrow? That way, it's one outing for you guys and then you can go back to nesting."

"I'd love that," Delaney said.

She was happy for a one-fell-swoop gathering. With both large extended families, there were lots of people to catch up with. And there were two other people she was missing as well.

"Is it okay if we invite Daphne and Frannie?" Delaney asked.

"They're at the top of my list," her mom said. "I thought this would be a great way for everyone to get to know them."

"That sounds lovely. Just let me know what we can bring."

Her mom laughed. "Just those babies. We'll take care of the rest."

Charlotte

IT HAD BEEN A WHILE SINCE CHARLOTTE HAD HEARD FROM Jake. She hadn't been on his Instagram for a while and lost track of where he might be—that's how much Peter had been occupying her time lately. The more they hung out, the more Charlotte realized how gun-shy Peter was about relationships, to the point she wondered if *she'd* have to be the one to make the first move.

Confident she'd moved on from Jake, but nonetheless curious about his whereabouts, she decided to play Where's Waldo with his worldwide adventures. Opening his Insta page, she found a post of him with a blonde on his boat. She zoomed in. Sure enough, Tori.

The caption read:

Happy to see my good friend on one of my stops again. Even happier to hear she's heading home to start her own business. Check out her beautiful photography and let me know which ones I should use on my blog. Wish you the best of luck, my friend!

Charlotte swiped through the photos. Each one was of Jake in beautiful settings, purportedly taken by Tori whenever he "ran into" her. Was it really by chance, or was one or both of them orchestrating their meetups?

Seeing them together was all Charlotte needed to make up her mind. That coming Wednesday night was about to go down in infamy as the night Charlotte Drysdale opened up her heart and told a boy she liked him. Only it wasn't the bare-chested sailor perched on the bow of his boat she'd confess her feelings to. It was the tailored-suited man at the helm of a restaurant franchise, who'd been showing her nothing but consistent, genuine interest. Even if he was a little slow on the take.

She spent days psyching herself up for her big disclosure, but when Peter called to reschedule their date due to a restaurant emergency, she felt relief. He promised to make it up to her when he returned from his upcoming conference.

As soon as she hung up with Peter, Jake called.

"Hey, I have to make this quick. I have a tour starting soon but wanted to let you know Tori's moving back to Cape May to start her photography business, and I gave her your name in case she needed legal advice. I hope that's okay."

"Of course," Charlotte said, hoping she sounded genuine. While she wasn't thrilled to sit down with the woman she'd harbored jealousy for all these months, it might be a chance to get to know her better. Especially if she was as good a friend as Jake claimed her to be. She couldn't wait to assess the situation for herself.

Cleo

CLEO STOOD ON THE CURB AT THE 30TH STREET STATION in Philly, waiting for Tori to pick her up. Her friend had just returned to the States permanently, planning to start her business in Cape May, the dust from her wanderlust finally settling. Cleo could hardly wait to see her.

A honk. She swiveled her head to see Tori's little red sports car heading right for her, pretending she was going to hit her but steering away at the last second.

"Ritz Carlton," Cleo joked as she threw her overnight bag in the back. "And make it fast."

"Sorry, ma'am. This car only goes down the shore."

"Okay. Ocean City it is." Cleo plunked down in the front seat. "I don't know why, but I suddenly have an urge to sit in a room filled with women, *ooh*-ing and *aah*-ing over onesies and diaper cakes."

"That's so weird!" Tori exclaimed, turning to face her in the seat. "I was thinking the same thing!"

"Oh, and please *please* let me be asked—a minimum of five times, no less—'When are you getting married?'"

"How 'bout 'whenever you lose that slacker of a husband?'" Tori suggested.

"Or my other favorite, 'When are you going to have kids?'"

"'Funny you should ask. I'm planning to steal an infant from the hospital next week.'"

Needless to say, attending a baby shower wasn't their favorite thing to do on a Saturday—or any day for that matter—even if it was for their mutual best friend. In fact, it took everything in Cleo's power not to leap from Tori's speeding vehicle and roll across all six lanes of the Atlantic City Expressway, knowing Tori would probably be right behind her. Not that they weren't excited about their friend having babies. It's just that, as single women, they knew the intrusive questions they'd be asked by women in attendance whose only goal in life was to marry off others.

"What did you get her?" Tori asked.

"That thing you put babies in to make them sleep. I forget the name of it."

"A swing?"

"No. It has a weird name."

"A crib?"

Cleo hooked an eyebrow at Tori. "I think I know what a crib is."

"Bassinette?"

"That's it. I had it shipped to her mom's house; hopefully it got there. How about you?"

Tori smiled. "Don't hate me. I made a diaper cake and a fake baby."

"Of course you did." Cleo shook her head and chuckled. "Wait, what the hell's a fake baby?"

"You stuff a baby outfit with washcloths, towels, and other things babies need and wrap it in a blanket."

"Oh, for Christ's sake. Let me out now."

"I was moved by the spirit of giving! It's a big deal, her having twins."

"I guess I don't have to ask if you made two fake babies."

Tori just smiled, then slapped her hand on the steering wheel. "Oh! Speaking of fake babies. Nigel wasn't lying to you when he said the chick he was hanging out with at the café was his lawyer. She'll soon be my lawyer too."

"Traitor." She pretended to be mad but was actually thrilled to hear Tori confirming Nigel's previous assertions about the mystery woman he'd been spotted with.

"Jake set me up with her. Charlotte's her name," Tori continued. "As soon as I'm settled, I'll be meeting with her."

"Charlotte." She mulled the name over in her head, trying to picture a pretty brunette with golden eyes, as Tori had described her. "Wait—Charlotte what?"

"Drysdale."

"Dude! That's Gus's Charlotte—the woman who took care of his cat. Did she move to Cape May?"

Tori shrugged. "I guess. Talk about a freakishly small world."

"You *go*, girl," Cleo said, recalling Charlotte's mention of quitting her job and moving on. "You sure Nigel's not dating her?"

"Pretty sure. I think Jake may have a thing for her, though."

"Jake...oh, you mean the sailor?"

"Yeah. We spent a lot of time together while I was traveling, talking. Mostly about Charlotte. I think he's in serious denial about his feelings for her. He's the male version of Cleo—thinking he's just in it for fun but not admitting to deeper feelings. With any luck, my matchmaking skills will take over."

"Oh, you have matchmaking skills?" Cleo asked, laughing. She felt giddy with Tori's revelation. All this time, Cleo had been hung up on Nigel having a new woman when, in fact, it was just plain Charlotte, the cat lady. A verified attorney. Someone sweet and kind, but nowhere near Nigel's type. She was warmed by the knowledge Nigel hadn't moved on. Yet, at least.

"Well, good luck. Hopefully, your skills get them together."

Tori cast her a look. "They aren't the only ones I was talking about."

Delaney

"HELLO!" DELANEY CALLED OUT AS THEY ARRIVED AT her parents' home for brunch.

"I'm in the kitchen," her mom responded.

Delaney turned the corner to a thunderous roar.

"*Surprise!*"

Jumping a foot in the air, she grasped on to Dalton, who laughed as he caught her.

Before her stood an interwoven gaggle of Ross and Brooks family members and friends. Among them, Daphne and Frannie. Judging by the blue and pink decorations that adorned the rooms, "brunch" was a front for "baby shower".

It also looked as if the families had fully embraced Delaney's twin and niece. Daphne and Kate had their arms around one another, and Frannie and Eli were jumping up and down, high fiving. It warmed her heart to see her newly discovered family being folded into the mix of their extended families and friends.

"Well, hello, everyone!" she cried out, giggling.

Frannie and Eli ran toward them, followed by five toddlers—Dalton's sister Nora's three kids and his cousin Amy's twin girls. Frannie threw her arms around Delaney's belly and Eli gave Dalton a fist bump.

She turned to Dalton. "Did you know about this?"

"I may have. They called me in as backup, in case you refused to come."

"Welcome home, little mama," a familiar voice came from behind her. "It's about damn time."

She turned to see Cleo and Tori, who joined her in a group hug.

After a buffet brunch, Delaney was ushered to a chair-turned-throne. Her sisters took seats next to her, Daphne handing her gifts while Kate recorded the bearers' names. After two hours of unwrapping gifts, Delaney was convinced she'd never have to buy the babies a thing.

Her favorite gift, by far, was the handmade puffy paint shirt Frannie had made her with the word "MOM" on it.

"I love it," she said, her eyes watering as she hugged her young niece.

"That's really cool, Frannie," Eli called out. "Can you teach me how to make one?"

"Sure," she answered. "It's so easy, even a boy can make one."

After the last gift was opened, everyone began mingling again. Except for Delaney, still on her throne, taking in the whole scene.

Kate and Daphne chatted animatedly as they organized the gifts. Bella held two of the toddlers, while two clung to her legs. Jordan picked up the fifth, tossed her in the air and caught her before leaning over to kiss Bella. Both sets of parents raised a toast, either to celebrate the success of the party, the anticipation of their first grandchildren, or both. Marley chatted with Cleo and Tori, while Dalton, Sam, and Ryan smack-talked each other over which team—Eagles or Commanders—would likely win next year's Super Bowl. Frannie taught Eli a special handshake, both succumbing to giggles each time they messed up.

While Delaney missed London, she wouldn't trade this for the world. Family. Home. A kick from one of the babies, reminding her just how lucky she was.

Soon, the party dwindled and only her parents and sisters remained. Her dad helped Ryan and Dalton load the gifts into their SUV. Frannie was in the kitchen with Delaney's mom, helping her wash dishes and put away the food as the child explained how to make a puffy paint shirt.

"The next one I'm making is for you, Grammy Faye," Frannie said.

"Oh, Frannie," she said, giving the girl a hug. Delaney could hear the love in her mom's voice. It was her first gig as a grandmother. Frannie had given her a joyous jumpstart, and a name they decided the babies would call her as well. "I'd love that. How about we have a sleepover some night, and we can have pizza, make shirts, and watch movies together."

"You say the word, Grammy Faye, and I'll be here," Frannie said.

Blinking back the tears in her eyes, Delaney turned to Kate and Daphne. "I'm so glad to have both my sisters together.

This has been one of the best days of my life."

"Let's go hang out on the deck," Kate suggested. "My weather app says its sixty-five degrees today."

The threesome headed outside and settled on the outdoor sectional.

"Well, girls, I have some news," Kate said, tucking her legs under her. "I'm gonna be joining you in motherhood."

"*What?*" Delaney jumped up from the couch. "Are you kidding me? Oh my God, that's fantastic!"

She swept her sister into a hug as Daphne joined in.

"Congratulations, Kate!" Daphne exclaimed. "When are you due?"

"Not sure yet," she said, laughing.

They gazed at her, confused.

"We're adopting."

Delaney and Daphne erupted in joy once more, demanding details.

"I've thought about this for a long time. I never would have had a sister had Mom and Dad not adopted you, Delaney," Kate said, then turned to Daphne. "And your parents wouldn't have become parents had they not adopted you. Ryan and I have been talking about it, even before we were married, and we both feel the same way. We want to give an existing child a home. Our home, among this huge, loving family."

"What a great family to bring a child into," Daphne said, beaming.

"How far along are you in the process?" Delaney asked.

"We've gone through the home study, found out we're eligible, and just received a referral. Now it's a matter of going back over."

"Back where?"

"China. That's why we were there earlier this year." Kate paused, smiling as she blinked back tears. "We've been matched with an eighteen-month-old girl."

"Welcome to girl-mom-hood!" Daphne cried out.

"What's going on out here?" Frannie asked as she joined them on the deck.

"Looks like you're gonna have to make another shirt, Frannie," Delaney said, wiping her tears.

"Are you having a baby, Aunt Kate?" the perceptive child asked.

"We're adopting a little girl."

"That's great!" she exclaimed, giving her a hug. "I'd better invest in puffy paint, the way this family keeps growing."

Everyone laughed as Kate held her glass up. "To motherhood, sisters, and nieces."

Daphne gave them a huge smile. "You don't know how incredible that sounds."

Delaney knew. While the gifts she'd opened that day were for the babies, the greatest gifts were the ones right there on the deck with her.

Cleo

THE SHOWER TURNED OUT TO BE A LOT MORE FUN THAN Cleo had anticipated. Despite being surrounded by married women with children, it wasn't the suck fest she'd envisioned. Instead, it was kinda cool to hear their stories about their meet-cutes, proposals, and babies. No one seemed ready to run for the hills, crying foul for being sold a bill of goods under the shackles of matrimony. Instead, everyone seemed— whole. Fulfilled. Happy.

For the first time in her life, the idea of marriage didn't make Cleo want to abscond like a fleeing felon.

It was as if someone had spiked the punch with a love

potion. Or tequila. Something. But after spending the afternoon surrounded by women seemingly content with their situationships, Cleo was struck with an overwhelming need to see Nigel. She missed him fiercely. Missed his easy smile, his strong arms around her, the passion they'd once shared. Their connection was forever etched in her mind. She hoped it was for him as well. There was only one way to find out.

She shot him a text.

> Hey! In town for Delaney's shower.
> Wanna meet for a drink?

His response came seconds later.

> Sorry Clee, in England visiting fam.
> Have fun with your girls.

Okay, not the answer she was hoping for, but at least he didn't tell her to fuck off.

A week later, she texted him again. This time, he didn't respond.

It broke her heart to think he was seriously done with her, and that this was the end of them.

Charlotte

CHARLOTTE HAD JUST RETURNED FROM WORK WHEN SHE found a small package from Jake at her door. Trying to squelch her feelings of excitement, she opened it to find a gift box wrapped in silk containing a necklace with a pendant made from a shiny green stone. It was shaped into a twist, almost like an infinity sign hanging vertically instead of horizontally. It was gorgeous.

Inscribed inside the lid of the box was a note about the necklace.

This greenstone Pikorua represents the eternal bond between two people, a connection representing friendship, family, love, or all. Wear your Pikorua to honor the beauty and strength of this relationship. With no beginning or end, its infinite shape symbolizes the natural ebb and flow of your connection that will persist through the unexpected twists and turns of your life.

She didn't want to make more of this gesture than might have been intended, but...wow.

Jake had included a note of his own.

My dearest Charlotte,

The second I stepped foot on New Zealand soil, I thought of you and how you should have been there with me to experience it. The country is gorgeous, you would've loved it. I picked up this little trinket at a shop in Auckland and decided that, if you couldn't join me, at least I could have you with me in spirit. I took this necklace throughout NZ and AUS, thinking about us and how much you mean to me. Please accept this token of our unbroken, eternal connection. Know that through the ebb and flow of our lives, whether together or separate, our connection will last through every one of life's twists and turns—and in whatever direction our 'ship goes.

Yours truly, Jake.

Charlotte laser-eyed the apostrophe before the word *ship*, her thoughts racing. Up until now, they'd only ever referenced the thing between them as a friendship. Was his use of the apostrophe an acknowledgment of something more? Otherwise, why not just write *friendship*?

She was overthinking this. She needed to calm down.

Something else in the box caught her eye. A stack of Polaroid photos. Each one featured the Pikorua in a different setting, with the explanation of each place noted on the back. He truly had taken the trinket around both countries.

The last photo was of Jake, fingers in a heart shape, framing the matching necklace he wore.

She put on her necklace, recreated the pose, and sent him a selfie. No words needed.

They were on a boat. She and Jake. His boat. The stars shined against a blackened night sky as they stood on the bow, looking for falling stars.

"There's one," she said, pointing to the streak of light falling gracefully to the earth.

She turned to see if he saw it, too, and met his gaze. Imploring, hungry. He pulled her in close, weaving his fingers through her hair.

"Charlotte," he breathed, his voice thick with lust.

His lips, full and parted, descended upon hers. This time, instead of stopping to answer a phone, he cradled her head in his hands, his probing tongue finding hers in a slow burn dance of fiery passion. The kiss lasted moments, perhaps hours, but the length of time didn't matter. They were finally, finally, expressing their hidden feelings for one another.

"I love you, Charlotte," he whispered as he came up for air. "And not just as a friend."

"I feel the same way, Jake," she said, just as a rogue wave, small but mighty, struck the side of the boat, sending them both into the black waters of the frigid North Atlantic.

She screamed as her body plunged—not into the icy ocean but her soft flannel sheets—awakening her with a start. She cursed Mother Nature for ruining her precious moment. The bitch.

She squeezed her eyes shut and tried to rewind her dream to just before the wave hit, so they'd have a chance to continue their steamy kiss, but it was too late. Reality took over, giving her the wake-up call she needed.

It may have only been a dream, but it told her all she needed to know.

The truth she'd been trying so hard to hide.

She was in love with Jake Brady. And there was no turning back.

Marley

IT WAS THE PHONE CALL THEY'D NEVER EXPECTED TO GET.

"You've got to be kidding me!" Sam exclaimed excitedly as he leaped from the couch where he and Marley were binge-watching *Love Is Blind*.

"What?"

"Uh, yeah," he said to the person on the line as he turned to her, his eyes as big as dinner plates. "Let me discuss it with my fiancée and I'll get right back to you."

Sam hung up and punched the air. "Yassss!"

"What?" she repeated, giggling at his enthusiasm as he broke into the floss dance to chants of "Oh, yeah! Oh, yeah! Oh, yeah!"

He took her hand and pulled her up, linking both his hands with hers. "That was Jesse Palmer. He's just called to see if I'm willing to be the next Bachelor."

It took Marley a split second of earth-shattering fear before realizing she was dealing with a practical joker.

"Sure, go for it," she said, voice dripping apathy. "I mean, it all worked out for Rick. Maybe you can find the next Jenna."

"I'm kidding."

"You *are*?" she mock-screamed in jest. "Oh my God, I thought you were serious!"

He picked up a magazine lying on the coffee table and rolled it into a megaphone.

"Remember that house in Cape May Point, the six-bedroom on Delaney's street?" he trumpeted.

How could she forget? They'd spent every free weekend since their offer was rejected seeking something as spectacular in their price range. To no avail.

He tossed the megaphone aside and clasped his hands with hers. "The deal with the buyer fell through," he whispered, tears welling in his eyes. "It's going back on the market tomorrow. Unless..."

Marley's eyes lit as she guessed what he was going to say next. "We put an offer in first?"

"You got it, babe. The agent said to start with our original offer. All you have to do is say the word, and I'll call him right now."

She reached down and picked up the magazine, rolling it back into megaphone status. "Word!" She didn't just say it, she screamed it. Then, "Oh, but wait...the money. How much do we need to put down?"

"I'm not sure," admitted Sam, disciple of the dive-first-ask-questions-later school of thought. "I'm sure my dad will help us out, float us a loan."

"But we talked about not doing that. Especially with everything going on..."

They'd recently hit a wall with a lack of incoming clients and were forced to crunch numbers, hoping they'd be able to pay next month's rent. If they needed to borrow money from his dad, it should be to float the firm.

They were silent for a moment, probably thinking the same thing. Wishing they hadn't given away that ten grand.

"It just makes me really nervous," Marley continued. "We can't bite off more than we can chew. The firm has to be our first priority."

"Trust me on this, Mar. Let's tell the agent to go ahead with the offer so we don't lose it a second time. I'll talk to my dad and see what he can do for us."

"I don't know…"

Marley didn't want to get into a habit of borrowing money, even though her in-laws-to-be were more than willing to help them out. But it was a pride thing for her. She didn't want them judging her family for not having the same type of cashflow to help them out. Nor did she want to appear to be taking advantage of their generosity.

"Trust me?" he implored.

She could tell by the look in his eyes she had no other choice.

Sam made the call. Now all they had to do was wait to see if their offer was accepted.

And then win the lottery.

The next day, Sam told Marley he'd received a voicemail from Andy. He put his phone on speaker as he played it for her.

"Hey, guys, Andy here. Hope you're doing well. The IT start-up I work for is growing in leaps and bounds. The owners are looking for a law firm to put on retainer, to help them with all the stuff they're going through with business expansion, human resources, contracts, purchasing new property… you name it. I recall you guys owned a law firm and, well, I wanted to pay you back for the humungous favor you did for us. If you're interested, my bosses would love to set up a meeting with you. They'll keep you pretty busy for the next few years, at least. Just let me know what you think."

Marley and Sam stared at each other, their jaws hanging open. Could they be this lucky?

They met with the owners of Andy's company a week later. By the end of the three-hour lunch, the law firm of Maguire Adams had landed its biggest account to date.

Hours before learning their house offer had been accepted.

Marley shook her head in disbelief, as if someone had just handed them a winning lottery ticket. "This proves everything happens for a reason. Everything works out in the end."

"Unbelievable," Sam agreed. "We gifted that money with no expectations of return, but we just got it back. In tenfold."

"And then some."

April

THE TEXT CAME THROUGH IN THE EARLY MORNING HOURS of April 2nd. Olivia had given birth to a healthy baby boy at 11:59 p.m., just in time to be an April Fool's baby.

After a congratulatory text exchange with Andy, and at his insistence, Marley and Sam made their way to the hospital to meet the baby. They knocked softly on the door, hoping they weren't waking anyone.

"Come in!" Andy ushered them in.

Olivia smiled up from the bed, a bundle of baby in her arms. "We're so glad you guys could come," she said. "Meet the newest member of our family."

"Hey, little man," Sam whispered to the baby. "Wow, he's so teeny. I had no idea newborns were that little."

"Thank God," both Marley and Olivia said at the same time, as the only two people in the room whose task it was to grow a human and eject it from their body.

"Can I hold him?" Sam asked.

Marley melted when Sam cuddled the baby in his strong arms, gently—almost instinctively—rocking back and forth as his hand patted the tiny bundle's bottom. Something shot right through her, from her heart to ovaries. If she thought he was sexy before then, watching him hold and coo at a baby was a whole level up. Dad looked damn good on him.

"What's his name?" Marley asked.

Olivia smiled up at Andy. "Go ahead, tell them."

"This little guy here is Baby Sam."

"What?" the baby's namesake exclaimed, his eyes glistening with emotion. "Are you serious?"

"Absolutely," Andy said. "We hope this baby grows up to have the same generous spirit you both have. And, of course, a little bit of your rizz."

"I am so touched by that," Sam said. His voice softened as he gazed down at the tiny person. "Did you hear that, Baby Sammy? Imma teach you how to win all the girls' hearts."

"God help us," Marley teased. "That's all we need is two Sams."

"Liv has a question for you," Andy said, prompting his bride.

Olivia smiled as her own eyes glistened. "How would you like to be Baby Sam's godparents?"

"Oh, my gosh," Marley gushed, "we'd love that, but...what about your family?"

"Between the two of us, we have three siblings. They're all spoken for with the other guys. We're out of options!" Andy joked.

"That's not all of it. You changed our lives with your generosity," Olivia said. "We'd love to have you be a part of our lives. Always."

Later that night, after they shared an M-n-S pizza night on the kitchen island, Sam cornered Marley as soft jazz filtered throughout the room. He swept her into a slow dance and nuzzled her neck.

"How about we make a little Sammy of our own?" he whispered as he pulled back to look at her. "I wasn't kidding. I think I'm ready."

The idea that the explosive, sexy passion they shared could result in the start of their future family hit Marley like a ton of bricks. Suddenly, making love took on a whole new meaning.

"Someday," Marley said, as he lowered his lips to kiss her, slowly, purposefully.

He picked her up and headed to the bedroom. "Until then, how about a little practice?"

Delaney

D ELANEY, NOW OFFICIALLY IN HER THIRD TRIMESTER, WAS starting to feel it. The babies proved not only to be soccer players, but wrestlers, boxers, and Black Friday shoppers as well. They'd already learned about sibling rivalry as they jockeyed for the best position in her belly.

She loved every second of it. Except when she couldn't sleep.

It was one of those mornings. Sleepless and groggy, she sat at the kitchen table of their Cape May home, sipping tea as she watched the breeze tease sea grasses in their sandy backyard. March and April had flipped scripts—March had come in like a lamb and out like a lion as it roared into April.

Her brain felt as blown around, as well. She was scheduled to start up again at her old firm the following day, but something nagged at her—the idea of returning wasn't sitting well. She couldn't help but feel another idea brewing just beneath the surface of her mind. She waddled to the kitchen table, pulled a legal pad from her briefcase, and began making notes. Hours passed before she put her pen down.

"That's it," she sighed, smiling at her outline. She drew a heart around it and at the top wrote, *My Dream.*

When Dalton woke up, she poured him a cup of coffee and shared her idea with him.

"It sounds amazing, Delaney," he said, shaking his head in disbelief. "You have every ounce of my support."

"Are you sure? I won't be bringing as much in as I used to," she said. "I'll be on a straight salary. Fortunately, I can do most of the start-up at home, so I can be with the babies."

"You could choose to never work outside the home again, if that's what you want to do. I got you in whatever you want to do, for the rest of our lives."

Delaney threw her arms around Dalton. His reward for having moved to London to open his company's new branch was that he was now heading up the Philly office. Now, as promised, most of his work was remote, with one day a week in the office, for which he commuted from Cape May. Perfect for their new family.

Next, she called her twin.

"Hey, Daph. Can you put me on speaker? I finally came up with my next goal and I want to share it with you and Fran."

"Yay! What is it?" Frannie asked as Daphne called her over.

Delaney told them about her idea for a new business—an organization that would assist in improving the adoption system from the ground up. She wouldn't be acting as a lawyer, but rather as an advocate for systemic reform. Thankfully, her degree wouldn't go to waste, because there'd be much legal knowledge she'd need, hurdles to mount, experience she could rely upon. While she was happy to have obtained her law degree and had loved her legal career, it was time for a new chapter.

"I'm so proud of you, Aunt Delaney," her wiser-than-her-age niece said. "I can't wait to see you achieve your dream."

"I hope you can include me in it," Daphne said. "I'd love to help in whatever way I can, so what happened to us won't happen to others."

Delaney couldn't wait to get started. She spent the rest of Sunday on her laptop, doing research and seeking resources. She'd put it all into action tomorrow.

The first thing she did Monday morning was drive to Philly, to the offices of Howe and Clemson. What was supposed to be her first day back as a practicing Pennsylvania criminal attorney turned out to be her last.

"I can't believe you're quitting," Jim Howe said. "Although with twin babies on the way, I expected you might want to take some time. Is that it? I can give you time to adjust to motherhood if that's what you need."

"No, Jim. I appreciate the offer but that's not what I need."

"More money? Better office? You name it, it's yours."

"It's too late for you to give me what I need," she said, chin thrust defiantly. "Needed, that is."

"Which is what?"

"I needed to know I was leaving my interns in the trusted hands of this firm. Instead, you pitted them against one another, yanking Marley out of a job she'd yearned for and, frankly, earned throughout the years. And you forced Sam to choose his job over his girlfriend, soon to be wife. They deserved better."

Jim sighed. "I know. I tried to fight for them, but the other partners were hell-bent on downsizing. And, well, as you know, the lowest hanging fruit goes first."

Delaney knew that's how business worked. She'd always been proud of this firm, treating their employees like family. Now that she and Dalton were starting one of their own, it was more important than ever they be shown the same respect. Judging by how the firm had treated Marley and Sam, not extending the same courtesy to them, Delaney had little hope.

She stood. "They deserved to be seen as more than low hanging fruit. Because how that translated to them, and to me, was they were 'baggage.'"

"I'm sorry," Jim said. "Please know you always have a place here if you want to return."

"No, thanks," she said, placing her resignation on his desk before letting herself out.

She'd thought it would be hard to quit her beloved firm, but instead, she felt as if a weight had been lifted. Now that she was starting her own nonprofit organization, there'd be no more billable hours. No more marching into the trenches of criminal court. No more worries that someone's freedom depended upon her knowing and manipulating the law in their favor. It had once been her passion, but with everything that had happened that year, her passion had shifted. Not only to the precious poppies growing inside her, but to a new role where she hoped to continue helping others.

Charlotte

CHARLOTTE HAD BEEN WEARING JAKE'S NECKLACE EVERY day. She'd become so accustomed to it, she'd forgotten to take it off for her date with Peter. It was her first time seeing him since he returned from his conference. She'd planned to tell him she had feelings for him that night. Instead, it would be the night she owned her truth.

Peter kissed her on the cheek when he arrived, making her heart feel heavy. She felt bad for closing the door on a potential relationship between them before anything had even begun.

His eyes rested on her necklace.

"This is beautiful," he said, running his forefinger over the polished stone. "I haven't seen it before. Is it new?"

"Oh," she said nervously. "I just got it. From a...friend."

Peter's eyes turned sad. "Jake?"

"Yes."

Peter continued to run his finger around the unbroken link. "Doesn't feel like there's an opening here."

"It's supposed to be endless. No beginning, no end."

He nodded. "No room for anyone else, either."

Peter deserved to know the truth. The whole truth, and nothing but the truth.

"I'm sorry. I haven't been honest with you, but only because I haven't been honest with myself." She took a deep breath before she continued, hoping she could trust him. "I do have feelings for Jake beyond friendship."

He gave her a defeated smile. "I had a feeling."

"We shared an intimate moment at Christmas, but up until then, we were only friends. Despite him backpedaling, I haven't gotten over it. I'm not sure if my feelings are reciprocated, but it's just not fair to lead you into something knowing I feel this way."

"I appreciate your honesty," he said. "That's exactly why I don't jump into things easily. I'm sorry if I haven't seemed more eager."

"But you have," she assured him. "In fact, I was willing to explore if there could be something here, but..."

"I get it."

She hugged him. "I hope we can still be friends."

She meant it. Peter had been such a breath of fresh air since she'd moved to Cape May. She enjoyed his company and hoped this wouldn't turn him away for good.

"Of course. Like I said, friendship is my jam."

May

Charlotte

WHEN TORI ARRIVED AT CHARLOTTE'S OFFICE, SHE OF-fered her a big smile and a warm embrace, which instantly melted away Charlotte's anxiety. For some reason, Tori felt like an old friend. Maybe for all the time Charlotte had crept on her Insta.

Letting go, Tori held her at arm's length.

"It's so nice to finally meet you, Charlotte. I feel like I already know you, from all Jake's told me about you."

Charlotte laughed. "I hope he told you good things."

"Oh, trust me," Tori said. The look on her face, her intonation, made Charlotte blush. "*All* good."

Whatever weirdness she anticipated between her and Tori was nonexistent. She found Tori happy, hopeful, and easy to talk to, which put Charlotte at ease.

"You're just as beautiful in person as Jake described," Tori added.

Charlotte almost swallowed her tongue as she tried to keep her heart from bursting through her ribcage. He...*what?* She almost asked her to say it again, and spare no details—what he said, how he said it, if he said anything more about her than her physical appearance. But she brought herself back to reality, recalling this was supposed to be a business meeting, and it was incumbent upon her to act like a grown-ass attorney, not a silly girl dishing over a boy.

As they launched into a discussion of Tori's business plans, Charlotte couldn't help but notice she was genuine and kind with sharp business acumen. The two readily agreed on Tori's business structure and the ways in which Charlotte could help her with legal aspects.

"Jake tells me you moved here from Philly," Tori said after she signed the last form. "How do you like it?"

"I love it," she said. "It's almost been a year. It's a completely different world than what I was used to, living and working in the city. Are you from here originally?"

"No, I grew up in Deptford, but my grandmother has a house here. I spent a lot of time in Cape May throughout my childhood."

"That's funny. My great-aunt had a place, and I spent much of my youth here as well."

"It's the perfect place to build my photography business, with all its history, culture, and art."

"I agree," Charlotte said. "For me, practicing law here is a dream come true."

"Jake said he's happy you made the move," Tori said, with an unmistakable gleam in her eye. "Which will be nice for you guys, once he returns."

Charlotte was about to respond, but the bell tinkling on the office door surprised her. She wasn't expecting anyone. Walking Tori to the lobby, she found Peter standing there.

"Hey, I didn't expect you back so soon," Charlotte said, giving him a hug. He'd been in Philly for the past few days.

"My meetings ended early, thank God. It's good to be back."

His eyes lit up at something behind Charlotte. Of course. Tori.

"I'm sorry I—I didn't mean to interrupt," he stammered.

"You're not interrupting anything," Charlotte said. Peter was still staring at Tori. "Uh, Peter, this is my client. Tori, this is—"

"Peter Stevens," Tori gushed. "Oh, my. It's good to see you again."

"Tori," he said softly, "the pleasure's all mine."

Charlotte looked from one to the other. "You two know each other?"

They laughed.

"I guess you could say that," Peter said, his eyes twinkling with the hint of an inside joke.

"I did the photo shoot for Peter's new business, back when it was a new business. How long has it been now?"

"A little over five years," he said.

"That long..." She sighed, shaking her head in disbelief.

"Too long."

His sentimental expression made Charlotte feel like a third wheel rolling into a special reunion. It was clear there was a backstory here, and it went way beyond a photo shoot. Charlotte remembered Bella once telling her that, if a man locks eyes with you for more than five seconds, he was clearly interested. She counted down the look Peter gave Tori.

Six, seven, eight...

Awkward! Charlotte backed up to leave them alone. Tori giggled and Peter cleared his throat.

"Anyway..." Peter turned to Charlotte. "I'm here to see if you wanted to grab dinner."

After witnessing their undeniable spark, Charlotte turned to Tori. "Would you care to join us?"

"I have a couple errands to run," Tori said. "Could I meet you guys in half an hour?"

They agreed to meet at one of Peter's restaurants. As soon as the door closed behind Tori, Peter sank into the chair behind him and put his head in his hands.

"Are you okay?"

"That was her," he mumbled from inside his hands, so softly Charlotte could barely make out his words.

"That was who?" she asked.

He looked up from his hands, eyes watery with emotion. "My person. Tori. The one who broke my heart."

Cleo

ANOTHER SATURDAY NIGHT. ANOTHER NIGHT OF MISSING Nigel like hell.

For lack of anything better to do, Cleo took herself to the bar where he used to work before he'd moved out of the city. She could still feel his presence. She was hoping to find Frank behind the bar and Gabriel on his regular stool.

Jackpot.

"Hey, Clee, it's been a minute." Gabriel hugged her. "How's my fave art*eest*?"

"I'm good," she said, hoping her smile didn't betray her melancholy.

He cocked his head to the side and shot her a knowing look. That's right—there was no fooling an ex-detective-turned-good-friend.

"Come, sit," he instructed, pulling out a barstool for her. "Tell the nice prosecutor all about it."

"First, let me tell the nice bartender what I want." She turned to a waiting Frank. "Whiskey, straight up, Pabst Blue chaser."

She glanced down at the rubber bracelet she'd been wearing since Gus's death, her order answering its question. *What would Gus do?* Why, he'd sit in a bar and drown his sorrows with JD and a PBR and talk with good friends. Just like she was about to do.

"I'm guessing I don't need to ask, but...are we still on a break from Nigel?"

"Yeah. Do we look forlorn or something?"

"We look heartbroken," Gabriel said. "Frank said Nigel's moved to Cape May. I'm guessing that's what's troubling you?"

That's right. She hadn't seen the guys since she'd turned down Nigel's proposal and he moved out. Nigel must have omitted those details when he gave notice he was leaving. She told them the whole story now, as Frank leaned on an elbow, enraptured by their conversation, while Gabriel made appropriate gasping sounds.

"Oh, boy. Don't tell me—Old Cleo showed up just as he got on a knee. Amiright?" Gabriel asked.

"You got it. I almost told him he didn't need to brand me. That's how I felt at the time. But now that I'm a few months from ground zero, my thoughts are...I don't know. Not changed completely. I'm still not ready for marriage. But... maybe chang*ing*? Or maybe I'm just wishing I'd pushed harder for a compromise."

There was that word again, only this time she'd be the one asking Nigel to back down from his hard-and-fast goals.

"What is it about marriage you're so afraid of?" Gabriel asked.

"Yeah," Frank piped in. "We have lots of friends who'd love to have that option, but their state legislators won't let them."

"That's not helpful, dude," Gabriel said as he placed a hand on Frank's. He turned to Cleo. "Could you see yourself with him for the rest of your life, but not married?"

"Yes."

Geez. Where did that come from? She didn't even hesitate.

"So, it's not committing to *him* that's the problem. That tells me something. First, you still love him. Second, your hesitation is about marriage itself. What is it that makes you feel that way?"

She shrugged, thinking of her parents' marriage. "I haven't known many that have worked out well."

Gabriel raised his eyebrows in disbelief. "Delaney? Kate?"

"Us?" Frank asked, thrusting his left hand out to display a ring.

"Wait, what?" Cleo demanded as she grabbed his hand. "When did this happen? And why the hell wasn't I invited?"

"Because it was spontaneous and simple, just like the two of us."

"Vegas, baby."

"Okay, what gives? Are you pregnant?" she teased, looking at the two marriage-phobic men. At least they had been the last time she checked. In fact, she recalled them both saying on different occasions they never saw themselves getting married. To each other, or anyone else. The three of them had that in common. "Were you drunk? Stoned? Both?"

"Drunk on love," Gabriel said. "But this isn't about us, even though we join millions of other happily married couples. So I'll ask again. If you're able to envision 'til-death-do-you-part with Nigel without a ring, what is it about the ring that makes it scary?"

"Don't hate me," she said, "but it reminds me of a noose."

"Damn, girl. We got some work to do."

"Go for it, babe," Frank said. "I gotta take care of these new customers, but when I get back, I want a fully cured Cleo, free from commitment-phobia."

"What do I look like, a fucking miracle worker?" Gabriel called out to Frank's retreating back. Turning to her, he took her hands in his. "Seriously, though. Let's work through this fear of yours. What's the worst thing you can imagine happening if you get married?"

"Losing myself. Becoming domesticated. Smothered."

He narrowed his eyes. "How many married people do you know who are any of those things?"

Cleo thought for a moment. Damn if she couldn't come up with anyone. Delaney and Kate were thriving in their careers, loving their lives, being independent when circumstances warranted or were desired. So were her other married friends. Daisy, the longest married of all the people she knew, had the most nontraditional marriage. She'd always worked outside the home; he'd taken care of everything else. Even Gus, whose marriage she'd mistakenly thought was awful, had been in a loving union. He was only bitter about love because his had been ripped away from him too soon. Cleo knew he wouldn't wish that bitterness on her if he were still alive.

In fact, of all the marriages she knew, it was only her parents' that was so fucked up. Which might have had more to do with addiction and other demons they battled, than the institution of marriage itself. Here Cleo had been operating with a set of beliefs that wasn't proven, realistic, or updated.

"I'm married now, and I don't feel any of those things," Gabriel pointed out. "Because when you find someone you want to do life with, it isn't scary or smothering."

"That's because you're nontraditional in your setup," she said. "Living between two cities, traveling back and forth together each week, allowing you both to pursue your careers."

Gabriel regarded her with raised eyebrows. "And what's stopping you guys from doing the same?"

Cleo's heart ramped up as she realized: he was right. Her ill-conceived concept of marriage had clouded her judgment to the point she refused to consider the options.

The ones Nigel had been trying to explore all along.

"Lots of people have nontraditional setups they make work," he said. "There's no one right way to do marriage. Instead, you get to define your situation and make it work for you."

"You guys make it look easy."

"Believe me, it hasn't been. We had to go through a lot of soul-searching, decision-making, talking out the wazoo, even fighting about it. I'm glad we both kept our own places; that's definitely made it easier for us to spend the week in Philly when I'm working, and here on weekends when he's working."

She recalled Nigel saying once that, with his business,

the weekdays would be the busiest, when he'd be harvesting his crops and delivering produce to the restaurants for their bloated weekend business. Conversely, her gallery would be busiest on weekends. On the quieter weekdays, she could have staff cover.

Gabriel excused himself to use the restroom. Cleo went to reach for her drink, but something stopped her hand. Gus's bracelet had caught on the corner of the bar, as if prompting her to look at it. She gingerly unhooked the band of rubber and looked down as she dared to ask herself the question.

What would Gus do?

But she already knew. He'd made it clear throughout the years he believed Nigel was her person, and she his. She thought back to their last conversation when she wasn't sure what to do about their situation and Gus offered his parting advice.

You'll know it in your heart when you're ready to answer that for yourself.

He was right. She knew.

And she was finally ready to answer.

Marley

MARLEY STOOD OUTSIDE CONGRESS HALL, WAITING FOR her girls to arrive for her bachelorette party. She couldn't wait to hit her favorite shore bars.

She was looking out for Delaney's SUV when a limo pulled up. From the sunroof popped out a familiar someone. Kate, holding a bottle of champagne.

"Get in here, bride-to-be!" she yelled. "Let the games begin!"

Marley laughed out loud. "I thought we were going lowkey?"

"We don't know how to do lowkey!"

The door opened and her cousin Kelly emerged, revealing a limo filled with women. "Surprise!"

"You guys!" Marley exclaimed. She'd expected it to be a mellow night out with just her bridesmaids.

Crammed inside the limo, in addition to her bridesmaids, was her friend Gwen from Philly, and a couple friends from college. Marley was blown away.

"We have one more stop to make in Stone Harbor," Delaney said.

"Who's in Stone Harbor?" Marley asked.

"You'll see."

Delaney laid out the plans for the night. They were heading north to the Deauville Inn in Strathmere, where Marley and Sam spent their summer weekends back in school. Then they'd travel down the coast to hit some of her favorite places: Ocean Drive in Sea Isle. The Princeton in Avalon. Fred's Tavern in Stone Harbor. They'd conclude their night in their favorite Cape May bars.

The limo pulled up in front of The Reeds hotel in Stone Harbor. Wells Abernathy stood out front.

"Wait, is that the new DA?" someone asked.

Wells had been named acting district attorney, effective immediately, after the previous one had announced her retirement. Knowing both Wells and his predecessor, Liz, Marley suspected she'd retired early to assist Wells in securing the vote. He'd won the primary, and now that he'd assumed office, would likely win the general election.

Marley laughed out loud, nearly spitting out her champagne. "Wells is coming with us?"

"No," Delaney said, "but his girlfriend is."

"Amanda!" Marley exclaimed, giving a little clap as her friend emerged from the hotel.

Wells kissed Amanda as someone unrolled a window. The women let out a collective "*ooh!*" and the happy couple laughed.

"Have a nice evening, ladies," Wells said as he opened the door and helped Amanda in.

The limo headed north on the Garden State Parkway to take them to their first stop.

Kate poured a round of champagne. "To destiny," she said, raising her glass.

"Not this again," Delaney laughed.

"It's like we're reliving your bachelorette party, Delaney," Marley said. "I'm here for it."

"It feels like ages ago," Delaney said, resting her hand on her belly. "Life can change pretty quickly. Just don't blink."

"What do you mean by destiny?" Amanda asked.

"Don't get her started," Delaney teased.

"Think about the relationships in this limo alone, and how we all came together. There had to be something out there, making it happen."

Kate gestured to Marley's friends. "You guys are all here because, somewhere along the way, you met and befriended Marley. I bet there are all kinds of interesting stories about meeting by chance, or something intervening that wasn't expected."

Marley looked at her friends and realized Kate was right. Each friend came with a backstory.

Kate continued, pointing to Delaney. "You hired Marley as an intern, and through you, I became one of her best friends. Amanda, you were the host of the segment Marley and Sam signed up for. You cousins, well, I guess we can't blame destiny for family."

Everyone laughed.

"My point is, I fully believe our destiny is found where choice and chance come together. We make choices in our lives intending to lead us in one direction, but other things happen by chance to bring us to where we end up. It's just crazy how often that happens."

Marley was introspective as she applied Kate's theory to

Sam. She'd met him in college in a mutual class that neither had originally registered for. The criminal law class she'd signed up for met on Tuesday and Thursday. Due to a registration snafu, the class had been overbooked and she'd been moved to the Monday/Wednesday/Friday session. It would have conflicted with another class for which she'd already registered had that class not been cancelled. Sam, on the other hand, had waited too long to sign up for classes in his major and was forced to take an elective. He was torn between astronomy and criminal law, eventually settling on the former. But the class had closed by the time he got around to registering, leaving him with the criminal class. He was late to class on that first day, and the only seat left in the crowded room was the one next to Marley. He'd forgotten a pen, so he asked to borrow one. The rest was history.

Now here she was, less than a month away from marrying him.

"I'm a believer," Marley said, raising her glass. "To destiny, and for all you wonderful women and the magical ways we've all come together. I'm honored to have you all be part of my special night."

Delaney

DELANEY STOOD ON THE BRICK SIDEWALK, LOOKING UP at the shingle hanging on the building. *Her* building.

She'd spent the past few weeks on the grind, true to her nature and impeccable organizational skills, wanting to get her dream jumpstarted before the babies arrived. In that time, she'd found office space, filed nonprofit documents, enlisted a bank of volunteers, and begun approaching potential board members. The president of which was her own flesh and blood. Her twin sister.

"Hey, boss," Sam's voice carried on the breeze from down the street. "Nice-looking sign you got there."

"That's *friend*, to you," Delaney called out, reminding Sam she was no longer his boss.

"Re*KIN*dle." Sam read the sign. "The name says it all."

Delaney had retained Marley and Sam as her lawyers. They were the ones who'd told her about available office space three doors down from their firm. Located on a quiet, tree-lined street, consisting of residences and boutique-style offices in Society Hill, it was the perfect location for her new venture. She would work most of the time from home in Cape May but would join Dalton when he commuted to the city once a week, leaving the babies in the loving care of their retired grandmothers.

"Ready for lunch?" Marley asked. "I'm starving."

The three walked a couple blocks to a small café on Walnut Street, where they were meeting Daphne. She and Frannie had relocated to the Philadelphia area to be closer to Delaney and their new business after her parents had retired to Florida.

Daphne was already waiting for them in a booth.

After they got settled and ordered their lunch, Marley dove into business. "The last time we met, we asked you guys to complete vision and mission statements for Re*KIN*dle so we can assist with legalities."

"I'll let the president handle this one," Delaney said, smiling at Daphne.

"Our vision is to reunite families separated by adoption."

"Nice and simple," Sam said. "I like it."

"Not too simple?" Delaney asked.

"Not at all. The simpler, the better. How about your mission?" Marley asked.

"Our mission is to guide adopted individuals and their

birth families on their journey to discover, rekindle, and embrace one another, in a cost-effective manner easily accessible for all."

Marley looked at the paperwork and furrowed her brow. "What's Frannie's Law?" she asked. "Is that something new?"

Delaney and Daphne smiled at each other.

"That's the name of the legislation we'd like to see pass, to make it easier and more affordable for Pennsylvania adoptees to find their families."

Delaney smiled. "We've partnered with a friend of mine from law school, who just won her bid for state representative after beating out longtime incumbent Ted Roberts."

"Oh my God, Tori's ex-boyfriend?" Marley asked.

"The same. My friend crushed him. And she's willing to sponsor the bill."

"That's great," Marley said, smiling as she turned to Daphne. "How does Frannie feel about being the namesake of an important piece of legislation?"

"She's over the moon. She's the sole reason I found my twin. She's why I'm sitting here now, pursing a dream I never knew I had."

"She's the reason we found each other," Delaney whispered, a tear rolling down her cheek as she clasped Daphne's hand. "Were it not for Frannie, we'd spend a lifetime not knowing."

Marley smiled. "Frannie's Law it is."

Charlotte

ON THE WAY TO THE RESTAURANT, PETER FILLED Charlotte in on his history with Tori.

"The photoshoot was how we met. Owen and I were about

to open our first restaurant, and she was assigned to cover the story for *Philly Mag*. I was taken with her from the moment she walked into the room. We hit it off immediately. As I told you earlier, we dated a few months but only casually. I was busy with the restaurant opening, and it seemed whenever I was free, she was doing photo shoots. That's how she met the jerk who would later become her boyfriend."

"Wouldn't she have known it was your dad's law firm when she came in today?" Charlotte asked, even though she'd changed the firm to her name.

"No, I never brought her here. How did she come to hire you?"

"Jake asked me to meet with her. They're friends."

When Tori joined them, Charlotte delighted in seeing the way she gazed at Peter.

At one point, Tori lifted her glass. "A toast. To Peter, for making your dreams come true. I've been following the media coverage over the years. I'm so proud of you."

The way their eyes locked, Charlotte sensed Tori hadn't quite gotten over Peter, either.

She finished her drink and excused herself, claiming to have a headache, to give them a chance to catch up.

As for Jake, Charlotte had been percolating with her newly acknowledged feelings after the dream had pushed her over the edge. She was growing accustomed to framing him in a different way in her mind and heart—as not just a friend, or someone she had to pretend was just a friend, but someone whom she finally, honestly and truly, loved. She wasn't quite sure what she was going to do about it. Probably nothing, as she wasn't a risk-taker. She just needed to get used to the feeling of being in love, for the first time in her life. Quite honestly, it was a heady, happy, hopeful feeling, something she'd never felt before, even if she was alone with those feelings. It was liberating to finally not hide her feelings from herself.

She and Tori met a few more times about her new business, always at Tori's request. And rather coincidentally, Peter seemed to know anytime Tori was there, finding whatever excuse he could come up with to stop by.

Finally, one day, they came in together holding hands. Peter told her they'd talked on the phone one night for two hours, and not only discovered they were both single, but neither one had gotten over what they once had.

Peter and Tori were officially an item. Once again.

June

Charlotte

THE GRAND OPENING OF PETER AND NIGEL'S RESTAURANT was rapidly approaching. Charlotte was excited for her two friends and their new partnership, and proud of how she'd used her legal skills to assist Nigel in chasing his dream. Now she was helping Tori do the same. Peter had signed on to be Tori's first client, displaying several photos she'd taken from around the world in his new global cuisine restaurant. A perfect match, in more ways than one.

In thinking about the dreams she'd helped others achieve, Charlotte couldn't help but think about her own. The road to her prior dream had broken, ultimately leading her to a better one. A dream come true beyond her wildest fantasies: practicing law, helping others, gaining their respect. She didn't need anything else. Except, maybe a love interest.

All in due time.

In the meantime, Peter and Tori occasionally asked her to join them for some of their outings. She felt uncomfortable accepting their invitations, not wanting to be a third wheel, but they insisted. One such day was spent at the Sandy Hook Lighthouse, where the three climbed together and witnessed a proposal at the top.

"So romantic!" Charlotte gushed, hoping someday she could experience something so special. A fairy-tale ending like in one of her many favorite romcoms; a happy ending Charlotte 1.0 could never have envisioned for herself. But as time went by, despair had given way to hope, causing Charlotte 2.0 to realize she, too, deserved to find such joy.

Later that afternoon, the three were enjoying drinks at

an outdoor bayside restaurant when Tori turned to her. "So, Charlotte. Is there anyone you're interested in?"

She was taken aback by Tori's abrupt, probing question. Peter gave Charlotte a subtle wink from across the table, as if to let her know her secret was safe with him if she chose not to reveal it to Tori.

"Not really," Charlotte fibbed. "Why, do you have someone in mind?"

"Actually, yes," Tori said, a teasing lilt to her voice. "Someone I think would be perfect for you. Say the word, and I'll fix you guys up."

Charlotte's heart lurched. Considering being fixed up with someone felt disingenuous. Like she'd be cheating on Jake—or at least, her feelings for Jake.

Tori and Peter shared a look. Charlotte felt her cheeks flush.

"Char-*lotte*," Tori sang. "Look at you, you're blushing. I'm guessing there *is* someone special in your life."

"Not yet," Charlotte admitted shyly. She shrugged. "But...hopefully?"

"Does he know?" Tori asked.

Charlotte shook her head.

Tori clasped her hands over Charlotte's. "Listen, girl, don't make the same mistake we did, letting someone special slip away. If you like this boy, tell him."

"Yeah, we were just talking about that the other night," Peter added. "I was head over heels for Tori, but never let her know."

"And here I'm thinking this guy is playing it so cool, so lowkey, he's probably not that into me," Tori added. "At that time in my life, I needed to feel cherished. In came my ex, who swept me off my feet. Unfortunately, the only thing he cherished was the idea of me, and the role I could play in his political gains. But I never stopped thinking about Peter."

"I've always regretted not being honest with you from the

start," Peter said, gazing at Tori before he shifted his smiling eyes to Charlotte. "Don't make my same mistake, Char."

"But what if he doesn't feel the same?" Charlotte blurted out.

Tori laughed. "Well, I guess you'll never know until you try, right? Trust in yourself. Trust in love."

Later that night, Charlotte replayed their conversation. Was she bold enough to take a chance? To lay her feelings on the line for Jake, and ask about his? While she'd contemplated doing that with Peter, this was different. They didn't have the same depth, history, and level of connection she shared with Jake. It made her nervous, thinking how much she could screw up their relationship if she'd misread every gesture, every look, every lingering touch that led her to growing feelings. But, as Tori said, she'd never know until she took a chance.

It was time. Time to trust in love. Make the big gesture like they do in movies.

She pulled out her phone and composed the text she'd been wanting to send him since he left in January.

> Dear Jake, I've been thinking a lot about us. In particular, the night you almost kissed me. If I could rewind time, I'd have grabbed that phone of yours and thrown it into the snow, because all I wanted you to do was kiss me, and that feeling hasn't gone away, no matter how hard I try. I don't want to lose your friendship, but I can't go another day without speaking my truth. Which is…I love you. As more than a friend. I'm ready to give you my heart and explore what else we could be together. If you feel the same, please send me a sign. If not, I'm sure we'll have a good laugh over this someday. Always friends, maybe more.
> All my love, Charlotte

It was finally the night of the grand opening. It had been forty-eight hours since she sent the text, and she still hadn't heard from him. But, for some reason, she wasn't worried. She did what she needed to do, and she was prepared to let things happen as they may. Strange twist for Charlotte, who never took risks. Especially where her heart was concerned.

Trusting in love just felt...right.

Getting ready for the grand opening gala, Charlotte paused in front of the mirror for a final inspection. Her chestnut brown hair was swept into a French twist and the long off-the-shoulder red dress clung to her in all the right places. It looked like the one Julia Roberts wore in *Pretty Woman*—another favorite movie featuring two characters who fell in love despite their differences. Maybe even because of them.

As pretty as she felt, she couldn't help but feel lonely. While she was accustomed to being a plus-zero for most social gatherings, she wished she had someone special to accompany her tonight. She wished Jake was here.

Charlotte's phone rang. It was Tori.

"Hey, girl," she said. "I'm heading to the party. Need a ride?"

"I was about to call an Uber."

"Don't. Peter had to be there early, so he went ahead without me. I'd feel more comfortable having someone to walk in with."

Charlotte smiled at the realization that even beautiful, confident women like Tori experienced social anxiety. She readily agreed. It might not have been a date, but at least it was a friend.

Minutes later, Tori arrived to pick her up.

"My God, you're stunning!" she exclaimed, her mouth taking an "o" shape. It made Charlotte giggle.

"As long as you have me back by midnight, we should be good," she joked.

Tori pulled out of the driveway and cast a look of whimsy at Charlotte. "Ever climb a lighthouse in heels?"

Charlotte laughed. "Not if I can help it."

"I have a huge favor to ask of you," Tori said, her eyes pleading. "I got a last-minute booking to photograph an engagement at the top of the lighthouse at sunset tomorrow."

"Ooh, how romantic!" Charlotte exclaimed.

"Except I just got a new camera and haven't been able to test the lighting. The sun's about to set, and I was wondering if you'd mind stopping off so I could test it out?"

"Sure," Charlotte said. "I can wait in the car."

"I actually need a subject, and it would be weird to use some random stranger. Would you mind standing in? I pay well."

Charlotte laughed again, wondering how on earth she was going to navigate 199 metal steps in high strappy sandals. But Tori had been kind enough to offer her a ride, and what was the worst thing that could happen?

Charlotte's brain started filling in the blanks: broken ankle, snapped heel, sullied dress...

Oh, shut up, Charlotte. Help a girl out.

"Okay, but if I break any body parts, I'm suing the hell out of you," she joked.

"Fair enough. Sorry this is so random. I promise I'll get you to the party as soon as we're done up there. Five minutes, tops."

Charlotte was out of breath by the time she hit the last step, relieved she hadn't broken a heel or any body parts.

Perfect timing—the sun was about to set. She turned to ask Tori where she wanted her to stand, but she wasn't there.

"Tori?" Charlotte called out to the empty staircase.

"Hey, girl," a voice came from behind her.

She spun back around.

It was Jake.

Cleo

CLEO RACED TO CAPE MAY, HOPING SHE'D MAKE IT IN time. She'd cut a break—the Friday night shore traffic wasn't as bad as she'd anticipated, despite it being June.

After contemplating her choices, she couldn't wait any longer. It may not have been the wisest decision to take a stand at an event where she wasn't an invited guest, but Cleo never stood much for ceremony.

After all, moxie was her middle name.

She was lucky to find parking not far from the restaurant. She was running late, so she yanked off her fuck-me pumps and ran in bare feet, making it to the restaurant just as they prepared to close the doors.

She stood in the very back of the crowded room. Glancing around, she saw Nigel at the front next to a podium and a group of men, laughing as they shook each other's hands. She recognized two of the men from the restaurant.

Someone approached a mic and began speaking.

As they announced their partnership, Cleo was mesmerized by Nigel's beaming smile, the joy in his eyes. He looked proud, and rightly so. He'd made his dreams come true.

After the speeches were over, she wandered through the crowd in search of Tori, hoping her friendly face would help calm her nerves.

"Cleo?"

His voice came from behind her. She turned slowly, uncertain what his reaction would be.

Nigel leaned in and kissed her cheek. "It's good to see you," he said, sounding genuinely happy. "Thanks for coming."

"I wouldn't miss it for the world. I know you probably don't want to see me—"

"Of course I want to see you."

Whew. That was a surprise, given he'd stopped responding to her texts. "I have some things to say, but this is your night. Mind if I hang, and we talk later?"

A smile spread across his face. "I'd love that."

Cleo was relieved Nigel was open to her being there and interested in talking. Thank God, or the night could have been a complete disaster. She didn't know how their talk would go, but at least he wasn't having her physically removed by security.

She laughed to herself as she thought, *Yet.*

Charlotte

CAPTAIN JAKE BRADY—WHO SHOULD HAVE BEEN SOMEwhere in the Atlantic—was standing at the top of the Cape May lighthouse. And he was wearing a tux.

"Oh my God!" Charlotte screamed, clasping her mouth with her hand.

"Surprise!" he exclaimed, opening his arms wide.

Charlotte began bawling at the very unexpected sight of him as she tumbled forward into his arms. He embraced her tightly, gently swaying them back and forth.

"What are you doing here?" she cried out, shedding happy tears all over his tux. "Did Tori know—"

"That I was here?" He gave her a shy smile. "Yeah. I kinda had her lure you here."

She gasped, clutching her hand to her heart.

"I'm home," he whispered. "For good."

He pulled her closer and gazed at her with a look she'd never seen before.

"For good?"

He nodded. "After that text of yours, there's nowhere in the world I'd rather be than where you are."

Her knees nearly gave out on her. Thank God his arms were wrapped around her, or she'd have puddled at his feet.

"Charlotte, I spent years preparing for this journey, eager to sail around the world so I could visit exotic places, meet fascinating people, experience once-in-a-lifetime things. But every night, I'd lay my head on my pillow—regardless of where I was or who I'd met—and my thoughts turned to you. How I wished you were there, experiencing it with me. No matter how fascinating my day was, all I could think about was...*you*."

His words left her breathless.

"I thought I needed to do this trip to prove something to myself, but I realized I already had what I needed. Someone who saw the real me and accepted me as I was. Someone who instilled the confidence in me I couldn't find in myself."

"You've done the same for me, Jake," she whispered.

"Turns out, you're the Jane to my Richard. The Terry to my Nickie. The Sally to my Harry. I promised you once, if we turned forty and weren't married to anyone else, we'd meet up here one day. But I can't wait seven years to share my truth. Especially now that you've shared yours."

Charlotte giggled. "I thought we'd settled on fifty."

"Even more compelling. I cannot wait seven*teen* years to tell you how I feel. I love the fact that you'd never had pizza until you were in your thirties, and now you can't get enough. I love how you single-handedly keep Purell and Wet Ones in business, too afraid to touch people's hands, but not afraid to touch their lives. And I love how you're terrified of heights, yet you find joy in climbing lighthouses."

His voice softened. "But most of all, I love the fact that

you've never given your heart to someone. I'm just hoping you meant what you said, that you're ready to give it to me."

"You already have my heart," she breathed in a bare whisper. "You've had it all along."

Exhaling with relief, he closed his eyes. "Good. Because I'm done traipsing around the globe trying to figure things out. I know what I want, and when you know, you don't want to wait any longer to make it happen."

He cupped her face, and she held her breath as he said the words she'd waited a lifetime to hear.

"I love you."

"I love you, too, Jake."

Charlotte crashed her lips to his so forcefully he toppled into the railing. She grasped onto him and pulled back, laughing.

"That would be my luck to push the only guy who's ever loved me off the top of a lighthouse." She linked his fingers with hers. "I promise I won't let you fall."

He gazed at her, eyelids heavy. "I already have."

This time, her approach was much smoother as she leaned into him, lifting her chin as she stared into his deep blue eyes. He held her waist, pulling her in tightly, touching his nose to hers.

"I'm all yours, Charlotte," he uttered as his lips fell softly on hers, teasingly at first, until years of denial, near-misses, and overwhelming temptation took over.

The sun dipped discreetly below the horizon as dusk rose up to greet them. From the corner of her eye, Charlotte saw a star shoot across the twilight sky.

Stars finally fell on Charlotte.

Cleo

CLEO RETURNED FROM THE BAR IN SEARCH OF TORI again, this time finding her talking to a woman in red.

"Hey, Cleo," Tori said. "You remember Charlotte?"

"Of course," she said as Charlotte turned to her. Trying to hide her shock, she gave Charlotte a hug. No longer just plain Charlotte, she was stunning. "You looked a little different last time I saw you."

"New and improved," Charlotte said, giving a little spin.

Cleo couldn't believe how much she'd changed. She was dripping in confidence.

"Congratulations on your new practice. And for having this one as a client," Cleo said, looping her arm with Tori's.

"It's been my pleasure," she said warmly. "And working with Nigel has been fantastic. I hear congratulations are due for your new gallery. Quite impressive."

"Look at us bosses, making our dreams come true." Tori raised her glass and Cleo followed.

A handsome dark-haired guy approached with drinks. Cleo recognized him as the infamous Jake.

"Hello, ladies. What are we toasting?" He handed a glass to Charlotte.

"Making dreams come true," Tori said.

Cleo saw the look he gave Charlotte.

"I know mine have," he said, wrapping his arm around her. "If you'll excuse us, I have some friends I'd like Charlotte to meet."

As the two walked away, Cleo turned to Tori, eyes wide over the new couple. "Are you serious?"

"Oh, girl," Tori said, grasping her wrist. "It's a whole thing. I've listened to him drone on about her for *months*. He's been in love with her since his trip started but was too afraid to admit it to her or himself. I'm glad he finally grew a set. Suffice it to say, I definitely have a career in matchmaking if this photography thing doesn't work out."

Cleo said a silent prayer she herself wouldn't need Tori's intervention.

As the party wore on, Nigel found Cleo and introduced her to his new associates, referring to her as his "friend." Which was a surprise, given his previous stance on never being her friend. But she'd take it. Better than ex, or fuckwad, or the other names she deserved.

"Are you staying with Tori?" he asked as the crowd dwindled.

"I'm hoping to stay with you," she boldly suggested. "Any room at the inn?"

"Oh!" he exclaimed, clearly taken off guard. "Of course."

They Ubered back to his place, and he gave her a tour. She was amazed at how he'd fixed up the farmhouse, making it his own. He asked if she wanted a drink.

"No. What I have to say can't wait." She took a breath, noting how fully she had Nigel's attention. "I've changed, Nigel. I'm done being commitment-phobic, and I'm sorry I've been so pig-headed, refusing to compromise. You were only trying to keep us together so we could both pursue our goals, but I was so afraid of losing myself and my dream that I cast away the one person who's always had my back, my heart, and my love. I thought the most important thing in my life was opening my own gallery, but I've come to realize a dream isn't worth achieving without someone special to share it with." She stepped toward him. "I love you, and I don't want to be without you anymore. I don't know how, or if you even want me anymore, but I would give anything to figure out—"

He grabbed her and kissed her before she could finish her sentence. Hard at first, then softly. God, it felt good. She'd gone so long without this great pleasure of her life, his touch. This is what she lived for, kissing Nigel.

"I was wrong to give you an ultimatum," Nigel said. "I don't care anymore if we get married or not. All I know is, I don't want to lose you again. I need you in my life, in whatever way you want to be here."

Cleo was struck with a lightning bolt of truth. Nigel wasn't here to brand her, make her change, or whatever her fear had been. Instead, he was—and always had been—choosing her for exactly who she was. She was in control of her life and her destiny, no one else, but she'd been so tripped up over her own archaic notions of marriage, she couldn't see the bigger picture. Which was that life wasn't worth living without this man standing before her.

"You won't ever lose me again. I promise."

He lifted her up and carried her to the bedroom, where he kissed her like he'd never kissed her before. They made up for all the time they'd lost. And then some.

The next morning, he led her outside to the little shack he'd once suggested could be her studio. It looked nothing like she remembered. The rotted wooden boards had been replaced and it had a fresh coat of paint. Purple, with yellow trim, her two favorite colors. Window boxes filled with pansies, her favorite flower, hung beneath tiny windows.

He opened the door to reveal a table off to one side, an easel on the other. Built-in shelving enveloped the room, filled with various art supplies.

Cleo's jaw hit the floor.

"I've been working on it for months, hoping someday you'd change your mind, and you'd want to be here."

She couldn't believe he'd done all this for her, even while they were broken up, just in the hopes that she might change her mind. If she didn't love him before...

"I want you," she said, kissing him. "Forever."

She pulled back and looked around, amazed at the lengths he'd gone to. "This is beautiful, Nigel. I'm blown away."

"Go ahead, check it out," he said.

She wandered around, noting he'd stocked her favorite brands of supplies. Without knowing it, he'd just made her loosely formulated plans come to fruition. Weekends in the city, weekdays here. This would be a perfect place to create, away from the city and the stress of owning a business. Seeing what he'd done for her made her want to give him everything he wanted. And then some.

Spotting a sketch pad, she picked it up, along with a paint pen.

"Are you painting me a picture?" he asked, chuckling.

Her back still to him, she answered, "Yes."

"What of?"

"Our future."

Two simple words she'd never wanted to hear. Two simple words she'd never thought she'd say herself. Two simple words she couldn't keep in anymore.

She turned and held up the pad containing those two simple words.

Marry me.

Delaney

MARLEY HAD ASKED DELANEY TO BE ONE OF HER BRIDES-maids long before she was pregnant with twins. When Delaney told her about the pregnancy and that her due date was around the date of the wedding, she offered to drop out.

"I don't want to take up someone else's spot if I can't walk," she explained.

"Nonsense. You're irreplaceable. It's 100 percent up to you. You can even decide the day of, but nobody's taking your place."

Now that the day was here, Delaney was feeling great, relieved she could partake in the wedding. The end of her pregnancy had been good to her physically, and she'd made it to the point where the babies were fully viable. They could come any day now, thankfully. She couldn't wait to meet her precious poppies.

She was in the bridal suite getting ready with the other bridesmaids when Dalton stopped by to check on her. The closer they got to the due date, the more attentive he'd become.

"Wow, you're stunning," he said, his eyes lighting up as she stepped from the room and joined him in the hallway.

She was wearing the same sleeveless turquoise dress Marley had chosen for the bridesmaids, altered to accommodate the growing fetuses.

Dalton addressed her belly. "You look great, guys. Ready for the wedding?"

Delaney held an imaginary mic. "Baby Emma is wearing a Dolce & Gabbana linen midi, while her escort, Baby Everett, is sporting a casual tux by Giorgio Armani. Looking just like his Daddy-O."

Dalton chuckled. "As long as you guys don't crash the wedding, we should be good."

Kate joined them in the hallway. "Everything good?" she asked Delaney. Like Dalton, her sister had become extremely doting of late. She leaned over to talk to Delaney's belly. "Anytime now, babies! Auntie Kate can't wait to meet you!"

"Not yet, guys," Delaney said to her own belly. "Let me get through the wedding first. I'm just so happy—" She winced and instinctively put her hand on her bump. "That was a kick."

"I came out to tell you we're doing pictures soon," Kate said.

"Okay, I'd better get back," Delaney said as she kissed Dalton. Turning away, she felt a stab of pain. "*Oof.*"

"What?" Kate asked, eyes wide with fear as Delaney doubled over. "Are you okay?"

Delaney caught her breath and inhaled, pulling herself upright. "Sorry, just a false alarm."

Until she felt another doubling-over stab.

"*OhmyGodohmyGodohmyGod,*" Kate said excitedly. "Is it happening? It's happening, isn't it. Oh my God, it's happening!"

"It's—" Delaney gasped between excruciating stabs of pain. "Happening."

"Come on, hot mama," Dalton said as he put his arm around her.

Delaney was impressed at how calm and collected he sounded.

"Looks like we got some wedding crashers on our hands."

Kate alerted Marley and the other bridesmaids, who joined them as they made their way to the elevators.

"Oh my gosh, call us the second it happens!" Marley said as she gave Delaney a hug. "Even if it's in the middle of the ceremony."

Delaney laughed as she felt another stabbing jab.

Kate accompanied her sister to the front door of the resort to meet Dalton, who'd rushed ahead to get the car.

"I love you," Kate called out after helping her inside. Wiping her tears, she said, "I'm so sorry I can't be there for this."

"Me too," Delaney said, squeezing her hand. "But we'll see you soon. Enjoy the wedding, I'm so sad to miss it."

Sad to miss out on their good friends' special day, but excited to make it their babies' birthday.

Kate blew her a kiss and off to Cape Regional Medical Center they went. Delaney recalled the last time she'd rushed to the hospital—two nights before her own wedding, when her dad was rushed there by an ambulance for a heart scare. This time, thankfully, it was for a happy reason.

To become a family.

Marley

AFTER THE EXCITEMENT OF DELANEY'S DEPARTURE, Marley sipped champagne as a stylist finished sweeping her auburn curls into an updo. The buzz in the bridal suite grew palpable as she and her bridesmaids prepared for her epic wedding.

"Are you ready for all this?" Kate asked, coming up behind her. Their eyes met in the mirror, and Marley felt her tears welling for the fiftieth time that morning.

"I was born ready," she said, recalling Sam's words. She wondered how he was feeling just then, trying to picture him in his tux. She was so excited to see him, waiting for her. Where the end of the aisle would become the beginning of their lives together.

When it was time to put on her dress, her mom helped guide it over her head, careful not to mess her hair. The room erupted in cheers as the women *oohed* and *aahed*, dabbing at their tears.

"Ready for the veil?" the stylist asked.

Marley called her mom over as the photographer snapped several mother-affixing-the-veil shots.

And then it was go time. Marley and her entourage made their way to the beach, where rows of white chairs, filled with guests, faced a simple white arch.

"Do you think it's weird we're replicating Delaney's wedding?" Marley had asked Sam one night as they were making their plans.

"I don't think so. Plenty of people get married on the beach in front of Congress Hall. And besides, we have to get married there, if the wish I made on a falling star that night is to come true."

Marley got goosebumps. "What was your wish?"

"That someday soon, you and I were going to stand under an arch just like theirs. I even told you that night, I just didn't reveal it was my wish, in case I'd jinx it. It took three years, but here we are."

If what Delaney and Dalton had created for themselves was any indication, they were in for a sweet life.

From the end of the beach path, Marley peered around the dune grass at Sam. He was standing alongside his groomsmen, looking hotter than he ever had in a tux, biting his bottom lip. The only other time she'd seen her uber-confident fiancé this nervous was when he proposed.

Marley and Sam had opted not to do the "first look," as he preferred to see her for the first time as she walked down the aisle.

"If I see you in a wedding dress before the ceremony, I'm going to marry the hell out of you right then and there, and rob everyone of the joy of witnessing it for themselves," was his proffered excuse.

And now, all the anticipation for that moment was reduced to mere seconds.

Marley blinked rapidly to keep her welling eyes from releasing tears of joy as she watched the women she loved most walk down the aisle. First, her mom, escorted by Sam's oldest brother. Then, her childhood friends and cousins. Marley reminisced over each bridesmaid as they made their way, acknowledging the place they held in her heart. She'd be nothing without them.

Kate reached over and squeezed Marley's hand when it was her turn.

"Next time I hug you, you'll be a married woman," Kate said, blowing her a kiss. "See you on the other side."

Marley laughed out loud, her tears now spilling forth. Thank God she'd practiced crying in her wedding mascara, instilling confidence it wouldn't leave streaks of black on her cheeks as she sobbed her way down the aisle.

When Sam's song began pouring through the speakers, everyone stood and turned to face her.

It was time. Time to join the love of her life and link their lives, their love, their hearts for all eternity. She was never more ready for anything.

Her dad held out his arm. "Let's go make Sam my son."

Sam was already teary by the time she began walking down the aisle. Their eyes locked, and they vacillated between laughter and crying. Suddenly, everything they'd ever experienced together flashed through her mind. Meeting Sam. Studying together. Laughing over coffee. Eating pizza on the kitchen island. Making love. Practicing law together. And now, at long last, standing under a wedding arch.

"You're gorgeous," he whispered breathlessly as he wiped his tears.

And then he took her hand and led her to the altar.

The place he'd been leading her from the moment they met.

Epilogue

TEN MONTHS LATER

D ELANEY LAUGHED AS SHE WATCHED THE KIDS SCRAM-ble around their backyard in search of Easter eggs.

"I found one!" Frannie yelled, holding one up.

"Me too!" Eli clicked his plastic egg with hers. "From now on, I'm following you, Fran. You've got that women's 'tuition.'"

"Come on, Everett, I see one!" Jordan said, racing with his baby nephew to pick up an egg.

"Not if we get there first," Bella teased, skipping to the egg, holding a laughing Emma.

The twins had just turned ten months old. Delaney and Dalton were thrilled to have such great babysitters in Bella and Jordan, grateful they'd be around this summer to help with the babies before they left for college—Bella as a fresh-man, Jordan as a junior. Parenthood had been more enjoy-able than Delaney had ever imagined it could be. Babies introduced chaos into an otherwise structured life, but she wouldn't trade it for the world.

"Don't blink," Dalton's cousin Lisa said as she handed Delaney a drink. "Before you know it, Emma and Everett will be heading off to college. Just like my baby."

"I can't even imagine it," Delaney said as they clinked glasses. "Congrats on Bella getting into Notre Dame. Are you going to be okay with the distance, Mama?"

Lisa sighed. "I'll have to be, although it'll be the hardest thing I've ever had to do. We've become really close this year, and I can't imagine life without her in it every day."

Eli ran up to them to show his mom the eggs he'd collected before he was off again in a flash.

Delaney laughed. "I can't believe how tall your little man's gotten."

"Crazy growth spurt this year. Hard to believe he'll be eleven this summer. Life's going way too fast."

"Party's here!" Cleo called out as she and Nigel arrived with a fresh salad.

"Thanks for bringing this, guys," Delaney said, taking the bowl from her friend's hands. "Doesn't get more farm-to-table than this."

"Did we miss the egg hunt?" Cleo pouted as she turned to Nigel. "I told you we should have left earlier."

"What, and miss out on our own intimate celebration?" Nigel asked, wagging his eyebrows at her.

Cleo blushed.

"Speaking of celebrations," Delaney said, "how's everything coming along for your big day?"

"Pretty good. Can't believe I'm going to be an old married lady next month."

Cleo and Nigel were planning a small wedding ceremony on the grounds of the farm, under a simple arch he'd constructed from grapevines he'd grown. Finally bitten by the Cape May bug, Cleo enjoyed spending weekdays here with Nigel, giving her a respite from the hustle and bustle of the city and a chance to create new art before they returned to the city on weekends. The best of both worlds.

"About time you made it," Tori, official photographer for

the event, said to Cleo as she joined them. "Oh my gosh, what a great shot."

Tori trained her camera lens on the twin babies, now sitting in the grass as Bella and Jordan placed their baskets in front of them.

"Maybe next Easter we'll have one of our own," Peter said as he came up behind Tori and hugged her.

"Gotta put a ring on it before that happens," she teased, spinning around to kiss him.

Delaney smiled knowingly at Peter. He'd enlisted her help in proposing to Tori on their upcoming anniversary of reuniting. She couldn't wait for both of her once-wild single friends to join her in happy matrimony.

Jake and Charlotte arrived next with a tray of her famous lasagna.

"Speaking of rings, let's see it, girl!" Tori gushed as a beaming Charlotte thrust out her left hand.

"Wait, when did this happen?" Cleo demanded.

"Last Saturday." Jake wrapped his arm around Charlotte's waist. "I lured her to the top of the lighthouse at sunset and asked her to be my first mate for life."

The women swooned as Charlotte giggled. "Looks like I'm going to have to get over my fear of rogue waves, sharks, and motion sickness."

"I got you, girl," Jake said, kissing his fiancée on the cheek. "Nothing's gonna happen on my watch."

The group was interrupted by Kate's two-year-old daughter, Destiny. It was the name given to her at birth, eighteen months before she met her adoptive parents. Kate, who attributed all good fortune to the concept, burst into tears upon meeting her.

When Delaney heard that, she finally decided to fully embrace Kate's moto. *Let go and let destiny.* As parents of twins, she welcomed a little magic in their lives.

"Auntie! Eggs!" the child exclaimed as she toddled toward them, holding out her basket, Kate in tow.

"Good job, Dez," Delaney said as Kate joined them.

Tori gave Kate a hug. "Girl-mom life looks good on you."

Kate smiled. "You're gonna have to add boy-mom to my title. We just got word we've been paired with a baby boy. We get him in June."

The group congratulated Kate, giving her hugs.

"Hey, where are Marley and Sam?" Cleo asked.

"Holland. Sam's so freaking cute, he surprised Marley with a trip for her birthday," Kate explained. "It's always been on her bucket list to see fields of tulips in bloom."

This time, it was Dalton who interrupted them as he announced dinner was ready. Their guests gathered around the table as Dalton gave a toast.

"We're happy to have you all here today, our closest friends and family. Thank you for all you've done to help us raise these babies. They've got some great role models."

Everyone raised their glasses.

"Wait! Marley's FaceTiming me," Delaney called out.

The room became silent as Marley and Sam's faces appeared on the screen. Delaney held the phone up so everyone could see.

"You finally made it to your tulip fields!" Kate exclaimed. "Show us around!"

Marley panned to show the tulips, a windmill, and the two of them on bikes.

"It's everything I dreamed it would be, and more," Marley reported with a smile.

"Everyone having a good Easter?" Sam asked. He was met with a chorus of affirmations.

"Check out what we bought," Sam said as he held up a pair of men's wooden shoes. "I think I'm gonna rock these in court."

Everyone laughed.

"Marley got a pair too," he said, holding up hers. "And we couldn't resist these..."

On the screen appeared a tiny pair of wooden shoes emblazoned with the words, "Dancing into our lives September 14...Baby Adams."

It took a moment to sink in, until everyone erupted in simultaneous cheer.

"No way!" Kate screamed. "I knew it wasn't gonna take you guys long! I call favorite aunt, since neither of you have sisters."

"No, I'm the favorite," Delaney said.

"Don't forget me," Cleo echoed.

Sam gave Marley a kiss. "You're all favorites. Can't wait to celebrate in person when we return."

"Oh, my gosh," Delaney sighed after they ended the call. "Marley and Sam are having a baby. They're gonna be amazing parents."

After dinner and more festivities, the guests began to leave. Daphne and Frannie, who were staying overnight, were the last ones remaining.

The sisters had just sat down to relax when Daphne grabbed Delaney's hand, her eyes gleaming. "I've got big news I've been dying to share," she said. "My book was just picked up by a publishing house."

"Oh my God, Daphne! That's amazing!" Delaney leaped up and hugged her. "I knew you were working on something, but I had no idea you'd finished it!"

"It all started in London, after you and Frannie encouraged me to follow my dream of becoming an author. I just haven't said anything about sending it out, because I wasn't sure anyone would be interested in publishing it."

"Of course they would be, and they are! I'm so proud of you."

Delaney was thrilled her sister was going to be a published author. "Tell me all about your book."

"It was inspired by the many conversations we've had about life and love. How love knows no limits, how important family is, how true friends have our backs no matter what.

"It's about destiny. How two people can spend a lifetime making choices, but it's only when those unexpected chances pop up that they find each other. Like you and Dalton. Kate and Ryan. Me and you.

"It's about keeping our eyes, minds and hearts open to those opportunities that present themselves in the weirdest of ways. A museum trip, a college class, an open bar stool, a lost phone. Taking a boardwalk ride, a boat trip, a DNA test. Random life events that, at the time, don't seem like much, but turn out to be monumental because they lead us to each other, our destiny."

"Wow," Delaney said. "I love that. What's the book called?"

Daphne smiled. "*The Way to Cape May.*"

Acknowledgments

ONE YEAR AGO TODAY, I WAS AN UNPUBLISHED AUTHOR with a laptop and a dream. Today I celebrate publishing the last book in a three-book series. Somebody pinch me! For many authors, regardless of the path they take and where they are in their journey, there's a team of people behind them. I feel so blessed for my team who, on both a professional and personal level, have helped turn my beyond-wildest-imagination dreams into reality.

None of this would have been possible without my publishing besties: editor Emily Ohanjanians and book designer/interior formatter, Jessica Kleinman.

Emily—you not only believed in me in taking on these projects, you helped me believe in myself as an author. You gave me suggestions when I was clueless, encouragement when I was uncertain, and LOLs when I needed them the most. I can't tell you how much that all means to me. I look forward to our next adventure with a whole new set of characters for us to know, love and ship (although there'll always be a special place in our hearts for Marley and Sam <3).

Jessica, you are amazing at what you do. Often the first thing I hear from people when they pick up my books is how much they love the design—proving we do, in fact, judge books by their covers. But of course, you knew that when you worked your magic, and for that I am so thankful. Can't wait to see your ideas for the next book!

Writing, editing and designing aren't all that go into making sure books end up in readers' beach bags. Many thanks to the brick-and-mortar bookstores and boutique shops who've graciously placed my books on their shelves. I am forever (and ever!) grateful to you.

That brings me to you, kind reader. Thank you for picking up my books and taking a chance on this debut novelist at a time you may have known nothing about me, my characters, or the worlds I create. I've been blessed to have garnered some loyal readers among you, and it's been my greatest pleasure meeting many of you at book signings, book club gatherings, and other events. I've thoroughly enjoyed discovering all our commonalities—our mutual love of the shore, places we grew up, schools we attended, people we've known. That's why I wrote this series—for you, my darling Shoobies (when you are one, you know). To all the readers who've picked up my books, kept turning pages, laughed out loud, cheered on my characters and saw them through to happy endings—I thank you from the bottom of my heart.

Most of all, I'm so very grateful for my family. Ya'll know who you are. You guys are truly the wind beneath my wings, and I love you all so very much. Special thanks to my mom, who's been by my side for every event, cheering me on, encouraging me to keep this forward momentum in my new chapter as an author. And my dad, a historical fiction kinda guy, who's read each of my books and provided feedback, even though romcoms are the last thing he'd normally ever read. You two are the absolute best friends a daughter and writer could ask for and I love being on your team, since you were one long before I came along.

As this is the final book in this series, I need to give a shout-out to the characters who've lived in my head rent free for the past few years, challenging me to think about love and the many challenges we face in finding it—whether that be love for ourselves, our friends, our soulmates...or some (even all) of the above. It can be a daunting trip for many of us but, like our characters, the journey to love—however you define your destination—is one worth taking. So thank you, Delaney, Marley, Cleo, Kate, Charlotte and Bella for teaching me about love and friendship and giving me (and others) hope. I'll miss you, my fictional friends, but I'm excited to get to know, love and introduce new characters as I journey forth in my writing career.

Til then...go forward with love in your hearts and be kind to one another.

Reader's Guide

ABOUT THIS BOOK
BOOK CLUB QUESTIONS

About this Book

AS I NOTED IN THE READER'S GUIDE SECTIONS OF *THE WAY to Cape May* and *A Cape May Kind of Love*, this series came about because I wanted to pay tribute to the Jersey Cape, home of so many real-life meet-cutes, proposals, and beach weddings. Where young parents bring babies to dip their toes in the ocean for the first time, and where families dress in matching outfits at sunset to pose for holiday cards. It's where grandparents share their beach houses and memories, passing them down as future generations are grown. In short, it's a magical place that brings much joy to so many. Inspired by the song, "On the Way to Cape May" written by Maurice "Bud" Nugent, these books are my love letters to the shore us Shoobies know and love.

But I was driven by more than just a desire to set a fun beach read in these quaint seaside towns. I also wrote these stories to explore the path to love that, for many, are riddled with twists and turns on our journey to happily ever after. Wanting art to imitate life, I created characters who each had an obstacle to mount, or something going on in their lives that hampered their ability to find and keep love. As what happens for so many of us.

Similar to Charlotte, I'm obsessed with all things romcom, and I suspect she and I are not alone. Many of us wish to see hopeful journeys end in happy results, regardless of whether it's our own or others'. Of course, we want it all to work out for ourselves, but while we're striving for it, there's nothing more hopeful and uplifting than a good juicy love story with some humor thrown in.

Also, like Charlotte, some may believe love is meant for others, not them. Nothing is further from the truth. We're all deserving of love—it's just a matter of finding it. Things ultimately worked out for our characters because they are but fictional beings dwelling within the pages of a romance novel; by the genre's very definition, they all must find their happily ever after. Yet, as we know, this isn't always the case in real life. The trick, I believe, is finding a happy-for-now, whether alone or with another person. As they say, the greatest love we can find is the one we have with ourselves. My purpose in creating these characters with real-life issues—abandonment, fear, hopelessness, self-doubt, to name a few—was to help those who may be facing the same or similar situations. So often, life gets in our way of finding happiness, which includes the fact that we sometimes get in our own way.

We may be like Delaney— so focused on controlling the outcome, we're not open to taking chances and finding joy in the unexpected. We may have had a troubled past like Cleo and are trying to heal so we can create a lasting connection with someone else. Perhaps we're distrusting of the world and the people in it like Charlotte, who only found love—both for herself and with another—once she was able to let down her guard and try new things.

Like Marley, we may not believe we're enough, a belief that thwarts us from achieving our goals or speaking our truth about our feelings for another, which just may turn out to be requited. Yet others may have been burned like Amanda, abandoned like Kate, or widowed like Daphne, and are afraid to take another chance on love despite that someone new may be waiting just around the corner. Perhaps, like Bella, we're willing to accept less than what we deserve before we find someone who mirrors the worth we see in ourselves.

Or...you may not have identified with any of these characters. At the very least, I've hoped you've enjoyed getting to know these guys, and they've helped open your mind to all the new possibilities that life may present to you.

May you find your happily ever after, or your happy for now, where choice meets chance. I hope that when you find what it is you're seeking, your "Exit o", it's the beginning of something beautiful.

Book Club Questions

1. If you could have brunch with just one of the characters in this series, who would you choose?

2. When Daphne tells Delaney about her book, she lists several scenarios where the characters had opportunities to find love. Can you match each character to their respective scenario?

3. If you could have given one character a piece of advice to help her in her journey to finding love, who would it have been and what advice would it be?

4. If you've been to the south Jersey shore towns featured in these books, which is your favorite, and why? If you haven't visited, what is your favorite vacation spot?

5. Did any of the characters' journeys to love and/or career help you learn anything about yourself?

6. Pick your favorite character and "write" the next chapter of her life. Where do you see her in one year? Doing what, and with whom?

About the Author

KIMBERLY BRIGHTON IS AN AWARD-WINNING ROMANCE AUthor, incidental humorist, and asparagus enthusiast from the Philadelphia area. *Cape May Ever After* is the third of her three-book Cape May series, following *The Way to Cape May* and *A Cape May Kind of Love*. She studied satirical writing and screenwriting at The Second City and is the author of *The Shore Blog*, a travel website focusing on the Jersey Cape, and *BlaBlaBlog*, a humor website. When not dreaming up swoony romance plots, she spends her time searching for food expiration labels and sitting at red lights. Married for 25 laugh-filled years, she's discovered the key to a lasting marriage: takeout.

To stay in touch and learn more about her upcoming releases, sign up for her newsletter at KimberlyBrighton.com or visit her on social media @KBrightonAuthor.

www.ingramcontent.com/pod-product-compliance
Lightning Source LLC
Chambersburg PA
CBHW032113310726
48972CB00001B/206